MW01093305

Harrison

VR Tennent

No part of this book may be reproduced in any form or by any electronic or mechanical means, without written permission from the author, except for the use of brief quotations in book reviews.

Please purchase only authorized electronic editions, and do not participate in or encourage the electronic piracy of copyrighted materials. Your support of the author's rights is appreciated.

This book is a work of fiction. Names, characters, places, and incidents either are products of the author's imagination or are used fictitiously. Any resemblance to actual events or locales or persons, living or dead, is entirely coincidental.

Harrison

Copyright © 2023 VR Tennent

Cover art by Kellie's Cover Design

Editing by Cath Lauria and Finishing by Fraser

Published by Frosty Enterprises Ltd

For everyone who thought
they knew who they should be.
There is no shame in change.

Author Note

Harrison is a steamy mafia romance and intended for readers aged eighteen years and over. It contains sexual scenes, violence and strong language.

Harrison

Violet Chase has always been off limits. The girl I wanted...but could never have.

In my teens, her father warned me to keep my hands to myself; boys like me don't get girls like her. His family saved me, and I owed them. Her brothers, my best friends, made it clear where I stood — below them.

We had one stolen moment of passion, then I ran. That was fourteen years ago, and I've regretted it ever since. Now, she's back in London, but life for both of us is very different. Her past decade has been filled with lies—things that she thought were true. The last place she ever expected to return to was here, begging her family for help.

As my career blossoms, my world darkens. Whether becoming

a lawyer for a mafia don was a wise move remains to be seen. A booming bank account is accompanied by an ever-enlarging target on my back. External pressures pull in all directions while my heart knows what it wants. It always has. Violet.

The question is, can we navigate the challenges to be together? Or once again, will we both run?

CHAPTER ONE

---◆◇◆---

Canary Wharf, London

June 2022

Violet

As I stand, gazing up at the glass skyscraper, my heart sinks. This is the last place I ever expected to end up—the doorstep of my brothers, forced to beg for their help. It's been over a decade since we laid eyes on each other. I only know they live in Canary Wharf through gossip. When I ran away to America thirteen years ago, setting foot back in London was never planned. Now, here I am, penniless and alone, praying they'll help me.

The double glass doors trimmed with chrome effortlessly slide open as I approach them. A tall, lean man wearing a suit with a black tie advances. His eyes narrow as he looks up and down my body. My attire is far from what the ladies who live in this building would usually wear. I imagine only designer labels make it past the threshold. But these were the only items I could grab before running and have acted as both clothing and a disguise for the past forty-eight hours as I got the hell out of Chicago.

The oversized Chicago White Sox shirt paired with boyfriend-style jeans drown my small frame. Weight has fallen off me in a matter of days—stress has that effect. I've barely eaten, even though I know I must. The tight braid my long dark hair was woven into hours ago is still in place and tucked snug under a black baseball cap, though errant strands escape all over the place. Being made to sleep on the plane, in the airport, and at the bus station on my journey hasn't been conducive to maintaining my appearance. The high-top trusty red Converse with the telltale star on my feet are the only items that are mine.

"Good evening, madam," the security guard says politely. His expression remains impassive as he speaks. "Is there something I can help you with?"

"My brothers live in this building. I'm here to visit them," I reply as firmly as possible. "Russell and Connor Chase." His arched eyebrow tells me he thinks I'm lying.

"Are they expecting you?"

"No, this is an unexpected visit. It's been a while since we met up, and I wanted to surprise them." His eyes move to the large black duffel bag in my hand. My shoulder sags as the bulk affects my stance.

"Can I take your bag for you? Ms. Chase, is it?" he asks, and I nod, then pass it to him. He turns and walks into the luxurious foyer of the apartment block. I follow behind, my gaze scanning the room, taking in the opulent wealth. Everything is either wrapped in leather or carved from marble. All surfaces are edged in silver.

Not that money is something I'm unaccustomed to. For the past thirteen years, I've gone to the best restaurants in Chicago, worn designer clothes, and dripped with expensive jewelry. The rewards all came at a high price. My future. My independence. My family.

"My brothers live on the top floor," I say, feigning knowledge I don't have. They like nice things too. I would bet the shirt off my back that one of them has the penthouse. "I've never actually visited. I live in Chicago, you see. The years pass so fast, before you know it, over ten have disappeared." He grunts, not agreeing or disagreeing with me. "Do you know if they're home?"

"I believe they are," he says. "I'll phone ahead for you. Mr. Russell lives in the penthouse. Mr. Connor has an apartment on the floor below." I smile to myself—pretentious bastards, always needing to have the best of everything, the flashiest cars, the most expensive watches and now, the highest apartments in one of the most expensive buildings in the city.

"Please don't," I interject. "I really do want to surprise them. I'll take the elevator up and knock on their door. I'll get them to call down to assure you everything is all right."

He pauses and gives me one last look-over, assessing me for threats. I think. Personally, I couldn't look less dangerous if I tried. Everything about me screams pathetic and dejected. I peek up at him with wide brown eyes from under my cap, pleading in pitiful silence. He sighs, defeated.

"Okay," he says, resigned. "But don't tell anyone. Your brothers would have my balls for letting you in here, unchecked and without invitation. I have bills to pay and kids to feed."

"Thank you, I won't tell a soul." I grab his hand between my two small, grubby ones and shake it enthusiastically before taking my bag from him. He wipes his palm on his pristine black pant leg. "What did you say your name was?" I ask.

"Matthew," he replies with a kind smile.

"Lovely to meet you, Matthew. I'm Violet. Violet Chase." With a small wave, I move in the direction of the elevator. He appears behind me moments later as I press the button frantically in an attempt to summon it. As he passes a small black card across a sensor, the doors part. "Thank you," I mumble, embarrassed by my idiocy. Somewhere like this will have high security, especially considering the type of people who live here and the circles they move in.

En route back to London, I did some research about who my brothers, both lawyers, are currently linked with. They certainly move in an ever-darkening world. Their law firm has been defending the Irish mafia in recent years. I always knew they had ambition; it looks like the firm keeps getting bigger.

I step into the intricate glass cube edged with chrome and hit the button for floor fifty-seven, one floor below the penthouse. Of my two brothers, I've always gotten along better with Connor—he's less bristly than Russell. Being the middle child, he was used to being overlooked while I threw a fit and our older brother had a pre-teenage meltdown. Connor would stand by and wait for the whole of hell to let loose, smile, then wander off to play Lego. I'd rather see him first.

The elevator is attached to the outside of the building and treats me to a bird's-eye view of the city as we rise. As beautiful as it is, heights are not one of my strong points, and my stomach somersaults. The further I go, the less well I feel, retreating as far from the glass windows as I can. Finally, pressed against the door, I crouch to the ground and close my eyes. *Will this fucking trip never end*?

I come to a stop, and the doors open silently, causing me to fall out into a lobby. I crawl across the navy and silver checked carpet, dragging my bag behind me. My legs shake from my unexpected brush with my phobia of heights.

When I glance up, I see a large frame on the wall. Inside it, the London skyline is painted in charcoal along the bottom edge. The words *The Level* are written above it. A solid wood door to the left-hand side of the artwork has a brass plaque telling me that behind it is the boardroom. The set-up surprises me. I thought I was visiting their home, not an office.

The small lobby has a blue velvet corner sofa, large enough to seat six people. There is a low, dark wood coffee table decorated with a fresh bouquet of summer flowers, all in whites and blues. The walls are painted a deep gray, with huge canvases depicting a famous city location hanging on every one. They're the type of paintings that you could get lost in, full of intricate detail.

After sitting on the floor for a few minutes, my head and legs stop swirling, and I'm able to stand. I stare at the closed elevator doors and my resolve wavers. Perhaps this wasn't the best idea. What if they reject me? I have nowhere else to go. They always warned me my impulsive attitude would bring me tears, and it did, though it took over a decade for the truth to come out.

Thirteen years ago, my brothers had both left home to study and practice law in London. I was eighteen and had recently secured a place to train in musical theatre at the *Royal Conservatoire of Scotland*. My final summer in Kensington was filled with lazy days at my parent's home and parties every weekend. My friends and I were moving on to new pastures after leaving school. All of us scattered across the world to study in our relevant fields.

During my first week at university, my father asked a business associate to check in on me to ensure I'd settled. That was when I met Aiden Marley. He'd appeared at my apartment on a Thursday afternoon, dressed in a sharp black suit teamed with perfectly polished shoes. He explained my father had asked him to visit while he was in Glasgow. I'd invited him into my home. He took up residence in my heart.

In his early thirties, I'd been blown away by his confidence and charm. He'd treated me like a queen every time he visited and made love to me as if I was the only woman on earth. For a year, he came to see me when he was in the city on business. We didn't tell anyone, knowing my father wouldn't approve of the vast difference in our ages. He told me once I graduated, I could move to Chicago to be with him.

I couldn't wait that long. At the end of my first year, I gave notice to the school and packed up, arriving unannounced at Aiden's office in his advertising firm the following day.

I now know that the shocked look on his face hadn't been because he was overjoyed to see me. It had been sheer and utter panic. He'd herded me into his office and closed the blinds. "What are you doing here?" he said sharply. I'd launched myself at him, wrapping my arms around his neck and kissing him fiercely. "Violet! This is my place of work. You can't turn up here unannounced."

"Why not?" I replied sexily, then ran my fingers across his crotch. He hardened beneath my touch. "You own the company, do you not?"

"Yes, but..."

"You're the boss. You can do whatever you like. And whoever you like." I'd unbuttoned the simple white shirt I was wearing, then slid it from my shoulders, exposing the see-through lace bra beneath. "Lock the door. I want you to give me an unforgettable welcome to America." His eyes had darted between the unlocked door and my breasts. His frame moved frantically to secure it. On returning to stand in front of me, he picked up my discarded clothing from the floor, handing it to me.

"Violet, what are you doing here? Why didn't you tell me you were coming? Put your clothes back on," he barked, his face contorted in anger.

"I wanted to surprise you," I said petulantly as I shrugged into my shirt.

"You've fucking managed that," he growled in my ear as he pulled me closer to him. "Fuck, I've missed you. Two weeks without you is too long." His arms wrapped around my waist, holding on tight.

"You won't have to worry about that anymore," I told him, and he looked at me warily.

"What do you mean?"

"I'm here to stay. I've packed my belongings, handed my notice to the school, and told my family I'm moving to be with the man I love." His jaw dropped spectacularly, almost hitting the floor. "Don't worry, I haven't told my father it's you." My fingers stroked his cheek in comfort. "I know you're worried."

"Your father is one of my biggest clients. I can't risk him pulling the contract. It will put dozens of staff out of work. You should have told me your plans. This is all very sudden." I blinked at him, shocked by his harsh tone. When I didn't respond, he sighed and asked, "Where are you staying?"

"With you of course, silly. I'll be keeping your bed warm every day," I purred. In an attempt to lighten the mood, I hooked one leg around his, grinding against him.

"You can't stay with me, Violet," he said firmly and stepped back out of my embrace.

"Why not?" I snapped. My heart was straining at the lack of enthusiasm my appearance received. "You have an apartment in the city, do you not? You told me you wanted to have a life together once I finished school. Now I'm done, I'm here."

"I said once you graduated. I didn't ask you to throw your career away to move here. You can't stay at my apartment. That's my personal space. We've only been seeing each other for one year. You've appeared here out of the blue. I'm sorry, but no." He fixed his gaze on me, his eyes narrowed as if daring me to challenge him. It was obvious he wasn't going to be convinced otherwise.

I sniffed loudly, trying to hold back the tears that were threatening to fall as my anger morphed into despair. In my mind, our reunion had been so much more. My huge romantic gesture had fallen flat.

He lifted his hands to my shoulders, sensing my distress. His eyes never left mine. "It's all right, Princess," he said. "I'll get you checked into a hotel nearby. Then we can meet later for dinner and discuss moving forward." I gave him a sad smile. He walked back to his desk, then pressed the button on his intercom. The machine rang out before a polite woman's voice echoed around the room.

"Mr. Marley, how can I help you sir?" she said.

"Stephanie, can you contact the Four Seasons and see if they have any rooms available, please? Make it a suite. I have a friend visiting from the UK, and they haven't sorted out any accommodations. Please put it on my card."

9

"Of course, sir. Is there anything else?"

"Please call a taxi to take Miss Chase to the hotel. She'll be down in the lobby in a few minutes. Any problems, do let me know."

"Yes, sir," she said and hung up.

Aiden walked back over to me and took my face between his hands. His azure-blue eyes pinned me to the spot as he dropped a kiss onto my lips. "You really are a bad girl, Princess. What on earth am I going to do with you?"

I ruffled his overly long dark hair between my fingers. The sting of him referring to me as only his friend fresh in my mind.

"You go to the hotel, rest, then freshen up. I'll be over this evening. We can discuss your future living arrangements then."

"Tell me you're happy I'm here," I whispered, my confidence knocked by his lukewarm reception. "I love you, Aiden. I want to be with you."

"I'm happy you're here," he said and kissed me again before leading me to the door. "I'll see you later." As he opened it, his hand dropped from my waist. He called to the woman behind a desk to see me out, then stepped back before there could be any further contact between us. It stung then—it still hurts me now.

As I think back to that day all those years ago now, it's clear all the red flags were there from the moment I arrived in Chicago. But at only nineteen years old and blinded by love, I'd taken his word as the truth. After a few weeks of staying in the hotel, I'd been moved into an apartment around the corner from his office. He would stay with me most nights during the week then disappear at weekends to have time alone or in preparation for business meetings. On key holidays, he could never be with me. "Advertising never stops," he would say. "I can't be distracted at these crucial times."

During my second year living in America, he encouraged me to join an amateur drama group. I threw myself into the club with gusto and appeared in every performance I could. Suddenly, I wasn't missing him on weekends as they were filled with singing, dancing, and cheering crowds.

So, life bumbled on—during the week we were madly in love, living together, eating in private restaurants, and making love in every room of our apartment. On holidays and weekends, I was a performer. Anytime I mentioned our future, or the possibility of marriage and starting a family, he would shrug it off. His excuse was that we were not born to follow convention. Our relationship was private. He didn't want to share me with the world; I was only his. I believed him. I always believed him. Now, I feel so stupid. Over a decade of my life was gone, an obscene length of time to live a lie blinded by a man who had no respect for me.

I move to sit on the corner sofa, needing a moment to collect my thoughts before I face my brothers for the first time in over a decade. Before I tell them the whole sorry tale of how I've ended up here, on their doorstep, after disappearing from my family to run after a man I thought loved me. The chances of my return being a happy one are slight—if I'm honest, most likely non-existent. My family members hold grudges, and traitors are seen as scum. My stomach flips at the thought of the worst-case scenario. Tonight, I may be on the streets if the next few hours turn sour.

***

Three days ago, I'd been sitting in my apartment drinking my morning coffee. The local news playing in the background as I scrolled aimlessly on my phone. I heard his name announced before I saw him.

Aiden Marley, the new owner of the Chicago White Sox baseball team, has arrived at his new business, the reporter said with enthusiasm. *Mr. Marley took ownership of the club one hour ago. This deal has been two years in the making and is an exciting development for the club. Mr. Marley has made his fortune within the advertising industry. He is a private man who is very rarely seen at public events. But with this newest purchase, I expect we'll be seeing a lot more of him. He is joined today by his wife of fifteen years, his childhood sweetheart, Marissa Marley. The couple have been together twenty years and have two young sons, who you can see playing catch behind them. If they weren't avid White Sox fans, they will be now.*

The reporter snorted at his own joke as I gaped at the screen. I watched my Aiden walking up the steps to the stadium with his arm around a beautiful blonde woman. Two boys around the age of eight skipped behind them, waving to the crowd. The family then disappeared into the building and the news cut to a story about trash collecting in the area.

I grabbed for the remote control and rewound the program, rewatching the scene I witnessed only moments ago. *He's married. He has children.* And I never knew. Shame engulfed me as the realization hit that I was the other woman.

***

The elevator sounding its arrival makes me glance up. Matthew from the foyer steps out, accompanied by another man. They're talking to each other, laughing as they speak. As they walk into the reception area, both sets of eyes fall on me.

"Ms. Chase," Matthew says, "I thought you'd got lost when I hadn't heard from you. I wanted to check you were all right and had found your brothers."

"Sorry, I was taking a moment to myself," I say apologetically, shaking my head.

"No harm done," he replies. "I believe you know this gentleman."

"Yes," I stammer, shocked by his appearance. Matthew nods, then returns to the elevator, waving as he disappears from view. I'm left staring at a man, a man I've not seen for as long as my family.

Harrison Waite stands before me in a sharp gray suit. His dark hair is styled precisely, not a strand out of place. His shrewd eyes look me over, then he cocks his head to one side and gives me a panty-wetting smile. "Violet Chase, long time no see. What brings you to the City of London dressed like you're ready to play baseball?"

Unable to speak, I mumble something incoherent to him. Not only is he my brother's best friend, but he is also a partner in the law firm they share.

The last time I saw Harrison Waite was the night I lost my virginity.

CHAPTER TWO

The Chase Family Home, Kensington

August 2008

Harrison

She's backed against the wall as I lay a hand either side of her head. I stare into deep brown eyes, almost the color of dark chocolate. We haven't connected yet—I'm in her space but not touching her. Every step I take closer causes her breathing to quicken. She disappeared upstairs while her brothers, our friends, and I played football out on the back lawn, enjoying the summer afternoon sun. Excusing myself to go to the bathroom, I'd followed her, then slipped into her room. I'd taken her by surprise. Now I'm caging her in, listening to the excitement build as her plump breasts rise and fall. She looks like a baby fawn caught in a lion's line of vision. In a way, she is.

"I know what you've done this summer, Violet," I whisper darkly, dropping my lips to her ear. "And I approve."

"What's that?" she says, her voice husky. She strains to control her breathing and push the words past her lips.

"Grown up." I snake one arm around her waist and pull her against me. My erection is hard against her stomach. Her eyes widen when she realizes what's caused the sensation. "When I left for university, you were a schoolgirl." My hand drops to her backside and I squeeze hard. She yelps. "You're not now. You've been cock-teasing me all fucking day." My focus never leaves her, and she gazes straight back with dazzling eyes and flushed cheeks.

"I've no idea what you're talking about, Harry," she replies demurely. "You have your wires crossed. I was simply having a lovely time with my friends before we all leave this week."

"Is that why you dropped a tissue and bent over directly in front of me? That fucking bikini should come with a warning. I nearly combusted on the spot."

She giggles. It's the sweetest sound. I shouldn't be here. If her brothers, or worse, her father, caught me in her room, they'd dismember me. But after four hours of drinking beer and watching Violet Chase strut around in next to nothing, sense isn't on my side. "Answer me," I growl, grazing her neck with my teeth.

"Maybe I was teasing," she concedes, then shrugs. "What are you going to do about it?"

"I'm going to satisfy my hunger." Her eyes pop open in surprise, but her hands move to surround my neck. "That's what you want, isn't it? Me inside you, making you crumble. You want to be fucked to hell and back before heading north to new beginnings." I remove her fingers from my hair, pinning them high above her head. She bites her lip. "I won't touch you until you tell me it's what you want." What feels like an eternity passes before she speaks. Internally, I'm praying for her to say yes. I need this as much as she does. This is a craving that needs to be satisfied.

"I want it. Lock the door," she replies, breathless and clearly aroused. I release her, then go to secure the only entrance with the sliding bolt. I remember her insisting on the lock being added when she turned sixteen to stop her brothers from entering her room. As I slide the metal, a cheer erupts from outside. She wanders over to the window to look down on the ongoing party. "More people have arrived. They won't miss us."

Her bedroom looks as it did when she was a preteen, the days when her brothers and I would chase her around the house. She would lock herself away in here for hours to avoid our torment. I always loved making her squeal—she would smile in a way that made my heart beat faster. Every damn time.

The walls are covered in pink floral wallpaper. A small white dressing table filled with bottles sits in the corner. The single white iron bed is covered with pale pink sheets decorated with daisies. Her collection of teddy bears sits on the pillow. Violet turned eighteen a few weeks ago; she's all woman to look at but younger edges still remain. It's endearing. Being two years older than her has meant I've seen her grow up. All my weekends have been spent here with this amazing family since I was a teenager. They supported me when my own mother couldn't anymore.

I move to sit on the edge of the bed and hold my hands out. She walks across to sit on my lap. I wrap my arms around her, and she places her palm on my cheek and leans in to kiss me. Our lips connect, and my heart leaps from my chest in response. At first, our kiss is slow and gentle, tentative even. We've never kissed before; this is new territory for both of us. As I slip the bikini strap from her shoulder, she stills.

"Do you want this?" I ask her. She doesn't respond, and I move the strap back into position. I pull back from her, her embarrassed eyes dropping away from mine. "Violet," I say quietly, "you don't need to do this. We can go back downstairs. No one needs to know this happened."

She stands, then walks around her room, twisting her fingers in front of her. As she turns back to face me, her fingers run slowly through her hair.

"I want to do this," she tells me, her tone firm. Her hands move to her back, unclipping the bikini top and letting it fall to the floor. I watch, entranced by the vision in front of me. Her nimble fingers unbutton the denim shorts she's wearing. She wiggles her hips, allowing the fabric to slide freely down her legs before stepping out of them. The pink plastic flip-flops she had on were kicked off earlier. She walks back to me, wearing only the black G-string bikini bottoms she tempted me with.

My hands move to her hips, pulling her toward me. I'm at eye level with her breasts and take one of the sweet pink buds in my mouth, sucking gently. She moans softly, and I increase the pressure. The noise gets louder. "I like that sound," I tell her. She glances down, and I bite, hard. She yelps, throwing her head back. Her dark hair glides down her spine finishing at her ass. I grab a handful and pull softly, and her body flexes on my command. "You look good like this," I say.

"Like what?" she asks, still looking at the ceiling.

"In my arms and at my mercy." I wrap her hair around my wrist, using my other hand to pull her ass closer. "Kneel on the bed. Straddle me." She climbs up as she's told. "Lower yourself down. I want to feel that pretty pussy of yours. I want you to feel how ready I am for you." My dick hardens further, straining against the fabric of my boxers.

"I can't see, Harry," she whispers, breathless.

"You don't need to. You only need to feel. Sit down on my cock and grind against me. Tease yourself. Tease me. Think about how it will feel when I remove those panties of yours and claim you. Because that is what is going to happen. I'm going to sink myself inside you, and not leave until I must." She rocks, moving in search of friction against my shorts. Her rhythm quickens as she chases the buzz. The delicate body I've lusted after is finally touching mine. It feels electric. Perfect.

"I bet your juices are flowing. Those bottoms of yours will be drenched. I'll need to clean you up with my tongue." My fingers soften, allowing the silky strands to be free. Her head falls forward, her gaze meeting mine. She kisses me again, biting my bottom lip as her lips retreat. I flip her over so she's lying on her childhood bed gazing up at me. "Spread your legs, I need to investigate my new favorite place. Ensure there's enough lubrication for what I have planned for you, Vi. Do you know how many nights I've dreamed of this?"

"Dreamed of me?" she whispers back. "You think about me?"

"Always."

My eyes run over her body as my fingers trail across her skin. "How many men have had you?" I ask and she blinks, startled. "How many have been here before me?" The number of sexual partners my previous conquests have had hasn't crossed my mind before or during sex. It was inconsequential. The relationships were purely physical. No real feelings involved. We had a nice time, but forever was never in my mind.

However, Violet means something, even though I know we can never be together. Her family will never allow it. This will be the one and only time we succumb to our desires. The sole day that I touch her like I want to, the way I've yearned to all summer. She is inexperienced, that much is obvious. I'm coaching her as we go. And she follows every instruction to the letter—either she likes being told what to do or doesn't know what to do. The thought causes a sense of unease to flit through my mind.

"Why does it matter?" she questions, annoyance lacing the words.

"It doesn't. I'm curious."

"Not many. I have specific tastes," she replies, then presses her lips together.

"Not many or none? And do enlighten me on your preferences," I continue playfully. She swallows but doesn't answer. "Violet, you have had sex?"

"Of course I have!" she snaps and scowls, annoyed. "Are you going to get on with it or not? I could boil the kettle quicker." She huffs; it makes her look even more beautiful, all rosy cheeks and smooth skin waiting impatiently to be touched. Devoured.

I've had a crush on my best friend's little sister since she developed tits. There's a picture of her in a bikini from earlier in the summer hidden in my underwear drawer. I use it for my extracurricular activities. Another fact her brothers, my friends, can never know. Protective is an understatement when it comes to Violet—if a boy so much as looks in her direction, they're warned off. Physically. Poor Brandon Hershaw didn't stand a chance last week; he and his bike ended up in the lake. I was happy to assist.

"Get on with it," I repeat back to her. "What would *it* be? I assume you mean fucking you." I grin at her, and she rolls her eyes. "Are you getting impatient?" My fingers stroke her stomach then slip under her panties. One finger plays with her lips—she's damp. I slide it inside. She's more than ready. I pump slowly, pressing my thumb to her clit. A gasp escapes through

21

gritted teeth—she's sensitive, bucking beneath my hand. Her knees bend as her feet lift from the bed. Encouraged, I add a second digit and increase my speed. Her initially tense body relaxes under my touch, hungry wet flesh sucking me in each time. My excitement heightens again at the unexpected event. The chance to have Violet beneath me, and under my control.

"You're ready. That pussy of yours is screaming to be filled with my cock," I tell her, removing my fingers and licking them clean. "Delicious." Her eyes pop wide. I move to stand then lift my t-shirt over my head. She watches me take my wallet from my back pocket and extract the condom I have tucked away for opportunities such as this. "We need to use protection," I say in hopes of reassuring her. She's nervous, that's obvious. I slip out of my shorts and boxers, then drop down between her legs, pulling her panties from her body.

"You have a pretty pussy. I knew you would." I lean forward and place a kiss on her pubic bone. My face drops lower, and I nuzzle greedily between her legs, tasting her gently with my tongue. She is everything I dreamed she would be—salty, sweet, and seductive. The taste of her coats my tastebuds as her aroma fills my senses. Violet Chase invades every part of me, securing her hold on my heart with each passing second. The girl I want but can never have.

After taking the condom from its wrapper, I slide it on. She's still lying on the bed, legs wide, with expectant eyes. I kneel between her thighs, lining up at her entrance, and press forward slowly. My dick nudges her pussy. She's tight, and groans softly at my intrusion. I flex my hips to enter farther, encouraging her body to consent, to allow me passage to where I long to be.

"Let me in Vi, take me. All of me. Now." Losing the thread of control I was clinging to, I surge forward, craving to claim her. My body screams to be connected fully with hers. Those beautiful brown eyes snap closed as a gasp escapes her lips. "Fuck, you feel incredible," I tell her.

Fine hands come to my shoulders; she holds tight as I move, sharp nails marking my skin. Slick walls encase my cock—she's the tightest woman I've ever been inside. Her legs wrap around my waist as I work, pounding her tiny body beneath mine. Dark strands are thrown back against the sheets, eyes screwed shut. My thrusts accelerate until I'm driving her into the mattress, chasing my release as she whimpers beneath me. Violet is the perfect combination of delicate and erotic. The ultimate forbidden cocktail I can only drink once.

Then it comes, that euphoric moment when sensation is at its peak, and I empty myself as she orgasms. Her body clings to mine then she slowly opens her eyes. We stare at each other for a few moments. Neither of us speaks, the emotion, the sensation, and the feelings of the situation swarming around us. Nothing has ever felt so wrong, but also, so right for me.

"Was I okay?" she asks, breaking the silence, surprising me.

I pause, considering how to respond. She smiles shyly before glancing away, then her eyes return to mine. "Not okay, Vi. You were breathtaking," I tell her. "Simply flawless. This will be a day I always remember." She chuckles, and her cheeks turn the most beautiful shade of red. I'm in no rush to withdraw, knowing this will be my one and only experience of having her. What seems perfect for me will not be mine.

After a few minutes, I move to stand while she lies motionless. The loss of her body is required but demoralizing. I look over her bare curves, enjoying the view, willing the image to embed itself forever in my mind. My gaze lands between her legs. It takes a second for me to process the telltale red marks on the bedding.

"Violet," I stammer, horrified, "are you? Were you?" She screws her face up, throwing an arm across her eyes. "Were you a virgin? What the fuck!" I pull the condom from my cock and throw it in the waiting trash can, then grab my clothes and dress. She scrambles under the blanket, wrapping it around herself protectively. "Violet, this shouldn't have happened," I snarl, panicked.

"I'm sorry," she says, not looking in my direction. "I wanted to, and I knew you wouldn't if..." She trails off.

"Too right I bloody wouldn't. Your brothers will kill me if they find out I was your first fuck." My anxiety and anger skyrocket at her deception, at being put in this position. Sleeping with her is off limits; being known as the man who has taken her virginity could be deadly. She will know that.

"They won't. I won't tell anyone. I wanted my first time to be with you, Harry." Her voice is pained, her distress obvious. Furious, I storm from her bedroom without looking back.

***

"Violet Chase, long time no see. What brings you to the City of London dressed like you're ready to play baseball?" I say to the woman who I deflowered the last time I saw her fourteen years ago. Her gaze runs over me, beginning at my eyes then dropping to my feet before returning to where it started.

"I'm here to see my brothers," she replies weakly. "I need their help. Things went sour in Chicago."

"What happened?" I ask, and she shakes her head. I know her family was furious when they discovered her living arrangements, but from the little I heard about her, she was happy. Her eyes are wide and watery—she keeps looking from me to the elevator. Nervous. I keep my voice level and calm. The last thing I want her to do is run. She's not stepped foot in London since she left. Her being here means she has no other options.

I notice her nails are dark with grime. The clothes she's wearing are creased as if they've been worn for days. "Are you in trouble?"

She crumbles before my eyes, dropping to the ground and sobbing furiously. I rush toward her, kneel, and bundle her into my arms.

"No, I'm not in trouble," she spits out between the body-wracking gasps. "But I've wasted thirteen years of my life. I'm lost, Harry. I have nowhere to go."

Not knowing what the issue is, I do the only thing I can—hold her. My lips drop to her hair in an attempt to console her.

"Russ and Conner aren't here," I tell her. "I doubt they'll be back tonight. There's a business meeting with entertainment planned afterward. They normally stay in a hotel to save the trip home." She peeks up at me but doesn't reply. Her body is fragile in my arms. It's obvious she's thin beneath her oversized clothes. "Where are you staying?" She shrugs non-committedly.

"I'll need to sort somewhere. Can you tell my brothers I called round?" She wipes at her face to clear away the tears now rolling down her cheeks, then takes a deep breath. Her body expands and contracts.

"I have a spare room. You're welcome to stay in my apartment tonight," I suggest. She gives me a curious look, then her shoulders sag. My instinct is to keep her close, protect her. Her leaving is not an option—she needs to be here, with me. Whatever has happened, I want to be the one to fix it. "You look like you've had a challenging trip."

"That would be an understatement," she replies quietly, wriggling from my arms to stand, then moving to collect the bag at her feet.

"I'll get that," I tell her, picking it up off the floor as I rise to join her. "My apartment is over here. Come on. You need a shower and a good night's sleep."

"You live here?" she asks, gesturing to the boardroom. I shake my head, not wanting to explain what's behind those doors.

"In the building, yes."

"Is that Connor's apartment?"

"No one lives in the boardroom. It's a business asset," I explain evasively. "We own the top two floors of this building between the three of us. Connor's apartment is next to mine. Russel has the penthouse." I signal for her to follow me in the direction of my front door before she can ask any more questions.

CHAPTER THREE

---◆---

Canary Wharf, London

Violet

Harrison picks up my duffel bag effortlessly, then turns and walks away. I follow behind him, unsure of where we are headed. The corridor disappears around a corner, and the hidden space comes into view. I'm left facing two doors similar in style to the boardroom, whatever that is. The way he spoke about it made my skin crawl. A business asset—maybe it's a vault where they all hide their gold bars. It wouldn't surprise me; this whole place screams obscene wealth.

The door to the left has a small plaque with the name *Waite* engraved on it. The other door has a matching one with my brother Connor's name. Harrison pulls a card from his pocket and swipes it across a small black pad, the same as the one at the elevator. He steps forward to a white rectangular box with a red light, similar to that of a shop assistant's scanner, and looks directly into it. The door clicks open audibly.

"You have an eye scanner to get into your apartment?" I say, astounded. He glances over his shoulder as he pushes open the door.

"We all take our security very seriously. When you work in the industry we do, you make more enemies than friends." He holds the door wide, signaling for me to pass. "Does anyone know you're here? Or were coming here?"

"No. I haven't even told anyone I've left America."

He nods, then follows me into the room, closing the door behind him. He drops my bag at his feet.

"Welcome to my humble home," he says, flashing me a smile. A smile that made me go weak at the knees in my teens is having the same effect now. "Make yourself at home. Your room is down here, third door on the right." He strides off, and I run behind him. Without warning, he stops, causing me to crash into him, my breasts connecting with his back. Hastily, he spins to face me, placing his hands on my arms. "Fuck, you're still the clumsy dolly you always were," he says, chuckling under his breath. I bristle at the comment. Rude bastard.

His hand takes one of mine, our fingers interlocking. We stare at each other for a moment. "My room," I prompt, and he startles. It's as if he wasn't even here with me, though he is looking directly into my eyes. "You were showing me to my room," I remind him.

"So I was," he says. "Sorry, got a bit lost myself there. It's through here." Not letting go of my fingers, he tugs me over to another dark heavy door sitting slightly ajar. As we step through, he flicks a switch on the wall, and a soft light coats the space. He lets go of me, then walks over to the floor-to-ceiling glass windows overlooking the River Thames.

"Your home is beautiful, Harry," I say honestly as my eyes scan the bedroom, absorbing the luxurious surroundings. It is an exquisite combination of modern and comfortable. A king-sized bed with a navy velvet headboard sits to one side on a raised platform. Pale pink silk sheets fall over the edge. The furniture is mirrored and polished to a high shine. Artwork on the walls compliments the navy and pink color scheme. A large navy rug sprawls across the dark wood floor between a matching velvet sofa and the bed.

"The view is the best part," he replies, continuing to look out of the window. "Up here, we are tucked away, looking down on the chaos below." His lips thin into a sad smile.

Night has fallen since I arrived. On the fifty-seventh floor, we look out into the darkness and down on the city's twinkling lights. I walk over to join him.

"I agree, the view is the best part," I say, but I'm not looking at the city. Harrison was my teen crush, my older brother's friend who was off limits. He was different from the other boys, rarely teasing cruelly and occasionally standing up for me in front of them. That day, when I'd given him my virginity, I'd hoped we would become something more. But as soon as he realized what he'd done, he fled my room, and we haven't spoken since. Until today.

The following morning, my brothers and him packed up and returned to London to continue their lives. I'd left for Glasgow within days, broken-hearted by his rejection. Sometimes I wonder if I'd have fallen for Aiden's charm if I hadn't been so devastated by Harry's dismissal. Aiden's appearance at my apartment had been a welcome distraction from my misery—an offer of attention when the man I truly loved didn't want me after having a taste. Sometimes I still wonder what I did wrong, why he chose to run.

"You must be so proud of yourself," I say to Harry, and he turns to face me.

"Why do you say that?"

"Well, look where you've ended up." I wave my hands, signaling at our surroundings. "If this isn't success, I don't know what is. And you've done it all yourself."

"No, I had your brothers' and family's support. I'd never have landed here without you all. I'm forever grateful."

"My father saw your promise. That's why he stepped in all those years ago. He knew you deserved a chance at a positive future. You've taken it."

"Why are you back, Violet?" he asks sharply, startling me. "You ran off all those years ago, and no one heard from you. Then you pop up unannounced claiming you've wasted years."

31

"I had nowhere else to go," I answer truthfully, and he rolls his eyes.

"What do you want? Money? An apartment? Russell and Connor aren't going to be overjoyed to see you, but I think you know that. As for your parents, I've no idea how they'll react. I've hardly heard your name mentioned in a decade."

"I know they hate me for leaving." My voice is meek as I drop my eyes from his, speaking to my feet.

"No, Violet, they hate you for running halfway across the globe. They are disappointed in you for throwing away your future. Never mind the fact you've been shacked up with a married man."

I blink up at him, stunned by his knowledge. "You knew," I whisper angrily. "You knew he was married."

"Of course I fucking did. Everyone did."

"Except me."

His eyebrows draw together as he looks at me, his gaze pinning me to the spot, furious. It's clear he doesn't believe me.

"Except you, what? I thought you had more respect for yourself," he snaps, then rubs at his forehead with his hand.

"I didn't know he was married. He never told me. I was kept away from everyone. Our life was private. That's why I'm here—I only found out a few days ago because of a news broadcast."

"You expect me to believe that you've been with Aiden Marley for thirteen years and the fact he had a wife never cropped up. Pull the other one—don't start lying to cover your ass. Your brothers are even less likely to accept your bullshit than me."

"It's the truth," I cry, throwing my hands in the air. "I was sitting in my living room in my apartment three days ago when he walked across my TV screen with his wife and kids. That's the fact of it." I glare at him for disbelieving me. "Now I see the red flags that I've been ignoring since the beginning, but until that moment, I had no idea."

"You're serious," he says, his tone softening in obvious surprise. I nod curtly, taking a deep breath to try and control my nerves, which have skyrocketed with the unexpected argument. "Shit, I'm sorry. We all thought you knew. When you didn't return anyone's calls or contact us, we assumed you didn't want to speak to us."

"What calls?" I ask, confused.

"For months we tried to contact you. The phone you had was disconnected but we called Aiden's office daily. He refused to speak to anyone. Denied you were there. But we knew—your father had a man on the inside. He saw you the day you arrived."

"He never told me," I say quietly. "I didn't know. He said my father couldn't know about us because of their business relationship."

Harry snorts loudly. "Aiden Marley is a salesman. He'd been chasing your father's business for years but was only ever thrown scraps. He is a wealth of information though, so your father kept him on his side. Marley got lucky with one contract that launched his career, and he's been treading water ever since.

I bet you never saw his bank statements. The man is in debt up to his eyeballs. Him purchasing that baseball team won't be legit. It'll be a cover for something darker."

"How do you know so much?"

"I've been keeping tabs on the bastard for years. He owes one of our clients money. A shit load of money. His clock is counting down. His name is getting closer to the top of the list."

"What list?"

"The list that no one wants to be on." His voice is low and ominous. "I'll go and get your bag," he says, changing the subject. "You have a shower, then meet me in the kitchen when you're ready. I'll cook us something for dinner." With that, he leaves my room, returning seconds later with my bag. "I'll see you in a bit." He retreats from my space, closing the door softly behind him.

I lift the bag onto the bed and rummage around in the contents. Simple black leggings and an oversized t-shirt will need to do. Tomorrow, I will need to go shopping and refresh my wardrobe. After laying out what I'm going to wear, I wander through to the bathroom. It's pristine white without a hint of color. There is a huge shower at the back of the room—jets point in all directions. It looks like a Tardis.

My clothes lie in a pile where I stripped in the center of the bathroom. Two decadent white towels sit poised on the side, waiting for me later. The water scalds my skin as I let it run over my body, washing away the previous few days of dirt and grime.

The shampoo I found in the cupboard smells of vanilla and is calming as I massage my scalp.

After an eternity of letting my worries flow away with the water, I step out of the cubicle and wrap myself in one of the soft towels. I make my way back through to the bedroom area, sitting down at the dressing table.

My reflection is unrecognizable. Sunken eyes and protruding cheekbones are far from how I usually look. But between the sickness and the stress, these past weeks have been difficult. With a glance down at my still-flat stomach, I sigh softly before the tears fall. Aiden doesn't know about our baby. I'd been planning on telling him, having only found out myself when he'd been away for two weeks on a business trip. Keeping the knowledge from him was torture, but I'd wanted to see his expression when I told him our news. Now, I will never get the opportunity. Not that he will want our child; he has his family already.

I lift the brush and untangle my disheveled hair. It's a laborious task, but Aiden never wanted me to cut it. He loved how feminine it is. He can't fucking stop me from cutting it now. Not that he cares.

I was sitting on the plane when the realization hit. Aiden kept me on tap but never made any effort. Yes, he looked after me financially, but emotionally I've been lost for years. The way my heart used to lift when he called. The way I would hang on his every word for his approval. My new knowledge infuriates me—I've been no more than a call girl. My youth has been wasted on a man who doesn't love me.

My tamed hair is piled on top of my head and secured loosely with a pin. Odd curls shoot off in obscure directions. One hangs blatantly across my eyes, no matter how many times I push it behind my ear. The black leggings hug my frame and sit flush against my stomach. I don't feel ready to share my news. My arrival is enough of a shock.

Resolving that I need to go and face Harrison again, I pull the blue cotton t-shirt over my head. In my bare feet, I pad out into the hallway and go in search of the kitchen.

Harrison is sitting on a bar stool at a sleek marble counter which sits on top of high glossy black units. The kitchen and living space are open plan, with the cooking space only feet from where you watch television. The whole area is mono-chrome—everything is black, white, or gray edged in chrome. The same floor-to-ceiling windows look out over London below. He glances up when he hears my footsteps.

"I thought you'd got lost," he says with a smirk. "Good shower?" His voice is deep and husky as he speaks.

"Delightful. I could have stayed in there forever."

His eyes darken. "I'd have had to come to find you. That may have been a dangerous situation."

"It's nothing you haven't seen before," I reply abruptly. His mouth drops open in disbelief. I'm taken aback by my own confidence. "Not that I've seen you since that day."

Redness explodes at the base of his throat. He's unbuttoned his crisp white shirt to expose the top of his chest. Tattoos peak out from the collar. His suit jacket is discarded over the back of the sofa. He wriggles uncomfortably in his chair and takes a deep breath.

"I'm sorry, Violet. What happened shouldn't have. I took advantage of the situation. It shouldn't have been me you had that experience with."

"I wanted to have it with you."

He goes to reply as the door to the apartment bursts open. My two brothers storm into the room, shouting nonsense at each other. Harry stands, stepping between me and them. If you didn't know they weren't related to him, you'd assume they were all brothers. All are similar in stature, with dark hair and shrewd eyes.

"So, it's fucking true!" my oldest brother Russell hollers. "The little harlot is back from across the pond. Have you run out of married men to fuck?" I recoil from the comment, throwing my hands to my mouth. "Get out, you're not wanted here." He steps toward me, and Harry moves in front of him, placing a hand on his chest. Russell glares at him, furious at the obstruction.

"Hear her out," Harry says, his eyes focused on my brother, who looks ready to explode. "Things haven't been what we thought they were." Connor stands at the back watching the situation unfold, assessing as he always does before making his move.

"Get out my fucking way, Waite. I want to hug my sister." Russell grins menacingly. "I want to crush her, like she did our mother."

"If you think I'm letting you near her when you're pissed and irate, you don't know me well enough. Go home, sober up, and we can talk in the morning. Violet can stay here tonight. Then we can discuss what's happened when everyone is fully awake and lucid tomorrow."

"She already keeping your bed warm?" Russell sneers. Harry's jaw tightens but he doesn't respond, simply stares the other man down.

"Come on, Russ," Connor says from the other side of the room. "Let's go and get some shut-eye. Or I can give Leila a call if you need some relief? We can deal with our errant sister tomorrow. Waite has it under control for tonight." He looks from me to Harry, then nods. The men make a silent agreement to get my mountain of a brother, who is ready to detonate, out of the room. "Come on bro," Connor says again. With a final scowl, Russell turns and follows him out of the apartment.

Once again, my emotions rush to the surface. I whimper pathetically as Harry turns to face me. "It will be all right," he says, wrapping his arm around my shoulders.

"How did they get in here?" I ask.

"For safety, we all have access to each other's apartments," he tells me. "That arrangement can have its downsides." He flashes me a cheeky smile. "Are you hungry?" I shake my head. "Bed for you then. Everything can be dealt with in the morning."

Chapter Four

The Level Boardroom

Harrison

Russell's fist crashes down on the boardroom table, the glass top vibrating violently. His brother hisses through his teeth and they glare at each other. "I don't want to fucking replace the table again. Get yourself under control," Connor growls.

"That bastard better start talking," Russell replies, then his focus moves to the man tied to the chair sitting at the opposite end of the room. He screams again as I hit him hard across the face with the black leather glove I was about to put on

"I bloody told you this place is soundproof. Save your cries. No one will hear them," I tell him again. For a member of a criminal gang, this guy is pathetic. "When did Devane say he'd be here? Why we have to do that fucker's dirty work I don't know," I mutter, annoyed that my day has started like this.

"He pays us handsomely for it, and stop complaining. This part is fun," Russell says with a dark smile. "You love it, Waite. I know you fucking do." I roll my eyes at him, then finish putting my glove on.

The intercom buzzes, announcing one of our associate's arrival. The hidden elevator doors glide open, and he steps into the room. This is the only floor it rises to, and the sole access to it is a single door hidden in a storage closet on the ground floor. The only people who know of its existence are our small team and Matthew, the security guard.

Hunter Devane's gaze roams over the room as he assesses the situation. "Thanks, lads," he says, a broad grin spreading across his face. "I knew it was a good call to have the bastard dropped here. The cops have been snooping around my place."

His long dark hair is scraped back into a rough manbun. Days of stubble coat his chin and cheeks. He's the oldest of our group at forty-two. With clear blue, astute eyes and sharp features, he emanates control. He's not a big man, both slim and lithe, but deadly. I've seen what he can do with a knife. His connections to the Irish mafia make him lethal, but he's London born and bred. The Irish connection is generations ago on his mother's side, but he uses it to his advantage daily.

"You're lucky you have deep pockets, Devane," I say crossly. "It's fucking Sunday. Some of us have places to be other than cleaning up your mess. Every bloody week you make our job of keeping you out of prison more fucking difficult. Next time, why don't you just kidnap someone in front of Buckingham Palace. It'd be less obvious."

"All right, Waite, you're pissed. I get it. I'll take over from here. You get back to whatever bit of skirt is in your bed. Is she paid for or here of her own volition?"

"Not every man has to pay for sex," I spit back at him, and he laughs.

"Sensible ones use prostitutes." He leers then grabs his crotch. "You can ignore them, kick them out, and call them back when it suits you. I'd rather have an on-tap pussy than a wife nipping my head."

"You have a fucking wife," I remind him. "Do you remember where she lives?" He shrugs, unconcerned.

"If you two are quite finished with your lover's tiff," Connor interjects. "Perhaps we could get back to our friend here." He gestures to our captive. "Did you let Damon know in case anything crosses his desk? He always prefers the heads-up if he's going to find a body."

"I texted him," Russell says. "Told him we had a fish on the hook. Are we going actual fishing this week? I miss our boys' afternoons. There's nothing better than a cooler box of beer and a salmon on the line."

"Fuck's sake," Connor says. "If you're all quite finished, I do have a bit of skirt to get back to and she's paid hourly. So, could we sort this out, and I'll return to getting my money's worth. She's still spread-eagled on my bed. You said it would take an hour maximum." He scowls at his brother. "That was two hours ago."

The sound announcing someone's arrival pings again. The doors open, and Chief Constable Damon McKinney, Head of the National Serious and Organized Crime unit, walks out. "Morning boys," he calls, running his hand through his close-cropped dark hair. He's huge at almost six and a half feet tall, with a physique a wrestler would be jealous of. "What shit are you dropping on my doorstep now? You do know it's the weekend."

"We know," Russell replies sharply. "These idiots have been moaning since we arrived. But work never stops, not in our world."

"Who's this?" Damon asks as his eyes land on our guest.

"This," Hunter replies, "is Michaels's man." Damon's eyes light up at the nugget of information. "Jarvis here was agreeing to help us with our inquiries."

"Is he being cooperative? Or does he require some encouragement?"

Hunter pulls his knife from the waistband of his jeans, twirling it between his fingers as he wanders over to the man in the chair. His eyes stay fixed on his prey. There is little chance of him getting out of here alive. The plastic sheet below the chair confirms it. Russell has prepared him for disposal on Hunter's say-so.

"Where's the product?" Hunter asks calmly. Jarvis shakes his head. The knife tip grazes his cheek in one swift motion, lifting a morsal of skin. He groans at the unexpected injury. "Listen to me, Jarvis, is it?" His victim nods.

"Today will be your final day on this earth. Everyone in this room knows it. I'm no liar, so I won't give you false hope. You have exactly..." Hunter turns to Connor, gesturing toward the large digital clock on the wall. Connor starts the countdown from one hundred minutes. "You have exactly six thousand seconds left in life. How they're spent is completely up to you. You have the choice of being put out of your misery with a final blow, or I can tear you apart piece by piece."

Our target visibly swallows as he listens to the maniac in front of him.

"What will it be?" Hunter smiles sweetly, then drives the blade into the man's arm. "The clock is ticking."

***

That afternoon, the five of us sit around our boardroom table in The Level. "It's still fucking Sunday," Connor mutters petulantly. He gave in a while ago and went to release the girl from his bed. She'd been furious, twisting his cock in her hand before storming off. When he arrived back in the boardroom, he was cradling both his crown jewels and his pride.

Our captive lies dead on the floor, wrapped in the sheet he sat on. Hunter got over-excited and finished him before we found out what we needed to know. This isn't the first time it's happened either. The man is an animal, even though the reasoning behind his actions is somewhat commendable. "You can't keep offing the witnesses before we get the information, Devane," I snarl.

"We have a rough idea where the product is," he says blandly, still playing with his blade between his fingers. Thank fuck he wiped it clean.

"Yeah, a farm building in Devon really fucking narrows down the search."

"At least we know the area they're cooking it. If we find the kitchen, we can take it down at the source. The stuff is lethal. It needs to be taken off the streets."

Damon clears his throat, then places his hands on the table. His forearms pulse as he clenches his fists then releases them. "We have the name of the man in charge," he says. "It's no surprise it's Michaels. He's been running dirty product for years; thousands of deaths are due to his drugs laced with anything they can sweep off the floor. Not that anyone knows who he is."

"I'd skin the bastard alive," Hunter says, then drives his knife into an apple sitting in front of him, uneaten. He lost his younger brother to bad heroin. That was when our crazy team began. Three lawyers, a Chief Constable, and a mafia leader working together to take dirty drugs off the streets. "Anyway, lads, I need to be going. I'll get Greyson to come past and dispose of that." He signals to the dead man, then stands and leaves. Damon follows behind.

"See you all Wednesday," Damon calls over his shoulder. "Make sure the beer fridge is full, Waite."

Russell, Connor, and I sit silently around the table, each sipping a beer. Greyson arrives thirty minutes after Hunter's departure and removes the corpse from the floor. He disappears without a word.

"We have a busy week ahead of us," Russell says, throwing each of us an agenda for the week. The room morphs from a torture chamber to a lawyer's boardroom in a heartbeat. "Everyone in the office tomorrow at seven. The stinking rich computer geek is coming in at eight to discuss the murder conviction he's up on."

"Roydon? Who did he kill?" I ask, and Russell raises his eyebrows.

"Innocent until proven guilty. Did you miss that class at law school?"

"They're very rarely innocent. Most likely guilty if he's paying our prices for a defense. Don't yank my chain, Russ. What's the details?"

"His much younger wife. Seemingly after a year of marriage, she wanted a divorce. The thirty-year age gap was too much for her. They grew apart, apparently." He chuckles. "Mr. Moneybags wasn't willing to give her up, so he drowned her in the Jacuzzi." I mutter some expletives under my breath. "It should be an interesting case for you. The evidence is concrete, so you'll need to do what you do best to get him off."

"What's that?"

"Sweet talk the jury, find a technicality, or simply convince them the truth is false. Don't let this case end your streak. What are we at now? Ten defense cases, ten wins?"

"Something like that." I turn over my phone, which has been lying face down on the glass. One message blinks on the screen. *Violet.* I'd left my number written on a notepad in the kitchen for her, next to a new phone. She'd still been asleep when I left this morning.

Will you be back soon? Violet.

"If we're done here. I'll be getting home," I say, standing and walking to the door. As I turn the heavy brass key in the lock, Russell's voice fills the room.

"Tell my sister I want to see her. She has some explaining to do." I turn to face him. He stares at me unblinking. "Is that a problem?" Connor watches us but doesn't volunteer an opinion. His eyes move between Russell and me, waiting for someone to make the next move.

"I'll tell her, but I'm not forcing her to see you after the idiot you made of yourself last night." His eyes narrow. "She's been through hell. Give her a day or so, then we can all sit down together."

"She's our fucking sister, not yours. This is family shit. It doesn't concern you."

"It does when you threatened her in my apartment." His hands clench into fists on the table as he attempts to control his temper. "All I'm saying is you don't know what happened when she left. You also don't know what her life has been like for the past thirteen years. Perhaps thinking with your brain instead of your fists may be beneficial. I'll see you both in the office tomorrow." Without waiting for their response, I leave and don't look back.

Violet is sitting on my sofa when I enter the living room. She's wearing one of my shirts. I gawk at her, taken aback by the sight. She looks up and gives me a soft smile. "I'm sorry, the clothes I brought with me needed to be washed. I stole this off the dryer. I hope you don't mind, Harry." She stands and walks over to me, her bare shapely legs protruding from the pale blue cotton. Her long dark hair lies in loose waves down her back. She's makeup free, and her skin glows under the soft light flowing in the windows. "Thank you for looking after me last night and standing up to Russ. He hasn't changed."

"It was no problem. He wasn't thinking straight. I've told him to take a few days to calm down. You can stay here until you feel ready to talk to him."

She stands under my nose, glancing up through long, fine lashes. Her cheeks heat with a rosy-pink flush. Unexpectedly, she wraps her arms around my waist and places her cheek against my chest. "Thank you," she whispers again. I place my hands on her shoulders, pushing her back softly so she lets go, stepping away. She frowns then rearranges her features.

"You're safe. Take some time to rest, then we can figure out where you go from here. Have you spoken to Aiden?" She shakes her head. "Has he contacted you?"

"No, I ditched my phone." The words are barely audible. It's as if I can sense her heart breaking. It makes me want to kill the asshole for hurting her. How can a man have a woman so beautiful and treat her like a whore? Over a decade of her life devoted to him for nothing.

"We'll decide what to do about him too," I say, almost to myself. She gives me a curious look but doesn't respond. The bastard is going to pay. I know his time is running out with our client he owes, but I may have to speed up the clock.

CHAPTER FIVE

Harrison's Apartment, The Level

Violet

"Good morning, dear," a kind, elderly woman says I as enter the kitchen. I grind to a halt and blink at her. She's removing a tray of freshly baked muffins from Harry's state-of-the-art oven. Her mouth moves into a wide smile, exposing perfectly bleached white teeth. They are in complete contrast to her wrinkled aged skin. Her whole persona emanates compassion and love. "Mr. Waite said to expect you at some point this morning. Judging by your expression, he never told you about me." She chuckles as she places the tray of delights on the counter. "Muffin?"

"Where's Harry?" I ask, not knowing what else to say.

"He'll be at work. It's Monday, there tends to be a seven o'clock meeting to plan the week ahead. Mr. Chase runs a tight ship, I believe." She glances at the clock. My gaze follows hers—ten-thirty in the morning. I must have needed sleep; normally, by six my brain is awake and ready to take on the day. "He's your brother, is he not?"

"Harry? No. He's an old family friend. Russell and Connor are my brothers."

"That's what I meant." She cocks her head to one side, her gaze running over my body. I'm still wearing Harry's shirt. I slept in it. "Mr. Waite said you've had a difficult few days. Oh my." Her hands fly to her mouth as her eyes ping open. "How rude of me. I've not even introduced myself." She wipes her palms on her pink checked apron, then steps out from behind the counter and walks toward me. Both her hands take mine. "I'm Mrs. D., housekeeper for The Level."

"The Level?" I repeat back to her. She smiles generously.

"The top two floors of this building. Your brothers and Mr. Waite own them. I look after them all. They're the sons I never had. I live downstairs, apartment twenty-five." Still holding my fingers, she tugs me to a bar stool at the kitchen worktop. "Now, come dear, you look like you need feeding, and I want to learn all about you."

An hour later, I'm still perched on my seat, eating yet another muffin. This is my third. Mrs. D. has talked continuously, asking questions about my likes and dislikes but never prying for information about my situation. The events which have led to me sitting here in front of her are left untouched.

"How long do you plan on staying with Mr. Waite?" she asks. I'm stuffing another piece of muffin in my mouth and pause, considering what to say. The suspicious part of me wonders if this is the interrogation starting. Is she snooping for my brothers?

"Not long," I reply ambiguously. "I'm only here to visit, then I'll be moving on."

"Back to America?" Her focus holds mine as I chew. She knows more than she's letting on.

"I don't know." My answer is honest. There's no point in me lying. At this moment, I have no plans to be anywhere. All I know is the man I have devoted myself to for over a decade is married to someone else and I'm pregnant with his baby. With no career, no friends, and a fractured family, a clear strategy isn't anywhere near the forefront of my mind. Surviving until tomorrow feels like the goal to be accomplished, not sorting out my life.

The front door swings open, ending our conversation. Harry strides into the room dressed in a sleek gray suit and white shirt. It's open at the collar—his tattoos are barely visible, but I see them as the material flexes when he moves. I wonder what they are. He didn't have them when we were younger. What made him feel the need to mark his body with a design, a statement?

Dark eyes fix on me. He runs them over my face, then down my legs to my toes before looking directly into my eyes once more. My mouth dries—he still affects me like he did all those years ago. One look, and I turn to mush.

"Good morning, Mrs. D.," he says smoothly, walking over then leaning down to place a kiss on her cheek. "You've met Violet. I hope she's not being too much trouble." He glances at me while flashing a sexy smile. "She was always a bit of a handful when we were kids." His words are laden with sexual innuendo causing my cheeks to heat. "She's all grown up, but still as much of a conundrum."

"We've been having a lovely morning," she tells him. "Girl time."

"Am I interrupting?" He raises his eyebrows at her, and she laughs. "I'm only home to collect some files then I'll be out of your hair. You can continue your girl time without my interference."

"This is your home," she reminds him, rolling her eyes.

"But we all know who runs The Level, Mrs. D., don't we? And it's none of us men." She scowls but doesn't respond.

"Did you sleep all right, Violet?" he asks, his attention turning to me.

"Yes, thank you. Have you seen my brothers?" I ask, bringing up the topic before I lose my nerve. My brothers are a situation I need to tackle soon.

"They're at the office, but they do want to see you. I told them only if you're feeling up to it. You can let me know later, so there's no pressure. After thirteen years, another few days won't kill them."

My shoulders sag as I think of what the meeting with my brothers may entail. Their welcome wasn't the one I hoped for, but it was what I expected.

"Thank you," I whisper, my voice soft and feeble sounding. All I've done since I arrived is thank him for helping me, standing up for me, looking after me in general. Back on London soil for twenty-four hours, and it's as if I've reverted to being a teenager—crushing on, while being supported by, my brother's best friend. But now, we're in our thirties, and life is much more complicated.

"Anytime, Vi," he replies. "I always was your security guard." Mrs. D. looks between us but makes no comment. Harry watches me, saying no more. I snap my eyes away from his, uncomfortable with the charged atmosphere. "I'll be getting those files," he says, then turns and walks toward a closed door on the opposite side of the room. My companion and I watch him go inside.

"He's a special man," she says, focusing on me. "Of the three of them I look after, Mr. Waite is always the warmest. It's a shame he's not met the woman meant to share his life." Her eyes glint as a soft smile plays on her lips. "In the eight years I've worked for him, there's never been anyone of importance. I wondered why." She pauses, the second hand on a clock the only sound. "Perhaps now I know."

***

That evening, Harry appears home as darkness has begun to fall. The summer heat hangs in the air. I've opened the apartment windows to allow the gentle breeze to circulate the rooms. He walks into the living area. I'm sitting on the sofa with my legs curled up underneath me reading a gossip magazine. The armchair directly opposite sags under his weight. His fingers move and undo two more buttons of his shirt, exposing a smattering of dark hair. One strong arm rises, and he runs his fingers through his already roughed-up hair.

"Tough day?" I ask, and he grumbles something incoherent. "Do you want anything?"

"A client who isn't guilty would be nice." He looks at me then closes his eyes before leaning backward against the cushions behind him. "And perhaps business associates who could agree with each other on something. Even what to have for lunch would do." I laugh out loud, and he smiles, but doesn't open his eyes.

"Russell and Connor have been giving you a hard time?" I surmise.

"Always." He sighs, then brings his focus to mine. "And they're on their way here to speak to you. Is that all right? Or do you want me to intervene?" The morsel of elation I felt from his arrival evaporates. "I don't mind telling them no, Vi. But Russell won't back down until he speaks to you. I suggest you're honest with him about what happened in Chicago."

"No, it's okay. I'll talk to them. Will you stay with me?" We stare at each other for a moment. Even though it's been years since I saw him last and we both have over a decade of experiences neither of us are aware of, my heart still skips with a glance from him. In his presence, I feel safe.

"Sure," he replies with a shrug. "Russell's already pissed off I've let you stay here. Getting more involved will give him plenty to beat me across the head with in the boardroom."

"Thanks," I say, and he responds with a nod. He rises from his chair, walks over to the fridge, and lifts six bottles of beer from the shelf before returning to place them on the coffee table in front of us. He offers one to me, but I wave it away as a strong knock rattles around the apartment.

"That will be them. You ready?" he asks. I swallow as nerves rise in my stomach. "Vi, last chance to say no. I'll turn them away at the door, but if I let them in here, they won't leave until they have answers."

"I'm ready." My voice sounds more confident than I feel. But I know to gain their support and reconnect with my family, this is a situation I need to face directly with honesty.

Harry walks over to the door and swings it open. Russell strides past him, making a beeline for where I sit. Uncurling my legs, I move to sit straighter in my seat. He stands above me, glaring down. Connor appears at his side, placing his hand on our brother's shoulder.

"Russ," he says, firmly, "sit down. It's Violet. Let's hear what she has to say. It's our little sister, and I don't know about you, but hell I've missed her." My heart strains as my brother's words filter into my brain. He missed me. Russell grunts but retreats to sit on the sofa opposite. Harry stands at the back then strolls over and casually sits down next to me, close but not touching. Connor positions himself on the armchair between the two sofas.

No one speaks. The men each take a beer, snapping the cap and drinking greedily. My gaze roams between them, waiting for someone to take the lead on the situation. Finally, Russell, clearly fed up with no information being forthcoming, speaks.

"Where the fuck have you been?" he snarls. "Thirteen fucking years with no word."

"Chicago," I answer simply. "But you know that." His eyes narrow to slits. Though my brother makes me nervous, I've never been able to resist poking the bear. My teen years were spent annoying him, either by defiance or kissing a boy. I've lost count of the number of broken noses my lips caused.

"Shacked up with a married man," he spits. Redness creeps from the base of his throat as his eyes darken. "You fucked off. Threw everything our parents gave you back in their face. Ruined your career. All to be the harlot of that bastard, Marley."

"I didn't know," I whisper angrily. Tears prick my eyes as the thin veil of confidence I had splits. "I loved him." He laughs out loud.

"Loved him," he bellows. "Was that before or after he told you about his wife?"

"I didn't know about her," I shoot back, furious that he would think I could. "Not until I saw them on the news." He

56

blinks at me, obviously confused. Connor looks from me to him, then back to me.

"You expect me to believe that for the past thirteen years you didn't know you were the other woman? That you cut all contact with your family, moved across the world, and were oblivious to it all? Do you think I'm a fucking idiot?"

"I believe her," Connor interjects. Russell scowls at him. He shrugs his shoulders in response. "Our Violet was never a liar. Spontaneous, forceful, and overzealous, but never a liar." He turns to me, leaning across and taking my hand in his. "I believe you, little sister, but I'm furious at you for living a lie for so long. For walking away and not contacting us." He squeezes my fingers. "Especially when we reached out to you."

"I didn't know," I say, never dropping my eyes from his. "Aiden told me you wanted nothing to do with me. That I'd let you all down and you had all washed your hands of me." Silence falls over the room as my brothers process what I've told them. Aiden Marley had duped us all and splintered my family in the process.

"The bastard's going to pay," Russell growls. "His lies and deceit will come full circle to land firmly at his door."

"I'm already on it," Harry states, and all eyes turn to him. "He owes our murdering millionaire money—a lot of money. Perhaps we could provide client satisfaction while giving Mr. Marley a taste of his own medicine." The men all look at each other, their agreement obvious to them but perplexing for me.

"We can discuss the possibilities at our next meeting, but let's just say I've become privy to some interesting information."

"I look forward to hearing it, Waite," Russell replies, then glances at our brother.

"Shall we go?" Connor suggests and they both stand.

"Violet, you would probably be better moving in with me," Russell adds. My skin prickles at the thought. I'd much rather stay here or somewhere else anyway.

"Living arrangements can be discussed another time," Harry says smoothly. "It's been a long day." He glances at the clock on the wall—it's almost midnight. Connor mumbles in agreement, then encourages our headstrong brother out of the door. I sigh in relief as the door closes behind them. Harry is still sitting on the sofa beside me, his eyes firmly fixed on the closed door.

"That went better than I thought," I tell him, and he chuckles.

"For you, yes. But for Aiden Marley, he now has a target painted clearly on his back." His beautiful and intense eyes bore into mine, pinning me to the spot. "Russell is a different man in some ways to the one you knew. Yes, he's still headstrong and a bully, but he's seen things he can't unsee. You have to understand, we move in circles a lot darker than they appear."

I blink at him, wondering how to respond.

"Our jobs are a mixture of light and dark. I defend some of the wealthiest men in the world. We rub shoulders with people who could end us in a heartbeat."

"I know you support the mafia," I tell him, and he smiles.

"We work for the mafia, there's a difference. But some of what they do isn't all that bad. Often the most ruthless men I've met have pristine principles. The world is all shades of gray—not everything is simply good or bad."

"What shade are you?" I ask him. His focus never leaves mine. He looks through me before answering. My heart beats hard in my chest. The young man who took me to bed for the first time is sitting in front of me. He's still the same kind generous soul I knew back then, but today I see a seam of iron running through him. He's still Harry but a harder version of him.

"Whatever shade you want me to be."

CHAPTER SIX

Harrison's Apartment,
The Level

Harrison

"Whatever shade you want me to be," I tell her, and she stares into my eyes. My common sense has taken a sabbatical. Tonight, all I can think about is getting close to her. Touching her. My instinct is to reach out and feel her skin beneath my fingertips. When Russell suggested her moving in with him, it took all my strength not to shout *no fucking way*. Before I can overstep the mark further, I stand, wish her goodnight, and disappear to my room.

In the shower, I run my hand down my shaft thinking of her, imagining her body joined with mine. How it has changed in the years we have been apart. My dick hardens to breaking point, my fingers pulling roughly as I visualize her out of her clothes. With one hand on the wall, I let the warm water roll over my body and pleasure myself pretending it's her, picture pumping her pussy as I pin her against the cool white tiles. Those shapely legs wrapped around my waist; firm breasts squashed against my chest. The sounds she makes with each orgasm, the sensation of her coming around me. I want nothing more than to find out what she feels like now, if our bodies will still connect seamlessly the way they did before. The one time we allowed it to happen.

***

My office phone rings, snapping me from the recollection of last night.

"Mr. Waite," my secretary Elspeth says, "Chief Constable McKinney has arrived for your eleven o'clock."

"Show him in, please."

The heavy oak door swings open and bounces off my wall. I glance up into Damon McKinney's furious eyes. "Five more, Waite," he snarls. "Five more deaths this weekend due to that fucking heroin." He strides across the floor and throws himself into the chair opposite me. His head drops to his hands, his elbows on his knees.

"Does Devane know?" I ask.

"Not yet. I don't want to start a war we can't win." He rubs his forehead. Tired eyes rise to mine. "When he hears, he'll be out for blood. Five innocent students on a night out, sold the product in a backstreet club. All of them dead within hours of taking it."

"Fuck," I mutter. "Same as Danny." Devane's little brother died on a night like that. He had no part in the criminal side of his family's life. Hunter spent his time keeping him safe in an attempt to allow him to live a normal existence. Not even the mafia don of London could save an overenthusiastic teenager from himself, though. At nineteen years old, he injected the wrong substance into his veins and dropped dead on the dance floor ten minutes later. Hunter has been out to find the source of the drug ever since—heroin laced with rat poison. The more weeks that pass, the more the deaths mount up.

"I need to tell him," Damon says, almost to himself. "But I've been juggling so much of the shit he's involved with across my desk, I'm worried I won't be able to control the fallout. There are only so many deaths and strange events I can explain away. There is going to be a point when someone will want answers."

"What do you need me to do?"

"Support me." It's a simple request. "When we meet at your place on Wednesday night and we sit down to discuss the project, all I ask is you support my suggestions on moving the operation forward." I nod, but leave room for him to continue. "Devane and Russell will want to use force. I don't think we can. This syndicate runs deep. There are a lot of people involved, and we don't know their true identities. We need all the evidence we can get before we take them down. Killing more witnesses won't help."

"Have you spoken to Connor?"

"Not yet, but I will. I'm not sure whose side he'll be on. The man plays his cards close to his chest. But at the end of the day, he is Russell's brother and will probably follow his lead."

"Connor is sensible. He knows when to fight a fight. I'll speak to him," I tell him.

"Good," he says and stands. "We need a combined effort, not fucking Robin Hood on a mission to stop whatever fucking injustice he isn't happy about."

"How are things at home?" I ask, changing the subject. He stills, looks at me, then drops his eyes away.

"Bad," he mutters. "Very bad. This month marks a year since losing her. Trying to juggle being a father along with what I do is like playing constant Tetris."

"You're doing an amazing job on all accounts."

He doesn't answer, only turns and leaves my office. My chest strains for my heartbroken friend. After years of trying to complete their family, his wife never lived to see the baby born. Twelve months on, he's lost and confused. If things continue as they have been, his life could become even more complicated.

When I arrive home, Violet and Mrs. D. are working together in the kitchen. There are umpteen pans on the stove bubbling away, and the smell of freshly baked bread fills the room. Lively chatter bounces between them about measurements and accompaniments to what they've got cooking. They don't hear me enter, only looking up when I stand across the counter from them. Violet gives me a breath-taking smile and my chest tightens. Hell, she is beautiful.

"Good evening, Mr. Waite," Mrs. D. says. "Dinner is almost complete. Chicken Dhansak with steamed rice, broccoli, and fresh bread. Violet knows what is to be done, so I'll get out of your hair. Let you both enjoy your evening."

"Thank you," I reply. Her eyes glitter as she speaks, moving between Violet and me. Are my feelings so obvious? Is merely being in a room with this woman a sign to everyone else how I feel about her?

Mrs. D. places a final glass on the counter, washes her hands, and leaves. Not before placing a gentle kiss on Violet's cheek, though. "Enjoy your night," she whispers to her conspiratorially.

***

Violet

Harry and I watch her leave, standing across the worktop from each other. My breathing deepens as I look at him. Fuck, he's gorgeous. His eyes run over my face and hesitate on my lips.

"Are you hungry?" I ask him. He smiles sexily then runs his tongue over his bottom lip.

"You could say that. How long will dinner be?"

"Ten minutes or so," I tell him.

"I'll go and freshen up. I'll be back," he says, then walks around the obstruction between us and places a soft kiss on my cheek. I melt under his touch, my heart exploding in my chest. "See you in ten minutes." He turns and walks in the direction of his bedroom. I watch his taut behind disappear out of view, then move to the oven, using it as a mirror to adjust the straps on the simple blue summer dress Mrs. D. arrived with after lunch today. She had popped out only to return with a few items to aid my failing wardrobe until I get to the store.

I'm scooping the last of the meal onto the plates when a knock at the front door distracts me. Assuming it must be Matthew or one of my brothers, I wander over and throw it open. Aiden stands on the other side, oozing confidence. "Good evening, Princess," he says with a sly smile. He's dressed in his black Armani suit paired with a pale pink shirt. His blue eyes lock on mine, and my body freezes in position. Seeing him is a shock I don't need. "You were much easier to track down than I thought."

"How did you get in here?" I stammer.

"I have a very persuasive personality," he replies with a sneer. I move to close the door; he slams a strong hand against it to stop me. "Don't fucking think about it. We have a lot to talk about." His hand snaps to my throat, strong fingers wrapping around my windpipe as he pushes me backward, into the apartment. I totter in reverse, trying to keep my balance as I match his long strides.

"Aiden," I gasp, pulling at his grip. "What are you doing? Please don't hurt me." His fingers tighten, reducing my access to oxygen. I panic for the child in my belly. "Aiden, please. You don't understand." I open my mouth in an attempt to draw in air; the reward is minimal.

"Imagine my surprise when I came to see you at our apartment and you were gone," he snarls, ignoring my pleas. "Just upped and fucked off. No note, no message. After everything I've done for you, Princess." His grip tightens further.

"Done for me," I spit between gasps. "You're married. I devoted myself to you for thirteen years. You lied to me. I never had a future with you. You never wanted one with me."

"Don't play the victim here, you little whore. Only an idiot wouldn't have realized what was going on." His lips contort into a vicious grin. "Perhaps I should have been more transparent with you, but I didn't want to lose that mouth of yours in my sex toy cabinet. You're one of my favorites." Tears fill my eyes. He is nothing like the man I fell in love with. Hard and detached, he chuckles under his breath. "And I want my little fuck buddy back. You're coming home with me. I doubt your family will want you. They'll hand you over no questions asked. What a disappointment you've become."

"I am not going with you! Go home to your wife!" I shriek. The sound is pathetic as my body struggles to take in air.

He flexes his fingers against my skin and pushes me hard against the wall. My back connects firmly with the plaster, and a book from the shelf beside me hits the floor. His knee comes between my legs, and he presses his hip against my stomach, imprisoning my body.

"Can you afford not to?" He drops his mouth to mine, biting my bottom lip hard enough to draw blood. The metallic taste of myself coats my tongue. "If they haven't disowned you already, they will when they find out about the bastard baby you have in your belly." His words knock the little breath from my lungs.

"How do you know?" My brain misfires—I haven't told anyone about the baby. Only my doctor in Chicago who ran the test for me.

"Did you think I'd let you leave, Princess? After all these years," he sneers. "When I couldn't find you, I called the doctor. I vaguely remember you mentioning an appointment during one of our boring phone calls. After the dozy receptionist confirmed you had been in, I told her I was concerned for your mental health. You being pregnant made your well-being a primary concern, and money can convince anybody to answer questions they shouldn't. Whose baby is it?" he asks, his mouth only inches from mine. The voice that used to whisper loving words has turned violent. Evil.

"What?"

"Who's the father?" he growls. "It can't be me. We always used protection. This is a disaster I was determined to avoid. Who were you fucking behind my back?" He leans toward me, applying more pressure to my body with his. His nose tip sits on mine, nasty eyes surveying my face for evidence of any deceit.

"No one!" I whisper, devastated once more at the change in a man I loved, one I had planned a future with.

"Liar! Was it your personal trainer? One of your weird friends from acting class? Who the hell was in my bed?"

"I was." Harry's voice breaks through the fear and terror coursing through me. Aiden stills and turns his head in the direction of the words. "The baby is mine," he confirms bluntly.

"Yours?" Aiden snarls. "Please do tell me how you managed to knock my whore up in Chicago when you live in London, Waite." They glare at each other. I'm alarmed that they know each other on sight.

"You aren't the only one who can jump on a plane, Marley. You playing happy families with your wife gave us plenty of time to enjoy one another." Harry flashes the other man a wicked smile. He looks completely at ease standing in the middle of his living room in only his towel. His hair is freshly washed, his skin still glistening with water. Determined eyes move to me, his expression never changing, then return to the man holding my throat. "I would appreciate it if you could release and move away from what is mine," he says.

Over his shoulder there is a tattoo of a tiger—it spreads down onto his chest. In its mouth, it carries a flower, a violet. The pattern can be easily hidden by a buttoned shirt, but now I can see the stripes that peek out occasionally from his neckline. He stands tall, never taking his focus from the other man. As the seconds pass, his eyes darken. "As I said, Marley. Please move away from my woman and child. I won't ask you again."

Aiden adjusts his grip fractionally, then resumes pushing me against the wall, prodding at my stomach with his other hand. "This asshole," he roars. "This is whose offspring you're breeding. Your standards have lowered somewhat, Princess. Imagine choosing a pauper over me. A whore's son who only ended up where he is by charity."

The pressure is removed from me abruptly. When I glance up, Harry has Aiden in a chokehold and is pulling him backward in the direction of the door to the apartment; his captive's arms flail around in an attempt to hit his attacker.

As they reach the door Aiden twists his body, taking Harry by surprise. He stamps on his bare foot and spins out of his grip, then uses a shoulder to slam him against the solid wood. The noise of the collision reverberates around the room, and another book falls from the shelf beside me. Miraculously, Harry's towel remains in place. I watch in horror as Aiden's arm draws back, then punches his opponent square in the stomach. A gasp of air bursts from Harry's lips. His expression changes immediately from annoyed to furious.

Harry lifts his hands to the other man's chest and pushes him away with force. Aiden steps back, but his heel catches the edge of a rug causing him to fall. He grabs Harry's wrist and pulls him down too. The two men roll around the floor, punches thrown in all directions. Harry's towel doesn't survive this part of the altercation and is left lying on the apartment floor next to them.

My eyes roam around the room, looking for something to intervene with and stop the ensuing madness. A small China vase decorated with pink flowers and a silver lid sits on the shelf next to the now disturbed books. Without thinking, I grab it from its resting place and smash it across the back of Aiden's head as he has Harry pinned to the floor by his throat. The porcelain shatters, and a cloud of what seems like dust fills the space, falling over both men. Aiden splutters and rolls off his victim. Harry takes the opportunity to stand and grab him into a chokehold before throwing him out of the door.

I crumple to the ground once more as Harry ejects him from the apartment. "I said hands off." I hear Aiden's body hit the floor outside. There is a gaggle of raised voices in the hallway. Harry is shouting something at who I assume are security guards. His fury is evident.

"How the fuck did that bastard get in here?" he bellows. "I'll be having someone's balls. Tell Matthew to be here at six o'clock tomorrow. I want fucking answers. Get that asshole out of here, now." The door slams closed. He appears in front of me moments later. He leans down to pick up his towel and wraps it around his waist. His dark hair and bare skin are speckled with gray dust. I'm curled in a ball against the wall, head in my hands, sobbing furiously.

"Violet," he says softly, crouching down beside me. His hand touches my shoulder. I peek up at him through tear-filled lashes, ashamed, embarrassed, and at a loss as to how I've ended up here. A concerned expression highlights his face. The confident lawyer has been replaced by a man not sure what to say.

"I'm sorry, I'll go. This isn't your issue to deal with. I've brought too many problems to your door."

"You're pregnant," he says, ignoring my outburst. It's a question but said as a statement. "Is Aiden the father?"

"Of course he is," I wail, brushing his hand from my shoulder and pushing myself up to stand. He rises too, dominating my space. He's tall above me—his gaze locks with mine.

I snap my eyes away, not wanting to have this conversation. Telling anyone about the baby had not been top of my priority list. Now, it's been blown into the open in front of the person who confuses me more than anyone, whose opinion of me, at this point, feels the most important.

"Vi, look at me." His hand cups my chin and lifts my eyes to his. He smiles softly. "It's going to be all right. You're safe here with me." I giggle unexpectedly as I look at him, and he frowns.

"What was in that vase?" I ask him. "It's everywhere."

"My cat," he replies with a smirk. "Jasper always was getting into places he shouldn't."

My hands lift to my mouth when I realize I smashed the remains of his pet over Aiden's head. The situation is nothing but obscene, and I'm at a loss as to what to say.

"It's okay, Vi. Jasper wouldn't have felt anything." He smiles again to reassure me. "The old cat would probably have enjoyed being the hero to be honest. He used to scratch and hiss at any visitors. He was a guard cat." I laugh out loud, then fall silent. He reaches for my hand, taking it in his.

"Why did you tell him you're the father?" I ask him, still in shock at the fact he did.

He takes a deep breath before speaking, his chest expanding and contracting. My eyes move to the tiger with the violet on his shoulder. He follows my gaze with his own.

"It means what you think it does. I've got you," he whispers before dropping his mouth to my forehead. I close my eyes, letting the moment wash over me. He draws back, and I raise my palms to his chest, the feel of his still-damp skin beneath my fingers. "I've got both of you." Our fingers intertwine, then he tugs me toward the sofa as he walks backward. "You sit here," he says, gesturing to the seat. "I'll go and rinse off again."

After what feels like hours, he returns showered and wearing only his shorts. He drops down beside me and wraps his arm around my shoulders. We sit together, my body curled around his almost naked one. As the minutes pass, my anxiety subsides. Being here with him makes me feel safe. I wriggle onto his lap, needing to be surrounded by him.

A film that has been playing in the background finishes—we must have been sitting like this for an hour, but I haven't noticed. Time with Harry is fluid. I enjoy him so much that it disappears. He is a sanctuary for me to be at peace within. So little time spent together, so much emotion between us undiscussed. My old feelings are reawakening with each breath.

"Are you hungry?" I ask, looking at our uneaten meal which sits on the counter, cold. He glances at me, and his eyes fire with arousal.

"Not hungry enough to stop what is going to happen now," he says. My breathing hitches, my brain joins the dots. He wants me. The look is the same one from that afternoon in my childhood bedroom—the carnal need for my body to be joined with his obvious. "Shall we go to bed? I think we both need this tonight. I know I need you."

"Okay." It's all I can say, both excited and terrified at the prospect of being with him again. He encourages me to my feet, then rises before taking my hand and tugging me in the direction of the bedrooms.

We arrive at his room; he pushes the door open. It is similar to the one I'm staying in, a bed draped in silk and filled with high-end furnishings. He walks me over to the bed, turning my body gently and maneuvering me to stand at the edge. The backs of my knees connect with the sheets.

With his limited clothing, I can see him fully. He's trimmed and toned with definition in all the right places. A dark trail starts at his belly button and leads beneath his shorts. He pushes the fabric down, letting it fall to the floor. His cock hangs between his legs, hard. I glance up at him, and he smirks.

"You've seen me," he whispers darkly, "now I want to see all of you."

He grabs the hem of the summer dress I'm wearing and lifts. I raise my hands above my head, allowing him to remove the cotton from my body. It drops to the floor in a pool of pale blue. His arms wrap around my back, masterfully unhooking my bra, and it joins my clothing on the floor. I stand before him in only my white lace panties. "Hell, you've grown up." He leans down and kisses me fiercely, holding the back of my head in his hands.

"Harry," I mumble against his lips, "this isn't a good idea."

"We've never been a good idea," he replies, "but I knew from the moment you arrived back, that you and I would end up here. You're like a fucking magnet, calling me. You always have been." He kisses me again, then encourages me to sit on the bed, tapping the sheet with his hand before dropping down beside me. "Over the years, no one has ever come close."

"We slept together once," I protest.

"Once was all that was needed. No one has ever made my body react the way you do. You only have to walk into a room, and I transform into a horny teenager. The feeling of that pussy of yours around me has been etched in my mind all these years. I need to feel you again."

"I'm pregnant," I say.

"And I'm here. I'm here for both of you. If you'll have me. That day, the day you gave me your virginity..." He trails off, and I flush.

"I should have told you," I mumble—the guilt still stings. If I'd told him, life may have turned out differently, but then again, he may never have touched me at all.

"And I should have contacted you after. But we were both young and unsure. You've always been the one that got away. I'm not letting you go again, pregnant or not."

His fingers trail down my collarbone, across my breasts, and land between my legs. As he strokes the outside of my panties,

I widen my stance to give him access. One finger hooks the fabric, pulling it to the side. His eyes never leave mine. "Lie down," he orders, and I comply without a thought. "Lift your knees." He pushes a finger between my lips, then adds a second. "Is someone excited?" he whispers. "Is someone remembering what it feels like to be claimed by a man who adores you? Who wants you with every molecule of his body?"

I groan softly as he pumps. Strong fingers reacquaint themselves with what has always been his, even if neither of us thought it would happen.

"That sound," he growls, "is one of the most erotic things I've ever heard. I want to make you do it again, but louder." He rips my panties from my body with his other hand. "These have to go." He throws them away, discarded as unnecessary.

The sound of my body sucking his fingers in triggers another moan. I draw my knees up further, spreading them wide. He lies beside me, propped on his elbow, naked. His cock is hard against my side, his hand encourages my pussy to give him more. "You're so fucking wet. I want to taste you." He extracts his fingers, sliding them straight into his mouth and sucking deeply. I swallow, completely aroused by the exhilaration on his face in reaction. "The sweetest flavor," he whispers. "I need more."

He grabs two pillows from the top of the bed, then shuffles down between my spread legs. "Ass up." I lift my hips, and he slips a cushion beneath my butt before kneeling with a leg on either side of him. He places one of my feet on each of his shoulders, pushing forward so my knees bend further toward my head. I stare up at him while curled up like a pretzel, my pussy open like a platter waiting to be eaten. "Keep those knees open. This is a fucking banquet, and I plan to feast."

His head lowers, a hungry tongue appearing on contact with my lips. His grip tightens, pushing my ass upward as his mouth presses hard onto my entrance. He allows me no mercy, eating as if I am his first meal in weeks. His strokes are deep, needing to sample every inch of me, his tongue sweeping across my skin in an effort to lap up every drop my body produces.

He leans forward more, folding me up further, the buzzing inside heightening the more pressure he applies. "I'm hungry," he murmurs darkly. "Feed me. I need more. Fill my mouth with your climax before I return the favor and fill you with my cock."

"Harry, this is intense," I whine. "I can't."

"'Can't' isn't a word in my vocabulary," he replies. His face is hidden—only the top of his head visible. He turns his lips to my inner thigh. Sharp teeth sink into my skin, reprimanding me. The unexpected pain sends me closer to orgasm; his grip on my body tightens further as his mouth returns to where it once was. I am pinned between his strong arms and ferocious tongue, both parts of him demanding my submission. He teases my clit relentlessly. I wriggle my ass in search of relief, but I can't get free of him. My orgasm builds to breaking point, and he withdraws, allowing a lull in the sensation. He repeats the process, taking me to the edge before not pushing me over. The alternating highs and lows are both seductive and infuriating.

"Shall I let you come?" he says softly, glancing up. The words that escape my lips are mixed with a moan, individually unrecognizable but begging him to allow it. He chuckles, then takes two fingers and slides them inside, holding me still with his other arm. My body spasms with the intrusion. I try to rock my hips, needing more friction as he pumps insanely slow. He senses my desperation, his dark, aroused eyes never leave my face as his thumb lands on the sweet spot. I come hard and fast around him on impact. He withdraws his fingers and immediately devours his rewards, furiously enjoying the refreshment. Once satisfied, he glances up again, my arousal still coating his lips. "I could do that every fucking day, watch you orgasm under my touch. You are truly beautiful." I gaze at the boy who could never be mine, both aroused and deliriously happy. "Can I have you now?" he asks in a whisper.

"You already do." I wriggle further up the bed, lowering my body back to a single level. He crawls over me, strong arms holding his lithe body along the length of mine. It's been years, but it feels so right, here and now with him. He is in control of me, using and enjoying my body for his pleasure. This may only be our second time coming together, but what's between us extends over years. It's clear the experience we are having now has been lived by both of us before, in our minds and hearts.

His tip nudges my entrance, firm hips pushing forward, his cock sliding deep inside. My body relaxes under his touch, softening on his command. Once we're joined together, he drops a kiss on my forehead. It's an intimate gesture that causes my heart to burst. Harrison Waite has always been the boy who broke my heart—it turns out the feeling is mutual.

***

Harrison

Almost every sexual dream I have had since I was a teenage boy has starred Violet. Tonight, my wish to have her again has come true. She is in my bed, both beneath me and surrounding me, her body yielding to my every suggestion. Now, we are connected. I flex my hips gently, and she groans softly.

"Is this okay?" I ask, concerned. Her eyes which closed when I took her, reopen, and she smiles. Her cheeks are the most stunning shade of pink, dark hair splayed across the silk. "Does it hurt? Tell me if you want to stop."

"The last thing I want is for you to stop," she replies with a giggle.

"Good. I'm not sure I could." Her pussy contracts around my dick, and I pump again, this time continuing as she recloses her eyes. Her breasts lift into the air as she arches her back underneath my torso, her plump rose nipples grazing my chest as I move. Delicate fingers that twisted the bedsheets as I worked on her lift to my shoulders. She squeezes softly then moves them upward into my hair, playing with the strands.

"Harder, Harry," she mumbles between moans, wrapping her legs around my waist. My hips work quicker with her encouragement. She wants this. She wants me. "I'm close."

"You're so tight, Vi," I tell her. "You feel incredible."

The tip of my cock surges deep inside her, her slick walls encasing my length. She screams as I thrust, driving her into the mattress, hard. Her grip around my waist tightens while her fingernails return to my shoulders and dig into my skin. The noise of her body accepting mine, wet flesh on flesh is the best aphrodisiac. Our slick bodies move together as if they've never been apart. Her pussy vibrates as I drive forward, pushing my body more, riding her hard through the orgasm. She whimpers again.

"Does that feel good?" I ask between labored breaths.

"Insanely good."

Every nerve on my skin is tensed and absorbed in the moment, determined to enjoy this unexpected event which I never thought I would experience again. Then it happens, my peak arrives, and I allow myself to fill her. My body releases all the arousal and excitement of today along with the years I've wanted this. After I withdraw, I move to lie beside her, and pull the sheet across us both then lay my head on her chest. She plays with my hair between her fingertips. Neither of us speak. We lie together, silent, the only sound is our strained breathing before drifting off to sleep.

Chapter Seven

———◆◇◆———

Harrison's Apartment,
The Level

Harrison

My phone vibrates on my bedside table, startling me awake. I lean across to reach for it, but my fingers miss, and I knock it onto the floor. "Fuck's sake," I grumble, annoyed, and extract myself from the duvet to go in search of it. Violet is snoring softly beside me, her head on the pillow, fingers curled around the soft fabric beneath her face. Her long dark hair is splayed across the silk.

Last night was incredible. I felt more complete inside her than I have in years. It was as if the past thirteen years disappeared, and we were right back in her childhood bedroom, enjoying each other for the first time.

The buzzing continues as I search for my lost phone. After scrambling around on my hands and knees, I find it beneath the bed. "Waite speaking," I answer louder than I intend.

"Mr. Waite, it's Matthew. I was advised you wished to see me this morning." I glance at the clock—six-fifteen. Shit, I'm late.

"Yes, Matthew. Meet me in the boardroom in ten minutes. We need to discuss a security breach yesterday. Someone needs their balls booted."

"Yes sir," he replies. I disconnect the call, still crouched on the ground beside my bed naked. As I rise to stand, Violet looks up shyly.

"Morning," she says softly with a nervous smile. I sit on the bed beside her and run my fingers across her cheek then down her neck. I'm caught off guard when I notice the bruising at her throat. "What is it?" she asks as concern flits across her face.

"He marked you," I snarl, and she gives me a curious look. "The bastard left bruises on your skin. I'll fucking kill him."

She pushes herself up to sit, and her fingers move to her collarbone. She glances at the wardrobe mirror that sits next to my bed. Her face falls when she sees the purple welts that mark where his fingers were.

"Oh..." Her voice trails off as she moves to the mirror. Staring at her reflection, her fingers trace the wounds. I walk over, stand behind her, and place my hands on her shoulders. Our eyes meet in the reflection.

"Has he hurt you before?" I ask, and she shakes her head.

"No, the man who arrived here yesterday is nothing like the one I knew. He was always distant but kind. He had no reason to be physical with me. I'd given him everything he wanted and barely asked a question."

"That's not a relationship," I tell her. She drops her eyes from mine.

"Do you have a proven track record of good relationships?" she mumbles, twisting her hands in front of her. "After sleeping with me, are you going to give me dating advice?" I laugh under my breath.

"That would be useless advice." She looks at me, once more. "I'm no expert, but I know one person holding all the cards isn't what it should look like."

"Have you ever been in love, Harry?" Her question takes me by surprise. I pause, unsure of the best way to answer.

"Love is a complicated emotion. Easily misunderstood. I suspect I have been." She sighs under my touch. "Have you?"

"I thought so, but now I'm not so sure," she says sadly. "I wasted a long time on a man who used me for his pleasure. Right now, love feels like something that will never be in my life. Perhaps I don't deserve to be loved."

Not knowing what to say, I drop a kiss on her shoulder then skim my fingers across her belly, a signal to her, I hope, that I am fully aware of her situation. Our situation. The secret that I am one of the few people to know. "Everyone deserves to be loved," I assure her. "You deserve to be loved."

"That goes for you too," she replies.

Uncomfortable with the statement, I drop my hands from her shoulders. She frowns in response. I care for Violet, more than I have for anyone, but love...no one will ever love me. What we have between us is special, but that could be down to the chemical balance of our bodies, hormones that attract one another. We are animals, after all—not everything is reliant on how we feel.

"I need to go. I have a meeting. You get back into bed," I say, walking over to my wardrobe. I open it and remove a fresh suit and shirt, then hang them on the door handle. She watches me as I dress, pulling on my boxers and socks first. "Mrs. D. will be here around nine. I'll be home tonight, but the boys are coming around for Wednesday night drinks."

"Okay," she says. I feel her staring, but I don't look at her, I can't. Suddenly, reality strikes. What happened between us last night was a terrible mistake. An added complication in my life I don't need no matter how good it was, how right it felt. She's heartbroken from betrayal and pregnant with another man's baby. What the fuck was I thinking? Never mind the fact she's the little sister I was never allowed to touch.

I've been warned before. This is a dangerous game to play for both of us. Protecting her means not having her.

"We normally watch football, and have a few beers," I tell her, braving a glance. She nods but says nothing. "Hopefully, we won't disturb you too much."

"I'll stay out of your way," she replies. "Is it only you and my brothers?"

"No, another two gentlemen are attending. Friends. Well, business associates really. Occasionally, there can be other company." I emphasize the word *company*, trying to warn her without saying the actual words. Her eyes widen as the penny drops. She understands. Her face twists in displeasure at the information.

"Female company," she prompts. I don't answer, not wanting to have this conversation with her. "I'll stay out of your way," she repeats. "It would probably be best if I move into a hotel anyway. I can't stay here after last night." She picks up the dress I removed from her, shrugging it on. "I'll go pack my things. Your message is clear, Harry, consider it forgotten."

"Vi..."

She lifts her hand to stop me from speaking. "It's okay, we don't need to discuss it. There was a lot of emotion. Things happened and were said that shouldn't have been. It was sentimental, you and me, a chance to remember a time when things were less complicated. A chance to be teenagers again—perhaps it was unfinished business that is now put to bed."

"You don't need to leave," I tell her. "Be here when I get home, please. We can talk about it."

She walks over to the door, pulling it open before looking over her shoulder. "Have a good day," she says with a sad smile. "See you later."

***

Later that morning, I'm sitting in my blue leather wing-backed chair behind the deep oak desk piled high with paperwork. My client sits across from me. He's in his sixties with thinning gray hair and a belly that protrudes over his belt buckle. He straightens the red checked shirt he's wearing again, then wipes at the coffee stain on the breast pocket. Looking at him, you would never guess he's a multi-millionaire media giant. He made his money through the creation of online advertising.

"Mr. Roydon, can we go over the incident again with regards to your wife's death?" I say. He mutters under his breath, then slaps both hands on my desk. "If we are going to fight these allegations, your story needs to be watertight."

"Waite, you and I both know there are more holes in my story than a sieve." He chuckles, then coughs explosively over the paperwork in front of him. It's hard to defend a man who has admitted repeatedly to being guilty. Luckily, it's only been to me in this room as far as I'm aware.

"Was anyone conscious of your wife's indiscretions?" I ask him, trying to keep the conversation on topic.

"Well, the bastard whose dick she was bouncing on would be. And quite possibly her personal assistant. How a woman with no job or responsibilities needed a fucking PA is beyond me." He rubs his face with his hands. "When I met her, she hypnotized me with her plastic tits and incredible blowjobs. I was a goner. Fuck, when she used to sit on my face while sucking me dry, what a memory. I'll die a happy man thinking of that. She could have asked for my kidney, and I would have agreed."

"Tell me again what happened the day she died." I ignore the digression about his sex life. In our brief conversations so far, it is a regular occurrence. It's as if he *wants* me to know that he still has sex. That he and his wife were still intimate, that he can still get it up.

"We were in the Jacuzzi. It was a normal Friday evening; a few bottles of wine had been drunk. I'd heard that she was fucking her personal trainer." He pauses, and I signal at him to continue. "She was under the water with her lips wrapped around my dick, and my hands were on the back of her head pushing her deeper." He smiles darkly. "She came up for breath, and I asked her."

"Asked her what?"

"If she was fucking the staff!" he snarls. "What else, you idiot?"

"Mr. Roydon, may I remind you I'm only here to help. I'm preparing you for questioning. We need to put our case to the jury that you are innocent and that your wife's death was a freak accident. There is no doubt she drowned in a Jacuzzi while sitting next to you, sir." I widen my eyes at him. "We need to portray her death as a tragic accident. Not a murder by a husband hellbent on revenge."

"Do you believe I'm innocent?" he asks, his focus firmly on me.

It's a stupid question considering he already told me he held her below the water. I don't like this arrogant, jumped-up asshole, but it's not my job to like him. It's my responsibility to provide him with the best defense I can. Now, there is the added benefit that he has connections to Aiden Marley, who I want to bestow some much-needed karma on.

"I don't need to believe in your innocence or guilt. It's my job to defend you to the best of my ability, and that's what I intend to do." He nods, accepting my answer. "I believe we can create a case that you were in the midst of intercourse with your wife. She was pleasuring you below the surface of the water with her mouth when her hair became caught in the filtration system."

"That is all true," he agrees.

"The question is, can we convince the jury your wife was under the water level of her own accord?" The uneasy smile returns to his face. His eyes narrow, challenging me to say what's on my tongue. "Or did you hold her there, and the vents sucking her hair in was dumb luck?"

"Luck?" he repeats back.

"A credible excuse is possibly a better description."

"I like to think that luck is always on my side, Mr. Waite. Chance and hard work have provided me with a life many strive for but few experience. Money sorts everything else, hence why you, the best defense lawyer in London, is sitting across from me today. That, sir, was not on account of luck."

"Congratulations on your success," I reply. "Now, can we finish our meeting?"

87

***

I pull into the underground parking lot at my building. The barrier to my space automatically drops as I approach it. Number plate recognition is an amazing invention. To access the rectangle of pavement that is designated for my car, I don't need to speak to anyone or press a buzzer. It's a joyous experience.

Climbing out, I pick up my briefcase from the passenger seat, then softly close the door behind me. The Ferrari was obscenely expensive, but I love how it makes me feel. It was the cherry on top to show I'd made it. After all the shit and heartbreak of my youth, I had something my mother would be proud of. If only she were here to see it.

Since working with the mafia—becoming part of it, some may say—the playboy lifestyle I once enjoyed stays in the shadows. Gone are the days of the boys and I living it large in the city, staggering from bar to bar and picking up women on the way. We frequent exclusive establishments with high security. Only those in the know are permitted entry; to most, these places don't even exist.

Russell, Connor, and I set up the law firm eight years ago. Russell had already been practicing for a few years, being slightly older than both of us. We worked long hours, networked at all times of day, and rubbed shoulders with those we needed to ensure our success. Now, we are one of the most in-demand firms in the city with a client list to rival the most established, with a staff of over one hundred relying on us to pay their bills.

Things grew exponentially the moment Hunter Devane walked into my office two years ago, looking to replace his current firm. He needed lawyers on call at all times of day for a wide range of duties. We've surpassed his expectations by burying charges and pushing deals through courts. He pays us handsomely for it, but the trade-off of walking a more dangerous course is an unnerving one.

For every benefit, there is a price. The deeper we move into ever-darkening circles, the larger the target on our backs becomes.

After swiping my card across the access pad, the elevator doors open, and I step in. It carries me smoothly to my floor, and I step out into the familiar lobby. My mind wanders to the meeting I had with Matthew this morning as I come face-to-face with the boardroom door.

The two men on duty last night will be sitting at home right now, jobless and sore. I wanted to kill them for letting that maniac into my building. When I saw the bruises on Violet's neck, it took every ounce of my control not to storm downstairs and end them on the spot. Matthew had calmed the situation but was left with no doubt what would happen if the mistake was made again.

A calming sensation washes over me as I think of Violet. Her being here in my home is something I could get used to. The emotion I felt waking up next to her this morning was either new to me or long forgotten. All I know is when I turned over and saw her asleep in my bed, my day felt better in all respects.

But then, after reality hit and I saw sense, I knew it couldn't happen again. She was always forbidden. Now, between her situation and my lifestyle, there is no way this could work. She needs a safe environment to live in with someone who adores her. That's not something I can provide.

As I enter my apartment, the now familiar smell of home-cooked food fills the air. "What's for dinner, Mrs. D.?" I call, dumping my briefcase at the door, then shrugging out of my suit jacket. She is standing, stirring a pot on the stove.

"Tagine," she replies, but doesn't say anymore. It's unlike her.

"Where's Violet?" I ask, my eyes scanning the room. I expect her to be sitting on my sofa, legs curled underneath her like she has been the past few days.

"Gone."

"Gone? Where?"

"A hotel, I believe. She said she told you this morning." She stops stirring for a moment, her gaze fixed on me, assessing my reaction.

"She said it might be best if she went to a hotel, but I never expected her to leave so soon." I return to looking around the room, half expecting her to pop out from a doorway and yell, "Surprise!" She doesn't.

"Well, she has," Mrs. D. snaps. "Her bag was packed at the front door when I arrived. She was gone by ten this morning."

"Do you know which hotel?"

She shakes her head. "There is enough food here for all you boys this evening," Mrs. D. tells me. "I assume it's the usual suspects you're expecting. The beer fridge is full, and the spare room remade in case anyone stays the night."

"It's not that kind of night," I mutter.

"Well, if the opportunity arises, the room is ready." She places the spoon in the pot, then walks out from behind the counter. One hand reaches into her pocket and extracts a bundle of white lace. "I was surprised to find these in your room this morning," she says, passing me Violet's ripped panties. I snatch them from her and stuff them into my pocket, annoyed at being caught out.

"Nosy bitch," I snap, and she scowls at me.

"They were tangled within your bedsheets on the floor. I didn't go looking for them," she says sharply, then adds, "Can I be honest?"

"Do I have a choice?" Though Mrs. D. is like the mother I lost in some ways, her familiarity can also be infuriating. Our relationship is at that blended point where employee meets friendship, and today I have a feeling that line will be crossed permanently.

"You don't share your bed with women," she states.

"I don't share my bed with anyone. It's my safe space."

"Why did you share it with Violet then?" Her question sits between us. "What was different about her?" I shrug. "Harrison," she says, her voice changing from hard to soft, as if talking to a small boy. "I've known and worked for you for a long time now. I know more of what goes on in this building than most."

"You're a treasured member of our team," I reply. "We all trust you."

"And I care for you. I want to see you happy, not only in business but personally. The way you looked at that woman yesterday was something I'd never seen from you. And I've met plenty of ladies the morning after over the years." I feel my cheeks heat in embarrassment. She smiles. "I don't know what happened or why she left this morning, but don't throw something away because you're scared or believe it will make life more difficult."

"Violet has been gone from all our lives for over a decade. Last night was a moment of madness. Nostalgia. It won't happen again."

"You're not a stupid man. Both you and I know those are complete lies." Her eyes narrow in annoyance. "I know you. It's time to grow up and stop being the playboy. Violet is back, she's here, and this is your chance." With that, she turns and leaves. As she closes the front door, she shouts over her shoulder, "Enjoy your boys' night. Don't leave all your shit for me to clean up tomorrow, because I won't."

"That's what I fucking pay you for," I mutter under my breath, but she doesn't hear me. She's gone too.

CHAPTER EIGHT

Wyecroft Pawnbrokers,
The City of London

Violet

"Five thousand?" I stammer. "That's it?" The man behind the desk shrugs his shoulders. "My father told me it was worth at least ten thousand, and that was years ago."

"Perhaps it was then, ma'am," he says politely. "But today I can offer you five thousand pounds, cash. No ID required, no paper trail. You said on the phone that is what you needed?"

I stare down at the gold ring that was my grandmother's. My heart breaks as I think about letting it go. But with no money and nowhere to stay at this point in time, I can't afford to be prissy about it.

"Okay," I say, resigned. "And it will remain in the shop for twenty-eight days?" He nods. Not that I think I will have the money to buy it back by then, but it feels better to have the option.

"I'll organize your cash. I'll only be a moment," he says before turning and scurrying away through a door behind him.

This was the only pawn shop I could find that would process my request: no documentation required. After leaving Harry's bed this morning, I realized I was on my own. The position I'd got myself into was my fault. No one else was going to fix it for me. Not my brothers. Not Harry. I had no right to ask that of them.

When I left, I considered going to Connor and asking for help. But the fact remains that so much time has passed, I don't know any of them anymore. Sleeping with Harry, my childhood crush, had cemented that. If I hung around, all that would happen is we would become more confused, more intertwined. His instinct is to protect me—it always has been, I see that. When I was a teenager, he stood up to my brothers. Yesterday, he claimed to be the father of a baby that isn't his. But when the smoke cleared and we'd had a taste of one another, reality returned, and he withdrew. Again.

In bed with him, I felt safe and wanted. Waking up next to him had given me a false sense of hope. The feeling lasted a matter of minutes before dissipating. As I watched him dress in his sleek suit, then speak of his night ahead, I realized my notion was ridiculous. My brothers and him are city boys living the high life, rubbing shoulders with men you'd rather not meet. The last thing any of them will want is a little sister and her baby hanging around.

As I shut the door of his bedroom, my decision to leave was finalized. Where, I didn't know, but somewhere I could fade into the chaos unnoticed.

The pawn shop owner reappears with a wad of notes. He counts them out deliberately in front of me, then places them into a brown envelope before passing it over. I drop the ring into his palm. "Pleasure doing business with you," he says.

After stuffing the envelope into my pocket, I turn and leave. I'll need to find somewhere to stay and a way to make a living. Five thousand pounds isn't going to last me long, not in the City of London.

***

Harrison

"Where's my sister, Waite?" Russell bellows. Our Wednesday night drinking session morphed into an interrogation as soon as he arrived.

"A hotel, seemingly." I try to be calm as I reply, but no one has heard from Violet since she left this morning. I'm furious with her for leaving. "She told Mrs. D. she was going to check into a hotel. I don't know which one."

"What fucking happened? What did you do to make her run?"

"Nothing!" I snap. "I opened my home to her when you were being a dick. She isn't my fucking sister. She didn't want to stay. She didn't need to. She's a big girl, Russ. She's managed without us all long enough."

"You seemed quite content playing happy families with her the other night," he snarls.

"I was trying to do the right thing." After taking another swig of my beer, I ready myself to tell him about the incident in my apartment. "Marley knows she was here; he turned up last night. Perhaps that spooked her."

The five of us sit in my living space, where a soccer match plays on my wide-screen television. Hunter and Damon are debating the strategy the winning team is using. They attempt to keep the mood light, but it doesn't work. Russell, Connor, and I are discussing Violet's sudden appearance, then disappearance, and what to do about it. An ice bucket of beer sits on the coffee table between us all.

"What did the bastard say?" he growls.

"He got handsy with her. I removed him from the premises and dealt with the hopeless idiots on the door who let him in."

"Why am I only finding out about this now? After my sister has run off, again? We need to fucking find her. I've only just told my mother she's back. It will kill her if I've lost her again." A concerned look flits across his face—genuine worry for his mum and his sister. I decide not to tell him about the pregnancy. It feels like a breach of Violet's trust. When we find her, she can tell him herself.

"What do you need?" Hunter asks, interrupting our conversation. "Between my connections and Damon's access to CCTV, we should find her no problem. What does she look like? Do you have a picture?"

"What's her financial situation?" Damon adds.

"Good question," Hunter agrees. "Does she have access to money? Or will she be relying on her bank cards?"

"I have a photo," I say, not looking at either of her brothers. "I'll get it." After rising from my chair, I go to my bedroom and remove the photo of Violet from when we were teenagers that's pinned inside my wardrobe. I still keep it; it's never felt right to throw it out. Sometimes over these past years I would take a moment to look at it and wonder, if I'd been braver, what could have happened.

On returning to the living room, Russell's eyes burn my skin. He watched me leave, and I'm certain he glared at the direction I took until I returned. I pass the photo to Damon and Hunter. "It was a few years ago, she still looks like this, but a little more grown up."

"I bet she is," Hunter says with a chuckle.

"Waite," Russell growls as he stands and walks behind the two men looking at the photo. "Care to tell me why the fuck you have a picture of my sister in a bikini in your bedroom?"

"You don't want to know," I answer firmly. "And it's none of your business."

He moves so quickly, I don't stand a chance to prepare. For a big man, he's athletic, jumping over the sofa in one move then grabbing at my shoulders, pushing me backward. He slams me hard against the wall. A fifty-thousand-pound painting crashes to the floor; the glass frame smashes, scattering shards across the room.

"If that filthy cock of yours has been near my little sister," he snarls, raising a fist into the air, "I'll end you, you selfish bastard." His hand crashes down across my cheek and being pinned against the wall, I take its full force.

"Are you done?" I say to him, glaring openly. "Do you feel better now you've cracked my fucking face? Your little tantrum is really helping us find her."

His hand moves to my throat. My eyes narrow—he doesn't frighten me. Considering Russell is a bully, he's never been able to take me on. I've seen so much worse than him over the years.

"My family took you under their wing," he growls, "when that lowlife mother of yours checked out. We supported you so you didn't get buried too. And this is how you repay me, my family, by fucking my little sister. Making her run."

"Leave my mother out of this," I argue. "I asked Vi to stay."

"Did you fuck her?" he asks again.

I can't lie to him. He'll know. He knows me better than anyone. Russell is the big brother I always wanted. It was he who brought me to his parents when he found me in a ditch at eight years old, half-dressed in the snow. That was the day my life changed for the better, the day I found the Chase family—or they found me.

"Fucking asshole," he mutters, then releases me. "Violet has always been a hard no. You were warned. Once we find her, you better fucking pray she's in one piece. I'm holding you personally responsible for any scratches on her." He steps back, allowing me room to move.

"We better get a move on," I retort. "Damon, can you get her face run through the system? See if she's been picked up on any CCTV?" I turn to the one man in the room I trust implicitly. Damon McKinney always has my back. Since I met him on a murder case a few years ago, he's become one of my closest confidants, though I've mentioned little of Violet to him. No one truly knows how I feel about her.

"On it, Waite," he says, typing furiously into his screen after snapping an image of the photo.

"I've sent her photo to my team on the ground." Hunter's voice cuts through the silence. "Once we have a location, we'll pick her up. Now, my question again—does she have money?"

"I doubt it. She turned up here with nothing."

"Anything missing from here?" he asks, his eyes scanning the room.

"My sister is not a fucking thief, Devane," Russell roars.

"I didn't say she was. But desperate people..." He trails off as Russell approaches him. "Don't think about it, Chase. I'm a lot quicker with a knife than you. Pick your battles wisely. You need me on your side. I fund your lifestyle. Remember that."

Connor chooses this moment to intervene. It's easy to forget he's here most of the time. "Russ," he says, "calm down. Everyone here wants the same result. We all want to find Violet safe and well." He glances at me. "For our own reasons. Let them help find our sister. Finishing anyone in this room isn't going to bring her back."

"Fuck's sake," Russell mutters petulantly. "Always the fucking voice of reason. Fine." He turns in my direction. "Keep your distance, Waite. I haven't forgotten what's transpired today. Business associate or not, you'll pay for overstepping the line." He raises his eyebrows. "Off limits, understand? My little sister will never be in your bed again. After this is done, you and I are finished." He storms off in the direction of the door.

"Where are you going?" Connor shouts to his retreating back.

"To find my sister."

I move to the sofa and throw myself down. Connor watches me, not speaking. I sit with my head in my hands. The sofa sags beside me as Damon comes to my side. His hand lands on my shoulder. "We'll find her," he says. The remaining men in the room never take their eyes off me—I feel every one of them.

"We need to," I mutter. "I need to apologize."

"How long?" Connor asks, surprising me. I lift my eyes to his. "How long has there been something between you both?"

"She's been away for over a decade. How can something be going on?" I reply.

"A person doesn't necessarily have to be with you to hold your heart. Be honest with me. When we find her, what do you want to happen?"

"I don't know," I answer truthfully. "I'm not exactly husband material."

"Husband material?" he says, lifting an eyebrow. "Fuck, Waite, I only meant do you want to date her?" Everyone laughs, the situation lightened for a moment.

"I've loved your sister since that last summer in Kensington," I say to Connor. "No one has ever come close. Violet Chase took up residence in my heart with her shy glances and sarcastic comments." I smile to myself. "She's one in a million."

"How does she feel about you?"

I shrug. "Confused, most likely. It's hard when what you want isn't what you can have."

"Let's find her before making any permanent decisions, Waite." He walks over and pushes my shoulder. "You've been like a brother to me for twenty years. I have no issue with you and her. Russell has always been territorial, but he'll come around."

"I'll always be the boy he found in a ditch," I mutter. I glance up and see the other men giving me a curious look. I look away. They don't know the story of how I found myself here. Only the Chase family does.

"That boy turned into a man I'm proud to call a friend. A brother. Where we start in life is not a roadmap to where we end up. You're proof of that." My gaze stays firmly fixed on the floor. He turns away from me and his feet disappear from my view as he walks toward the door. "Now, let's find Violet."

Chapter Nine

Farringdon, London

Violet

"What did you say your name was?" the girl behind the counter says. Her crazy blonde curls are pinned high, twisted into a messy bun.

"Violet."

"What brings you to London?" she asks, flashing me a beaming smile.

Hell, I only came in here to buy some clothes that actually fit me. I'm desperate to get back to feeling more like me, whoever me is.

"Life," I reply evasively, and she laughs. It's warm, filled with joy. She's the type of person you look at and immediately like. I suspect she's in her mid-twenties, still having that rosy glow of youth. The thought is depressing; I've missed out on so much.

"I reckon we're all living life. It likes to chew us up and spit us out so we land completely where we never expected. It makes things interesting, I suppose. Where do you stay?"

"A hostel for the moment. My original plans went a bit wrong. I'm having to pivot."

"Pivot?" she repeats, her eyebrows drawing together in obvious confusion.

"Yes, pivot. If something doesn't work out, you change direction. Try something else. Find where you're meant to be." Her mouth breaks into a wide smile and she nods, now understanding. "Right now, I have no permanent home or a way to make a living. But I'll get there. For once in my life, I'm actually in charge. It's freeing." I volunteer information she didn't ask for. It feels good to speak to someone.

"I hear you," she says. Her gaze runs over my face then drops to my toes before rising again.

"What kind of work are you looking for? I may know of somewhere that's hiring."

"Anything," I tell her. "I'm not in the position to be choosy. I need to be able to eat."

"Me neither. I arrived here a few years ago with big dreams of entertaining audiences in the West End. The closest I've got is an elf in the local shopping center pantomime."

I laugh out loud then snap my hands over my mouth. "Sorry," I mumble, "that was insensitive."

"Don't worry about it," she says kindly. "If I didn't laugh, I would cry. I may be able to help you with somewhere to stay too. I'm Samantha." She holds her hand out across the counter in the small cheap clothing store I found while walking the dreary London streets. I take it, her grip is surprisingly strong. Summer has taken a day off today. The sign in the window said everything inside costs one pound. It does, and it looks like it.

"Lovely to meet you, Samantha."

She scribbles on a small white notepad with a bright pink pen. Her clear blue eyes dance as she passes it to me.

"Here's my number," she says. "I finish work at five." She glances at the old clock on the wall, the second hand ticking around the face slowly. "Message me, and we can meet up for a drink. We're looking for a roommate. I live with another three girls not far from here. The apartment isn't pretty, and the neighbors can be a handful, but it's dry, clean, and cheap."

"Sounds good. And you said you may be able to help me with my lack of job situation?"

"I'll tell you about that later. It's better if you see it rather than hear about it. It will be less..." She pauses then taps her lip with a finger considering her words. "Overwhelming." She nods to herself, happy with her assessment. "Yes, overwhelming. But I think the management would be interested in hiring you. You have what they are looking for."

"What's that?" I question, confused how she could assess me for a job from our brief conversation.

"Promise," she replies with a wink. "I'll see you later."

I leave the shop with a bag filled with poor-quality clothing, no idea what I'm walking into, and potentially a new friend.

After debating for over an hour, I decide to send the random woman I met in the clothing shop a message. What do I have to lose? If this was meant to happen, I'll only find out by following the trail. Samantha messages back within minutes with a location to meet at half past five.

***

The coffee shop sits in an alleyway behind the store I visited earlier. It's small with only eight tables crammed into the tiny space. Each one is covered with a red plastic tablecloth. Samantha sits at the furthest table from the door—her hand shoots into the air when she sees me. I wave back shyly, not wanting to draw attention to myself. There aren't many people inside with two tables taken. The only sound is quiet conversation.

As I approach her, Samantha stands and steps out from her chair, enveloping me in a hug, which takes me by surprise. "I'm so glad you came," she says, giddy. "I was worried you wouldn't show up." I try to smile at her, not knowing what to say. Overfamiliarity is something I'm not used to. "You looked like you needed a friend today. I remember being like that. London is a scary place on your own."

"It is," I agree.

"Anyway, sit. Let's order some coffee and cake. We can discuss anything or nothing at all then I can show you what's available." She beams. "I've set up a meeting with the boss at the club about the job. He's keen to meet you. It's the main man too, down from Glasgow. If he likes you, you'll be in. You would never think he is what he is."

"The club?"

"Yes, unfortunately the wages from the clothes shop don't cover my living costs. So, I need to dance too."

"Dance?"

"Yes, dance at a gentleman's club. We all do. That's how I met the other girls." My heart sinks as she describes her role. "Don't panic," she says, leaning forward and placing a hand over mine. "It's a lovely place to work. You don't need to do anything you don't want to, and the owner looks after us. As I said, he's incredibly normal for such a connected man. You'll understand more once you see it."

"I don't know," I mutter.

"Just come and meet the girls. See the club. You don't sound like you have many options, Violet," she says, fixing her shrewd eyes on me. There is nothing stupid about this woman. She saw me coming this morning. A woman in need. A woman who needed possibilities when she had none. "This could be the answer to your prayers. In a few months, you could make enough money to be back on track. I clear at least five hundred a night."

"Five hundred," I splutter. She grins at me wickedly.

"And all I need to do is swing around a pole with my tits hanging out. Easy money," she says, widening her eyes.

"Do they ever touch you?" I ask, nervous that I'm even considering the possibility of this. My only knowledge of gentlemen's clubs and strippers is from movies. It doesn't help to squash my worries.

"Who? The clients?" She shakes her head. "No, they're not allowed to. Mr. Parker would have them out on the street with a broken arm. As I said, we're looked after."

"Okay, I'll come and look," I concede, figuring I have nothing to lose.

"Excellent," she shrieks, slapping her hands together. "Drink up so I can take you to meet everyone."

An hour later, I'm standing in the most luxurious nightclub I've ever seen. The entrance had been completely inconspicuous, a single blue door nestled between a takeaway and a launderette in inner city London. A man in a tuxedo stood on the other side of the doorway. We scaled a narrow staircase toward another blue door, but once we walked through, it opened into the most amazing space.

A circular stage with a pole stands in the center of the room. Booths in blue velvet line the edges. Every wall is mirrored. On the far wall, there is a bar with every conceivable bottle stacked behind it. Samantha struts into the empty space, holds her hands above her head, and turns three-hundred-sixty degrees. "Welcome to Guilty Pleasures," she says with a smile. "Mr. Parker will be in his office. It's just through here. He's expecting us."

I follow her behind the bar where she knocks on a mirrored door—you wouldn't notice it unless you knew it was there. "Come in," a deep voice calls. Samantha pushes the door open, and we walk into a large office space with a heavy wooden desk at its center. Behind it sits a man in a sharp blue suit. He looks to be in his late thirties with dirty blond hair and dazzling green eyes. "Hello Samantha," he says, his tone welcoming but authoritative.

"Good evening, Mr. Parker. I've brought the new candidate as you requested."

"Very good," he replies, then turns to me before standing and stepping out from behind his desk. He holds one hand out, and I take it. His grip is firm—this is a man in control. "Joel Parker," he says, introducing himself. "And you are?"

"Violet."

"Do you have a surname?" he asks with a smirk. "Or are you like one of those pop stars who are so well known you don't need one?"

"Brown," I reply. Instinct tells me not to use Chase. If this man is the type of person I think he is, he may know my brothers. I don't want him connecting the dots. For my new life to work, no one can know who I am. I need to be anonymous.

"Nice to meet you, Violet Brown." He gives me a look that lets me know he knows I'm lying. "Has Samantha explained the opportunities available at Guilty Pleasures?"

"She said this was a dance club."

"It is. But you don't need to dance if you don't want to. We have a position available at the bar, or some of the girls do offer private entertainment. Where you choose to start is completely up to you."

"Private entertainment?" I say, my chest tightening with nerves. He nods.

"We provide a safe space. The girls choose if they want to provide our gentlemen with optional extras. As I said, it is your choice. If it makes you more comfortable, you could start the bar, meet some of the clientele. The gentlemen who come here are wealthy men looking to unwind. We provide a high-end service and total discretion; they pay us well for it. In return, we pay you handsomely."

"Do you sample your product?" I snap, and he chuckles.

"No, I'm a happily married man with a son at home plus another on the way. These clubs," he waves his arm around, "were my family's. I inherited them. It's not my favorite part of the business, but I manage them in the fairest way possible."

"Oh, that makes it all right then," I mutter.

"The clubs would operate whether or not I owned them. This way, I know the girls who work here are well looked after. Sex is one of the oldest trades in the world. Making it illegal won't stop it." He raises an eyebrow. "Miss Brown, if the opportunity is not for you, I understand. Normally, one of my cousins manages our London establishments. I live in Glasgow, myself, and return home tomorrow. Have a think, and if you want to try an evening behind the bar, you can let him know."

Samantha moves to my side, bumping my shoulder gently. "Do you have any other options, Violet? You don't need to do anything you don't want to."

I sigh, resigned. She's right. This opportunity has landed on my lap. I need to take it.

"Apologies, Mr. Parker," I say, and he glances up from his phone which buzzed a moment ago. There is a photo of a little boy with his arms around a pretty brunette on the screen. "I would like to accept your offer of a trial."

"Excellent," he replies. "Samantha will show you where everything is and explain how we work. Rest assured, our clients are well warned to behave, and if you feel uncomfortable at any point, alert one of the security staff. They'll take care of it." He looks at Samantha and nods. "Thank you, Samantha. A good job as always."

She takes my arm, and we turn to leave. Once out of the office I stop, and she spins to face me.

"What's wrong?" she asks.

"What exactly is your job description?"

"I told you; I dance." I narrow my eyes. "And recruitment."

Chapter Ten

---○---

Chase, Chase and Waite
Law Offices, Canary Wharf

July 2022

Harrison

"How the fuck could she have disappeared without a trace?" I snap, as I pace around my office. Damon holds his hands up, shaking his head.

"There's no sign of her since she left your building back in June. Four weeks have passed. She's either in the Thames or using an alias somewhere far away from here." He shrugs his shoulders, again. We've had this same conversation every week since Violet vanished. Russell isn't speaking to me. Even Connor is beginning to lose patience. The blame for her leaving is being firmly placed at my door. "Have you spoken to Marley?"

"No," I tell him. The same answer I've given him every other time he asked me. "It's not that simple. Reaching out to him for information will bring complications I don't need."

"There's something you're not telling me," he says sharply. "Stop hiding whatever the hell it is and tell me what we're dealing with."

"She's pregnant." His mouth twists in displeasure. "She was pregnant in June anyway."

"It's Marley's?"

"Yes, and he knew about it. When he appeared at my apartment and had her pinned against the wall by her throat, I told him the baby was mine." His eyes pop wide.

"Did he believe that bullshit?"

"I'm not sure. She was left alone a lot in Chicago, so it's perfectly plausible someone else is the father. However, I believe her when she says the baby is his. She loved him. Thought he was her future." The familiar green-eyed monster raises its head when I think of her with him. Violet's time in America is something I try not to reflect on. Her life with another man. When she had her hopes pinned on someone else. Not that it would be wise to have them set on me—her being with me wouldn't be much better.

"Why the fuck would you tell him you're the father?"

"Impulse," I say with a shrug. "My protective instincts went into overdrive. I wanted that madman as far from her as possible. Honestly, Damon." I sit back in my chair and run my hand through my hair in frustration. "The woman turns me crazy. She always has. I only need to be in the same room as her, and I lose my head. I'd take a bullet for her. She's all I fucking think about lately. Not knowing where she is, or if she's safe, is driving me insane."

"I'm surprised Marley didn't kill you on the spot," he says, but nods in understanding. He adored his lost wife, though they had their issues. Not being able to get pregnant being one of them.

"When she turned up in June, part of me hoped it was our chance to try." I laugh at myself even thinking about it. "Russ would never allow that to happen." I glance beyond the glass wall that separates my office from the main floor. Russell is storming around throwing random files on people's desks as he shouts at them. "He'll never forgive me for driving her away, again."

"Once we find her, wherever she is," Damon says calmly. I notice he manages my expectations with the word, *wherever*. "It will give you all some closure."

"She can't be dead," I reply quietly. "Her family has missed her for thirteen years; she was back a matter of days and left again because of me. She's out there somewhere, and we need to find her."

"You don't know she left because of you." His eyes bore into mine. "You can't take the blame for everything. It's not always your fault. Her brothers didn't exactly welcome her with open arms."

"I took her to bed when she was vulnerable and pregnant with another man's child. The safe space I provided for her disintegrated the minute I did. It was stupid and selfish. I was an idiot with her." He rolls his eyes. "You and I both know that's the truth. She was never mine to have but I couldn't help myself. First her virginity and now, this." I'd told Damon about our previous encounter one rainy afternoon while we were brainstorming. Russell and Connor still don't know, and I'd rather they didn't.

"You didn't force her onto her back," he reminds me. "She was a willing participant. It sounds like both of you need to keep your hands to yourselves or fucking make a go of things. Her family's opinion is irrelevant if you want each other." He sighs then rubs at his forehead.

"The time has come to speak to Marley," he continues firmly. "He may know something we don't. Bring him to The Level; it will give us more leverage. He still owes Mr. Moneybags, doesn't he?" I nod. "Perfect, bring him too. You're his favorite human on earth after getting that bloody murder charge dropped. You're like a hound with fucking technicalities, finding a morsel of doubt and then exposing it. I dare not mention your name at headquarters. Every officer who works a case you take on withers when they hear the name Waite."

"Eleven out of eleven," I tell him with a wink.

"Cocky bastard," he mumbles. "Wednesday at The Level. No excuses. Get everyone gathered, and let's find this bloody woman once and for all. She has some explaining to do. And you both need to decide what the fuck is going on between you. Thirteen years is a long fucking time to be stuck on a woman you've been with once. Romantic asshole."

***

Marley sits in the chair at the top of the boardroom table. His hands are on the arms, a wide grin across his face. He spins the chair around, then brings it to a stop so he can look at us all. The two men he brought with him stand at his shoulders, poised and ready for battle if required. They both must be over six foot and a similar width. Their dark suits stretch uncomfortably over the bulging muscle beneath.

"You've certainly upped your security," I say. "Are you feeling exposed?"

"I do what I must," he replies mildly. "You and I both know, Waite, the darker the world becomes around you, the more at risk your life is. I would imagine you may be considering doing the same, if the information I have is correct."

"What information would that be?"

"One word: heroin." His mouth moves precisely as he pronounces the word. "You and your vigilantes are getting closer to the source. It's been noted. I'd watch your back if I was you. Keep poking the hive and prepare to be stung."

His knowledge surprises me. Often in business, people are connected in ways you don't expect them to be. But Aiden Marley having knowledge of a drug ring we're looking at wasn't something I expected. His life is changing as much as mine is. Not always in the direction I want it to.

The atmosphere since we arrived in the boardroom has been frosty, two sides of a war brought together because one needs the help of the other. I'm furious to be asking my enemy for information. I like to be the one holding the power—being the underdog is not something I plan on being again.

"Where's my money, you useless piece of shit," my client, Mr. Roydon, growls, losing the thread of control he possessed. He's been attempting and failing to hold his temper since Marley arrived. Once we won his court case by getting the murder charges thrown out, his focus moved immediately to Aiden Marley and the two million pounds he is owed. This is a fact I plan to use to my advantage.

"I invested it like you asked me to," Marley replies.

"Where?" he snaps.

"In the best investment available." He grins wickedly. "The same operation that these boys are trying to shut down."

"Drugs!" he hollers. "You invested my money into a product that's killing innocent kids. You're over the line, you bastard. That money was for your business. To be invested in advertising."

"This is my business," he replies, shrugging his shoulder in feigned disinterest. "It was a solid investment."

Roydon stands, placing his hands on the table and narrowing his eyes at the piece of shit across the room from him. The two heavies step forward protectively. I place my hand on Roydon's arm, willing him to relax—this meeting can't go south. What is at risk is much greater than two million pounds. Violet.

"Marley, I want my money back within ten days or there will be consequences. Your men can't watch you day and night. I could still buy and sell you ten times over. There are plenty of resources at my disposal," Roydon snarls.

"He recently had you released from one murder charge," Marley shoots back, gesturing to me. "Perhaps it's not the best idea to threaten me so soon. I doubt you would get away with it again. Especially if the lawyer is here when you pull the trigger." He chortles. "It would almost be worth dying to see all you bastards behind bars. The vigilantes banged up for trying to stop the criminals they consider worse than them. You're all a bunch of fucking hypocrites. When you look in the mirror, I'll be staring back at you."

"Careful what you wish for," I tell him. "I'm a good defense lawyer. I'd be happy to prove it again."

"Your death could be easily arranged," Hunter adds quietly. He's standing behind the three men. I'm not sure how he got there. He lifts his blade and places it against one of their throats.

I tense along with every man in the room. Eyes dart around, surveying the situation, each person trying to guess the next move. This is the type of action that could send our meeting into a spin. There is every possibility it could create a bloodbath.

Hunter is unpredictable at the best of times, but when he can smell blood, he's in his element. The predator in him appears and won't leave until satisfied.

"Devane," Connor warns. Hunter glances in his direction, smirks, then returns his focus to his captive.

"Gentlemen, I believe you were invited here to provide us with some information which, as yet, you've not been forthcoming. If you would be so kind as to answer Mr. Waite's questions," he prompts.

"I'm telling that bastard nothing," Marley hisses.

Hunter presses the blade into his security guard's throat. Blood trickles down his neck from the cut, coating a deep blue tattoo then staining his white shirt collar. The man stands stock still, terrified to move. Marley glances up in the direction of the moan that escapes the hostage's lips. He looks impassively at his employee, bored almost.

"Let's try that again, shall we?" Hunter says. "If you don't agree to answer our questions, your man here will lose his head. Not long after, you'll lose yours too. Trust me when I say I'm good with a knife. The best."

"He is," I agree. "Terrifyingly fast, but what I always find most impressive is his accuracy. His ability to remove the smallest portion of skin to create the greatest torture. We made a sensible decision in soundproofing these walls."

"There's one of you and three of us," Marley argues, feigning confidence, but the sweat on his brow says otherwise. Hunter has him rattled.

Damon appears at his elbow and places a loaded gun to the other security guard's head. He clicks the safety off.

"I think we have the advantage," Damon advises. "Now, start fucking talking."

"Violet," I say, and Marley's eyebrows shoot up. He wasn't expecting her to be part of this conversation. She is the sole reason for this meeting as far as I'm concerned. If we gain unexpected information on the drug ring that would be a bonus but finding her is the only thing that matters. Since her disappearance, she has become the most important factor in my world. After years of denying how I feel, I've accepted what I knew all along. She's the woman I'm meant to be with. She's my responsibility to keep safe. "Where is she?"

He screws up his nose, confusion flitting across his face. "I don't know. You should have a better idea of that than me. Being the father of her child, after all." He smiles darkly. "Or are you?"

Russell tenses on my other side. I told him about the altercation at my apartment in full last night. He dealt me a blow to the stomach in reward for finding out his sister was pregnant with this maniac's baby.

"Let's face it, the little bastard could be anyone's. From my experience, she was always open for business. She is a good fuck. I kept her around long enough to ride plenty of times. I've had her in every position you can imagine." He grins at me. "I especially liked when she was gagged, then I didn't need to listen to her. Or when I was deep down in her throat. She can take it. Bear that in mind the next time she's servicing you. I would give her five stars in that department. That mouth of hers is something else."

"Don't fuck with me, Marley. Tell us where Violet is," I growl.

"I wouldn't tell you where the little bitch was even if I knew. I've not seen her since you threw me out of your apartment." He stands then wipes his hands on his pants. "If you brought me here to talk about that little whore, I'll be going. You're welcome to her and my bastard offspring. She's not as appealing as she once was. Tainted goods."

Russell shoots out of his seat. Connor stands behind him and places his hands on his shoulders. "Relax, bro," he cajoles. "Don't rise to the bait."

"Now, if that's everything, my men and I will be leaving. Please remove your weapons." He glances at each of them. "Or don't. They're easily replaced. I have plenty of possessions at my disposal." He looks at the man he owes money to and smirks. Damon and Hunter lower the weapons to their waists, and we watch as our only link to Violet disappears into the elevator and out into the night.

"Trust that bastard to be involved with the heroin too," I mutter. "Everywhere we turn, he's there sticking his fingers in the pie. I'm beginning to think everything is interconnected. The drugs, Violet, and your missing money," I say, turning to Roydon.

"Possibly," he replies. "The drugs and the money make sense. Your missing girlfriend doesn't though."

"She's not his fucking girlfriend," Russell growls. "Waite is only still walking because he's needed at the firm. If he wasn't so good at his job, he'd be buried under someone's patio. I'd personally make sure of it. When we find my sister, he'll be nowhere near her."

"Shut the fuck up, Russ," Connor interjects. "You need to stop all this big brother bullshit. Violet is a grown woman who we haven't seen in over a decade. Whether she's with Harry or not, it doesn't matter. We need to get her back in one piece."

"You'd be happy for her to be with him?" he snarls, and they glare at each other.

"Why not? He's like a brother to us."

"He's no brother of mine," Russell hisses. "He's only here because of the charity of our family. Because I dragged his sorry ass out of a ditch as a kid when his Mum finally cracked with the drugs. When she was too bloody high to care where her precious little boy was and crocked it." He turns to me and prods at my chest with his finger. "You would be nothing more than a whore's son without us, Waite. Probably living in some shitty house, shooting up coke, and adding to the death statistics." His gaze roams over my face, then he narrows his eyes. I stare at him, unblinking. Russell is a bully; he always has been. Backing down now would be giving in. I never relent control to anyone. Not even the man who saved me. "It doesn't matter how good a lawyer you are, how expensive your suits are, or what car you drive. You'll always be the boy from the ditch. Remember that."

Chapter Eleven

Golborne, London

Jan 11, 1996

Harrison

"Happy birthday, sweetheart," my mother says, her mouth drawn wide into a bright smile. "Eight today, where has my little boy gone?" She wraps her arms around me as I sit at the shaky kitchen table. There are ten beer mats placed under one leg to stop it from wobbling. A single cupcake with no icing sits in front of me, a lonely blue candle almost burnt out on top. "Make a wish," she tells me.

I close my eyes and wish with all my heart that when I open them, we will be somewhere else. That the big purple bruise surrounding her eye will have disappeared and the house will be warm. My lungs fill with air, and I blow out hard between my lips. She claps her hands, cheering loudly.

When I open my eyes, everything is still the same. Devastation fills my chest. I used to believe in magic, but with each day that passes, I'm beginning to think it's all a lie.

Our room in the shared house is miniscule. There is a single bed stuffed into the corner, and I sleep on an old mattress on the floor with an ancient red cover stained from years of use. It's winter, and ice lines the windows both inside and out. Food is rationed between all who live here. We receive three small meals a day made from scraps collected either from restaurants or rubbish bins. It's one of the jobs we children are given while our mothers work. They call us a family, but we're not. I'm sure families don't live like we do.

The men visit at all times of the day and night. My mother has a lot of regular visitors, the same people. The same men. I don't know their names, but I recognize their faces. She never tells me what she does—just that she spends time with them, they're her friends. If I'm not playing outside with the other children, I need to stay in the living room. I'm not to go upstairs, as children are not allowed in the bedrooms when their mothers are working.

Once, I forgot my toy truck. I went to our room, but the door was locked. I could hear my mother talking on the other side of the door, then the sound the springs make when I jump on the bed. I'd gone back downstairs without my toy.

Our house is home to eight ladies and five children. There are no daddies here. Only Jeff, our owner. He keeps us. He's tall, as big as a skyscraper. When he stands in front of me, I have to crane my head back to see his eyes. A tattoo that looks like barbed wire runs down the side of his face and across his cheek. His knuckles have words on them, but I can't read, so I don't know what they say. He always wears dirty jeans that are ripped at the knees with a black t-shirt. Normally, there is a picture of a skull or a naked lady on his chest.

If we all do everything he asks and follow the house rules, we get chocolate sometimes.

The rules are...
- Don't speak unless spoken to.

- Don't go to your bedroom when your mum is working.

- Never take food from the kitchen.

- Always tell him if you see a policeman near the house.

The rules are easy to follow, most of the time. But on the days I'm ravenous, it's hard not to steal something from the kitchen. There are packets of biscuits in the cupboard and chocolate in the fridge. Often, I stand in the doorway and watch Jeff eat biscuit after biscuit. He stuffs them into his mouth, one by one, and chews slowly. He knows I watch him—his eyes dance as he eats, never looking at me directly but enjoying the teasing.

"What did you wish for?" my mother asks, interrupting my memories.

"A bike," I lie as I look at her. The joy on her face disappears for a moment, then reappears when she realizes.

"Maybe one day," she says softly. "One day, you will get out of this place and have everything you wish for."

"You'll be with me," I argue. She only smiles sadly in response.

That evening, the children are all sent to the living room to watch a film. It is a story about a magic lamp and a genie who gives you three wishes. We all watch the tiny screen, our eyes glued to the miracle being portrayed. A scream resonates through the house—a woman's voice, one I know. The most important person in my world.

"For fuck's sake," Jeff yells as a man wearing nothing runs down the stairs, stopping in the hallway. We all run to the door to watch the chaos.

"The whore is dead," the naked man growls. "She shot up when I was getting busy then she passed out. She won't fucking wake up."

Jeff grabs the man by the shoulders, wrestling him to the front door then throws him out onto the street.

"I'm naked, you dickhead!" the man shouts, furious as he batters the door. Jeff pulls a woman's coat from a hook, opens the door, and tosses the garment outside. He slams the door shut. Jeff bounds up the stairs, and I follow behind him, my eyes frantically searching for my mum.

When I reach our bedroom door, Jeff is standing over the bed looking down at something. He leans down and shakes it violently. "Mummy!" I shout as I realize who it is. He spins to face me, then snatches my shoulders as I run into the room.

"Fuck off, you stupid boy," he snarls. "She's fucking dead." I scream, and he hits me hard across the face. "Shut the fuck up."

"Mummy!" I wail, trying to wrestle from his grasp as he throws me over his shoulder. I grab for the small blue teddy bear on the shelf as we pass, then stuff it into my t-shirt. As we turn out of the room, my head cracks off the doorframe and everything goes black.

When I wake, I'm wrapped in a blanket. The motion of the car makes me feel sick. It's dark. I try to move my fingers, but my hands are tied behind my back. Too frightened to shout, I lie still until we pull to a stop. The car turns off, and I hear the door close. The trunk opens above me; soft light filters through the sheet to my eyes. I stay silent. I am picked up and then thrown into the air. I hit the ground with force, water and mud surrounding me. I hear the car door once more, the sound of the engine, then tires screeching against the pavement.

Cold and wet, I lie motionless, too frightened to move. It's nighttime. I hear the hoot of an owl in the distance, but the light from what I think must be a lamppost flickers above me. After a while, I wriggle in my bindings—my hands are secured fast. It's then I hear the sound of voices, young voices—boys I think.

"Russ," one of them shouts, "look here. That pile of trash is moving."

"Shut up, Connor. We better hurry up. We're late. Mum and Dad will ground us...again." The voice that responds sounds older, more forceful.

"I'm telling you, bro. There's someone down there." The sound of metal hitting the ground tells me they've stopped and dropped what I assume are their bikes. "You go take a look."

"Me? Why me? You're the one who wanted to stop. Maybe it's a monster." He cackles with laughter, then I hear the sound of footsteps in mud. Something kicks at my leg, and I pull it away. Two screams echo in my ears.

"It's alive!" the younger boy shouts. "Run."

"Wait a minute," the older voice replies. He prods me again with his foot. "Hello, are you human? If you're a vampire, please don't bite us."

I don't speak. I can't. Feeling like I do, I want them to go away. To leave me here to rot in the mud, wherever I am. My eyes are tightly screwed shut, but I blink them open as I feel him crouch next to me. Something moves the cover at my face, and I look up into the eyes of a boy with dark hair, older than me but not grown up.

"Connor," he says, "ride home as fast as you can and get Dad. Tell him we found someone. He needs help."

CHAPTER TWELVE

---◆◇◆---

Farringdon, London

Violet

My room certainly is the definition of cozy. It's the smallest room in a four-bedroom apartment located only a few minutes' on the tube from Guilty Pleasures, my new place of work. The girls who live here are welcoming but standoffish. Samantha is the social butterfly of the group. Two of the girls are sisters and share a room—identical twins. The other is more my age, in her thirties, with a craze of red hair. All of them have incredible figures and bouncy tits. Samantha introduced them all so quickly, I didn't catch their names. I'll ask her later.

I've packed away what I can in the chest of drawers pushed into the corner of my private space. I tidy the roughly straightened bed in an attempt to make the worn sheets more appealing. Thankfully, the room is warm and has a small window that looks out onto the city below. People rush around carrying shopping bags and talking on their phones. On the opposite side of the street, black bags of trash are piled high. A rat nibbles at the edge of one, and my stomach somersaults. It seems there is a strike in the local council this week and nothing is being collected.

A soft knock at the door distracts me from the chaos below. "Come in," I call. Samantha walks in with a steaming mug of tea, passing it to me with a smile.

"Welcome to your new home," she says. "The girls will let their guard down once they get to know you. You're our fourth roommate since April." She rolls her eyes deliberately. "Let's just say we've met some interesting individuals."

"What are the girls' names again?" I ask, embarrassed. My cheeks heat violently, but she squeezes my arm in reassurance.

"Mia, Diane, and Steph."

"Thank you. They went in one ear and out the other."

"No problem," she says. "We need to be ready to leave in twenty minutes. We change at the club. All your outfits are kept there. We have access to a dressing room with every conceivable hair product and lipstick." She beams at me. "You'll be at the bar tonight. Have you worked in a bar before?" I shake my head.

"Don't worry, you'll pick it up in no time at all. I'm working there this evening, so I'll keep you right. Meet you in the living room in twenty." She turns and leaves, closing my door softly behind her. I look back to the darkening sky outside.

Today is day one of my new life. A new home. A new career. In the coming weeks, I need to get myself sorted and in a position to not only look after me, but the dependent growing in my belly. This solution will be short-lived but may provide a few weeks of income and a safe place to stay until I find an alternative.

***

Samantha skips into the preparation room at Guilty Pleasures. An expanse of mirrors runs along the back wall, floor to ceiling. On the opposite side is a row of six dressing tables, each with individual Hollywood mirrors. Shelves hold rows of hair-styling products and makeup. She grabs my hand and drags me through another open door. My jaw drops as I take in the surroundings. Rack after rack of costumes and wigs are crammed into the room.

"Welcome to the closet," she sings. "In here, you can turn into anyone." She struts over to a rack on the far wall and picks up a bright-pink outfit. It's barely a scrap of material, only enough to cover your necessities. "Try it on," she says, waving it in my face. "You'd look fucking awesome." I grimace at the thought of wearing the garment but accept it from her. No one will know me here; I can be whoever I want.

After struggling with the miniscule outfit, I stand, looking at myself in the wall of mirrors. The Lycra starts at my shoulders and runs south in a deep V-shape, covering my nipples then between my legs. "My tits will fall out," I mumble. Samantha laughs and winks.

"You will get extra tips if that happens." She walks over to a drawer, pulls it open, and extracts a roll of tape. "Don't worry, once I've stuck the bastard down, it won't be moving." Her face breaks into a beaming smile and she waggles her eyebrows, then pulls some tape from the roll. "Arms up," she orders. "Stand there and don't bloody move." Her hand moves fast, lifting each strip of fabric and applying tape to my skin. She lays the clothing down then presses firmly. "This stuff is like concrete when it sets. Take a shower with your outfit on after you're finished work, that will lift the tape safely from your skin." She stands back and surveys her handiwork, then nods to herself. "Fucking hot," she says.

Now, standing behind the bar, dozens of clients approach, one after the other, with dark eyes and appreciative smiles. "Who is this, Sam?" one man says. He's tall and slim with wide green eyes and close-cropped gray hair. It's hard to judge what age he is, but I would guess in his fifties.

"This is Violet. Isn't she gorgeous?" she replies, strutting over to stand beside me and placing her hand on my shoulder. She walks effortlessly in the eight-inch heels on her feet. I nearly broke my neck leaving the changing room in mine. Luckily, Samantha caught me under the arm and I managed to grab the wall in support. For the past hour, I've been shuffling around attempting to stay upright. I'm not sure how long I will last.

"Hello, Violet," the man says. He brushes an invisible hair from his insanely expensive blue-checked suit. As he focuses on me, I drop my eyes away, uncomfortable. He chuckles softly in response. "I love it when a new girl starts. You're all so fresh in the beginning. Ripe for the picking." My eyes return to his as he runs his tongue over his bottom lip.

"Can I get you something?" I ask him.

"Perhaps," he replies. "It depends on what is on the menu."

"Drinks only."

"Shame," he says with a smirk. "Hopefully in a few weeks, you'll loosen up and be willing to offer me some entertainment." His eyes fire. "I'd love to see what's under that poor excuse of an outfit. You might even enjoy the process."

My skin crawls—this guy is a creep. Briefly, I consider walking out of the bar, going back to my brother's apartment block, dropping to my knees, and begging for help.

The image of them loving my pathetic situation stops me. There is no fucking way I'm going crawling back. Violet Chase needs to toughen up and take control for once.

"Apologies, sir," I reply, placing my hands on the bar and leaning toward him. His focus drops to my breasts but immediately returns to my eyes. "I am most certainly off the menu. If you want a beverage, I'd be delighted to help. Otherwise, please move to the side and allow me to serve someone else." I glance at the girl I don't know, swinging around the pole in the center of the club. "Perhaps you should take a seat and enjoy the entertainment that is on offer."

"Feisty too," he says with a nod. He places an elbow on the bar, locking his gaze with mine. "I bet you're a screamer, Violet. You and I could make some sweet noise together."

"In your dreams."

"You most definitely will be."

Samantha passes him a scotch on the rocks. "Behave," she scolds him. He takes the drink, nods to her, then turns and walks toward the stage. "Jeez," she says, "I'm surprised he didn't beat his chest and jump the bar. That man has his sights firmly set on you. You do know who he is?" I shake my head. "Marshall Blake. One of the wealthiest men in the city. He owns a football club or something. And girl, you are on his radar." She lifts her hand to high-five me. I laugh, waving it away.

"That creep will be getting nowhere near me," I tell her. "He made my skin crawl."

"Don't be so hasty," she advises. "That creep there could be your ticket to a new life. And in all honesty, he isn't awful compared to some."

***

In the four weeks I've worked at the club, Marshall Blake has become my biggest fan. It turns out, he isn't so bad as first impressions appear. Every night I work, he's here, sitting at the bar, chatting while I pour drinks and serve the never-ending stream of patrons. He asked me out, and I said no. He's a good-looking man, but my heart doesn't beat the way it should when I see him. Only two men have ever made that happen in my life, and neither of them are here. But Marshall has sort of become a friend to me—he's lonely, that much is obvious. Him coming to the club is for company, not sex. I've never seen him take a girl to the private rooms; he barely watches the dancers. For all his alpha-man talk, he's a sweetheart who is looking for love. I wish he would realize that Guilty Pleasures isn't where he will find it.

On my first night on stage, he'd been unimpressed. "Why do you feel the need to do it?" I shrugged. "Violet, if you need money, I'll give you it. You don't need to shake what God gave you in front of these assholes."

"May I remind you, you are one of these assholes?" I retorted.

"No, I have standards and the ability to have a conversation with the woman I'm looking at without constantly looking at her breasts. Most of these apes." He signaled to the men sitting surrounding the stage. "Are barely capable of drooling and swigging whiskey. The expensive suits they wear only cover up what they really are. Neanderthals."

"Marshall, most men who come here have high-level jobs or run businesses that would make your eyes water with the money they earn. I'm not sure neanderthal is an accurate description." He flashed me a smile, which from another man would be endearing. From him, it feels like my uncle is trying to flirt with me.

"You can dress an ape in Armani, and it's still a fucking monkey," he said, pushing his glass from hand to hand on the bar top. "Promise me you won't sell yourself to them." He looked at me, his expression pleading. "Please don't sleep with them for money. You're a bright woman, Violet. You don't need to lie on your back to earn a living."

"Of course I won't," I snapped, furious he even thought I would.

"This is how it begins," he continued firmly, never losing focus on my face. "Girls arrive here, work the bar, then progress to the pole. When enough men have waved fifty-pound notes in their faces for more, one blowjob becomes full-time prostitution. Very few leave the cycle. Once they're in, they tend to be in for life. I've seen it happen so many times over the years."

"Why do you come here?" I asked him bluntly. "It's obvious you don't agree with the trade, though you gave a good impression that you did the first time we met. If you don't like it, why come?"

"To keep an eye on things," he replied evasively. "The girls in this establishment are some of the best-treated in the industry, but issues still arise. Joel Parker and I have an understanding.

"Understanding? Care to elaborate on what that is exactly?"

"I get free membership, unlimited food, drink, and conversation. He has eyes on the ground. None of the staff know, except you, that my presence here is a business arrangement. Most think I'm a lonely businessman, desperate for female company. I've never been with any of the girls."

"You're telling me that you come here for free food? I wasn't born yesterday." My sarcasm bounced between us, and he snickered. "There's something else."

"My sister walked this road and suffered the consequences." He paused, then took a glug of whiskey I poured into his glass moments ago. "We found her tied to a bed in an abandoned whore house. She'd been there for weeks. Most likely died from dehydration." He winced at the memory. "I've spent the years since then trying to support women in this industry. Sex will always be a trade, but that doesn't mean it can't have regulations, even if those regulations are imposed from within. This is something Parker and I agree on—the women, the product, are of the utmost importance. By being known as a regular here and in a few other places in the city, I'm privy to information others aren't."

"So, let me get this straight," I said, resting my elbows on the bar and placing my chin in my hands. "You expect me to believe that you're not a randy old man here for kicks. That even though you're a multimillionaire businessman, you spend your nights and weekends fighting for the safety of women in the sex industry."

"That's a fair summary. You're a good judge of character, Violet," he said with a smile. "Reading people is something that comes naturally to you."

"You wouldn't think that if you knew my history," I muttered. "I haven't managed to read men particularly well. My current condition is proof of that."

"Condition?" He raised an eyebrow in question.

"Situation," I whispered quickly, placing my hands on the bar. My eyes darted from side to side to ensure no one heard our conversation. He placed one hand over mine.

"Know this, you have a friend here who can help. If you're ever in trouble, you tell me. I like you, Violet. Being here is something you don't need to be doing." He stared at me, unblinking, his authority palpable. "But I think you already know that, and for some unknown reason, you're choosing to be here and swing around that pole. Just don't get lost in the fog. Know when it is time to leave."

I nodded to him, unable to speak. My words caught in my throat.

"Anyway," he said, "I have places to be and other people to chat with." His lips broke into a cheeky grin. "But you're always my favorite conversation partner. I'll see you soon, Violet Chase." It was only when he turned and left that I realized he used my real name.

Fuck, he knows who I am.

CHAPTER THIRTEEN

Chase, Chase and Waite
Law Offices, Canary Wharf

August 2022

Harrison

"I've found her," Damon says as he walks into my office. "But you're not going to like what I have to tell you."

"Where is she?" I snap as my heartrate increases to hyper in a split second. "Is she alive?"

"Yes, she's breathing. Though if her brothers find out what she's been doing for the last few weeks, she may not be for long." I narrow my eyes at him, confused by his statement.

"What are you talking about?" I ask, rocking back in my chair. "Is she hurt?"

"No, she's definitely in one piece and has plenty of witnesses to confirm it."

"For fuck's sake, Damon, spit it out."

"She's working at Guilty Pleasures." My jaw drops, and he smirks.

"Parker's place?" He nods. "Doing what?" My fury skyrockets. I've been there. I know what the girls do for a living. If she's been offering lap dances or more, I may spank her ass myself if Russell doesn't get to her first.

"Dancing as far as I know." He shrugs. "Seemingly, she started on the bar then progressed onto the stage within days. She has quite a fan club."

"Is this some kind of sick joke?" I snarl, and he shakes his head.

"No joke. I spoke to Joel Parker today and sent him a photo. He confirmed he hired her in July. She called herself Violet Brown."

"Brown, that's original," I say, sarcastically.

"She's working tonight," he tells me. "I was thinking we could go pay her a visit. It would probably be best not to tell her brothers. I don't think I'll be able to control the three of you."

"What time does the club open?"

"Midnight."

"I'll pick you up at twelve-thirty. We can let the festivities get underway before surprising her."

"What are you planning to do?" he asks, raising an eyebrow.

"Bring her home."

***

I wash my face again before looking in the mirror and roughing up my hair. My phone beeps.

Let me know when you're leaving.

Damon's message sits on my screen beside the time, which is midnight. I message back that I'll be with him in twenty minutes. After shrugging on my suit jacket, I head downstairs to the garage and slide into my car. The automatic barrier lowers, and I speed off into the night to go and retrieve Violet Chase from whatever situation she's entangled in.

Since Damon told me she's working at Guilty Pleasures, I've been caught somewhere between relief, guilt, and fury. The past hours have been spent contemplating every life choice I've ever made and what my relationship with the Chase family will be when I finally bring their daughter home. The girl has always been completely off limits, but I ignored the rules. Twice. Both times resulted in her running away from her family.

Tonight, I'll bring her home to them once and for all.

Damon is standing on the pavement when I arrive at his house. His nanny and son were already in bed; he didn't want to disturb them with me sounding the horn when I arrived. "You ready for this?" he asks as he climbs into the passenger seat. "Are you calm?"

"Yes," I reply, not looking at him.

"What is the plan?"

"We go to the club and see how things stand. Hopefully, she'll be behind the bar, and we can approach her quietly."

"I don't think she works the bar now, Waite," he warns. I feel him staring, but I don't look in his direction. Tonight, I'm fucking praying she's working the bar.

Our drive to Guilty Pleasures is made in silence. There is nothing to say or discuss. Damon knows exactly what's on my mind. As we pull up outside the club, the doorman approaches me and takes my keys to park my car. I hand him a fifty-pound note. He climbs into the Ferrari, then drives off down the road to the off-street parking area.

Damon and I pull our member's cards from our pockets as we approach the entrance. This is somewhere I've not been in years, but in my twenties, I was a regular. I probably should have canceled my membership, but it is a place many well-connected men frequent, and having the option to come here can have its benefits. It's known for discretion. The security staff wave us through, and we climb the familiar staircase to the club above.

"Good evening, gentlemen," a pretty blonde says as we enter. She's wearing a fitted black corset dress with insanely high heels. Her hair sits in perfect curls around a heavily made-up face. "How can I help you this evening? Are you in for a drink or, perhaps, some entertainment?"

Damon speaks before I have a chance to. "Can we have a table near the dance floor?" She nods. "And two beers."

"Beer," I mutter. "I'm going to need fucking tequila if tonight is going to turn out how I think it will."

"Of course," she says with a beaming smile. "Follow me. I'll show you to your table then get your drinks. Two beers and a tequila." I don't argue—the liquor will be welcome. We file behind her, weaving through the already busy club. Men in suits with open-neck shirts laze about, drinking and watching the pretty girls strut around. "Here you are, gentlemen." She signals to a table for two next to the stage, then heads in the direction of the bar. We both sit and remove our jackets.

I glance around the room. No one is recognizable, but no doubt there will be people here I know or who know me. A man sits on his own by the bar drinking a whiskey. He's not watching the stage, only talking to the woman serving the drinks. The music changes and my attention is brought back to the pole in front of me.

The girl who was there before has disappeared. The lights drop, and it casts the stage into darkness. As they lift, a figure comes into view. She's turned away from us at the back of the platform. Dark shiny curls flow down her back, glimmering under the lights. She's wearing sky-high heels on the end of long sexy legs. Her ass looks incredible in a glittery pink thong. When she turns around, she's topless. My jaw drops in shock. She struts to the pole on the stage, hooks a leg, and swings around with insane confidence.

The fiber of control I have snaps.

Chapter Fourteen

Lammerton Home for Boys

January 1997

Harrison

"This will be your room, Harry," says the woman who looks terrifyingly like the teacher from the storybook *Matilda*. She's a large lady with scraped-back black hair in a bun. Her features are strong, her nose slightly too large for her face. She's wearing a dark gray jacket that is so tight the buttons have popped open three times since I arrived. The white shirt underneath is pristine, the collar standing tall at her neck. She places a heavily booted foot into the tiny bedroom in front of us and signals for me to follow her. "Come on, don't be shy. This is your bedroom. Your own space."

I walk forward as she stands at the door, holding it open. As I peer around the corner, I expect someone to jump out and surprise me. That was a common occurrence at the last boy's home I was in. Inside, there is a single bed with a light blue blanket, a chest of drawers, and a table with a lamp. I notice the gray shade sits canted, obviously broken. All the walls are white—there are no pictures or designs. One small window looks out into the English garden below filled with rosebushes and trees.

Over the past twelve months since being found in the ditch, I've stayed in two foster homes and one boy's home. None of them were a suitable fit for me; seemingly, I need extra support. That's what the grown-ups say. I wish other children would stop yanking my chain.

The last straw with the Reynolds Family was when I threw their son, James, in the garden pond. He stole the biscuit I was eating from between my fingers as I sat on the swing, enjoying the spring sunshine. Ever since I'd arrived at the house, he had been hassling me, teasing me about being the boy who was found in a ditch. After three weeks of torment, I snapped. As he'd walked away munching on my snack, I ran up behind him and pushed him straight into their custom-made pond with exotic fish. Social services collected me that evening.

"Now, Harry," the woman says, snapping me from my memory. I raise my eyes to hers. She did tell me her name, but I can't remember. Possibly I don't even want to. No doubt this will be a short-lived placement too. Each day that passes, my anger grows. My mum has left me on my own in a scary world. No one wants me. No one loves me. Hating everyone and everything is easier than trying. "Harry," she says again firmly. I looked away without realizing it. "Do you understand where you are? And why you're here?"

"Suppose," I say with a shrug. "My mum's dead, and I have nowhere to live. So, you're stuck with me." She studies my face, her bland expression never faltering. "I'm a bad boy who threw someone in a pond?" I suggest when she doesn't say anything. She stares at me for another minute before offering an explanation.

"You're here in Lammerton because your other placements have not been successful." I know this—the social worker explained it. "But you have to understand, there is nowhere else after Lammerton. This is it. So, whether you're happy or sad, good or naughty, you will remain here at this home with us."

"What if someone wants to adopt me?" I ask and she smirks.

"Little boys are always bottom of the pile. Especially little boys with bad tempers. You need to start behaving or this will be your home until you're an adult." I blink at her, stunned. All the other adults I've met since losing my mother have been overly nice, offering me treats and taking my hands in theirs. They all want to console me, help me "come to terms" with my loss. It makes my skin crawl. This woman is offering nothing of the sort. She's warning me to behave or I'll be stuck here, forever. A bad boy discarded in the landfill.

"What's your name again?" I mutter petulantly.

"Matron Deliah. Now, you get settled in. Dinner will be in an hour. I'll send one of the boys to collect you." She places my black trash bag with the few belongings I've collected on the bed. None are mine—all have been gifted to me by the families I stayed with. The only item I still have is my little blue bear; he's kept safe in my jacket pocket all the time. "See you at dinner," she says as she turns, leaving and closing the door behind her. Once again, I'm on my own.

***

Four weeks after moving to Lammerton, I've started to adapt to the strict routine we live under. Every morning we are woken at six o'clock. Breakfast is at seven, then lessons start at eight. Weekends are spent carrying out chores around the grounds or helping in the local community, if they trust you. I'm not trusted. But Matron Deliah has told me she is happy with my progress since I arrived. My temper is more in control, especially when one of the other boys annoys me.

On my second day here, an older boy tried to steal my lunch. I responded by tipping his soup in his lap, then jumping onto the bench next to him and punching his nose. The blood had spurted out across the table, ruining his friend's meal too. Now, no one approaches me. I've not made any friends, but it's better that way—you can't lose them.

It's a warm afternoon in June when Matron tells me I have a visitor. "Harry, there is someone here to see you," she says.

"Who? I don't have anyone to come and see me."

"Patience, wait and see. Now, go and wash your hands then come to the visiting room."

"Where is it? I've never needed to go before."

"Next to the front door. Run along, don't keep him waiting," she prompts, waving a hand at me.

"He?" I question.

"Yes, he. Go." My mind races as I run across the garden toward the bathrooms inside. He. Who could it be? I don't know any grown-up men that would want to visit me. No one who would even know I was here.

The thought I don't want to recognize jumps forward, waving its arms. *Perhaps it's your dad?* I try to bat it away, but I can't help but hope. Not that I know who he is, but if anyone comes to visit, I wish it would be him.

After washing up and changing my t-shirt, I head off in the direction of the front door. The visiting room is clearly marked by a black sign with white letters spelling VISITORS ROOM. The door to the room is ajar, and I hear voices inside talking excitedly. When I walk in, there are already three tables of boys who live here with whom I assume are their family members. Many boys only stay here for a short time before going home after whatever issue is sorted.

Matron is sitting at a table in the corner talking to a man wearing a black suit with a white shirt. She looks up and upon seeing me, she signals for me to join them. I walk over, nervous about what is about to happen. The man turns to face me and gives me a kind smile. He extends a hand; I take it, and we shake. I've seen people shake hands on television; it feels strange to do it in the real world. His hair is dark but graying around the edges. He has sharp brown eyes the color of chestnuts. I notice his shoes are polished to a high shine.

"Hello, Harrison," he says. "It is lovely to see you again. And this time under better circumstances." I gawk at him, both stunned and confused.

"You know me?" I ask.

"Yes, we've met once before. Back in January last year. It was my sons who found you that night. I was the person who took you to the hospital. My name is Mr. Chase."

"Harry," Matron interrupts, "sit down. Mr. Chase wanted to come and visit you. He has been keeping up with how you've been doing since he found you. When he heard you moved here and were now settled, he wanted to visit you."

On autopilot, I move to sit opposite the man who most likely saved my life. His eyes run over my face, but he doesn't speak straight away. I stare right back at him. I've learned never to drop my gaze if I can. It's a sign of weakness, and bullies love that, so I don't ever look away.

"I'll leave you both to it," Matron says. She walks over to another table and engages in conversation with them. Mr. Chase and I watch her leave then our focus returns to one another.

"So, Harrison," he says firmly.

"My friends call me Harry."

"Well, you don't know me, so we're not friends. For now, I'll call you Harrison, and you call me Mr. Chase." I scowl at him. "Don't contort your face like that. If the wind changes it will stick."

"What?"

"Do you not know that, Harrison? If you make a horrible face and the wind changes direction, you risk keeping that face forever."

"That's not true," I argue, and he smiles.

"Maybe it is, maybe it isn't, but are you willing to take the risk?" He raises an eyebrow in challenge. "Shall we start again? I'm Mr. Chase, it's lovely to see you again under better circumstances."

"Hello, Mr. Chase," I mumble. "It's nice to see you again."

"So, tell me, what has been happening this past year? I hear you've had a few different places to stay."

"No one wants me."

"Is that true? Or have you been misbehaving?" he asks. I slap my hands on the table between us and open my mouth to argue. He raises a hand. "Don't lie to me, Harrison. I've heard everything about your vigilante escapades. You like to dish out your own punishments, I hear."

"He stole my biscuit."

"That one event. What about the other times? The broken window. The cut-up clothes. The boy with the broken nose. Are you telling me they all stole a biscuit? And that their punishments were deserved?" I shrug, unable to justify my actions. "Answer me."

"I get angry," I say as an attempt at an explanation.

"That's no excuse. You are not the judge and the jury. It is not your responsibility to distribute a sentence to offenders. Do you understand?" I nod, completely lost as to why this man is sitting across from me, giving me a lecture. "Answer me."

"Yes, Mr. Chase."

"If you want to work in law enforcement," he says, "you need to become someone who is allowed to serve the punishments. That means becoming a policeman or a lawyer or even a judge. Do you know what those people do?"

"Yes, Mr. Chase."

"Do you want to work when you grow up, Harrison, or do you want to be in jail?" The question sits between us for a moment as I process what he is saying. When I don't answer, he continues. "What I'm saying is, if you don't stop this bad behavior now, it will follow you into adulthood. Now is when you decide whether you're putting people in jail or going to be in jail yourself."

"Okay, Mr. Chase."

"This is your life. It is your responsibility to live it the best way you can. It is unfair that at such a young age I'm having to say this to you, but this is where you are. Now, tell me, can you read?"

CHAPTER FIFTEEN

Guilty Pleasures
Gentlemen's Club

Violet

My song starts with the lights coming up. I turn and strut to the front of the stage feeling incredible in my minute thong with my tits hanging out. Never did I think I could do something like this and feel in control, but hell I do. Men literally drool over me and offer their money for a night.

I fucking love saying no.

Part of the reason I've enjoyed my short time at the club so much is that I know it can't last long. The doctor told me I'm past twelve weeks now and will start to show soon. A pregnant pole dancer isn't a sought-after entertainer, so I'll enjoy it while I can.

Being Violet Brown is fun. Having my freedom is life changing. No one tells me what to do. No one advises when they'll see me. I live with girls I now consider friends. Apart from my shifts here, my time is my own. No one demands it. No man is a higher priority in my life than I am. That is a change I plan to keep, whatever happens next.

When I dance, the crowd is invisible to me. Sure, I hear the calls of appreciation, but my eyes never look to the men below. I keep them fixed firmly above their heads. But this time, I feel his focus on me. Moving to a basic invert, I'm upside down on the pole as my eyes meet his furious brown ones. Harrison stands immediately in front of me, his arms crossed over his chest.

"Get the fuck down from there," he mouths.

"No," I snap back silently. "I'm working." He moves to climb onto the stage when I see Marshall striding over from the bar and taking his arm. Harry glares at him, pulling it out of his grasp. Marshall leans forward and whispers something in his ear. I try to ignore the altercation in front of me and concentrate on my dance. After finishing a spin, I look at the men and see Marshall cradling his nose. A larger man has joined the group and is herding both of them toward the bar. The girl behind it already has three glasses of what looks like whiskey lined up in preparation. Shit.

His eyes never move from me the whole time I'm on stage. He's furious, that much is obvious. The other men speak to each other, but Harrison never joins in the conversation. He sits and watches my every move while sipping whatever amber liquid is in his glass. If steam could rise from someone's ears, it would be from his.

After my set is complete, I retreat to the dressing room.

"Who was that?" Samantha shrieks as she bursts through the changing room door. I'm sitting at a dressing table removing the heavy makeup from my face. My eyes remain fixed on my reflection.

"Who?" I ask, feigning ignorance.

"Um...the hottie that was glowering at the stage while you were dancing." She holds her hands out. "Then who proceeded to punch Marshall square in the face when he tried to move him."

"Oh, him," I reply with a shrug. "That's Harrison."

"Harrison?" she says, raising her eyebrows. "Why would Harrison be so upset to find you performing? I assume you know each other."

I laugh then promptly burst into tears. She walks forward and wraps her arms around my shoulders. We look at each other in the mirror. "Violet, what's going on?"

"He's..." I trail off, not knowing how to explain who he is. *My friend. My ad hoc lover. My brother's best friend. My soul mate I can't have.* He's always been forbidden. I was warned constantly throughout my teenage years to stay away from him. Though my father supported him, he's always seen him as a charity case to a degree. Something to show off as a work in progress, a success story he can boast about to his friends. "He works with my brothers."

"And what do they do?"

"They're lawyers." Her eyes pop open. "Harrison is one of the best defense lawyers in the city. The three of them own a firm in the financial district." My explanation tumbles from me. The truth I've been hiding for weeks spills out into the open. Who I am. The type of people I'm connected to.

"Well, I'm assuming by his little outburst that isn't all he is, a colleague of your brothers." She narrows her eyes, willing me to volunteer more information.

"We have history, but things are complicated. We hadn't seen each other in fourteen years until June. I suspect someone told him I'm here and this is him come to take me home to my family." The thought is depressing. "I ran away to Chicago when I was nineteen. I've only just come back."

"You don't need to go anywhere you don't want to," she tells me firmly. "You have a place to stay with me, always. Us girls have got to stick together." I smile at her in thanks; this woman has become a closer friend than anybody ever has in the past few weeks. Female companionship isn't something I'm used to having. A friend to rely on isn't an attribute I want to lose.

"Things aren't that simple," I whisper. "You see, Sam..." As I go to tell her about my precious cargo, the dressing room door swings open, and Harry storms into the room.

"Violet," he growls, coming to my side and taking my elbow. "Put some fucking clothes on. You're coming with me, now."

"No," I shout back, and he glowers in response. "Take your hands off me."

"This isn't a fucking question. I'm telling you, you're going home." I pull my arm from his grip and push him hard in the chest. "Don't push me. I'll drag you if I have to." His eyes are dark, and not from arousal. He's livid.

"I told you, I'm not your problem. Now fuck off. I'm doing fine without you and my masochistic brothers. Go back to your boys' nights and 'female entertainment.' You shouldn't be in here. Samantha, call security." The woman beside me is gazing at an irate Harry, who is continuing to lecture me. I'm not listening. "Sam, security." I tap her arm with my hand. "Fucking focus, will you."

"Would you put some bloody clothes on?" he mutters again, running a hand through his hair. A familiar redness appears at the base of his throat, the color creeping up to his cheeks. He's panty-wetting to look at when he's mad.

"Why?" I snap. "It's not as if you've not seen it all before. You've definitely been up close and personal with these." I shake my tits at him, and he opens his mouth to respond when Marshall and the other tall man I saw appear in the doorway.

"Waite," the man barks, moving between Harry and me. "Come with me, now. You're going to get yourself thrown out of here and then you won't have done what you came to do."

"And what would that be?" I ask sharply. The unknown man turns to me. His eyes run over my face, and he smirks.

"To take you home to Mummy and Daddy, sweetheart. They know all about your little predicament." My stomach falls—shit, my parents know I'm back in Britain and pregnant. "Daddy is not too pleased, I believe. I can't say your brothers are particularly overjoyed with the news they're going to be uncles either."

"You're pregnant!" Samantha whispers in my ear crossly. I wave her away with my hand. "Is it his?" she says, signaling to Harry.

"No."

"Whose is it then?" she asks, her face contorted in confusion. "How many men do you have, Violet?"

"I'll tell you later. At this point, none, and I don't want one."

The tall man takes Harry by the shoulders, turns him around, then pushes him out the door leaving Marshall standing with Samantha and me. I drop to sit on the bench next to the nearest dressing table and my head falls into my hands. Samantha places my pink silk robe over my shoulders. The tears fall freely as my reality surfaces. Marshall crouches down beside me, and I glance at him.

"Did you tell them I was here?" I ask him quietly and he nods. "Why?"

"I've worked with Damon for years," he starts to explain.

"Is Damon the big guy?"

He nods again. "Chief Constable Damon McKinney, Head of the National Serious and Organized Crime Unit," he tells me. "He put a call out to his men on the ground to look out for you.

Imagine my surprise when I found you here. I didn't tell them straight away, but then he told me about the baby." He pauses, considering his words. "Violet, I couldn't in good conscience not tell him. This is not somewhere an expectant mother should be working."

"That's my choice," I stammer as my tears fall harder.

"Sometimes we need people to take control," he continues. "Especially when we end up somewhere we never expected to be. I didn't want to break your trust, but I had to decide what was the priority. *Who* was the priority. The innocent party in all this was that baby." His eyes move to my stomach then back to my face.

"I wasn't planning on working here long," I justify, and he smiles softly.

"Most girls never do. In the beginning they enjoy the buzz this life offers, then it becomes an obligation. I've told you this before. It's hard to get off the wheel once you're strapped to it." He sighs sadly. "My sister is proof of that in both life and death. I couldn't save her, but I had the opportunity to help you. So, I took it."

I open my mouth to argue when Samantha squeezes my elbow. "He's right, Violet. You have a lot more to think about and consider. Someone else who needs to be your priority. It maybe doesn't feel like it now, but tonight was meant to happen. It's time to go home."

"I don't have a home."

"You do." Harry's voice cuts through our conversation as he re-enters the room. "You always have a home with me, if you need it. Both of you." He walks over and stands between me and Marshall. We rise, and he focuses on Marshall. "I'm sorry about your nose." The bruising is starting to show across the bridge of it, a purple arch highlighting beneath his eyes.

"Completely understandable in the circumstances," he replies with a chuckle. "If I'd found my lady in a similar position, I would have gone postal too."

"I'm not his woman," I hiss, annoyed. Harry glances at me but doesn't argue. His attention turns back to Marshall.

"Thank you for alerting Damon to Violet's whereabouts. Her family and I are very appreciative of your assistance in this matter. If I can help you at all in the future, don't hesitate to ask. Violet is very precious to me, even if she doesn't realize it." A sad smile appears on his lips and my heart strains slightly.

"Perhaps there is something you could do for me," Marshall says. Damon stands silently watching the proceedings. He is the epitome of quiet domination. "I believe you and a few colleagues are involved in some investigative matters that are of interest to me."

"Perhaps," Harry replies evasively. "Do elaborate on what they are and where your interest lies."

"Heroin." Harry's face doesn't change with the word—he looks impassively at the other man. Everyone stands so silently you could hear a pin drop. "You and your friends are trying to dismantle one of the biggest drug rings in London. That's the word on the street anyway."

"And if we do want to do as you say, why would that be of interest to you?"

"I want in," he answers simply. "Innocent people need to stop dying at the hands of evil bastards to line their pockets."

Harry looks at Damon, who nods. "I'm sure that can be arranged," he replies. "Damon will contact you regarding the next meeting. There has been new information—things are heating up and we are getting closer to the source. Someone such as yourself would be an asset to our team."

"Excellent," Marshall exclaims, rubbing his hands together. "Good old-fashioned justice. I'll see you boys soon." His gaze moves to Samantha and me. "And ladies, until the next time we meet." He bows exaggeratedly then leaves.

Samantha's jaw has almost been touching the floor during this whole discussion. My fury has been rising fast, ready to explode to the surface the next time someone tries to tell me what I need to do. Damon moves to Sam's side and taps her shoulder. She looks to him and he signals they should leave. Before moving, she turns to me.

"You don't need to do anything you don't want to do," she says. "You and baby can stay with us until you figure things out. Remember what we said, Violet. You are putting yourself first, no one else." She glances at Harry, who is standing silently listening to our exchange. "No one." Then she walks out.

As soon as the door closes, I spin to face him. Stepping forward, I rise onto my tiptoes so I'm standing directly under his nose. "You," I say, poking at his chest with my finger, "you are the most confusing bastard on the fucking planet." His eyes meet mine, then drop to his feet. "Why the fuck do you care if I'm dancing here? What has it got to do with you? You're not my boyfriend. You're not my baby's father. You're..."

"What am I?" he whispers softly. His lips drop to my forehead, kissing me gently, the intimate gesture startling me.

"You're Harry." It's all I can say. There's no other way to explain who or what he is to me. There aren't enough words to describe how he makes me feel, so safe and so unhinged in the same moment. Both centered and confused. The emotion this man sends surging through my body is deliciously unbearable, but oh so addictive.

"Who is Harry?" he asks, and I glance up at him, my eyes filled with unshed tears. "Because in all honesty, Vi, I have no idea. The more I meet him, the more I think he'll always be just the boy your brother found in a ditch."

"Don't say that. You're so much more than your past."

A sad smile plays on his lips. Tonight, he looks like the young man I fell for all those years ago, not the hardened version I've met now. His vulnerable edges are visible once more.

"This is why I've always adored you," he says, and my heart beats harder. "When you look at me, you don't see a peasant, you see me." He leans down and kisses me softly on the lips. When he withdraws, they tingle with the loss. "But I'm dan-

gerous and not the right man for you. I should never have insti-
gated anything romantic between us. I've been cautioned often
enough since you were fourteen. Not that I fucking listened."
He laughs, lifting his focus to the ceiling before it returns to me.

"What's so funny?" I ask. My eyes search his face for a clue
as to where this conversation is headed. I was given the same
warning. *If I find out there is more to this than friendship, Violet,
you won't be seeing him again. He won't be welcome here.* My
father had watched us like a hawk when Harry came to visit. If
there was so much as a look he didn't like, I was told to leave the
room. *Go do something girly. Leave the boys to it. You shouldn't
be here.*

"Nothing is funny," he replies, shaking his head. "It's ironic
that the man who saved me, helped me become the best version
of myself, is also my greatest hurdle in life. He puts the barrier
between me and what I truly want."

"And what's that?"

"You."

CHAPTER SIXTEEN

Lammerton Home for Boys

August 1998

Harrison

"C..o..m..p..l..i..c..a..t..e..d." I screw my eyes up as I try to read the word on the page. "Complicated," I shriek, knowing it's correct.

"Well done, Harrison," Mr. Chase says enthusiastically. "Complicated. Your reading is improving magnificently. I'm proud of you, boy." I beam up at the man who has become a father figure to me, though he doesn't realize it.

"Complicated," I repeat then focus on the next word on my list. Every week he visits for two hours on a Friday and helps me with my studies. I still call him Mr. Chase and he refers to me as Harrison. It makes me sad he doesn't consider us friends yet, but he comes, which is what matters.

I'm trying to decipher the next eleven-letter word when he speaks. "I've been thinking, Harrison, maybe it's time you meet my sons. How would you feel about that?" he asks. I stop focusing on the paper in front of me and turn to him.

"Russell and Connor?" He nods, confirming my statement. "I don't know. Why would they want to meet me?"

"Well, they were the ones who found you, and they always ask about you when I've been here. In the last year and a half, I've watched you grow into a young man I'm proud to know. You could be a good friend for them and them for you."

"Maybe," I say with a shrug. "I don't have any friends. People don't like me."

"They don't understand you, Harrison. There is a difference. You have a quiet determination that is disconcerting for some people."

"Disconcerting?" I repeat. The word rolls off my tongue. "What does that mean?"

"It means you make them nervous."

"But I don't do anything wrong," I protest. I've learned to keep quiet in the home, not stand out from the crowd. If I slip through my life here, no one annoys me.

"You don't need to. You have a presence about you that makes people take a step back. No one messes with you, but no one approaches you either. I've seen the other boys and the way they look at you. You have control even if you don't realize it."

"Possibly," I reply, confused.

"My sons are like you. Strong willed. Confident. Argumentative."

"I'm not argumentative."

He laughs out loud. "Yes, you are. You're also one-hundred-percent confident in your own opinions, which in a young man is an excellent quality and will stand you in good stead for life ahead. But you need to be spending time with other boys like you, boys with promise. You have promise, Harrison. In your life, you will be successful. I'll make sure of it."

***

September 2022 – The Level

"Harrison, I am very disappointed that you ignored one of the most important rules of our friendship," Mr. Chase states. Tonight, I know I'll be paying for the time I enjoyed with Violet. "When I supported you as a young man, I did it because I knew you would be an asset to both me and my family. I saw you as someone who could be incorporated long term into our business. A loyal associate that could be relied on."

He walks over then around the chair I'm tied to. They haven't gagged me, yet. His fingers are clenched around the knuckle-duster on his right hand.

"You have surpassed every challenge I've set for you, then gone on to become one of the most influential lawyers in the city. Sometimes, I feel prouder of you than I do my own sons."

Russell and Connor watch their father as he strolls around. They visibly bristle with the comment. "Your success has not only been of benefit to the law firm and its amazing growth, but also to our family operations. The clients you attract have allowed us to gain information previously never at our disposal. For that reason, I respect you as a professional man and partner in business."

I look over to the men I consider to be like my brothers; they divert their gaze from me. My focus returns to the man in charge. The man who is always in charge of the Chase family. Edward Chase.

"However," he says turning to face me. He leans down and looks me directly in the eye. "Violet was always fucking out of bounds; I told you that as a sixteen-year-old boy with a hard-on. Nothing has changed. You and my daughter are a no-go area. She will not be with someone from your background. She deserves better."

"Sir," Connor says, stepping forward. His father spins to face him. "Waite was the one who found her and brought her home to us. She ran again, we've only just got her back. Surely, we should be thanking him."

His father straightens his shoulders and shakes his head. "No, from what your brother has told me, she ran because of him." His furious scowl lands on me. "In our family, those who cause the problem, pay. You will suffer a debt of your misguided actions and your complete disregard of my orders. Whether an instruction is ten minutes or ten years old, it is still a fucking command. Do you understand me, Harrison?"

"Yes, sir," I respond firmly, never dropping my eyes from his. Like his son, this man is a bully who rules both his family and businesses with an iron fist.

"Once I've delivered this penalty, the matter will be put to bed. It won't be discussed again, and you will not be in the same room as Violet for the rest of your lifetime."

"Yes, sir."

"Good. We have an understanding once more. You play your part but stay in your fucking lane. Diversion will not be tolerated." His arm draws back and the metal crashes down on my cheek. "One," he growls.

***

"Harry," Mrs. D. whispers as she dabs at my eye. Fuck, my head hurts. My hand lifts to my cheek, the skin stinging. "Harry," she says again, "can you hear me?"

"Yes," I reply, my voice almost silent. "How long have I been out? Where am I?" I blink my eyes open, and she's smiling down at me, but there is no hiding the concern in her eyes. The last thing I remember is Mr. Chase lifting his fist to bring down the fourth blow.

"You're at home. Connor brought you in an hour ago. He wouldn't let me phone an ambulance. You're a mess. What happened?" I chuckle under my breath, causing my ribs to strain.

"Shit, don't make me laugh. It bloody hurts."

"Who did this?" she asks again.

"The Chase family." Her eyebrows draw together in confusion. "I broke the rules, and this is my punishment. When Edward Chase tells you something is off limits, it's fucking off limits."

"What are you talking about?"

"Violet," I reply sadly. "He found out that she and I were..." *What are we?*

"In love?" she suggests, and I glance at her, startled.

"No, of course not. Intimate, or had been. He told me as a young man she would never be mine. And I didn't listen. This..." I signal to my face with my hand. "Is this what happens when you go against the rules."

"It's barbaric," she wails, her hands covering her mouth. "You and Violet are adults. It is none of his business. This can't happen. We need to phone the police."

"He owns the police," I say. "Everything anyone does connected with the Chase family is his business. I've seen it with my own eyes since I was a boy. Mrs. D., I knew I was playing a dangerous game. This hasn't come as a surprise. Edward Chase has been both my savior and my captor since childhood. Without him, quite honestly, I would either be in jail or dead. But the day he decided I was his pity project sent me down a path where I would always be beholden to him and have to dance to his tune."

***

Monday morning rolls around. I walk into my office to find Damon McKinney and Hunter Devane sitting waiting for me. Both of them are holding takeaway coffees in one hand and a doughnut in the other. "I hope you pair of assholes brought refreshments for me too. Doughnuts are a bit cliché, are they not McKinney?" I snap as I throw myself into my chair.

"Eat what you're bloody given. What the fuck happened to you?" Hunter says as he places a coffee and my favorite apple cake in front of me.

"I had a debt to pay," I reply.

"For what?" Hunter sits back down in the seat across from me, Damon beside him.

"For sticking his cock where he's not allowed to," Damon suggests and Hunter laughs. "Am I right?"

"Old man Chase dealt out the punishment himself," I mutter angrily. "And he fucking loved every minute of it." Damon gives me a knowing look. He is aware of the Chase family's underground businesses and connections. As I've come to know him better, he's told me stories of Edward Chase and his punishments that would curl your toes. His reputation precedes him. Get in his way and prepare to be disposed of. "Anyway, to what do I owe the pleasure of this unexpected visit?"

"McKinney wanted to make sure you were still alive after the other night. He said your rescue mission didn't quite go to plan." Hunter sips at his drink as he watches me. "You got the girl out but put a target on your back in the process."

"She's back where she needs to be," I say, not acknowledging the comment. "The beating was something I had to take. I knew it was coming since Russell found out I'd slept with her."

"You're sure about that?" Damon asks. "You think her being back at her parent's house is the best place for her at the moment?"

"Where would be better?" I ask, glaring at him.

"You told her she always had a home with you. Your words, Waite."

"It was an empty promise to get her to leave Guilty Pleasures. We can't ever happen; you and I both know that. Even if I wanted it to, it would never be allowed. I owe Edward Chase and his family my life; this is a wish of theirs I need to honor."

"Why?" Hunter interjects. "Do you not think you've repaid them enough over the past ten years? How many cases have you won for them? How much money have you earned them? How many times have you done their dirty work?" He pulls a knife from his waistband and starts twisting it between his fingers. He presses the blade into the tip of his middle finger, a drop of blood beads on his skin. "Once the debt is paid, Waite, the debt is paid. The Chase family can't hold you in indentured servitude for your whole life for a few years in school and university. There comes a time where both parties are even."

"I doubt he will ever be of that opinion," I say with a smirk. "Though the thought is sweet."

169

"Allow people to use you, and they always will." He fixes me with a stare. "You don't owe them fuck-all. It's time you both realized that. Anyway, I'll see you at The Level on Wednesday. We have lots to catch up on. My team are getting closer to finding the kitchen. That shit will be off the streets. We're going to win this one, boys, I can feel it in my bones." He jumps up and strides toward the door. Before leaving, he calls over his shoulder, "The bastards behind this will pay for every death that shit of theirs has caused. Painfully. With their blood."

Damon and I stare at the closed door. He turns back to me and laughs. "That idiot is a fucking madman. How have I ended up on the same side as him?"

"How have any of us ended up here?" I say, dropping my eyes to my hands which are twirling a pen. "We spend our days balancing light and dark. Walking in circles we'd rather not. Working with men who become more ruthless with each day that passes. We pretend that our little mission to rid the streets of dirty drugs cleanses us of our own bad behavior. We're all criminals at the end of the day, only dressed differently."

"That's an awfully deep sentiment for a Monday morning," he mutters.

"If this weekend has taught me anything, it is that I will always be the boy from the ditch in everyone's eyes. I can earn more, learn more, and win at every opportunity but at the end of the day, the life you're dealt is the one you're stuck with. It defines who you are."

"I don't think that is strictly true," he argues, crossing his arms across his chest. "Everyone has the option to change direction. Part of the reason you're sitting here in front of me is that you met Edward Chase as a small boy. The other reason is you're a shit-hot lawyer and fucking good at reading people."

"Today, I'd rather be a trash collector."

He laughs out loud. "I doubt you could afford a Ferrari on that wage." He stands. "People will stop looking at you like that boy from the ditch if you stop appearing like him. He's gone, and you're here. It's time to take control. You think you need them. I promise you, it's the other way around." He walks toward my door, pulls it open then closes it again, turning to face me. "And Waite, one more thing—Violet certainly didn't look at you as if you were a charity case." With that, he leaves.

CHAPTER SEVENTEEN

The Chase Family Home, Kensington

Violet

My childhood bedroom is the same as when I left it at the age of eighteen. Over the past fourteen years my mother has changed nothing. The posters of the boybands I loved so dearly still hang on the walls, and everything else is either pink or white. After a heartbreaking speech from my parents, I've locked myself in here away from my family. My father spoke in a tone he uses when truly disgusted with the person he is talking to. My mother cried as she sat next to him, every so often taking a white linen handkerchief from her pocket to dab her eyes.

"Fourteen years, Violet, with no word from you. Do you know what your selfishness has done to this family? To your mother?" he growled.

"Father. Sir. I..." There were no words that could justify my actions all those years ago. I walked away, that much is true. Aiden Marley turned my head, and I ran after him like a puppy, begging him to love me.

"I don't want to hear your pathetic excuses." His eyes started at my face then ran down my body to my toes. His face screwed up as if smelling something unpleasant. "Then you appear back here with no warning. Pregnant, no less, with a married man's baby. The man you walked away from your career and your home for. The man whose cheap slut you've been for over a decade."

His fist slammed down on the dining table next to us, making me jump. We hadn't yet moved to sit down. Standing felt safer—I could run if I needed to.

"Your brothers then report that you absconded again only days after your return, but not before playing the tart for another man who has always been prohibited." His furious eyes focused on mine again. He leaned forward, invading my space. "But my darling daughter, the most devastating details were finding out you have been working in a strip club after running yet again." He grabbed the tops of my arms roughly in his hands, pulling me toward him and lifting me off the ground so we were nose to nose. "Your return should be a happy occasion. It is anything fucking but," he snarled. "I feel nothing but shame when I look at you."

So now, at the age of thirty-two, I am sitting on my childhood bed with my knees pulled up to my nose, rocking to the sound of pop music from my teen years. Life could not be any more fucked up if I tried. A quiet knock at the door interrupts my pity party.

"Go away," I shout, but the knock sounds again, louder this time. "I said go away."

"Violet, it's your mother. Open the door, please," she calls, her voice wavering with emotion. Sighing, I uncurl myself from my wretched position and climb out of the bed, then walk over to unbolt the door. She opens it immediately, sliding in, then closing and relocking it behind her. Her arms wrap around me, and she pulls me close, holding me like she did when I was a small child. "My darling girl," she whispers fiercely against my ear. "Oh, how I have missed you. I'm so happy you're home."

I pull back and stare at her. She blinks then smiles kindly. Her face has changed considerably with the years, but her dark hair, now gray, sits in the same simple style in waves to her shoulders. She's wearing a plain cotton dress, like she always has, with a round neckline and hem to her knees. It's my mother, but she's aged, like all of us.

"Mother, I'm sorry," I say, dropping my eyes from hers.

"Darling, I don't want your apologies. All I want is my daughter here with me. These years without you have been empty." She takes my hand, leads me to the bed, and we sit down together. "I want to learn all about my grown-up girl," she says with a smile. "Tell me everything."

Time passes unchecked. I tell her every detail I can remember of my life since leaving. It feels good to unload, to explain how I felt meeting Aiden as a young woman and what made me go to Chicago in the first place. How I thought they wouldn't want to speak to me. All the wasted time in between. She listens silently, squeezing my hand to encourage me to continue when I stop.

"I enjoyed working at the strip club," I say honestly. "It was freeing."

"That is understandable, though I don't like the idea of you selling yourself for men to enjoy." Her voice is calm—there is no judgment. My father is a hard man, but my mother is his opposite, a soft soul in a terrifying world. With her, I've always felt safe and loved. Over the years, I had considered attempting to contact her, but the fear of my father was too great. I assumed it would never be allowed. The risk of losing her again was one I wasn't willing to take.

"Harrison wasn't too impressed when he found me either."

She laughs, taking me by surprise. "I can imagine he wouldn't be. Is it true, Violet, about you and him?" I look at her warily. "You won't be in trouble with me if it is. I would rather know if the information your father was given is correct."

"Yes," I answer truthfully. There is no point in lying.

"Since when?" Her gaze locks on me. She is silently warning me not to tell an untruth in the way only a mother can.

"We've been apart for fourteen years, Mother," I reply dismissively. "It was a single night. Too many emotions passed between us, and we became carried away with each other. It meant nothing."

"That's the only time you've been with him?" she questions as her eyes narrow.

"Mother, I don't want to have this conversation with you. There is no Harrison and me. There never can be." I divert my focus to my fingers on my lap, unable to continue lying and look her in the eye.

"He took a risk telling your father and brothers where you were and that he was the reason you ran."

"What?" I stammer.

"Before he left to bring you back. He called your father, told him he'd seduced you then disregarded the incident the following morning. He promised to have you home with us. Harrison assumed full responsibility for your disappearance." She places a finger under my chin, encouraging my eyes to lift to hers. "Violet, be honest with me. Is there more between you both than a single night?"

"It can't happen," I whisper.

"That doesn't answer my question. I need to understand why after one night with him you ran."

"Because he withdrew again."

"Again?" she prompts. I wince, knowing I've said too much.

"We happened once before, that final summer before I left for Glasgow. I hadn't spoken to him since then, until he found me outside his apartment in June." My cheeks heat with embarrassment. This isn't a discussion I ever wanted or expected to have with my mother. "I've always felt safe with him," I tell her, unsure if that explains anything. "Growing up, I thought he cared."

"He always looked at you as if you were the most beautiful girl in the world," she tells me and my jaw drops. "Since you were both teenagers, that boy has been crazy about you. It didn't matter how many times your father warned him off, his eyes still followed you around. He searched for you in every room. I always wondered if anything had ever happened."

"Will my father ever forgive me for leaving?" I ask her.

"The answer is yes; he will come to terms with what has happened. Your father is a proud man. Your leaving was difficult for him to accept."

"And Harry? Will he forgive him?"

She swallows, then looks at me directly before answering the question. "Your father and your brothers had a meeting with Harrison to discuss his behavior."

"Discuss his behavior?"

"You and I both know this family isn't a normal one. There is the family, then those who work for the family. Harrison is the latter and has rules he is expected to follow in return for his position."

"What does that mean?"

"It means that he has broken the code. That he had a debt to pay, and your father is the one who executed the penalty."

"Did he hurt him?" I wail, my hand holding hers tighter. "Did he kill him?"

She shakes her head, a sad smile on her lips.

"No," she says, "he didn't kill him. Most likely he will be roughed up, perhaps a broken bone or two. Harrison is too valuable for your father to dispose of, but he had to pay for what he'd done. Entering into a relationship with the head of the family's daughter without permission is a..." She pauses. I see her considering what to say. "It's something that other men would lose their lives for. Harrison is lucky that at the moment, he appears indispensable."

"Indispensable? In what way?"

"He has connections. In the city, his work is unmatched. The law firm is gaining clients from esteemed companies and individuals due to his reputation alone. At this point in time, Harrison Waite is an asset your father will not be willing to sacrifice."

I sit and listen to her; all the while terror builds in my belly. My father will hurt him because of me. I've seen and heard the type of pain my father can inflict on someone. I've felt it. It stays with you long after it ends.

"What does the law firm have to do with my father?" I ask, confused. The little research I did before returning to London had shown no apparent connection between him and the business. Not that I should be surprised there is. The thought he would allow my brothers' autonomy within their careers is laughable. He would never allow them the freedom to expand beyond his control. There must always be a benefit with every action for Edward Chase.

"Darling, enough talking for one day. Your father has always supported his children. You know that," she says, squeezing my fingers in reassurance. "None of this is your concern. You rest. Have you seen a doctor recently?" I shake my head. "That is something we will need to arrange. Whoever the father is," she nods to my stomach, "this baby is still my grandchild, and I plan to support you both from now on. I love you, my child." She leans forward and places a kiss on my forehead. "Now, sleep and rest. It will all seem better in the morning. Your father will be home. The situation will have a line drawn under it, and we can all move on." I watch her stand and leave my room before climbing under the duvet.

Sleep doesn't come. At three in the morning, I'm lying staring at the ceiling. My mind races as I think about what torture my father and brothers could have inflicted on Harry.

***

When I was around the age of twelve, I had risen from my bed in the middle of the night needing a glass of water. On my way to our kitchen, I heard a whimpering noise coming from the living room.

As I peered around the old wooden door, a man came into view. He was tied to a chair, his wrists and ankles secured with cable ties. My brothers stood in the corner watching on as my father plus two other men stood around the prisoner. "You see, my boys," he said. "Sometimes in business, we must play hardball. Sometimes, punishment is needed to ensure the right people stay in power. This man here was a member of our family. A key person within our delicate organization, but he has broken our trust by liaising with our enemies, providing them with information on our inner workings."

He placed his heavy boot on the man's foot and pressed down, and the man squealed in pain. It was then I saw the knife already lodged in his ankle.

"It is important that everyone, both comrades and enemies, know who is in charge. This man's death will act as a warning to others who are tempted to usurp the chain of command." My father had then taken a knife from his pocket and dragged it across the man's throat. We all watched as he bled out, though they never knew I was there. From then on, my father, the man meant to protect me, became a terrifying individual. Someone I didn't know. A dangerous man to be aware of at all times.

***

My mind returns to my current situation. To Harrison and what could have happened or was happening to him tonight, what sort of justice my father and brothers have chosen to inflict. My chest strains as I think of him, knowing the risks he's taken to be near me and to protect me. All I know is I have to see him. Being away from him permanently isn't an option.

The following morning, I descend the stairs to the smell of frying bacon. My mother is in the kitchen wearing the same apron she had when I left years ago. It was a present I gave her for her birthday when I was thirteen, a pink gingham contraption that ties at the waist with the words *Best Mum in the World* across the chest. "Good morning, darling," she says as I enter the room. My father is sitting at the table drinking his morning coffee while reading the newspaper. He glances in my direction then returns to his task.

"Father," I say sweetly. The words stick in my throat. He grunts. "Please, may I have my phone?"

"No."

"I want to speak to my friend, Samantha. Tell her I'm all right."

"No."

"She said if I didn't contact her, she would call the police after I was taken from the club." He looks at me, his eyebrows drawing together skeptically. "For all she knows, the men who took me home weren't who they said they were." I'm careful not to use Harrison's name. "I need to tell her I'm safe. You wouldn't want the police at the door."

Without a word, he stands and pulls my phone from his pocket, then passes it to me.

"I want to see all communication you make with anyone," he barks. "And you are not to leave this house. Do you understand me?"

"Yes, sir."

"Any funny business and you will be locked in your room until that." He signals to my belly. "Is born and we decide what to do with you both." My skin prickles at his derogatory tone. My temper threatens to flare. I push my anger down, not wanting to upset him. I won't be able to do what I want to do if he's watching me.

"Yes, sir," I say again. He was always *sir* when distributing orders to us. Father was a term rarely used, and anything more endearing was unheard of in our home.

"To ensure you behave and don't run away again," he says as he lifts an eyebrow, "You will remain in this house for the foreseeable future. You will not be left on your own until I am happy that your behavior has been amended. But I doubt you would be stupid enough to flee once more."

He picks up his phone and presses a few buttons. My handset beeps in my hand. A photo of Harrison pops onto my screen. He is tied to a chair. Blood runs from his mouth, and there's a deep cut across his cheek. I scream, dropping the phone on the floor. When I pick it up again, a large crack covers the glass, but there is no hiding the broken man below.

"That was his warning, and it is also yours," he says with a smirk. "Next time, I'll make sure his pretty face is permanently disfigured. Stay away from him." I stare, unblinking at the image in my hand, tears welling in my eyes. My father leaves, then I feel my mother's arms around me as I cry.

CHAPTER EIGHTEEN

The Level Boardroom

October 2022

Harrison

Yet another clear plastic sheet is spread out across the floor underneath a man tied to the chair. He knows he won't be leaving this room alive. Everyone in here knows that. I secure his wrists with a further cable tie. He's strong. His arms pull at the bindings, causing his muscles to flex, the intricate blue tattoos that cover his arms ripple beneath.

"I'll ask you one more time, asshole," Devane growls. "Who is Michaels? We know it's an alias. We know he is top of the tree, and you are one of the bitches doing his dirty work." The brute in the chair draws back his lips, and what could be a smile or a sneer appears. Stumps of dirty white enamel line his mouth—each one has been filed to a point.

"Why would I tell you fuckers anything?" he replies. "I'm dead anyway. You lot have been trying to hunt us down for years. You've still not worked out who the man at the top is." He laughs, throwing his head back, and his Adams apple bobs furiously. "Those law degrees need to be ripped up. A bunch of fuckwits, that's all you are. Pathetic."

Hunter steps forward, standing between the man's legs. Our prisoner is tall—his knees bend beyond a right angle with his feet flat on the floor. The knife moves swiftly, cutting the remainder of his t-shirt open. Hunter removed the sleeves earlier. He places the tip of the knife below his sternum, angled upwards, and pushes gently. It pierces the skin. His captive doesn't flinch.

"I've found after much research that I can create multiple injuries here without killing someone. By the time I'm finished with you, you'll be begging me to end your life." He smiles sweetly. "But I'll be getting every bit of information I require first."

"Nothing you can do will make me talk. You don't frighten me. I know this vendetta is all to do with that pathetic excuse of a brother of yours dropping dead on a dancefloor." He widens his eyes, leaning forward slightly as far as his bindings allow. "Play with the snakes and prepare to get bitten. You'd be better fucking killing me. Save yourself time."

Damon places his hand on the knife and removes it from Hunter's grasp. I pull him away and move him to sit in the furthest seat. Russell stands behind the prisoner's head and places his hands on his shoulders. "If you don't mind me interrupting," Russell says, "I would suggest you listen to what Waite here has to say before wishing your life to end. It may interest you personally."

After settling Hunter and warning him silently not to move, I walk back over to the trussed-up man. "Mr. Taylor," I say, and his eyes spring open in surprise at the use of his real name. "I believe you have a daughter." The same eyes narrow instantly. "Lisa," I continue, "she lives with her husband in Barnsley and their two young children."

"Bullshit," he growls. "You've got the wrong man." I ignore him and continue.

"Their children are avid ballet dancers and attend Swinson's Dance School. Neither of the adults are in work, but they live a nice life funded by money from an unknown source."

"Oh, we found the source," Marshall interrupts, rising from his seat and coming to join my side. He smiles knowingly. This man has proven himself to be a fantastic asset to our team within a matter of weeks. He has connections in the world of business across a variety of global markets. His close relationship with the police force and politicians means if he lifts the phone, the person at the end of the line listens to what he has to say. "It's an off-shore account in the Cayman Islands." He places the paperwork down in front of our guest. "The same account that has been linked with the dirty drugs business."

"You can't prove fuck all," the man known as Taylor hisses, but uncertainty marks his features.

"Mr. Taylor, I can assure you, if we are showing you the evidence here, we can prove it," I say firmly. "Please remember you are a small cog in this dark machine. Scapegoats are always set up to take the blame if the tower of cards falls. It looks like you and your family have been allocated that position."

"Tell us what we need to know," Marshall says, "or I'll pass my findings to the necessary departments at the tax office. Your daughter and her husband will be locked up. Your grandchildren will end up in care. Is that a risk you want to take? Do you want to be the reason their lives are ruined? I would imagine they don't even know where the funds come from. They will be innocent victims in all of this, while you protect the evil bastards that run it."

"And at the end of the day," I add, "you will be dead. That is a fact that no one here is hiding from you. Do you think the men you work for will protect your family?"

***

A matter of hours later, the six of us sit on smooth leather sofas drinking whiskey and watching a curvy redhead gyrate around the pole in Guilty Pleasures. After not being here in years, this is my second visit in weeks. At least this time, I won't be begging Violet to leave with me and go home.

Connor is salivating as the dancer drops to her hands and knees, then crawls across the stage. He stands, walks over, and stuffs a fifty-pound note into her G-string. He whispers something in her ear, and she smiles, then returns to her dancing.

"I'm seeing her later," he says, dropping back into his seat and clinking his glass with Russell's. Marshall rolls his eyes. Hunter lifts his hand to congratulate him with a high-five. I glance at Damon, who has ignored the whole conversation.

"You fancy some pussy tonight?" Connor asks, looking at me, and I shake my head. "I'd have thought you would be up for celebrating after our win this afternoon. Between you and Marshall, we now have some prime intelligence."

"We still don't know who Michaels is," I argue, and he shrugs.

"We have the names of a few higher up the tree though." He raises his glass toward me. "The poor bastard today didn't seem to hold any more information. For all his bullshit talk, I don't believe he knows who is at the top. He doesn't have high enough clearance. He was running the product but not dealing with the organ grinder."

"I'd say that's right," Damon interjects. "The names he gave us, I've passed to my contacts. They'll see what records they have on them, known crimes or suspected. The web is a lot greater than we first thought. These drugs are being distributed UK-wide in all major cities. We are looking at gangs working with gangs, but there is always a man in charge."

"I think we need to visit the main kitchen," I say, and all eyes fall on me. "We know where it is now, exactly. Perhaps some surveillance would be beneficial. We could see who is coming and going. How they move the product. What sort of weapons they have."

"You want to go undercover, Waite?" Damon says with a smirk. "Dress all in black and wear a balaclava." I glower at him, and he holds his hands up in surrender. My eyes move to the mirrored wall beside me. The raw line of where my cheek was split four weeks ago is still there. My anger bubbles again the same as it always does when I think of what Edward Chase did to me that night—when he laid down the law and demonstrated I was his puppet.

"I think you're right though," Damon continues, interrupting my frustrating thoughts. "We need to understand more about how they're operating and who is running the day-to-day business. We should set up a schedule to watch them." He turns to Hunter, who has been listening silently to our conversation. "Do you have men that could be utilized?" Hunter nods. "Excellent, we can firm up the details on Wednesday at The Level, but let's move to the next phase of taking these bastards down."

After another hour of watching women I'm not interested in dance on stage wearing next to nothing, I make my excuses and leave. Damon catches up with me as I reach the pavement outside. "Not your thing?" he asks. "Mine neither. I prefer what I have at home." I glance at him, surprised at his admission.

In recent months, I've suspected his situation had changed but never asked.

"Years gone by, I'd have been in a back room with one of the girls, waving notes around and enjoying every minute. Now, I can't get the bloody woman I can't have out of my mind," I say, and he gives me a sympathetic smile. "Connor keeps me updated on how Violet is, as far as he knows. Her father won't even let her leave the house. She's locked up day and night, not allowed past the front door."

"Do you want her?" he asks. "Is trying to have her worth risking your life for? Because that's what we are talking about, Waite. Being with her will draw a target on your back. Your networks will be severed."

"Even if I wanted to be with her, how am I going to get near her? That house is like a fortress. They have security guards surrounding the perimeter now. Each year that passes, Edward gets more paranoid." I flag down a passing taxi. We both climb into the back, and I give the driver my address. "Connor and Russell are more wary of him than they've ever been. He has always been vicious, but now he seems to have no limits. Their cousin ended up at the bottom of the Thames last week. Edward strapped his feet with blocks and put him in alive."

"Why?" Damon asks, completely unflustered by the information.

"Questioned him during a family meeting. Edward was having a bad day," I answer bluntly. "He was disposed of before the old man even considered another solution."

When the taxi pulls up in front of my building, I see a woman in a long trench coat standing at the entrance. It's now one in the morning—the doors will be locked with no one allowed in who doesn't live here. After saying goodbye to Damon, I walk up the pathway and pull the key card from my pocket. She turns to face me, and I recognize her instantly. It's the girl from the strip club who seemed to be friends with Violet. Her astute eyes fix on me, and I stop in front of her.

"Harrison Waite?" she says sharply, and I nod. "Violet needs you. She's in trouble."

"Why should I trust you?" I ask her, and she smirks.

"Do you have any other option?" Her tongue darts between her lips. "You love her, no? Or was your little jealous rage at Guilty Pleasures an act?" I bristle at her comment and narrow my eyes at her. "You know that power-crazed father of hers is holding her prisoner?"

"I heard he wasn't letting people see her. I'm not exactly welcome at the house, so haven't tried myself."

"You know she's getting married?" she asks, and my jaw drops open. The jealousy that I've been burying for weeks, the rage at not being considered good enough for her, explodes from me. I'm furious.

"Married!" I spit. "To who?"

"Her worst fucking nightmare."

CHAPTER NINETEEN

The Chase Family Home, Kensington

October 2022

Violet

Six weeks. Six long weeks of being under house arrest with my parents. Every day is the same. My father disappears most mornings before the sun is up and returns after dark. My mother spends her days in the kitchen or preparing something in the house to please him. Men patrol the gardens holding guns with knives strapped to their waists. In the little time I've spent outside, they watch me intently as I wander the vast gardens. I couldn't run even if I wanted to—there is no way out.

I was able to keep my phone. My mother checks my call history and messages daily. The only person I've been in contact with is Samantha. She has been essential for my sanity. We talk about her work and the other girls at the apartment where I lived for a short while. She tells me stories that make me smile, especially about her horrendous dating experiences, which seem to be a weekly occurrence. I'm hopeful she will be allowed to visit soon. My father doesn't watch me with the same disdain he did in the beginning. I'm being a good girl.

***

It's a cool autumn afternoon when I receive a message from my father to meet him in his office at four o'clock. He wants to discuss my plans moving forward. I take a shower and slowly dry my hair before applying a layer of makeup. My dress is a simple floral design that finishes at my knees. The soft material skims over my stomach, which has developed a small bump in the past few weeks. After slipping on my ballet flats, I take one final look in the mirror and head to my father's study.

His door is closed. The dark wood is old but has been sanded and polished to a high shine. I stand outside for five minutes, not wanting to go in and face him. I can hear his deep voice on the other side talking to someone on the phone. His tone is abrupt and annoyed, but it always is. He runs his business the same way he does his family—brutally. Once the talking stops, I gently tap the door.

"Come in," he barks, and I push open the door. He is sitting in the red leather wing-backed chair behind a heavy wooden desk. Rows of bookshelves line the walls, filled with ancient volumes. My father's rare book collection is valued in the millions, and it's his pride and joy. No one is allowed to open a book without his permission. I received the cane at the age of twelve for removing one from the shelf. "Violet," he says as he meets my gaze, "thank you for being so punctual." He glances at his watch. "Bang on time."

"You wanted to see me, sir," I say meekly, dropping my eyes from his. If I look at him too long, my face will be true to my thoughts. He'll know I have no respect for the evil dictator that he is.

"Yes, I did. After six weeks of being home with your mother and me, you seem to have settled back into our lifestyle. Your cooperation has been appreciated." He leans back against his chair and crosses his arms over his chest. "Sit down, make yourself comfortable. You won't be leaving for a while. We have a lot to discuss."

"Thank you for taking me back after embarrassing you and my mother so badly. After abandoning my family and my responsibilities as your daughter." He smiles darkly at my words. "I'm sorry, Father. Sir." I take a seat in the identical chair opposite him.

"Your apology is appreciated," he says, "but in some ways, it is unnecessary. What started as the heart-breaking devastation that my daughter had left turned into an opportunity. A lucrative business arrangement." My face contorts in confusion, and he laughs. "As I said, we have a lot to discuss. But first, I have some good news for you." He leans down and presses a button on his intercom, then speaks into the microphone. "You can come in now."

The door opens immediately, and a man I never thought I'd see again walks in. Aiden Marley comes into my father's office dressed in his trademark designer suit with a perfectly pressed white shirt. He smiles, the way he used to when he would see me after weeks apart, back when I was desperate to see him, the days when my heart filled with joy at his presence.

My father stands and strides over to him, shaking his hand dramatically. "I'm glad you could join us, Aiden. It would be best if we tell Violet the incredible news together. I know she is going to be overjoyed."

My hand rises to my throat in memory of the last time I saw him, when he pinned me against the wall in Harry's apartment. When he reduced the airflow to my windpipe, even though he knew I was pregnant with his child. The bruises he left behind marked my skin for days as a reminder of how violent he had become. A man I never truly knew.

"Violet," Aiden says, "you're looking radiant. Pregnancy suits you." He walks over to me, leaning down and placing a kiss on my cheek. I recoil from him; he bristles but doesn't say anything. I look to my father for guidance. He ignores me and moves back to his chair. Aiden takes the seat beside me. He moves to take my hand, and I pull it from his grasp, placing it on my knee.

"You may be wondering what this is all about," my father says, and I glare at him. "Don't look at me like that young lady," he reprimands. "This situation is a result of one you created fourteen years ago. Even if you weren't aware of it."

"Father, sir, I don't understand."

He holds his hand up to silence me. "If you keep your mouth shut, I will inform you," he growls. "I'll tell you the plans from now on and how your life is going to progress. But understand, my daughter, nothing is up for discussion. The deals are done, and the paperwork is signed. Your life and the life of the child in your belly is mapped out."

My focus moves from my father to the man sitting beside me. A man I used to adore and now despise. A man who ripped my youth from me with lies. A man whose child is in my womb.

"As you know, back when the two of you started a relationship," my father gestures to the two of us as he begins his tale, "Aiden and I were loosely business associates. His advertising agency headed up the sales team of our property business. It was a successful venture in a lot of ways. We both were seeing a good return on our work and investment, as well as making positive connections in many major cities across the globe."

"That we did," Aiden agrees, and the men smile at each other. My father rises from his chair and walks over to the cabinet where he keeps his prized whiskey. He pours two generous glasses, passing one to Aiden and keeping one for himself, then retakes his chair. The men toast silently to each other.

"Then you took it upon yourself, Violet, to follow your childish heart across the Atlantic and turn up on Aiden's doorstep. He was shocked to say the least. I was aware your relationship had progressed beyond him checking in on you, not that I was best pleased." My father chuckles to himself.

"I remember that phone call," Aiden adds. "I'm glad we weren't in the same city that night. My body may have been found in a watery grave. You were thermonuclear." The men raise their glasses again in silent agreement.

"That evening you arrived in Chicago," my father says, "he called me and told me where you were. Over time, we came to an agreement. Something that suited both of us."

"An agreement?" I ask, confused.

"Aiden being fond of you, he wanted to keep you. You honestly don't think I could have brought you home if I wanted to, Violet. You were able to stay in Chicago because I allowed it." He tents his fingers and places his elbows on his desk, then leans forward. "This man has been a loyal business associate ever since. I consider him one of my closest friends. We have worked well together. He has run some of my most lucrative operations, and all I had to do was give him my daughter. It was a sacrifice well worth making."

"I still think I got the best part of the deal," Aiden replies. He turns to face me, lifting his hand to my cheek. I close my eyes under his touch, unable to look at him. "We were very happy together, weren't we Princess." I reopen my eyes and blink at him with a bland expression on my face. What I really want to do is spit at him, but I know that would not be a wise move. The situation I am in is a dangerous one. I need to be compliant.

"Then everything went to shit in the summer with the news report and that bloody baseball team," my father continues. "I told you that deal was a bad move." Aiden holds his hands up and nods toward my father in surrender. Both men laugh. "You disappeared without a trace, sneaking out of the country and turning up in the apartment of Harrison Waite. Only to run again." He rolls his eyes. "There is a bit of a pattern here, my child. When things get difficult, you bolt."

"That won't be required anymore," Aiden interrupts. "Our predicament is sorted."

"Predicament?" I hiss, and he grins wickedly.

"Unfortunately, Marissa wasn't overjoyed to discover I had a mistress. She took the children and filed for divorce." He shrugs. "Someone called her and told her about you. My suspicions are it was one of your brothers. Not that it's an issue—family was never one of my goals. It was a good thing to have for appearances' sake. I always preferred being with you, Princess."

My father taps his desk with the small hammer he keeps to restore order when meetings spiral out of his control. We both return our attention to him.

"So, as Aiden is now in the process of a divorce, our original agreement is being reinstated," my father says bluntly. He looks at me, awaiting my reaction. "You will return to America with him and resume your life at his side. He is the father of the child you carry. Once his divorce from Marissa is finalized, you will marry quietly. Life will return to a better version of what it was. You will have your man, and your child will have their father. These past months will be as if they never existed. They will be gone and forgotten."

"You're speechless, Princess," Aiden says with a dark smile. "I felt the same. Complete euphoria that you will be returned to me. Once again, you'll be mine."

"I'm going fucking nowhere with you," I shout, pushing myself to my feet. The anger bursts from me. Aiden rises. I turn to him and prod at his chest with my finger. "There's a small fact you're forgetting." He smirks and raises an eyebrow in question. "I didn't know about your fucking wife and kids. You lied to me. I don't want you."

He grabs my wrist in his hand and squeezes. "It's not your choice, Princess. It never has been. You've been sold. You're mine in exchange for my loyalty to your father and his operations. We will be returning to Chicago together."

"I don't feel well," I say, turning to my father. "Please, can I go to my room? I need to lie down. I feel nauseous." He nods but smiles nastily.

"Before you go," Aiden says, "there is one other bit of good news I have for you." I glance at him. "I've booked our wedding for February next year. Our baby is due in January I assume, from what I've been told and working out the dates. My divorce will be finalized before the year is out. This time next year, you will be my wife. We will be a family, the three of us."

"Incredible news. We will celebrate now as we discuss business," my father interjects, once again raising his glass. "Sleep well, my daughter," he calls to my retreating form as I leave the room.

Back sitting on my bed, I pull my phone from the drawer in my bedside cabinet. The only contact number I have is Samantha—I know my messages are monitored. I can't risk being caught, but I am *not* going back to Chicago with that lunatic. Praying that my father hasn't gone as far as recording my calls, I dial her number. The phone rings twice, then disconnects. My heart sinks. A few minutes later, my handset buzzes to life.

"Hello, Samantha," I answer.

"Violet," she trills down the line. "Lovely to hear from you. It's been like three hours since we spoke." She laughs, and my lips move to a sad smile. Talking to my friend is the only light in my life right now. "Do you miss me already?"

"Always," I say. "I need your help. I'm in trouble."

"How can you get in trouble locked in a mansion? Have you run out of tea?" She giggles at her own joke.

"My father has agreed I'm to return to Chicago and marry the man who is the father of my baby." She falls silent. Over the past weeks, I've come clean about my situation during our phone calls. "Please listen. There is a lot you don't understand, but I need you to get a message to Harrison and my brothers. You need to tell them I'm in trouble. I need them."

Chapter Twenty

The Level Boardroom

Harrison

"Tell us again what she said," I say. Samantha screws her face up, annoyed, then flicks her blonde hair over her shoulder.

"She said," she speaks painfully slow, emphasizing each word. "That her father had agreed she is to move back to Chicago with the married man who knocked her up." With her head cocked to one side, her eyes focus on me and widen. "You know, the bastard who pinned her to the wall in your apartment by her throat."

"Yes, I'm aware of who he is. It doesn't make any sense."

"This is bullshit!" Russell barks, jumping to his feet. He storms around the table and leans over the woman sitting in the chair. We are all in The Level, our little band of six vigilantes and this woman we don't know who turned up on my doorstep telling me Violet is being married off to the man who she ran away with years ago. "My father wouldn't allow it."

"Are you calling me a liar?" Samantha hisses. "Get out of my face, you arrogant piece of shit." Russell gawks at her. She pushes his chest. "I said fucking move." He steps backward. We all watch on in awe. Samantha stands and looks up at him, openly furious. He's much taller than her—he dwarfs her slim frame. "Don't ever invade my space again, you creep. Who the hell do you think you are?"

"My father wouldn't allow Violet to go back to Chicago with that asshole," he says, sounding like a petulant schoolboy. Crossing his arms over his chest, he narrows his eyes at her. She doesn't move.

"He isn't allowing it. He's fucking arranging it. Catch up, you absolute idiot," she says bluntly. Hunter bursts into laughter, and Russell glares at him. "Were you not listening to a word I said? Your father has been complicit this whole time. He left Violet in Chicago because the arrangement suited him."

"Oh, she's gutsy," Hunter shouts across the room. "I like her." Everyone ignores him.

"You're nothing but a cheap whore," Russell spits. "Why should we believe you?"

Before Samantha can reply, Connor steps forward and places a hand on his brother's arm. His eyes run over her from top to bottom. As usual, he has stood in the shadows until now. "Why would she?" he says, turning to his brother. "What benefit is it to this woman to come here and lie? It doesn't make sense. We both know our father can't be trusted. We both have felt the sharp end of his retribution." His focus moves to Samantha. "Is my sister still at our parents' house? How are you able to communicate with her?"

"She has a phone. Your mother checks her messages daily. We call each other when we can. She's told me pieces of the story over the past few weeks. Today, she took a risk and phoned me as soon as your father told her what was to happen. She said to contact Harry and tell him she needs his help." Her eyes focus on me and narrow. "You need to get your shit together and stop running away from how you feel. Step up."

"I'm not running anywhere," I reply sharply. "Things aren't straightforward. And you have no idea what I feel."

"I know a jealous man when I see one," she says with a smirk. "And the thought of Violet with another man is eating you alive. When I mentioned her getting married, your eyes all but popped out your head."

I'd moved to stand with my back against the wall to give myself a full view of the room while Russell had his meltdown. Hunter and Damon sit opposite me in deep leather chairs. Marshall is at the head of the glass table, out of his seat but in his position. Russell and Connor stand next to Samantha to my right. She turns away from them and walks over to me, stopping directly under my nose. Her eyes search my face.

"Harrison," she says, "are you trying to tell me that you don't love her?" The words said out loud are terrifying. *I don't love anyone, and no one loves me.* "Did you storm into Guilty Pleasures like a bear because you don't care for her?" she asks. "You dragged me upstairs here and phoned all these men to come help in the middle of the night because your feelings for Violet are nothing but platonic." Her lips widen into a grin. Bright-white teeth glint between ruby-red lips. "Is that what you're trying to make me believe? Because I'm telling you now, it's not working."

"I don't need to explain myself to you," I answer. My voice is level but inside I'm in turmoil. Samantha has me worked out. I love Violet, even if I don't want to admit it to myself.

"Perhaps not," she says with a shrug. "But you and she are owed at least honesty about how you feel about each other. And." She pauses and her hand swipes through her hair. Though she's brazen, this woman is nervous being here with us. "She doesn't deserve to be left to a life of being the second choice for some bastard who has no respect for her, an evil asshole who has bought her. We need to get her out somehow."

"That I agree with. We need to stop him taking her back to America." I look over the top of Samantha's head to Russell and Connor behind. "Will you help me?" I ask them. "I'm doing this with or without your support. I believe what Samantha is telling us."

"I'll help you even if these boneheads don't," Marshall interrupts, walking over to stand beside me. "There is no way on this earth I'd let that woman on a plane back to where she ran from. Whether Edward Chase is involved or not, if there is any truth to what is being said, then we need to intervene." He looks at Samantha. "We've known each other a while—you're not a liar. I've seen you deal with awful situations at the club and maintain your dignity. I believe you're telling us what you've been told. And, it's our responsibility to find out the truth of the situation."

"Thank you, Marshall," she says, and her body visibly relaxes with his words.

Damon and Hunter rise, walking around the table to join us. A strong hand squeezes my elbow. "Whatever you need, Waite," Damon says, "we will both be there at your side."

"Too right," Hunter agrees. He glances at the Chase brothers, who are standing watching the events unfold. "What do you say, boys? Is it not time your father learned that he can't push all you kids around? If what this lady is saying turns out to be true, and if your sister was left in Chicago on your father's orders, then you've all been lied to, too."

"We need to find out the truth, Russ," Connor says. His brother nods but doesn't speak. He moves to sit on the chair nearest to him, and we all follow his lead and take our seats around the table to discuss our next move.

An hour later, Samantha holds the handset in both hands as she looks out over the city. The sun has started to rise over the rooftops. She messaged Violet thirty minutes ago, but there's been no response yet. "She normally replies within minutes," she says, her voice laced with anxiety.

"It's still the middle of the night," I tell her. "She's probably sleeping, and I would imagine her phone is on silent. She won't want to bring too much attention to it. Violet is smart. Do you know if she is speaking to anyone else outside the house?"

She shakes her head.

"You don't know or she isn't?"

"She isn't."

"How can you be sure?"

"My number is one of the few allowed on her phone. It's only mine and her parents, I believe. Everything else is blocked. They only let her speak to me because she managed to convince them I had no connections that could help." Her eyes stare at the blank screen as though willing it to light up with a message. "What if they've been listening to her calls? What if they know she asked me to come here? To get help?"

"If that is true, they'll move her. They will need to anyway, with the progression of her pregnancy. I would imagine Aiden will want her back in Chicago soon." As I go to open my mouth, her phone lights up with the name *Violet*. Samantha answers and lifts the handset to her ear.

"Hello, Violet, is that you? Are you all right?" she asks rapidly. I tap her shoulder; her eyes flick to me.

"Put the phone on speaker," I tell her, and she does as I request.

"Yes, it's me," Violet whispers. My nerves steady slightly on hearing her voice. "I'm all right. Were you able to get help? Things are progressing fast here—there are a lot of men in the house. My father came ten minutes ago and told me to pack because I would be leaving tonight." A sob escapes her, and I pluck the phone from Samantha's grasp.

"Vi," I say firmly, "we are going to get you out of there. You can't panic about this, it's not good for you or the baby."

"Harry," she gasps, "she found you. I need your help. I can't go back to Chicago. He'll lock me up. I'll be his prisoner." All the men in the room watch on silently. "I'm scared."

"Where are you now?" I ask her, ignoring her panicked tone. We need as much information as possible from her to create a plan. I need to keep her calm.

"In my room. I've locked the door, but they will be coming for me soon."

"Do you know how they plan to move you? Where to?"

"No," she replies, her voice rising. "He won't tell me anything." She starts to lose control, her breathing quickening.

"Vi, you need to stay relaxed," I tell her, my voice firm. I look at Hunter. "Can you get men down there? Watch the gate, and if anyone comes and goes, report back to us." Hunter salutes, then pulls his phone from his jeans pocket. He stands and disappears out into the hallway to give his men their instructions.

"Harry," Violet calls down the line, bringing my attention back to her. "Please don't withdraw from me again. Don't leave me on my own."

"I won't. I'm coming to get you, and this time I'm not letting you go." My mouth dries. The thought of losing her is chilling. "Violet, I…"

"Someone is coming," she whispers, interrupting me. "What if they're here to take me?"

"Listen to me—I'm not leaving you on your own. I'm coming to get you. Leave the phone on so we can hear what is happening. Put it in your pocket." My words are clear and sharp. "Vi, leave the phone on," I repeat. "Stay calm and do as they say. The most important thing is that you and the baby are safe. Let us take care of the rest."

"Are my brothers there?" she asks. I glance at the men who have moved to stand beside me.

"We're here," Connor says, his eyes fixed on the phone in my hand. It's still on speakerphone; they've heard it all. I can tell by their faces that they know she is telling the truth. They know their father has been playing them this whole time. "We're all coming to get you, Sis. Hang in there and do as they say." He nods to me. I switch the speakerphone off and walk into the corner of the room.

"Vi," I say softly, "we will figure this out." Her breathing hitches. "I love you. I always have." Now is not the time to pretend I don't. Now is the time to stop being scared of my emotions and embrace them. Embrace her. If things go wrong, this may be the only chance I have to tell her how I feel. How I truly feel.

"I love you too," she replies. A smile flickers on my lips with her admission. "Come for me."

***

Violet

The door handle rattles. "Princess, open the door. I want to see my girl," Aiden calls through the barrier. The elation I felt with Harrison's words vanishes, and the terror that has been coursing through my body since my father told me of his plans returns instantly.

"Go away," I shout back.

"Open the door or I'll knock it down," he snaps angrily.

"Who's there?" Harrison asks. The phone is still pinned to my ear.

"It's Aiden," I whisper. "I need to go."

"Leave your phone on. I'll mute this end so he won't hear us. It's going to be all right. Just do as he says." He pauses. "Within reason. Protect yourself if you need to." He doesn't say what he's thinking, but I know what it is. He's worried Aiden is here to collect some overdue time with me. Time with my body. The thought of him touching my skin is revolting.

"Okay," I reply, then slip my phone into the breast pocket of the striped pajamas I'm wearing.

"Princess," Aiden barks. He's furious—I know by his tone. "Open the fucking door now or I won't be held responsible for my actions."

Steeling myself, I walk over to the door and release the bolt, then retreat to my bed, sitting on the edge. The hardwood swings open, and Aiden strides into the room. He's dressed in his usual business attire. I touch my pocket to ensure my phone is still there—the screen is turned against my body so he cannot see the light.

"Hello," he says, sitting down next to me. He wraps a hand around the back of my neck and pulls me toward him. His lips crash into mine. I pull back, but he holds me tight, not allowing me to move. "Princess," he growls, "don't disobey me. You don't want to make me angry. We wouldn't want a repeat of what happened in Waite's apartment. He isn't here to interrupt this time." He grins nastily. "Though that pretty little neck of yours in my grasp is somewhat appealing."

"I'm sorry," I mumble, dropping my eyes from his. "It's early. You surprised me being here."

"It's five o'clock. The sun is coming up, and we have places to be. Get dressed."

***

Harrison

I switch the phone onto mute so we can hear what is happening but there's no risk of us being heard on Violet's side. "It's fucking Marley," I hiss. "Devane, are your men there?"

"They're sitting down the road from the entrance. No sign of life yet, but the place is like a fortress. High walls and cameras everywhere," he says. "We won't be able to get in. If we are going to intercept her, it will be in transit."

"Russ, do you have any contacts on the inside you trust?" I turn to Violet's brother. "Is there anyone who could tell us what is going on? Help her, if she needs it."

"I'm not sure who to trust," he replies. "They all work for my dad. It would risk him finding out we're on to him."

"Fuck," I mutter. Violet's raised voice brings my focus back to the phone in my hand. "If he touches her, I'll kill him with my bare hands."

"No, Aiden," she shouts, terrified. "Take your hands off me. Please."

"Oh, come on Princess. You need to get undressed anyway," he replies, then laughs loudly. "Let me see that pussy of yours, it's been too long. I've missed your slick walls being wrapped around my cock."

"Aiden, please. When we happen again, I don't want it to be like this. I want it to be special." She's stalling, trying to slow him down. "I want to wait until we're home in our own bed."

"Home," he repeats. "It will be good to have you back where you should be. Underneath me. The way things were. Though this is new," he says. "The belly will take a bit of getting used to." I imagine the bastard touching her growing bump and my anger rises a notch. The thought of him with her makes my skin crawl. If he forces himself on her, I'll tear him limb from limb.

"That belly holds my child," she hisses, losing a little control. Stay calm, I will her silently.

"Our child," he corrects her. "My child, and you will be my wife." There is the sound of skin hitting skin.

"In your fucking dreams," she shrieks. "I'll never be yours, whether you force me to marry you or not. I hate you. You lied to me. Used me."

"And I'll use you whenever I want to, Princess. Don't fucking hit me again," he growls. "I'll let you off this time. I understand the past twenty-four hours will have been a shock for you. But do it again, and you'll regret it. Reject me once more, and I'll pin you to the bed until you realize you're mine." There is a rustling noise. Him standing, I think. "Now, get dressed," he demands. "We will be leaving soon." The line goes silent, then a few seconds later, a door slams closed.

"Harry," Violet's petrified voice whispers. "Did you hear that? We're leaving." I take my handset off mute.

"I did," I tell her. "We're coming. Do as he says for now. Charge your phone and leave it on. I'll see you soon. I love you."

CHAPTER TWENTY-ONE

The Chase Family Home, Kensington

25th December 2004

Violet

I've heard so much about the boy sitting across from me. Harrison. My brother, Russell, pulled him from a ditch eight years ago and my father took him under his wing. I know he lives in a children's home, but my family will fund his final years in education at a private school starting next year. Every Friday, my father goes to visit him and help him study. I've never been allowed to meet him until today. He is the most beautiful boy I've ever seen. My eyes are magnetized to him; I can't stop staring.

"Violet," my mother snaps, "pass the potatoes to Connor. Are your ears full of wax?" Harrison flashes me a cheeky smile, and my stomach flips.

"Sorry Mother," I mumble, passing the plate then dropping my eyes to my meal. I eat silently for the remainder of our dinner.

At eight o'clock my father's driver arrives to take Harrison back to the children's home. He walks over, takes my hands in his, and places a kiss on my cheek. "It was lovely to meet you, Violet," he says. We've hardly spoken, but I've been aware of him watching me since he arrived. "Merry Christmas." My heart beats harder as he speaks.

He wishes my brothers goodbye with high-fives. The three of them are close and socialize regularly on weekends—never here, they meet at parks or where he lives. My father squeezes his shoulder and promises to see him soon as my mother passes him a box filled with treats. With a final goodbye, the first boy I've ever openly crushed on walks out of the door.

***

October 2022

Harrison

Hunter sits across from me in my kitchen. His phone is lying on the counter, silent. He has multiple cars in position surrounding the Chase mansion. There has been no obvious movement. Damon and Marshall went down to join them on the stakeout. Russell and Connor have headed into the office and are awaiting an update. It's ten in the morning and Hunter is on his third whiskey. None of us have slept—Samantha was offered a bed in my spare room by Mrs. D. who arrived for work at nine.

"Alcohol at this time in the morning, Mr. Devane," Mrs. D. says, disgusted, as she piles a load of washing into the machine.

"If I must," he replies with a grin, and she rolls her eyes.

"Is there anything I can help you with, Mr. Waite?" she asks. "This doesn't feel like a normal morning. If you need me to carry out different duties, do tell me."

"It's Violet," I tell her, and she glances at me. "She's in danger, and we're trying to get hold of her. Bring her back before she's taken back to America." Mrs. D. knows most things that happen here in our glass tower high in the sky. She knows we aren't normal lawyers and law enforcers. She knows Hunter Devane isn't a businessman who always stays on the right side of the law. The woman isn't stupid, and I am not prepared to treat her like she is.

"America?" she questions, her eyebrows drawing together. "Why would she have to go back to America?" Before I can answer, Hunter's phone lights up with a call. He picks it up, accepts it, and raises the handset to his ear.

"Devane," he barks down the line. The person on the other end speaks rapidly and Hunter nods along. "We'll catch up with you," he says. "I have you on tracker." He cuts the call and turns to me. "Three black Mercedes have left the house. The windows are darkened, so they can't see who the passengers are. My team is going to follow. Damon and Marshall will sit tight in case of any further movement."

"Okay, what direction were they heading in?"

"The airport," Hunter says. "We need to move now."

As I am grabbing my keys, I look at Mrs. D. who is watching me intently. "Can you stay here and look after Samantha when she wakes up?" She nods. "Thank you."

With a sympathetic smile, she says, "Go and bring her home. I'm ready to look after Violet too once she is here." We stare at each other for a moment, her withered eyes holding my anxious ones. "Go get your girl. Your family."

"Waite, come on," Hunter snaps, and I run out after him.

Our journey down to the garage in the elevator is made in silence. My companion's focus is on the blue dot traveling across his phone screen which stops moving as the elevator descends – connection interrupted. As soon as the doors open, we run to my car and jump in. Hunter connects his phone to the navigation system, and the little blue dot reappears on my car's screen. With a turn of the key, the engine comes to life and we head off in search of the woman I love.

London traffic during the day is torture. I weave among the cars as best I can. "They've arrived at the airport," he says. "All three vehicles have stopped outside the private entrance to the airfield."

"Are your men there?"

"Of course. How do you think I know? And Damon has just arrived." He eyeballs me then focuses back on his screen. "Put your foot down, Waite." I push the accelerator further to the floor as we join the motorway traffic. It's busy but moving freely, and within ten minutes we are driving up the side of the airfield. It's a small private one, not the airport we initially expected him to be taking her to.

There is a private jet with the name *Marley* painted along the side. Fuck, he must be doing better than we thought, or taking his clients' money and spending it for personal use. The three black vehicles sit beside it, all the doors still closed. We pull to a stop behind Damon's inconspicuous gray Ford Focus which he uses when he doesn't want to be noticed. I push open my driver's door at the same time he does and we climb out, walking toward each other.

"You brought the Ferrari," he says, his face contorted in annoyance. "So much for a fucking stakeout. Under the radar." He lifts his eyebrows to emphasize his point.

"It's the fastest car I have," I snap back.

"Come on, you come with me," he mutters and signals for me to follow him. I climb into the back seat of his subdued car as Hunter jumps in the other side.

"I'm coming too," he declares.

"No you're not," Damon tells him. Hunter ignores the comment and settles himself in the seat. "Devane, get out."

"No," he says. "I'm not missing out on the fun." Marshall laughs as Damon sighs then drives toward the entrance to the airfield.

"There is going to be a fucking mess to clean up after today," Damon mumbles. "I can feel it."

As we pull forward to the entrance, a security guard approaches the car. "Good morning gentlemen," he says. "Can I help you?"

"Yes," Damon answers—we've all been warned to keep our mouths shut. "Chief Inspector McKinney." He passes the man his badge. "I have reason to believe that an airplane on your premises is holding stolen goods. I need to gain entry to assess the situation."

"Do you have a warrant?"

"Do I need one?" he replies. "If there is nothing to find, this should be a short visit."

As the men debate, one of the rear doors of the waiting black cars opens. Marley steps out wearing a sharp suit and carrying a briefcase. He turns and leans down into the car, speaking to someone. He shakes his head, then leans in, reaching into the vehicle.

"McKinney," I say, not taking my eyes from the unfolding scene. "We need to get in there." He's still arguing with the security guard.

Violet steps out onto the tarmac. Her dark hair is loose around her face—it blows off in all directions with the light wind. She's wearing a simple, black, long-sleeved dress that hangs off her slim frame. It looks like something her mother would wear. Aiden has his hand wrapped around her wrist; he pulls her to his side then slams the door closed. She pulls her arm from his grasp, and he spins to face her. I can't hear what is being said, but it's obviously an argument underway. Two of his men then come to her sides. They take an arm each and escort her toward the plane steps.

"We need to get fucking in there," I snap, and Marshall turns in his seat to look at me.

"Come on then, Maverick," he says, pushing open his door. Hunter does the same. I follow their lead and we make a run for the partially open gate. The three of us make it and slide through the gap, running for the plane as fast as we can.

"Stop," a man's voice sounds from behind us. We ignore him and keep running for the private jet. I watch on as Violet climbs the stairs with the two burly men behind her. Aiden went up first and has already disappeared into the cabin. "Stop or I'll shoot," our pursuer shouts. A gunshot rings out and all the people on the stairs turn in the direction of the sound.

Violet's two escorts descend, heading for us. Aiden reappears. I'm only feet from her now. Hunter pulls his gun from his waistband and shoots one of the heavies in the leg, causing him to fall to the ground. Violet screams, and I look up to see Aiden manhandling her up the stairs as I reach the bottom.

"Get in here, you stubborn bitch," he yells. I hear commotion behind me but don't turn to look. My only focus is getting her away from this maniac as I jump the steps two at a time. She disappears from view.

The aircrew gape as I enter the plane. They step in front of me, stopping my progress. "Sir," a perfectly dressed blonde woman says, "this is a private plane. You're not meant to be in here."

"I'll collect what's mine, and I'll leave," I tell her, pushing past and walking into the luxurious cabin. My eyes dart around the space—there's no sign of Violet or Marley. "Where did they go?" I snap over my shoulder.

"Sir, you shouldn't be in here," she argues, and I twist to face her, pulling my gun. "The bedroom at the back," she stammers, terrified, gesturing toward the rear of the plane. I charge between the leather seating and marble counters to the closed door.

"Aiden, no, please," Violet's cries come through the door.

"You're fucking mine," he snarls. "Behave, stop struggling, and lie here quietly until I ensure the inconvenient assholes that have followed us are disposed of."

My shoulder slams against the barrier between me and the ongoing altercation. It flies open. Violet is laying on the bed. He's on top, straddling her to keep her pinned down. She is struggling beneath him. He grabs her hands and holds them above her head.

"Fucking get off her," I yell, lifting my gun and aiming at him.

"How the hell did you get in here?" he barks. "Security. Get this asshole out of here. I have a whore to claim."

"I said, get off her." My words are slow and clear.

"What are you going to do about it?" he says with a grin. "She's mine to do with as I please. Her father said so. Now, fuck off. Or do you want to watch?" I take a step forward, my gun still aimed at his face. "Are you going to shoot me? Is the pauper boy going to dish out his vengeance?" He laughs, throwing his head back. Violet takes the opportunity of him being distracted to use a free hand and grab his genitals through his pants. Her hand twists furiously, and he squeals like a wounded animal. I fire. The bullet hits his shoulder, and he falls backward as one of his security guards appears behind me.

Violet climbs off the bed. I grab her hand and turn, hitting the man across the face with the butt of the gun. We push past him as he stumbles and make our way back down the cabin past the startled cabin crew, who have found themselves in the middle of a gunfight. Their jaws hang open, bodies frozen in position ready to work.

"Violet," Aiden's voice says from behind us. "Another step and he's a dead man." She stops. I pull her hand, but she resists. "Good girl, Princess. Now, listen. Come back here immediately, and I'll let him live." As I turn back to the man I despise, I become aware of the little red dot on my forehead. The red laser cuts across the space between me and the bodyguard with the gun. Violet looks at me then back to Marley.

"Don't hurt him," she whispers gloomily. Her voice is strained. "I'll go with you if you let him live."

"Good girl, Princess," he repeats. "Now, let go of his hand and come here." She goes to drop my hand, but I hold on tight, not releasing her fingers.

"Let me go, Harry," she says quietly, diverting her eyes. "This is a fight we can't win."

"Listen to her," Aiden agrees. "Your friends are outside at the end of the barrels of my men's guns. Take a look." I glance out the window and see Damon, Hunter, and Marshall all on their knees, weapons trained on them. "Turn around and admit you've lost. Walk off this plane and forget about Violet. You and your friends can leave without anyone getting killed"

"Harry," Violet says, "you need to save your friends. Go. I'm meant to be with Aiden." Her wide watery eyes blink up into mine. She takes a step toward me then rises on tiptoe and places her free palm against my cheek. Her lips touch mine momentarily. "I need to go with him."

"I promised I wouldn't withdraw again," I whisper fiercely.

"You're not. You're doing the right thing. It isn't your choice to leave."

I look at the bastard who is in control of the situation, and he raises an eyebrow in question. If I refuse, we could all be dead. If I walk off this plane without her, chances are I may never see her again.

"I don't want to leave you. I love you," I say, and she smiles sadly against my lips.

"We were never going to work. You said so yourself. We've always been a bad idea." She kisses me again. "Now, let me go."

"This is all very touching," Aiden says, sounding bored. "Go now, Waite, or my man will shoot." I release Violet and step backward. The space between us feels enormous. Aiden is holding a towel to his shoulder where my bullet must have passed through. The security guard behind me grabs my elbow and pulls me in the direction of the stairs. He pushes me hard, and I stumble down them, only to be caught by another goon at the bottom.

My friends are still on their knees, hands tied behind their backs. "Kneel beside them, eyes on the ground," the goon barks. As I move into position, I take one final glance up at the plane and see Violet looking down at me through the window, devastation clear on her face.

Trussed up on the ground beside my friends, we watch the plane take off into the air with Violet inside.

CHAPTER TWENTY-TWO

---◆◇◆---

Chase, Chase and Waite
Law Offices, Canary Wharf

Harrison

"Where the fuck were you?" I roar, storming into Russell's office. "She's gone. That bastard has her on a plane to Chicago as we speak." He raises an eyebrow and leans back in his chair. The smug look on his face needs to be removed, fast. My nerves are shot, anger bursting from every cell. As I laid there on the damp ground, secured like a pig waiting for slaughter, I promised myself that if I got out alive, the Chase family was not going to run my life from now on. It was time to put myself and my wishes first.

"She chose to go," he says simply. "She chose him. Typical Violet, running off when it suits her. If you ask me, we're better off without her."

"Fucking lies," I growl. "Did your daddy tell you that? Has he managed to convince you yet again that he's not the bad guy in the situation? That someone else made the decision." He scowls, straightening himself in his seat. "And you're a dumb enough fuck to believe him."

"Watch your mouth," he snaps. "Remember who you're speaking to."

I walk forward to his desk, placing my hands on the highly polished glass; it will leave finger marks and that will piss him off. Russell's office is cleaned twice a day—it's always pristine.

"And who am I speaking to?" I ask, glaring at him. "Russell Chase, the man or Russell Chase, his dad's bitch?" He shoots out of his chair and reaches across the desk, grabbing at my shirt collar. He pulls me toward him so we are nose to nose.

"Don't push me," he warns, tightening his grip.

"What are you going to do, Russ? Kill me? Dispose of me? Or merely beat me up? You don't frighten me, you're nothing but a fucking bully." He snarls like a dog as I mock him. "But you can't get rid of me, can you? I'm worth too much in here. Clients would walk if I did, and you know it. I own a third of this firm, and I'll take it if I need to. Let go of me before I make your life more difficult."

He chuckles then releases my collar. "And how would you make my life more difficult? You're the lap dog, not me. My father's charity case. You only have what you do because of my family. Nothing more than the boy from the ditch."

"I'd tell your father about your little sideline," I tell him, ignoring his jibes, and his eyes pop open. "I'm not sure he would be pleased to know his son is sleeping with the enemy."

"You know nothing," he spits, striding over to a glass fridge filled with beer in the corner. He pulls the door open, removes a can and drains it, then takes two more from the fridge.

"I know you've been selling information on your father's businesses to his competitors. That's how he's been losing out on his recent property bids. The bids you've been making for him."

"Bullshit." He looks at me warily though, which tells me I'm right. The accusation was a stab in the dark, but someone had to be giving Edward Chase's competitors the information on what his offers were on property around London. He's lost four in a row—it's a situation he's not used to. With every loss, his anger increases a notch. "I've been buying it myself," Russell concedes. That admission I wasn't expecting. I try to stop my jaw from dropping.

"Why?" I ask, genuinely perplexed. "Why would you risk that? Him finding out could be deadly for you."

"Because I wanted to teach him he can't win every bloody competition. That he is not the most powerful man in the world. That he can be beaten," he says with a sigh, then throws himself back into his chair. I sit down opposite him. The confrontational atmosphere disappears instantly.

"I can understand that," I say honestly. "It's hard when you feel like your life isn't your own." He tosses me one of the beer cans he's holding. I catch it and snap it open; it fizzes over my fingers. "You're playing with fire, Russ. If he finds out, I hate to think what he would do to you."

"He'd kill me. I'd be seen as a traitor to the family. Pocketing individually what should be part of the family fortune." He sniggers. "The fortune he controls."

"Violet is being taken against her will," I say, attempting to get the conversation back on track now that he's subdued. "When I got to the plane, Marley had her pinned to the bed." He smirks. "She wasn't happy about it. I shot him in the shoulder."

"You shot him?" Once again, his eyes widen in shock.

"He won't die from it; I think it went through the muscle. But he threatened to kill me if she didn't go with him," I continue. "Then his men tied the four of us up and left us on the ground to be found later." He listens intently as I go back through the events of earlier, when I lost Violet yet again.

"I phoned my father this morning. He told me she went of her own accord. She's been with Marley for years," he says.

"Under false pretenses. It's not him she's in love with," I argue, keeping my gaze fixed on him. I need to own this, own the truth of it all.

"And in your opinion, who does she love?" he asks sharply.

"Me. She loves me." I pause to let the words sink in. "And I love her."

"How is that even possible?" he replies, rolling his eyes. "You slept with her once and haven't seen her in years. It's a ridiculous notion. You need to get it out of your head. One time with a woman doesn't make you love her. Go and buy yourself some pussy. Get over Violet and let her crawl back under her Chicago rock."

"The time in my apartment wasn't the first time we've been together," I admit.

He narrows his eyes. "When?"

"The final summer before she left for Glasgow. Just after she turned eighteen. I've been crazy about her ever since." He goes to open his mouth, but I raise my hand to silence him. "Let me speak. Listen to what I have to say before you explode." He bristles but holds his tongue. "That summer, it only happened once, but it was special. I'd been resisting her for months, stealing glances when I thought no one was looking."

"We all knew you were fucking looking," he mutters. "How many times were you advised to keep your distance?"

"I tried, Russ, but..." I trail off, not knowing how to explain what I feel.

"How can you be sure?" he questions. "You don't know each other. You've barely been together."

"She's the only woman who has ever made me feel this way."

He shakes his head as a smile plays on his lips. He doesn't believe me. Russell doesn't believe in love.

227

"What I do know is, she isn't with Aiden Marley through choice. And even if she doesn't want to be with me, she definitely doesn't want to be with him," I state firmly. "Help me bring her home. Then if she decides she doesn't want me, I'll walk away. I'll sign over my part of the firm to you and Connor, hand over my clients, and go." His eyes search my face, looking for a catch. There isn't one. I'd give up everything I have to make sure Violet Chase was safe, she and her child. But I pray she wants me if I offer myself to her, if I get the opportunity to. "What do you say? I know our relationship has disintegrated in recent years. You don't see me as the brother I see you as." He visibly swallows. "Help me save your sister. We both love her."

"I'm not sure my sister needs saving," he says. "She made her bed; let her lie in it."

"She is lying in it," Connor announces as he walks into the office, catching the end of our conversation. "Literally. She's in her old room at the mansion. I've spoken to Mother." We both gawk at him. "Seemingly, the bullet you put into Marley did a little more damage than you thought. They had to divert the plane before he bled out." He laughs loudly. "Shame really, it would have been a good way to get rid of him."

"Where is he now?" Russell asks.

"He is also at the mansion, being cared for by Father's private nursing staff." Connor looks between us. "Mother says Violet has locked herself in her room again and is refusing to come out. I asked her what the situation was with Marley. She told me she doesn't want to move back to Chicago." He focuses on his brother. "Father has agreed that Aiden can keep Violet in return for his continued service."

"Service?" Russell spits, clearly confused. "What kind of service?"

"Business I assume. I don't know the details and neither does Mother. But she's worried about Violet, and she wants us to help get her out." He takes a breath. "Russ, our sister needs us. For once, we need to stand up to our father and do what we think is right." Russell nods but doesn't speak, the blood draining from his face at the thought of challenging his father. Connor turns to me. "If you love my sister the way you say you do, I'll support you being with her."

"I love her entirely," I tell him decisively. "I want her to live the life she wants, whether that includes me or not." He doesn't acknowledge my words, just looks me up and down. Quiet, reserved, and deep, that's Connor Chase.

"Violet has an ultrasound at the private maternity clinic in the city on Friday," Connor continues. "Mother is taking her. There will be a few guards, but they won't be allowed into the hospital."

"Friday? That's three days away. What if he touches her before then? He was practically forcing himself on her when I found them on the plane," I say. My anger bubbles under the surface. I want to go and get her now.

"He's in no fit state to do anything at the moment," he replies with a smirk. "Drugged up to the eyeballs while he heals, apparently. Mother will keep him away for a few days under the pretense of looking after Violet and the baby. She has a plan; we need to trust her."

"Trust your mother? Does she not follow your father's instructions without question?"

"Normally, yes. But this is her daughter. She wants what's best for her, and for some obscure reason she seems to think that's you." He widens his eyes. "Take the offer of help. You don't have to fix this on your own." He grabs my shoulder. "We will get her out of there, and then she can reject you herself."

"I'm assuming you have a plan?" Russell interjects.

"Of course," Connor replies, "but we can discuss it tonight in The Level."

CHAPTER
TWENTY-THREE

━━━◆○◆━━━

The Chase Family Home,
Kensington

Violet

As I lie on my childhood bed and stare up at the ceiling once again, any hope of getting out of this godforsaken situation disappears.

I sat on the luxurious leather seat staring out of the airplane cabin window at Harrison as we took off. He and his friends looked completely helpless, bound and gagged as they were, their rescue attempt squashed. He came for me like he said he would, but I never got to go with him. In that moment, all I prayed for was that Aiden's men wouldn't kill him. All I wanted was for them to let him live.

We had been one hour into the flight when Aiden passed out from his injuries. Harrison's bullet nicked the brachial artery in his shoulder. The injury wasn't bad enough to cause his death, but he'd lost enough blood that we needed to turn around. We had been brought straight to my parent's home where a medical team was waiting. I walked through the front door and up to my room with no concern for the bastard who will be my life partner. My husband.

The only person I've engaged with is my mother. She brought me breakfast the following morning. We didn't speak—there is nothing to say. My life is planned out. I need to survive it.

***

Friday morning arrives. I've spent my time here in my room. I've not seen Aiden or my father. My brothers have been strangely absent too. They weren't at the airfield, so I assume they took no part in my failed escape. Perhaps they agree with my father that the best place for me is Chicago. No one tells me from day to day the future arrangements being made, not that I have any plans they would affect. Every few hours, someone will appear with a tray of food and a glass of water, either a member of the house staff or my mother. This morning, it was my mother's turn.

I hear the key in the lock. They took the bolt off the inside of my door and started to lock me in the day after I arrived back.

"Your father says if you're going to lock us out, we'll deadbolt you in," my mother told me. "If you want to start acting like a grown up and coming downstairs, the door will be opened for you, but until then you'll be treated like the irritable teenager you're being." She repeated his words exactly. "This is the message from your father," she said, her tone softening, "not me. I would stay in here too." She had placed the tray of food she was holding on the floor and embraced me before resuming her standoffish approach. The small glint of emotion took me by surprise, and I was forced to turn away from her to control my tears.

Now, she walks into the room not holding a tray. In her hands is a soft, pink, long-sleeved dress and my Converse trainers. I am still in bed with my duvet wrapped around me. There is nothing to get up for. She places the garments over the bed rail and then sits down next to me.

"I've arranged for you to have a private ultrasound at a clinic in Westminster today," my mother says simply. Her hand rises to my face and moves a stray piece of hair from my eye. "Now, get dressed and come down for breakfast."

"Why?"

"Why not? You've had a stressful week, and I want to make sure my grandchild is safe." She stands then wipes her palms on the white skirt she's wearing.

"You'll stain that," I mutter, and she chuckles.

"My clothes are not my priority today. You are, Violet. We need to go to the city for this ultrasound to ensure both of you are all right. It will only be us and a couple of guards—we may even be able to do some baby shopping." She smiles happily as my heart sinks. The last thing I want to do is go fucking shopping. "Today is an important day."

"It's only an ultrasound. I'm fine, mother," I argue. "It's not needed."

"You might find something there that you're not expecting," she replies. "It is always better to check." Perplexed, I watch her skip out of the room, more upbeat than I've seen her since I arrived back in London.

The soft pink dress skims over my curves, the material stretching to allow for my growing waistline. The hem finishes an inch below my knee. My trusty Converse are like wearing slippers—it feels good to have them back on my feet. They'd been taken off me when I arrived here as girls shouldn't wear casual shoes according to my father. Heels and feminine wear at all times. I'd been surprised to see them in my mother's hand, but I wasn't going to argue. After running the brush through my hair, I apply a light layer of makeup then head down for breakfast.

My mother is standing at the stove stirring something. "It's cold outside," she says. "I've made us some porridge." My lips automatically contort at the thought. I remember my mother's porridge, so thick you could stand on it. "Don't screw up your face," she scolds. "You need your energy for today."

"Mother, it's an ultrasound. We'll get driven there and back. Father will probably insist I'm handcuffed to one of his goons during the whole fucking process," I reply, sounding like the petulant teenager she accused me of being earlier.

"Language," she says sharply, tapping the edge of the pot with her wooden spoon then lifting it to point at me. "The rules in this house haven't changed, Violet Chase. Ladies do not use bad language under my roof."

"But boys can swear like fucking *Mick Jagger*," I mutter.

"Violet," my father's booming voice bellows, "you heard your mother. Watch your language." His next words are quieter, but anger is clear in his tone. "It's nice of you to grace us with your presence. I was beginning to think you didn't want to be here." He's behind me, but I haven't turned around to look at him yet. The sight of him may make me laugh, cry, or explode. I'm not sure which response would be best. So I stay focused on my mother, the woman who I think is on my side—but I can't be sure.

"Turn around and look at me, you ungrateful little bitch," he growls. I swallow and straighten my back, then turn around.

"Good morning, Father," I hiss through gritted teeth.

"It's hormones," my mother says. "Edward, you remember what I was like when I was pregnant. One minute as happy as a lark and the next sobbing into my pillow."

His lips quip into a sly smile. "Yes, but you weren't defiant. This one is, and she needs to learn to toe the line, as all women should. She's not even asked how her future husband is after being shot." He looks from me to my mother and back to me. "He will be fine and should be able to return to your bed this evening, you'll be pleased to know. When you return from this ultrasound, you'll be moving into the guest quarters with Aiden. He will update you then on the arrangements for your return to Chicago." He snickers. "Hopefully without any interruptions or near-death experiences."

I go to speak, but my mother interrupts me. "Perfect," she sings, clapping her hands together. A burning smell starts to emanate from the pot of gunk in front of her, and my stomach twists. "Once we have eaten, Violet, we will go up to your room and move your things to the guest room." I glance at her, and she beams in reply. "You will be so excited to have him back with you after these challenging few months. Just think, thanks to Aiden's ongoing love and your father's patience, you will get your happy ever after." I turn fully this time and gawk at her, not knowing what to say. The scenario playing out couldn't be any fucking further from happily ever after if it tried.

"Listen to your mother," my father snaps. "She knows what's best for you. She is the epitome of a wife for a man like me. You should try to do the same for Aiden. Accept the outcome and mold yourself into the best version of what is required." Without another word, he turns and leaves.

My mother scoops a ladle of porridge into a bowl and hands it to me across the counter with a spoon. I move to sit on a stool. "Eat," she encourages, then glances up as if checking for onlookers. "Everything will be all right, my daughter. Trust me."

***

The dark Range Rover sits on the perfectly paved driveway waiting for us. The windows are black so no one can see in. A man dressed in a trademark black suit with a white shirt and wearing an earpiece opens the door for me to step into the back seat. Another man, dressed the same, sits in the driver's seat. My mother slides in beside me and smiles. She takes my hand in hers as the first man gets into the passenger seat.

"Good morning, ma'am," he says to my mother.

"Good morning, Jonathan," she replies kindly. "Do you know where the clinic is?"

"Yes, ma'am. Mason will drop us at the front entrance. I will escort you inside then return to the front door to wait," he says. "Then once you're both ready to leave, you can message me to come inside and get you."

"That's perfect, Jonathan. Thank you. I appreciate you gaining clearance not to come into the facility. There will be other ladies there, and I felt you both would not be a suitable presence in the waiting room." He laughs, his whole body vibrating slightly. "A few babies might be born early with a glance at the two of you." She raises an eyebrow at him and winks.

"Understood, ma'am," he says. I look at my mother, and she grins. Her familiarity with the staff is surprising—especially the jovial nature of her comments. My father never speaks to his employees with anything but professionalism and disdain.

The privacy screen rises between us and the men up front.

"Are you excited?" she asks me, squeezing my fingers. "You get to see your baby. Do you want to find out the sex?"

"I've had an ultrasound before," I say. "I think this is all an overreaction."

"Nonsense." She waves my comment away. "The sex?" she prompts.

"No, I don't want to know. At the least that will be one thing in my life not planned for me. That will be a surprise on the day I meet them, whether I'm imprisoned with a son or a daughter." I sigh, air passing gently between my lips. "The poor little mite has no idea what they are being born into. A family which isn't real with a mother who doesn't want to be there."

"You do want this baby?" my mother questions, taking me by surprise.

"I did, but I don't have much to offer them, do I?" She cocks her head to one side as she listens. "When I discovered I was pregnant, I couldn't wait to tell Aiden. As far as I was concerned, we were together and happy. Now I see how stupid I was, how many red flags I've missed."

"Don't be too hard on yourself, darling," she says. "Life is complicated. The men we love are not normal men. They live in a very different world to most."

"But I didn't know about that world or about his wife," I wail, losing a little control. "My whole existence in Chicago was a lie. The day I saw that news report, I ran." Tears prick my eyes; I wipe them away with the tip of my finger. "Like I always do. Then you know what has happened since then. It's been one big shit show with a lot of conflicted emotions, but it looks like I'll end up back where I started. In Chicago with a man who doesn't love me."

The car passes through two tall black pillars holding heavy iron gates open.

"But to answer your question, I don't know if I want this baby. I've barely had time to get excited about the prospect of becoming a mother. What kind of life can I offer them? One filled with restrictions and dangerous men."

"Maybe things won't turn out as badly as you think they will," she says. "I can't wait to meet my grandchild."

The car stops outside what looks like a residential home in the affluent area of Westminster. After driving through the gates, the red brick building comes into view. A large fountain with a fish that has water shooting from its mouth sits in front of the house like a roundabout. A wide stone staircase leads to the heavy oak front door.

Our driver cuts the engine, and the passenger gets out, opening my door then my mother's, and assisting us out onto the red gravel. My mother walks around the car, then slips her arm through mine. We walk up the front steps together, our escort following behind. There is no signage, no obvious detail that this is a hospital. My mother presses the brass doorbell, and it sounds loudly. A few minutes later, the door swings open.

On the other side is a short woman with graying hair and a kind smile. Perched on the end of her nose are delicately framed round spectacles. The white coat she is wearing strains at her bosom, obviously a few sizes too small.

"Good morning," she says. "I'm Nurse Saffron. You must be Violet. Please come in." Before I can answer, she takes my hand and pulls both me and my mother through the door, closing it immediately behind us. Inside the building is more like a hospital, modernized with clean lines and white space. We stand in what must be a waiting area. Dark leather sofas surround coffee tables piled with magazines. A few women, obviously pregnant, sit with whom I assume is either their partner or a family member.

"I'll check you in," Nurse Saffron says. "You take a seat, then we will call you through when we are ready for you." She gestures toward a plain gray sofa. My mother takes my hand and guides me over. We both sit down.

"You do know there are a few months to wait before this little one is born," I say, placing my hand over my stomach. Mother is almost bouncing next to me with what I think is excitement. "You'll only see a picture today. Not even a picture, a white blob on black."

"Oh Violet, you have no idea how important today is for me." She stills, then her eyes meet mine, strong and focused. "Whatever happens, promise me you will follow your heart."

"Mother, you're acting very strange. What is going on?"

"Violet, promise me you will make decisions in your life based on what your heart wants."

"But..."

"Promise me," she repeats. "It may not seem plausible, but I promise you, you will have options."

"Okay, I promise," I concede, unsure what else to say.

"Violet," the nurse calls, breaking the moment. "We're ready for you. This way please." My mother and I stand, then follow her down a long, completely blank hallway with white walls and doors. At the end of the corridor are double doors with a simple black sign telling us this is the Ultrasound Suite. The nurse pushes open the door, holding it wide for us to walk through.

"Please climb onto the bed," she says, "and lift your dress to your bust." I do as she says, and my mother comes to my side. The nurse lays a blanket across my bottom half, leaving only my mid-section exposed. We watch on silently as she squirts gel onto my rounded stomach then sits the scanner on the gloop.

"There's baby," she says, a smile in her voice. The whooshing noise of the heartbeat is loud and clear. We all stare at the screen, mesmerized by the messy blob. I don't notice the door swing open. It's not until he's standing next to me that I realize he is here.

Harrison smiles down at me then looks at the screen. He takes the hand my mother isn't holding. His chest rises and falls as he watches the blurry image. My mother lifting and kissing my knuckles brings my attention back to her. "Goodbye, darling," she says simply and leaves.

I look back to Harry, and he leans in and kisses me softly before whispering, "Are you ready to run Violet?"

Now I know why I have my Converse.

CHAPTER TWENTY-FOUR

Walker Private Maternity Clinic, Westminster

Harrison

Her big brown eyes blink back into mine like a stunned owl. She is looking at me as if I'm a figment of her imagination. She searches my face, then lifts her free hand and touches my cheek. I close my eyes under her touch. Hell, it feels good to have her fingers on my skin.

"You're really here," she whispers under her breath. I lean in and kiss her again.

"Yes, I am, and you're coming with me." My focus moves to the midwife. "Thank you for all your help, Nurse Saffron."

"My pleasure, Mr. Waite," she replies. "I'm delighted to be of service after what you did for my brother. Now, you'll need to move quickly so they don't realize Violet has gone."

"Harry, what's going on?"

"I'll explain later. We need to go. There is a car out back. We will slip out the rear gate. Your mother will give us ten minutes before sounding the alarm."

"Where is she?"

"Probably at the nurse's station having a cup of tea," I tell her with a grin. "Come on, I'll tell you everything later. We need to go, Violet."

"Are you here by yourself?" she continues as the nurse wipes the gel from her belly. She climbs off the bed then smooths down her dress.

"Do you honestly think I would be stupid enough to come here on my own?"

"No, but..." She trails off then shrugs her shoulders. "After last time, why would your friends want to help?"

"Because they care. Damon, Hunter, and Marshall are all in a car which will follow us. Russell and Connor are outside the front gates in a second vehicle. We are leaving via the back entrance, but I would imagine your father has other men nearby. I very much doubt he has only sent two with you." I link my fingers through hers, pulling her beside me. My other hand lifts to her chin, then I run my thumb across her lower lip. She gazes at me; I could get lost in her eyes. It's been a risk since I was a sixteen-year-old boy. "I thought I'd lost you," I whisper. "We need to go now so I can keep you."

"I'll check if the coast is clear," Nurse Saffron says. She smiles broadly at us, then disappears out of the door. I lead Violet toward it, and we stand in the ultrasound suite awaiting the nurse's return. Minutes later, the door cracks open. "Okay, your mother is making her way to the waiting room now. Go."

We run. I pull her along with me, and we burst through a fire exit at the back of the building. My black Ferrari sits waiting, a larger, sleek car behind it. I pull open the passenger door and guide her inside. As she is doing up her seatbelt, I climb in beside her. The engine is already purring beneath us. I hit the accelerator, and we fly out through the back gate into the residential London streets, the second car hot on our tail.

My telephone starts to ring. I press the accept call button on the steering wheel and Connor speaks. "They know she's missing," he says. "The two security guards have run down the front steps with my mother screaming behind them. She's playing her part well."

"She's fooled them all," I agree.

"My mother is involved in all of this?" Violet says, the tone evidence of her shock.

"It was her idea. Between your mother and Connor, we were able to come up with a plan to get you out." I take her hand in mine, resting it on my thigh.

"Where are we going?" she asks.

"The Level for now, but we may need to change plans. At least it's secure. Hunter has men stationed around and throughout the building." She nods but doesn't look at me. Before I can speak, Connor does.

"We have company. Put your foot down."

I flex my foot, pushing the pedal further toward the floor. Violet's grip tightens on my fingers. A look in the mirror tells me three vehicles are traveling behind the boys, all large dark jeeps with matching windows. Another one pulls in front of us. Violet squeaks.

"That's Russell and Connor," I tell her. I try to remove my hand from hers, but she tightens her grip. "I could do with having both hands on the wheel." Her cheeks flush as she releases me and places her palms in her lap.

The car in front increases in speed then swerves around a taxi which blares its horn. I follow. The speedometer rises again, now well over the limit. Traffic is heavy in the city center as usual, but it's moving. We weave in and out, a convoy of black vehicles all headed to the same destination.

"We're five miles out from The Level," Russell barks.

I don't see the black van; it appears from a side street and catches the back of my car. We spin, out of control across the lanes. Another dark vehicle hits the front. Violet screams, then goes silent. My head crashes against the window—I hear the sound of smashing glass and crumpled metal. The accident is over within seconds but feels as if it is lived in slow motion. The world around me swirls, cars, people, and buildings disappearing into a haze. We come to an abrupt stop next to a crash barrier.

"Waite, can you hear me?" Connor calls, trying to rip open my door. I glance over to Violet. She's lying in the passenger seat, her forehead against the window. Blood trickles from her hairline down her face. I'm aware of men in suits surrounding the car.

"Get them away," I snarl at Connor as I try to push myself up to sit straighter. My car is twisted around me, but I don't feel injured. Russell appears at Violet's side; her door opens, surprising him. He stumbles backward. There is the sound of sirens, and the suits disperse. I think I see Hunter holding something to one of the men's backs—his gun no doubt.

Russell crouches down beside his sister, supporting her head on his shoulder. "Is she breathing?" I ask him, frantic as my panic rises.

"I think so," he responds. The look he gives me is one of terror. "But her leg looks bad. There's a lot of blood."

"Excuse me," a deep voice says from behind him. "Please let me in to see the patient. If you could move back, please."

"Who are you?" Russell snaps.

"I'm a doctor," he replies. "My name is Dr. Ben Jones. If you would kindly move to the side so I can assess the lady's injuries." As Russell moves away, a man comes into view. He seems to be in his late forties with dark hair and bright blue eyes. He focuses on me. "What's her name?"

"Violet," I answer. He nods and goes to speak. "She's pregnant," I add. His eyes move to her stomach, the soft pink giving way to the curves.

"How far along?"

"Um...." I stammer and his brow creases in confusion. "Five months or so."

"Okay," he says, speaking to her as if she's awake. "Violet, my name is Dr. Jones. You're safe. You've been in a car crash outside Guy's Hospital. The emergency services are on their way. I will be taking care of you." He checks her pulse and heartbeat as he speaks.

"Will she be all right? And the baby?"

"Right now," he says, "I don't know. But I'll do everything I can."

***

Violet

The regular beep becomes annoying. It's incessant, droning on and on as I try to sleep. "Would someone shut that bloody noise up," I mutter, easing my eyes open. The room is bright, and I immediately snap them shut again. My head hurts—actually, everything hurts. I wiggle my fingers and toes; they flex, slowly.

After turning to the side, I'm met with a head of dark hair. He's snoring softly as he sits on a chair bent over with his forehead on my pillow. The door opening makes me glance up. Samantha walks in and smiles broadly.

"You're awake," she says in a dramatic whisper.

"What happened?" I ask, my brow creasing as I think. "Was there an accident?"

"Do you not remember? Harrison was driving you to The Level. Some of your father's men were following you, and one ran into the car deliberately. Then another one hit you for good measure." She walks around to the side of the bed without Harrison and takes my hand. "If you're going to have a crash, outside a hospital is a good place to do it." She presses the call nurse button beside her. "We better tell them you're awake."

"Do you know if my baby is okay?" I ask her and she smiles.

"Yes, Violet. Your baby is fine. They did an ultrasound as soon as you were brought in. Wait till you see the doctor who treated you. Fuck, he's hot. Old but hot." I laugh then wince, and Harry stirs.

"Do you have to discuss how hot the doctor was?" he mutters.

"He was though," Samantha argues. "Trust Violet to end up in a crash and get saved by him." She fans herself with a hand, and I giggle again. Harry sits up as the door opens, and a tall, dark-haired man walks in. If this is the doctor, I agree with her.

"It's good to see you awake, Violet. How are you feeling?" he says, walking over and picking up a clipboard hanging on the end of my bed. He flicks through the pages.

"Okay, I think."

"I'm Dr. Jones. It was me who treated you at the scene. You've been lucky. No serious injuries or broken bones. A few scratches where the window smashed, but nothing required stitching. You hit your head hard, so I'd like to keep you here to monitor your progress for a while to ensure there are no lasting symptoms of concussion and safeguard your baby as well." I try to focus on him—he's slightly fuzzy. Once I've closed my eyes and reopened them, he sharpens. "Everything is looking good at the moment," he adds reassuringly.

"What day is it?" I ask.

"It's Saturday," he replies. "Ten in the morning, to be exact."

"And you work here?" It's a stupid question, but seemed sensible before it left my lips.

"I do, but in the oncology ward. I was off duty when the accident happened, but I like to see my patients through their treatment so I said I would oversee your case. I hope that is all right?"

"Yes, of course," I respond, then look at Harrison who is watching me. "Are you all right?"

He smiles then leans forward to kiss my cheek. "I am now." He turns to the doctor. "Thank you for everything. For coming to the scene of the crash and for treating Violet. I can't thank you enough."

"Just doing my job," he says. "I'll request you're kept here until Monday. I'd like to scan the baby again then, to be sure all is okay. Would it be all right if I checked some of your vitals?"

"Sure." He walks over and places his stethoscope on my chest, then my stomach. He smiles then checks my pulse. I glance at Samantha who is watching him with her jaw almost on the floor. She signals to his back and mouths the words *hot fucking doctor*. When I look at Harry, he's glowering at her.

"All good, as I said," Dr. Jones advises. "Now get plenty of rest, and I'll see you on Monday." He turns and leaves.

"Fucking sex god doctor," Samantha announces. "I wonder if he's married. I'd call him daddy any day." Harrison groans in disgust.

"He was wearing a wedding ring," I tell her, and she pouts.

"Shame," she mutters with a shrug.

"Why would you notice if he had a wedding ring on?" Harrison interjects.

"Jealous much?" Samantha jibes. "Anyway, I best be off and leave you two lovebirds to it. I have to say that was an extreme way to get together. Have you never heard of dating like normal people?"

"Unfortunately, things are never that straightforward," I say with a chuckle. She kisses my cheek, rises, then skips out of the door.

"Can you help me sit up?" Harrison stands, then supports me to sit straighter before pressing the button to raise the bed's back. He props pillows around me too. As he leans over to my other side, our gazes meet. We stare at one another, our eyes searching each other's. My breathing accelerates with my heart. He touches my face gently, then places a kiss on my forehead.

"I love you," he whispers. I move my hands to his forearms to hold on. At this moment, I never want him to leave.

"I love you too."

"Do you want anything?" he asks. "Water? Something to eat?" I shake my head. The thought of food turns my stomach. I retch, but nothing materializes. "Shit, Violet. Are you okay?"

"Pass me that bedpan," I mumble. He places the gray cardboard basin in front of me, and I promptly spew the contents of my stomach into it. Harrison's hand moves to my back, gently stroking up and down my spine. "Sorry."

"Nothing to be sorry for," he says with me curled over the container and him still massaging my back. "Do you think you'll be sick again? I'll get you a fresh one." He picks up the disgusting item and disappears out into the hall, returning a few minutes later with more. Then he walks into the bathroom and appears back with a glass of blue liquid. He places one basin on my lap and passes me the water. "Mouthwash, swirl and spit," he instructs. I do as I'm told. "Again." After I comply, he removes the basin once more, putting it on the floor.

"What happened?" I ask him.

"What do you remember?"

"The clinic. The car. Then something hit us, and we spun across the road. I banged my head, I think." He nods. "But after that, nothing."

"We were lucky," he says. "The bastards hit us outside the front of the hospital. Dr. Jones saw the accident and came to help within minutes. You were unconscious, and your leg had been injured by glass from the smashed windows. I'm sorry, Violet. I didn't see the van. You, me, the baby, we all could have died." He visibly tenses. His hand moves to his hair in frustration then he pinches the bridge of his nose.

"But we didn't, and we're here. You came to get me, Harry. After everything, you took a risk and came for me." I sigh softly. Fuck, I love him more than I realized. "What is our plan now? Has my father been in touch? My mother? Is she okay?" The events come back to me at once. My mother took a risk helping us. I hope she's not suffering as a consequence. I pray my father doesn't suspect she was involved with my escape. I want to ask Harry a million questions.

"Your mother is fine. The police came to the accident quick enough that your father's men left. Hunter has people watching the hospital, and Damon is on your door. He wanted to guard you personally." He smirks. "Didn't think I was up to the job."

"Russell and Connor?"

"They've been here to visit, but they're at The Level now. Do you want to see them?"

I shake my head. "The only person I want to be with is here," I say, and he holds my hands in his.

"I'm so sorry, Violet, for..." he pauses, "for everything. When we had that night in June, I didn't want you to leave. The way I acted in the morning was ludicrous. I fully expected you to be in my apartment when I got home. Then you were gone, and we couldn't find you."

"I shouldn't have run again. It was immature of me. I should have stayed and spoken to you. Discussed our situation and what we both wanted from it."

"We both made mistakes." He swallows. "Back when we were practically kids and now. That time, your first time, it was special. You and me together like that. I'd adored you since that first Christmas we met, when you sat across from me at the table and I had to pretend not to look at you."

I chuckle. "The feeling was mutual." One hand lets go of mine, then traces my shoulder and down my arm.

"When I came back from university, you were eighteen, all grown up." He flashes me a panty-wetting grin. "Well, you thought you were." I slap his arm. "You'd gone from the girl I crushed on every weekend when I visited to a woman I wanted to be with. It unnerved me. Then the lake happened..." I laugh out loud remembering the incident.

"Poor Brandon," I say, shaking my head. "The boy got one hell of a shock when you threw him and his bike into the lake. All he did was say hello and ask me out for ice cream."

"That's the right day but the wrong incident you're remembering."

"You mean behind the ice cream shop?" He nods. "You all took me for a cone after throwing my date in the lake." His gaze runs over my face. I cock my head to the side as I remember. "When you tried to kiss me, and I rejected you? That incident?"

"You didn't reject me," he argues. "I told you no."

"Nonsense," I mutter, and he laughs. He's beautiful when he's happy. I want to be the reason he smiles. "You could barely keep your hands off me. If Russell hadn't walked around the corner, I may have had my first sexual experience there, pinned up against the wall next to the recycling bin."

He bristles at my comment. "Your first time shouldn't have happened the way it did. A stolen moment in your bedroom with no conversation afterward. It was incredibly selfish of me. You should hate me." He drops his eyes from mine.

"Look at me, Harry," I tell him, and he peeks up through beautiful dark lashes. The man in front of me isn't the strong in-control lawyer with all his ducks in a row. He's vulnerable sitting here, having this conversation. "Perhaps how it happened wasn't the ideal way, but it was with the right person. I wouldn't change it."

His lips crash into mine, and he kisses me deeply, — strong hands cupping my head, holding me to him. I pull back, breathless, my chest visibly rising and falling.

"Fuck, I want to take you home," he whispers against my lips. "But I can't."

"Not for a few days," I tell him.

"No, Violet, you're not moving in with me," he says firmly.

"Why?" I snap, pulling away. "Is this you withdrawing again? You haven't even got my panties off. It must be a fucking record for you running."

"I'm not running. Listen to what I have to say." He stands then walks over and makes sure the door is closed tight. "Your father will look for you at my house," he says, turning back to me. "I need you to be somewhere safe with someone who can support you through the remaining months of your pregnancy."

"You could do that if you wanted to. That apartment is like a fucking fortress."

"Listen," he repeats, walking back to my side. "Mrs. D. lives in the same building. She has a spare room. I've arranged for you to stay there."

"But I don't want..." He raises a hand to stop me from speaking.

"Violet, I want this to work between us. It's you I want to be with for the rest of my life. But." He widens his eyes. "You only came back to London in June. You've been in a long-term relationship with a man who lied to you. Do you think jumping into one with me is a good idea?"

"You're not Aiden," I argue. "You love me."

"I do, and that's why I'm doing this. At Mrs. D.'s you'll be safe, and I can see you every day, but you'll have your own space more than two doors away. If you stayed in my apartment, I doubt I'd keep my hands off you."

"I wouldn't want you to."

He smiles sexily and my heart beats harder.

"You're six months pregnant. You've been through hell. I want you to take some time for yourself. I need you to figure out if it's me you really want, because I can't lose you. I'd rather not start this at all if that's what happens."

"So, you want to be friends?" I splutter, my thoughts completely in disarray with our conversation. He saves me, then rejects me.

"No, I want to be a lot more than friends," he says, sitting down on the bed beside me. It sags slightly under his weight. "I want to take you to bed every night. I want to get down on one knee and ask you to be my forever. I want to have a home with you." He stops speaking and places a hand on my swollen belly. "I want to call this amazing little human you're growing mine."

"I don't understand, Harry," I whisper as tears fill my eyes. They escape down my cheeks.

"Know this," he says. "I want you forever. All I'm asking is you take some time to be sure that's what you want too. In the meantime, you stay with Mrs. D. I'll see you every day. We can talk. We can kiss. We can pretend to be teenagers." He pecks my cheek. "This is me giving you time. This is me wanting you to have a choice. Enjoy being in control of your destiny." He lays his forehead against mine. "But I pray you choose me."

CHAPTER TWENTY-FIVE

<hr />

The Level Boardroom

Harrison

Marshall, Damon, and Hunter all sit around the boardroom table in The Level. Each of them holds a bottle of beer. As I walk into the room, they lift them in my direction. "Congratulations," they yell in unison. "Mission accomplished." I laugh and shake my head.

"Albeit with a few blips," Damon adds.

"But we got her out, and she's alive," Hunter says, taking another swig of his drink.

"How is she?" Marshall asks.

"Shaken but all right. Not happy at having to move in downstairs." I shrug out of my suit jacket then lay it over the back of a chair before getting myself a beer from the fridge. I snap the cap, drain it, and pick up another one before sitting down opposite them. Hell, I'm tired. It's been a stressful weekend and today in the office was no better.

Our boys' Wednesday evening has been moved to Monday, as Violet is being discharged tomorrow. I plan to spend the day with her, ensuring she is settled in Mrs. D.'s apartment. Tonight, we're getting back to the job at hand—dirty drugs and how the fuck Aiden Marley is wrapped up in all of this. With everything that's been going on, I've lost sight of the current situation. Hopefully the team will get me up to speed.

"I'm not surprised she's annoyed, and I would guess confused too," Damon says. I glance at him. He's sitting in the leather chair, leaning back and watching me. With the darkening London sky behind him, the sunset creates an orange glow around him like an aura. The top three buttons of his shirt are undone, and his tie hangs loose around his neck. "You're giving her mixed signals."

"Mixed signals? Is rescuing her from an arranged marriage not enough of a sign that I care?" He laughs out loud. "I'm trying to do the right thing by not forcing things between us."

"Waite, do you not think the situation is complex enough without throwing in a few more curveballs? You tell her you love her, try to rescue her and fail, then manage to extract her on the second attempt." He turns to Hunter who is nodding along at his summary. Marshall listens with a blank expression on his face, not giving away his thoughts. "There's a crash, she ends up in the hospital. She then wakes up and finds you asleep at her bedside. I'd assume at this point you were the doting potential lover." He raises an eyebrow. "And, amid all those pheromones swirling around the room and feelings..." Hunter lifts his fingers to his throat and fake gags. The men all snort with laughter. "You tell her...yes, Violet, I love you, but you can't move in with me."

"Are you watching me on a fucking camera?" I mutter, miffed by his assessment, which is on point.

"Violet told Samantha, who told Connor, who told me," he says. "And yes, she's pissed at you."

"Samantha speaks to Connor? Since when?" I say, perplexed by the connection and mildly disturbed that my love life is being discussed freely by those in our group and on the outskirts of it.

"Since her little power play up here," Damon advises. "He's quite smitten with her. Though, I don't think anything has happened. He maybe wants some tips from her on how to control Russ."

"No one can control that maniac," Hunter pipes up, and we all gape at him.

"Ever heard of the phrase 'pot and kettle'?" I ask him. He shrugs, then goes back to skinning a banana with his pen knife. What is it about him and knives? Actually him, knives, and fruit. I do wonder how the fuck I ended up here, working with him.

"Are the Chase brothers gracing us with their presence?" Marshall says, diverting the topic of conversation. "We have a lot to discuss. Some of us want to get the business out of the way so we can drink beer and get plastered. My nerves are still shot from last Friday, then my weekend was filled with idiots."

"What happened to you?" I inquire.

"Jumped-up men that I pay a small fortune to close business deals failing to do what they're paid for. It's cost me four million due to one missing signature and not completing on time. Typically, they are all blaming each other rather than sorting out the fucking problem." He blows out heavily. "Fuck the beer, pass the whiskey."

The decanter of the amber liquid sits at the center of the table surrounded by six glasses ready for us. Mrs. D is an angel—everything is prepared as it always is. She'll be in soon with a mountain of food for us to munch on while we discuss tactics.

"So, are Russell and Connor coming or not?" Marshall prompts, his irritation at being kept waiting obvious, and in complete contrast to his normally calm manner.

"They're coming," I tell him. "I left them arguing in Russell's office."

"What about?" Damon asks.

"Their father and what to tell him. He knows they were involved in Violet's removal from the maternity clinic. Their phones are ringing constantly—he's demanding to speak to them. He wants retribution."

"Has he contacted you?" I shake my head. "Do you expect him to?"

"No, I doubt I'll hear from him. He'll probably try to manipulate my situation in some way or make things difficult for me in the firm. Whatever Violet decides will dictate what happens next."

"What do you mean?" Damon's brow creases in thought.

"I told Russell that if Violet decided she didn't want to be with me, I'd give him and Connor my shares in the company and walk away. Our relationship has been gradually getting worse since my career overtook his. Day-to-day work is hard, and we don't gel anymore, but I needed his help to free her. So, I played the only card I had. The firm." Damon's jaw drops open. "That's why I've told her she's to stay with Mrs. D. I need to be sure if she chooses me, she chooses me because it's what she wants."

"You can't do that," Damon growls. "And you can't be expected to. That business is as much your success as it is the Chase family's." He crosses his arms over his chest. "So what you're saying is, you've gambled it all on the decision of a woman. A woman who has been through more shit in the past few months than most people in their lifetime. And..." He pauses, focusing on me with shrewd eyes. "She is currently six months pregnant with hormones raging fucking everywhere."

"Her being pregnant won't affect her decision."

"Pregnant women are fucking crazy. Their opinion swings from day to day, minute to minute. Trust me, I lived with one.

None of them can be trusted to be lucid. This is one hell of a gamble you're taking."

"Well, I have to hope when she says she loves me, she means it," I tell him.

My three friends gawk in unison, obviously stunned.

The law firm has been my life since I was a young man. Becoming a lawyer is what defines my success. Thousands of hours of work to build it up, and I've risked it all for love, the one thing I said wasn't required in my life, the experience I was adamant I didn't need. That belief flew out the door the minute Violet Chase walked back through it in June. When I stepped out of that elevator and saw her in the lobby, all the old feelings came rushing back. The ones I pretended to never have.

For years, I filled my life with work and women—chasing the thrill of earning more, winning always, and having a good-looking woman in my spare room. I loved how they hung off my every word, the way their eyes danced as I pulled out the gold credit card. Now, as I accept how I feel about Violet, how I've always felt, it all seems so meaningless. Selfish and pointless. If I'd contacted her after our first time together, perhaps we both could have been saved from all the heartache. But then again, maybe we would have ruined it anyway. This is our chance to be happy—I won't run again. Hopefully, she won't either.

Raised voices divert my attention from my thoughts. The door swings open; Russell and Connor stride in, side by side. Connor sits down beside me, then leans forward and pours out two large measures of whiskey. He passes the bigger one to his brother. "Fucking sit down and drink that," he snaps. "You really are a dickhead."

"He deserved to be fired," Russell shoots back. I look between them, confused. Who the hell has he fired now? I hope it won't be another case of unfair dismissal we need to navigate—the last one was bad enough.

"He ate your sandwich," Connor says, slowly and deliberately. "It was in the staff fridge and didn't have your bloody name on it. What do you expect to happen? And why the fuck are you bringing lunch to work like an intern?"

"It was my favorite one. Mrs. D. made it for me from the leftover meatballs," he replies like an adolescent schoolboy. Russell raises the glass to his lips and drinks greedily, then refills it before sitting down. He places himself at the top of the table, ready to be in charge as always. "It was theft." Connor rolls his eyes.

"Who did you fire?" I ask.

"Kevin in the administration department," Connor responds. "For sandwich theft. That's the fucking reason that idiot wrote in the email. How he ever became a lawyer, I don't fucking know."

"I'm sitting right here," Russell interjects, crashing his fist down on the table.

"Are you all quite finished?" Damon says, taking advantage of a pause in the conversation. "Perhaps we could start talking about something other than sandwiches."

Not waiting for a challenge, Marshall hands us all a sheet of paper with the details of a company on it: Aimsbury Holdings

Ltd. We all stare at it, scanning the address and known directors, and my eyes land on one name. Aiden Marley. "What's this?" Russell says, snarky. "Are we meant to guess?"

"It's details of a limited company," Marshall replies with a sly smile. Russell mutters something under his breath. "This is the company which owns the kitchen located in Devon. As you can see, our friend, Mr. Marley, is a director and also the majority shareholder."

"Is this the building on the farm we found?" I question, and he nods. "But not the main kitchen located here in London. Do we know who owns that?"

"My men have been monitoring both properties," Hunter says. "The Devon farm is dormant as of this weekend. The building is empty, and no one has been at the site for days. We set a match to it so they couldn't return and use it again."

"That's subtle," Connor replies sarcastically.

"Not subtle, effective." Hunter's face lights up, and his eyes dance. "The main kitchen is located in an industrial unit outside the city. It's a run-down estate—very few businesses still operate from it. They're using a delivery firm as cover. Vans and lorries move at all times of day. HBK Removals, I think it's called." He pulls his phone from his pocket and swipes at the screen. "Yes, that's the name of it. The industrial park is out toward Basildon."

"What information do we have on them?" I ask.

"This is where it gets interesting," Marshall says. "Hunter phoned me with the details when we uncovered where it was.

The company itself isn't registered to anyone of interest—a few low-level criminals that dabble in a bit of this and that. What was interesting is who owns the building."

"Marley?" Russell suggests and Marshall shakes his head.

"No, your mother." Silence falls across the room as the words sink in. "The industrial park is owned by a company called Hesdale Assets, and your mother is the sole director."

"No fucking way," Connor growls, standing and slamming both hands on the table. The glass vibrates frantically. "This is a joke. My mother would never be involved in something like this."

"I'm not suggesting she is," Marshall continues, completely unflustered by the outburst. Russell's jaw hangs open—he's speechless. There's a first time for everything. "But what I am suggesting is your father has assets lodged in her name and is using them to push drugs around the country. I believe that the man we've been searching for, Michaels, is actually Edward Chase."

"You're suggesting my father has been playing us this whole time?" Connor asks.

"I'm saying that the evidence shows he is involved in some way."

"I don't believe it," Russell argues. "My father is a lot of things, but he's not a drug dealer. He might undertake corrupt business deals, but he wouldn't allow young people to be murdered by dodgy drugs. It's not his style."

"Anything that makes him money is his style," Connor says to his brother. "If this is true, it changes things. I always knew my father was involved in the underworld, but never did I think he could be behind something like this." He runs a hand through his hair. "Or at least he wouldn't have an operation of this caliber and we wouldn't know about it. If he's hidden this, what else could he be hiding?"

"We're not involved in all our father's business arrangements."

"Obviously," Connor shoots back. "First Marley and now this. Russell, we need to consider breaking ties with him."

"What about Mother?"

"Perhaps we could encourage her to leave him? She's not safe there. If he is involved in the drug business as deep as we think he could be..." He trails off. The brothers stare at each other, conversing silently.

"What is it?" I prompt, confused.

"She'll kill him if he's been dealing drugs. It was her one stipulation when they married," Connor explains, but it doesn't make the situation clearer.

"Stipulation? How was your mother in the position to make that?" This is a story I've never heard. How Mr. and Mrs. Chase met has never been discussed. I always assumed it was young love.

"She was payment for a debt," Russell says, solemnly. My skin crawls. "Her father owed my father a lot of money. He was young and powerful and took a liking to his debtor's daughter

who had just turned eighteen. He chased her, but she rejected him, over and over again, until the debt came due and my
grandfather couldn't settle it."

"My mother sacrificed herself. She agreed to marry him if he
wrote off the debt. Her only other stipulation was he didn't deal
in drugs. She lost a cousin in a similar fashion to how Hunter
lost his brother. As far as we were aware, he never has. Money
laundering, corrupt business deals, loan sharking, and murder,
yes, but never drugs." Connor speaks slowly as we all listen on.
"We need to find out," he states plainly. "We need to know if
our father is the man behind all this."

"And if he is?" Russell says, for once following his younger
brother's lead.

"We take him out."

CHAPTER TWENTY-SIX

Guy's Hospital, The City of London

Violet

Harrison's hand is strong and stable on my back as he leads me to the underground parking lot. Four men in suits with earpieces surround us as we walk. A large black Range Rover sits waiting for us—it's parked as close to the exit of the hospital as it can be to limit my need to walk—or our exposure. I'm unsure which.

As we reach the rear door, Harry opens it then offers me his hand to balance as I climb in. My bump seems to get bigger by the day. It feels alien to have this extra weight in my middle, and occasionally, I lose balance. The driver smiles kindly in the mirror. "Good afternoon, ma'am," he says with a nod.

"Hello," I reply as Harry climbs in the other side. He takes my hand, and I pull it from his grasp. He glances at me but doesn't say anything. I'm still not speaking to him for putting yet another roadblock in the way of us. Part of me wonders if he wants it at all. His little speech about me taking some time to think was cute but fucking annoying. All I want to do is go back to his apartment and curl up on the sofa with him, watching terrible television to forget any of this shit happened. I want to pretend that after we slept together months ago, we woke up the next morning and decided this was it for us. That we were going to be together. But no, like a record stuck on repeat, he withdrew, and I ran.

"Mrs. D. has your room made up for you," he says, startling me from my thoughts. "She asked whether you want to eat with her tonight or with me in my apartment?"

"I'll eat where I live," I reply sharply, then place my palms over my belly protectively. "Where we live."

"Violet, this is only a short-term arrangement. Please see it as it's meant to be."

I turn to look at him. He's pleading with me silently. "How short is short-term? Is there a document I need to read to understand the parameters of the decision I need to make? If I decide to be with you, is there a cooling-off period?" His face twists in annoyance. "Do I have to spend a set number of days in my holding apartment until you decide it's all right for me to move upstairs?"

"We will know when the time is right." He reaches for my hand on my stomach, but I shrug him away. "I love you, Violet."

"You have a funny fucking way of showing it." Since our discussion in the hospital, I've stewed in my thoughts. It's only made me angrier. I'm bordering on furious with him at this point. It's like a carrot being dangled before a donkey—*this is what you could have*—only for it to be snatched away. I want the bloody carrot.

The remainder of the journey is made in silence until his phone rings, and he gets involved in a debate with a lot of legal jargon I don't understand. I sit and stare out of the window at the passing buildings. People fill the pavement, rushing to get wherever they are going. The familiar building comes into view, and our car drives around the back before coming to a stop at what looks like an industrial entrance. We all sit until Harry finishes his call. Without a word, he opens his door and steps out before coming around to open mine. I take his hand as he offers it. He leads me to a heavy steel door, and behind it is the storeroom with the elevator that takes us straight up to the boardroom of The Level.

Mrs. D. is waiting for me along with Samantha. As I step out into the room, they both run and wrap their arms around me. Harrison stands behind us, not speaking. He hovers but doesn't interrupt as the women hold me and cry. Once they let go, Mrs. D. takes my face in her hands and looks me straight in the eye.

"I'm overjoyed you're back with us. I'm going to wrap you in cotton wool until this little angel is born." Her eyes flick to my stomach, then move to the man behind me. "Is there anything you need Mr. Waite? Or am I all right to take Violet to my apartment and get her settled?"

"Focus on Violet," he says. "But could you both give us a moment, please? I'll bring Violet down to you."

"Of course," Samantha and Mrs. D. reply together then leave.

I move to the window and look out over the city. He comes to stand behind me, placing his hands on either side of my waist then rests his chin on my shoulder. He pulls me against him, and I feel him harden against my back. "I do want you," he whispers softly, then places a kiss on the side of my neck. "More than anything I've ever wanted in my life."

"You can have me," I say back, hoping the honesty in my voice is obvious.

"When I was a boy, living in the whorehouse with my mother..." I still, unsure where this conversation is headed. He's never spoken openly about his childhood or past to me. Everything I know is through my brothers. The three of them used to be so close, but from the little I saw of them together, I know this isn't the case now. "I never knew where my next meal was coming from. There was no guarantee we would eat. Children were a product of the job."

"Harry, I..."

"Let me speak," he scolds, but his fingers flex on my hips in reassurance. "I was an inconsequential item which was discarded as soon as my mother died. Throughout my time there, I was treated as such. On the days we weren't fed, the hunger was all-consuming. It was an obsession. More than once I was punished for stealing from the kitchen." He chuckles. "That need and determination helped me become what I am today."

"You were always special to me," I tell him. "Mesmerizing even." His grip tightens possessively. I submit, allowing him to pull me to him further.

"My hunger is back, Violet. And it's you I'm ravenous for." He trails one hand from my collarbone down my body, resting it back on my waist. "Don't take my reluctance to move you in as a negative. Don't convince yourself that somehow I don't want you. This is me being sensible. This is me giving us the best chance I can."

His lips touch the side of my neck as his arms wrap around my expanding middle. My body relaxes in his embrace, and my heart slows as I calm. He always could make me feel safe, both as a sixteen-year-old girl when my brother tormented me and as a young woman having her first sexual encounter. Now, in my early thirties, pregnant and at a crossroads, he's managed it again. He's got me, all of me. I turn in his arms and look up at him. He rewards me with a gorgeous smile.

"We've been apart for fourteen years and never truly been together. You are undertaking one of the most important journeys you can in becoming a mother. Life has changed unrecognizably for you in a matter of months." He stops speaking and his eyes search mine.

"What is it?"

He gives me a look that tells me he is unsure whether to say what he is thinking. "I can't be your rebound." The statement sits between us. "I'm not a stupid man. I know you loved Aiden. It makes my blood boil what he did to you. I know you will grieve for what you had, whether it was real or not. He was who you saw your future with. It is him that fathered your child. This child."

Unsure how to respond, I lay my head against his chest and tighten my hold around his waist.

"When I heard you left for Chicago from Glasgow after quitting school, then discovered why, I was furious. In my mind, you and I would always come back together, though I admit to never making the effort to do so. We were both so young, I always thought there was time, and perhaps when we were older it would be possible. Then I found out you fell in love with someone else. The knowledge broke me. I broke myself."

He leans his chin on the top of my head as I listen.

"Love became something I didn't want or need. Relying on someone else was out of the question. I threw myself into work and life being one of the boys alongside your brothers, while trying to surpass my own ridiculous expectations. There has never been anyone else who made me feel like you do from a single look.

Over the years, I've never had a relationship the way you have. I've never been with someone who I truly saw a future with. Now, I do. That's why I'm being cautious with us, because 'us' is so precious. I'm terrified we will break."

"We love each other, Harry. Committing to anyone or anything is always a risk," I say quietly into his chest. "I've known since I was a teenager you were my boy. Even when I was in Chicago, planning a future with Aiden, I would think of you and wonder if you'd found what you were looking for, and why I'd fallen short for you."

His hands lift to my shoulders. He pushes me back slightly and my eyes flick upward to him.

"You have never fallen short for me." He drops to a knee in front of me, taking me by surprise. "If I ever have made you feel that way, please forgive me. It was never my intention. I ran because I was scared, and you were all-consuming. It frightened me. And now we have this little one to consider too," he says. Still on his knee, he takes my hands and kisses my belly. "I may not be your child's biological father, but if you choose me, I promise to be the best daddy I can be to them."

"I've already chosen you," I tell him. "No amount of time apart will change that. I understand your concerns and why you want us to happen this way." I pull at his hands, encouraging him to stand. "But, know this—you are not a rebound. Aiden was my rebound. He appeared in my life when I was nursing a broken heart because of us. You have always been the one I wanted. Deep down, I've known it all along. My stupidity backed me into a corner and kept me in Chicago. My pride too. Refusing to see what was obvious in front of me." I reach up and run my fingers across the back of his neck. He closes his eyes.

"Kiss me," I whisper. "Be the last and only man I kiss from this day forward because I'm telling you now, this is it for me. You are everything I'll ever need. There will only ever be you."

He takes my hand and guides me to the long glass table, then turns me to face him. His hands move to my backside and lift me gently onto the cool surface. I wrap my legs around his middle as he stands between them, my swollen belly pressing against his toned abs. He kisses me, tenderly at first, exploring my mouth gently. With my arms around his neck and his surrounding me, I enjoy the sensation of being enveloped by him. Wrapped in him. I feel the tears on my cheeks before I'm aware they appeared.

"Don't cry," he says quietly against my lips. "I've got you." After a few more scattered kisses, he lifts me down. "I better take to you Mrs. D.'s or she will be sending out a search party." I giggle, and he smiles before taking my hand once more, leading me to my new temporary home.

A short ride in the elevator brings us to the twenty-fifth floor. Security guards are stationed in the lobby. Harry nods to the man then takes me to the apartment. He knocks on the door firmly, and it immediately swings open. "I thought you'd got lost," Samantha says, looking between us. "Were you both getting reacquainted?" she sniggers, then waggles her eyebrows.

"None of your bloody business," Harry mumbles.

"It's okay," she replies with a cheeky smile. "Violet will give me a blow-by-blow account later. Nothing is sacred when it comes to us girls."

"You will be dreadfully disappointed," he tells her. "And yes, I've learned already that discretion is not your strongest point." She sticks her tongue out at him, and his eyes pop wide. "You're a pain in the ass," he tells her. "Why the hell are you still here?"

"I'm Violet's wing-woman," she answers without missing a beat. "And without me, you'd have been one step behind. I'm here to stay, so get used to it. I've always got my girl's back."

Before he can respond, Mrs. D. appears in front of us with her token apron and tray of goodies—freshly baked chocolate-chip cookies this time. She passes them around as we stand in the hallway. "Your room is down here," she says. Harry holds my hand firmly as we walk. She pushes open the door when we arrive at it, and he leads me in. It's a simple double bedroom, all white linen and voile. Understated. Simple. Clean.

"It's beautiful," I say, "and thank you for having me."

"You are welcome as long as you want or need to be here." Her shrewd eyes move between Harry and me. "I'll leave you to get settled. Dinner will be at six. The men already dropped your case here. It's by the window."

She leaves, and Harry walks over, picks up my case, then places it on the bed. I open it and start to put my meager belongings away. A few summer dresses, a pair of jeans, two thin-strapped tops, and my hoodie. It's not much, only what

Connor seemingly managed to get via my mother, but it's something.

"I meant to ask you," I say, and Harry looks at me. "The nurse at the maternity clinic. How did you know her?"

"I didn't, but we got lucky. Her brother is a recent client that I got acquitted. He is also owed a large amount of money by Aiden. It's a small world, so he was happy to help when I spoke to him."

"Everything and everyone do seem to be interconnected," I muse. "So many pieces of the puzzle fit together but don't."

"More than you could imagine, but I don't want you to worry about that. You're here and safe in this apartment. Promise me you will rest. Promise me you will put yourself and this little person here first." He touches my stomach again; it seems to be a common theme. The baby kicks, and he pulls his hand away. I laugh, and he smiles nervously, then places his hand back where it was. I put mine over his.

We stand together like that as my baby moves within me. Both of us feel it. I know we do. The new life within me and the new life starting between us. The three of us. Hope for the future blooms tentatively. Today feels as though we are finally following the correct map to where we need to be.

CHAPTER TWENTY-SEVEN

———◆◆◆———

The Level, Canary Wharf

Harrison

Life has been relatively quiet in recent weeks. The Christmas lights are blinking throughout the city, and everyone is full of festive cheer. The drug ring seems to have gone quiet—little movement is being reported by Hunter's men, and no further deaths linked to them have been conveyed. The lack of information makes me uneasy.

Violet's stomach grows from day to day. Every time I see her, she is slightly rounder. She looks stunning wandering around in her fitted tops and leggings, her bump proudly on show. Mrs. D.

keeps her busy baking and chatting throughout the day. They have become firm friends; she's the mother Violet doesn't have to help her at this crucial time in her life. As Mrs. D. undertakes her duties in our various apartments, Violet follows her around doing small tasks.

Her evenings are spent with me. She is always there when I get home, either cooking or sitting on the bar stool as my housekeeper does. We eat then retire to the couch; she lies in my arms until it's time for bed, then I escort her downstairs. It feels like we are living our teenage love story, doing all the things we should have been able to do. Our relationship hadn't moved beyond a kiss until last night, until we couldn't resist any longer.

***

We had been sitting at the dining table eating the remnants of a strawberry cheesecake Violet had made. Cream had trickled from the corner of her mouth as she missed it with her spoon. On impulse, I'd lifted my hand and wiped it from her skin with my thumb, then popped in it my mouth. "Delicious," I said, and her eyes fired as she looked at me. "Best-tasting dessert I've ever eaten."

She laughed, and her firm breasts rose then fell beneath her soft cotton t-shirt. My dick hardened instantly as I watched her.

"I'm not a patisserie chef," she chided.

"I wasn't talking about the cheesecake." She bit her lip, and I was a goner. Having her sitting in my home opposite me, teeth denting pale pink flesh with her nipples poking through the soft material of her clothes, was too much. I needed to touch her, hold her, and have her surrounding me. She knew—her breathing hitched then deepened. I stood and held my hand out.

"What are you suggesting, Mr. Waite?" she asked, a cheeky smile playing on her lips. Her hand came to mine, and she rose to meet me. Those beautiful eyes that speak directly to my cock ran over my face. She stepped forward and placed her free hand over my heart. "That's quite a heartbeat you have there. Has something got you excited?"

"Every damn day. Watching you wander around here. Coming home and finding you waiting for me. You sitting next to me while I do the things I used to do alone." She went up on her tiptoes, I lowered a little, and we kissed—softly, gently, tenderly. "Can I take you to bed? I want to give you pleasure the way you have me, by being here. We don't need to do anything you don't want to do. But I want to be with you, sleep with you. If you'll allow it."

"I'll need to ask my supervisor," she replied, her mouth quipping again. "Mrs. D. will storm up here and demand you return me if I overstay my curfew."

"She's implemented a curfew?" I teased. She let go of my hand, that palm coming to rest on my chest beside the other. My arousal heightened as we stood there, looking at each other. I moved my hands to her hips, her palms moving up and down with my chest as my excitement surfaced.

"Yes, she was concerned about me spending every evening with a certain man. Told me he was a morally gray individual with questionable tastes." I raised an eyebrow at her. "She didn't want me to get into a predicament I can't get out of. She even offered me some pepper spray."

"Pepper spray." I snorted. "So, tell me about this morally gray character you've spent all your evenings with."

"Well…" She paused, her mind whirling before my eyes. She's such a fucking cock tease—that hasn't changed in the past fourteen years. "He is a family friend. A little older than me. Quite good looking."

"Quite good-looking?" I growled, then leaned in and nipped her neck with my teeth.

"Extremely hot," she corrected. "He only has to look at me and I melt. One touch is enough for me to do anything he wants. One kiss and I'm gone, I'm his. He has complete control of me, body and mind."

"He sounds like a powerful man." She dropped her gaze away; it settled on my crotch. My dick was hard against my jeans, my current desires bold and obvious.

"When it comes to my heart, he is," she whispered, still looking downward. Her hand moved over the bulge; she drummed her fingers over the smooth material. "I'm not sure how I feel about going the whole way, now I'm so big," she said, her cheeks flush embarrassed. I placed a finger under her chin to raise her eyes back to mine.

"Whatever you let me do, however I can enjoy you, will be enough for me. I want to give you pleasure. I want to watch you come over my fingers as I find your buttons."

"Find my buttons?" she replied with a smirk. "I'm not a remote control."

"No, you're a woman with needs and specific preferences. When I take you to bed, I want to know which spots give you the best rewards, and in return, you can find mine." She giggled. I picked up my phone from the table beside me, and she frowned. "I'm messaging the supervisor for permission for you to stay." After discarding the handset on the surface again, I took her hand and led her to my bedroom.

We arrived at the already open door, silk sheets spread on the bed with perfect precision. The only light came through the window from the city outside. It wasn't bright—our building is so tall that nothing looks onto us. The room almost had a romantic feel without trying. I noticed a candle that wasn't there before sitting on my bedside table, a lighter strategically placed beside it. Mrs. D. thinks of everything.

I encouraged Violet inside with me, closing the door behind us. She was makeup free in her leggings and my t-shirt, with bare feet. "You look incredible in here," I told her. "This is exactly where you're meant to be, sharing my space, my life."

"I'm glad you've realized that," she said.

"You being for me wasn't a doubt I had. You wanting me was. Me being good enough for you more so."

She took both my hands and wrapped them around her waist. Our lips locked. She tasted of cheesecake and sexual promise, two decadent flavors intermingled to create perfection. My fingers moved to the hem of the t-shirt. I lifted it slowly, wanting to give her time to refuse. She didn't, raising her arms willingly as I pulled it over her head. She was braless beneath. I suspected as much, but it was exhilarating to have it confirmed.

Lowering myself, I kissed her collarbone, then trailed my tongue down her chest 'til I arrived at a pert pink nipple. It was already elongated, aroused. I took the bud in my mouth, sucking deeply, and she moaned softly above me. Her round breasts sat perfectly above her swollen stomach. She was every inch a woman—feminine, raw, and stunning.

My lips moved to the other nipple. Her fingers played with my hair. I bit down gently; she gasped, and her fingers flexed on my scalp. I released her from my mouth then maneuvered her toward the bed, encouraging her down onto it. She lay back, her tits free but pussy still covered with a simple strip of black Lycra.

"I want to see all of you," I whispered, pulling the leggings from her body. Beneath her bump was a lace G-string. "This is pretty," I said, running one finger beneath the waistband. "But I'd rather see you bare." I slipped it off so she was naked, lying on my bed. Where she should be. "Bend your knees," I instructed, then stood.

Looking down at her, lying open and exposed, my need for her peaked. She blinked up with wide eyes, watching intently as

I undressed before her, leaving on my boxers. My dick strained against the material, desperate to be free, but there was no guarantee we would get to that this evening, whether inside her pussy or wrapped in her hand. She was fully aware of how I felt. If she wanted to give me pleasure, she would instigate it. Hell, I hoped she would.

Lying back down beside her, I propped myself up on one elbow before taking her mouth with mine. My hand moved down over her stomach, hesitating between her legs. I placed my palm over her, holding the most intimate part of her as I explored her mouth with my tongue.

"You will feel me in every part of you," I told her. "Tonight, I'm going to take my time and enjoy each inch of you. Lay claim to all of you. No place on your body will be missed. When we finish, I want you to have no doubt who you belong to, which man is yours, and who will be there for you for every day we wake together."

***

Violet

Last night, Harrison showed me I was his. He made love to me with a gentle but dominant tone. Every touch, kiss, and suck was placed on my body as another sign of his ownership.

He respected me not being comfortable with full intercourse. Though I wanted to, my child moving inside unsettled me about full penetration. Instead, he used his fingers and mouth to bring me to orgasm. Once he had finished kissing me, his lips moved south over my skin to between my legs. He pulled me to the edge of the bed, spreading my thighs wide and crouching down between them. His tongue started at my ankle, gliding over my skin painfully slowly until he reached my pussy, then he repeated the process on the other leg. By the time he touched my clit with his tongue, I was wet and ready for him to enjoy me. He flicked my sweet spot, increasing the sensation between my legs until I reached for his hair to encourage him to move lower—to eat me, enjoy my flavor.

"Patience," he scolded, batting my hand away. "I want you to be gagging for my tongue inside you. I want to concentrate on this perfect button first." His finger pressed my clit, and I bucked beneath him as my body buzzed. "I wonder if I could make you come, just by playing with this using my tongue."

My mouth was dry, my legs open, and my nipples hard. The vibrations running through my body were intense. "I'm not far away," I whispered, breathless. "Please, Harry, touch me inside. I want to feel your fingers in me."

"Next time, perhaps," he replied darkly. "But now, I'm going to return to playing with my first button, and when you come, I'm going to watch your juices flow free. I love having a front-row seat." He returned to his task, and the sensation of orgasm increased at an alarming rate. Then I felt it, the release, as I let go and my body shuddered violently. "That's my girl," he praised, then buried himself between my legs to taste the rawest part of me. His statement was simple and light, but it meant the world. Now I was his, and I always would be.

He took me to my peak three times throughout the night, either with his mouth or his hands. He never suggested anything more, and I appreciated that—it made me love him more. It made me realize that a man can be dominant but gentle. In charge but listen. Respect your boundaries, satisfy you, and gratify himself.

Then I'd wanted to pleasure him, show him what he meant to me. He had moved to stand, and I followed him, dropping to my knees and sliding his boxers down his legs. His cock hung at my eye level, hard and angry. Desperate for attention, desperate to be sunk within me. I offered him what I could. I took him in my mouth, wrapping my hands around his taut ass and encouraging him deeper.

"Fuck my mouth," I told him. He moved gently at first, wrapping my hair around his fingers and holding me to him as his speed increased. I dug my nails into his skin, encouraging him to take what he wanted. "Use me," I said fiercely. He thrust forward. His cock hit the back of my throat as he rode my mouth, his control slipping with each stroke. The sounds coming from his lips, the deep growl of a man on the edge. His strong hands held me steady as he chased his release, jerking forcefully as he emptied himself. I closed my eyes, enjoying the taste of his seed, maintaining my holding on what was now mine. Relishing the fact I made him feel this way. He withdrew, and I licked him clean. His hands took mine, pulling me up-ward.

"I love you, Violet," he said, kissing my forehead. He guided me to the bed, laid me down, and wrapped himself around me. It was the most peaceful night's sleep I had ever had, encompassed by the man I never thought I would regain. In the morning, I woke up and he was still there, encasing me, but awake. He never ran, and neither did I. We lay together, unspeaking, knowing that this morning was the first of thousands.

Chapter Twenty-Eight

Harrison's Apartment,
The Level

Harrison

"I have an ultrasound today," Violet says. "Do you still want to come?"

I glance up at her over the bowl of muesli I'm eating. She appeared at my door ten minutes ago. She's been spending more time here, but still retreats to Mrs. D.'s apartment every other night. The time is coming closer for her to move in permanently, I can feel it.

"Wouldn't miss it," I reply, and she beams in response. The possessiveness I feel for the child growing inside her is shocking. Never did I think another man's baby could mean so much, be so important in my future.

"Do you have a busy day ahead?" she asks.

"With us shutting down for Christmas holidays this week, I have back-to-back meetings. Mr. Moneybags is coming in to discuss how we can apply more pressure on Aiden to get his money back. I'm not feeling hopeful."

"How come?" she says.

"He paid him in cash." Her eyes pop from her head, and I laugh. "Two million pounds handed over in a suitcase for an investment. Not much shocks me, but that did. No traceability, no electronic records detailing the agreement. He literally handed him it with no strings.".

"I'm not a lawyer," she says, "but even I know that's a bad idea."

"What time is your appointment? I'll arrange for security to collect you and bring you home. Don't go anywhere without them—at least one man within arm's reach of you at all times." She rolls her eyes, already bored by yet another speech on keeping her safe. "Violet, this is serious. The threat is still there. You need protection at all times."

"Even in the bathroom?" she asks, portraying innocence. "Do I need a bodyguard in the stall as I urinate? You know, in case Aiden pops his head up the toilet to steal me away."

"Be fucking serious," I tell her, then move on quickly before she can annoy me any more. She smiles sweetly. "Is there anything else you need to do today?"

"Samantha might come to visit. I'd love to go out for a hot drink and a huge piece of cake." Her eyes rise to the ceiling, and she rubs at her stomach. "Cake would be nice, in a café, with other people."

"I'll tell you what. I'll meet you at our ultrasound." She grins manically with her plump pink lips. "What?"

"Our ultrasound," she mouths, then walks over and wraps her arms around my neck, standing behind me as I sit in my chair.

"Our baby, our ultrasound," I tell her, then continue with what I was going to say. "I'll arrange for Samantha to meet you somewhere with mountains of cake and sweet treats. As long as the security team know, they can prepare for it. Leave it with me. Your wish is my command."

"You really are like my own personal genie." She squeezes me and drops a kiss on my cheek. "Except you're not blue and aren't a very good singer."

"It's good that those two features are not on your list of requirements in a life partner," I say, then place my bowl on the table and tap her arms with my fingers. "I need to go. Work is calling, I'll see you at..."

"Eleven."

"Eleven it is. It's a date at the ultrasound clinic." She removes her arms. I stand then grab my briefcase and leave, calling over my shoulder, "Love you." It feels incredibly surreal but right.

***

Two minutes past eleven shows on the clock as I pull into the hospital parking lot. Not caring who sees, I dump my car at the entrance and toss the keys to one of my security team standing at the door. "Second floor. Out of the elevator and turn left," he shouts behind me. I take off at a run and try to navigate my way through the hordes of people currently trying to pass through the carousel doors. "Excuse me," I mutter as I slide by them. None of them seem to be in a rush to be anywhere.

As I enter the hallway, an old woman with a stick is in front. She holds it out to the side as I pass, causing me to promptly trip over it. Stumbling forward, my highly shined Italian leather shoes slip on the tiled floor. After two more staggering steps, I land in the arms of a security guard who is glowering openly. His badge tells me his name is Fred and he is hospital security.

"Sorry, sorry," I say, quickly pushing myself back up to stand from his embrace. He sighs and releases me.

"Excuse me, sir, can I ask where you're headed? And what has you so flustered? We take patient safety extremely seriously here. If you don't calm down, I may have to ask you to leave," he tells me, then puffs out his chest like he owns the fucking planet.

"The ultrasound suite. My girlfriend has an appointment." I glance at my watch. "Like now. I need to go." As I try to push past him, he places a hand on my chest. "Don't touch me. I think you'll find that is outside the parameters of your job description."

"What would you know about my job description?"

"Enough that I could prove a case to get you fired if you piss me off enough. Now, let me pass." He laughs and shakes his head.

"Jumped-up prick," he says, looking me up and down. "You might have a big wallet and be used to people kowtowing to your demands, but within these walls, I'm in charge."

"Are you fucking kidding me?" I spit as my phone starts ringing. I pull it from my pocket. "Hello."

"Where are you?" Violet hisses down the line. "I've been called in. They're waiting for you."

"The security guard is holding me hostage in reception."

"What did you do?" she says, and I scowl at the phone. Why bloody assume I'm at fault?

"I didn't do anything. I'll be with you in a minute. Let me discuss the options with this gentleman." She sighs then mutters something under her breath. "What was that?"

"Hurry the fuck up."

I go to snap back at her, but she disconnects the call before I can respond. I turn back to the idiot playing God in front of me. "Now, thanks to you, I have a pissed-off pregnant woman

293

to deal with. Give me the name of your supervisor. I'll be discussing your conduct with them after my appointment."

"Fred," someone calls, distracting him. I take my chance to dodge past him and run for the staircase, taking them two at a time.

"Stop!" he blares behind me. I ignore him and keep running. Pushing the double doors open, I burst into the waiting room and find Violet sitting with her arms crossed over her bump. She glares at me and stands, then marches over. Her gait is wider than it once was to allow for her changing shape. She stops directly under my nose and looks up at me, openly furious.

"Fuck, you look as hot as hell," I tell her. "All frustrated with pent-up rage and bursting hormones. Is there a store cupboard around here?"

"What?" she stammers, confused by my statement.

"I know how to relieve that fury." I grin at her then quickly pinch her nipple. Her mouth drops open.

"People are watching," she hisses.

"All I need is you with your legs spread and my fingers in that slick pussy of yours. What do you say?" I continue. "It could be just what you need."

"No fucking chance. You're late." Her tone is annoyed, but I see a smile playing on her lips. There is the sound of rushed footsteps.

"Quick, which room are we meant to be in?" She gives me a curious look. "That could be security coming to throw me out, and I don't want to miss seeing our baby today."

She grabs my hand and leads me to a white door standing ajar beside the chair she was sitting on. On the wall to the right-hand side, there is a small TV screen with her name in white lettering on a blue background. Violet Chase. That is something I want to change in the future. Violet Waite sounds much more appealing.

Her small hand lifts and knocks gently on the plastic surface, then she pushes the door open. As we step through, an elderly man with wispy gray hair and a long white coat stands at the prepared medical bed. He smiles kindly and introduces himself as our sonographer. We both say hello in unison, and everyone laughs.

"If you could lie on the bed then pull your dress up to expose your stomach," he says. He points to a pale pink sheet folded on the cabinet beside him. "This is to cover your lower half during the procedure. I'll give you a moment to get ready." He nods then pulls the blue curtain around the bed to give us some privacy.

Violet stands on the small wooden step placed next to the bed. She climbs up then hitches her dress above her bump before lying down. I grab the sheet from the bottom of the bed and lay it over her panties and legs. Moving to stand at her head, I twist a stray curl between my fingers and bend down, placing a soft kiss on her lips.

"Are you ready?" I whisper softly, and she smiles in answer. "That's us ready for you," I call, and the curtain opens as the man who will show us our baby walks back in.

"Wow," I murmur in Violet's ear. We both have our gazes fixed on the screen in front of us. "It's like a real baby." She giggles softly, and I kiss her cheek. "You know what I mean. In the last one they looked like an alien, but this 4D image is amazing. You can see everything."

"Do you want to know the sex?" the sonographer asks, and Violet shakes her head.

"No, thank you. I want it to be a surprise for us both." She smiles, her face filled with complete joy. "I can't believe this is happening, Harry," she says. "After everything, I'm here with you and we are planning our little family together. Doing all the normal stuff we should be doing." I lower my lips to her temple, closing my eyes and breathing her in. She smells beautiful as usual—the perfume she wears is instantly recognizable.

"Never change your perfume,". I tell her.

"It's a cheap bottle from the local pharmacy," she replies. "I don't even know what it's called."

"Whatever it is, it's you. When the scent hits me, I know you're near and everything calms." She glances at me. "You've saved me, Violet, as much as I saved you. This is a two-way process." We stare at each other for a beat. The sonographer clearing his throat breaks the moment. Violet's cheeks pink at being caught in what is an intimate exchange. Our focus returns to the screen.

***

Twenty minutes later, we are walking from the hospital hand in hand. Violet chatters on about how amazing the experience of seeing our baby was, how she can't wait to meet them. She clutches a scan picture in her hand and every so often lifts it to look at it; a beaming smile appears on her face every time. The second photo is safely stored inside my suit jacket pocket. It is going on my desk next to the only remaining photo I have of my mother. We arrive at my car.

"I thought you were going back to work?" she says.

"I am, but I'll take you to meet Samantha. The team will follow behind. I don't want to leave you yet." She squeezes my fingers, and I open her door for her. My new Range Rover means she needs to step up to get inside. She balances on my arm as she does.

"I miss the sports car," she mumbles.

"You could have probably got into it but struggled to get out in your current condition." She swipes at my arm, and I pretend to dodge out of her way. She turns to grab her seat belt. "I'll get that." I lean over her and clip it into place. As I retreat, she kisses me fiercely, grabbing my face between her hands.

"Thank you," she says, "for staying. For being here."

"I wouldn't be anywhere else. Wherever you need me, I'll be there."

"I'm getting fed up now of being pregnant," she admits. "There are only so many days of swollen ankles and morning sickness a girl can take. And I'm looking forward to wearing jeans again." I place my hand on her stomach, and our baby kicks hard. "And I won't miss my insides being treated like a football either."

"I like you pregnant. It suits you," I tell her. "I'm kind of hoping this won't only be a one-time thing. That when the time is right, you and I will be able to create our own little bundle too. Maybe a few."

"A few?" she repeats back to me, eyes wide. "How many did you have in mind?"

"I was thinking we could have four boys. Though I would like a daughter too."

"They aren't made to order," she chides. "You get what you're given."

"It could be a lot of fun trying," I say, brushing her lips with mine again. "There is something incredibly sexy about you, rounded and carrying a gift so special."

"So basically, you want me either with child or nursing one for the foreseeable future," she says, snarky. "Is this your kink, Mr. Waite? Pregnant women?" Her palm rises to my cheek.

"There is only one woman I want to carry my children, and I'm looking at her."

"Children plural again," she says, raising an eyebrow. "Remember, I grew up in a house with two brothers. It's not all it's cracked up to be."

"I didn't have anyone," I reply honestly. "I never want my family to be left the way I was. Alone." She holds my gaze with hers. Honesty passes between us, an understanding that we've both been broken in our own way. Our pasts are messy, but this is real, and always has been.

"Our children won't be, and you won't be," she murmurs against my lips. "We are here together now, Harry. You and me, the way it was meant to be. I'll give you a bloody football team if it makes you happy. Hopefully, we will be blessed with some multiples to save time." I laugh and kiss her, deeply and meaningfully. My tongue invades her mouth, wanting, needing to consume every part of her.

"If you weren't already cooking number one, I'd suggest we make a start. What a place to have a conversation about family planning—the hospital parking lot is quite apt," I point out, and she laughs.

"Nothing about us is conventional. But as long as we are together, I don't care."

***

Samantha is waiting for us as she said she would be. As we approach her, I see she is flirting shamelessly with the two security staff I assigned her. They're sitting at a table in the coffee shop, all with a tall latte between their hands. The two men hang on her every word. Samantha leans forward, giving them full view of her bosom. Violet chuckles, and I glance at her.

"You saw that too?" I say, and she nods.

"Samantha is suffering from some sexual frustration," she explains. "She needs a good ride to get it out of her system. I think she has her sights set on a man in a suit with an earpiece. She has an ongoing fantasy about it."

"Are there no boundaries in women's conversation?"

She snorts, shaking her head, then lifts a hand to push a strand of hair out of her face. "Don't worry, I always give you a good review. A solid four stars every time."

I stop dead, turning to face her. "Four stars?" I step forward and wrap my arm around her back. "You've combusted under my touch every fucking time," I growl, dropping my mouth to hers. "And that's only with my fingers and my mouth. Imagine what it will feel like when I have you pinned to the mattress and filled with my cock." Her breathing hitches. "Plus, I know those orgasms are real. You leave enough evidence on my bedsheets to prove it."

"I very rarely give anything five stars," she replies with a smirk. "There is always room for improvement."

"Fuck's sake," I hiss, "don't push me. I'll drop your panties and make you come here in the middle of this café. Give the patrons a blow-by-blow account of how I've made you scream my name every night you've stayed in my bed." Her cheeks color. "I especially liked the sound you made last night as you came on my tongue. It was an all-encompassing experience. Taste, touch, sound, and smell. You were fucking perfect."

"Harry," she whispers, breathless. Her eyes are round, pupils dilated. She's turned on. I harden against her hip.

"I'll promise you this." She peeks up, curious. "Tonight, I'm getting those bloody five stars."

CHAPTER TWENTY-NINE

―◆○◆―

The Level, Canary Wharf

Violet

Samantha and I arrive back at The Level with armfuls of baby gear. We have shopped 'til we literally dropped and ate two helpings of cake at different coffee shops. The guards followed us around but kept their distance. It was nice to be able to do something somewhat normal. As we walk into the foyer, she asks, "What apartment are we taking the baby things to?"

"Um…" I stammer. "I don't know. Harry will probably want to see them. He did pay for it all."

"I can't believe he handed you a bloody limitless credit card and told you to enjoy yourself." She rolls her eyes. "I need one of them. Deep pockets, high patience threshold, and preferably a big dick that has stamina."

"You best keep looking then," I tell her. She gives me a curious look as if about to say something else but doesn't. I know she's been talking to my brother, Connor, but neither of them has mentioned anything.

"I'm sure he'll turn up," she says with a shrug. "Preferably before I'm too old to enjoy him."

"Good evening, Miss Violet, Miss Samantha," Matthew says as we enter. He is a constant in this building. Always on the door, ensuring the people who live here can go about their business safely and with no challenges. "Let me take those for you." He plucks the bags both of us are carrying from our grasp. "Do you not have someone to help you?" As he glances up, our two security staff walk in, also laden with bags. He chuckles. "Ah I see, preparing for the new arrival. Where would you like to go?"

"Mr. Waite's apartment please," I say, and he nods. "Is he in?"

"I believe so, ma'am. Arrived back an hour ago, I think. Maybe around six."

"Perfect. Thank you, Matthew." We all follow him to the elevator and once piled inside—Samantha, me, our guards, and the bags—he sends us upward, into the clouds. I turn my back on the view outside and close my eyes. The tactic seems to be working to calm my fears as we rise.

Samantha prances in front of me toward Harry's apartment when we arrive. She is so comfortable now in these surroundings. Recently, she was able to give up her job at both the clothes shop and Guilty Pleasures. She told me she'd come into an inheritance. It was enough to live on for a year while she returned to her studies and figured out her next steps. She still lives in the same apartment we shared, but life is looking so much brighter. Her nursing degree course starts in January. She is incredibly excited to be moving forward in life.

Harry is waiting at the front door when we turn the corner. He walks out into the hallway and takes me in his arms, kissing me ferociously. "I've missed you," he whispers. Samantha groans loudly.

"Pass the sick bucket," she says. We ignore her. I don't bloody care. This is what life is about, having someone who wants you.

"Did you get everything you wanted?" he asks, then looks up and sees his men starting to carry the vast number of bags around the corner and toward his apartment. "I see you made a good start anyway." Harrison nods to his head bodyguard, who was assigned to me today. "Put them in the living room," he instructs then looks at me. "I want to see everything you bought."

"That'll take a while," I tell him.

"I'd be disappointed if it didn't."

After two hours of combing through bags and coming across things I forgot we bought, Samantha stands to leave. She kisses my cheek and hugs me tight. "I'll see you after Christmas," she says. "Have the most amazing day together." She looks from Harry to me then back to him. "I hope you've bought her something special."

"It's all in hand," he replies with a wink. They give each other a knowing look.

"Have you both been conspiring?"

"It's all for your benefit," Samantha says, hugging me once more before leaving.

Harry and I watch her leave, then he takes my hand and leads me to the sofa. We sit down as we do every night, him in the corner with his arm around me as I lean back against him. It's become our thing, our position. When we do it, I know I'm home.

"Mrs. D. is going to spend Christmas with her family," he tells me. My eyes flick to him, hesitating on his expectant eyes. "I was thinking it might be quite a good time for you to move in full-time."

"Really?"

"Only if you want to," he adds quickly. "No pressure."

"I'd love to." Nothing else needs to be said. He knows how I feel about him. I settle back against his chest, and we sit and watch a drama TV show neither of us is really concentrating on. Every so often he strokes my arm or squeezes me a bit tighter.

"Are you ready for bed?" he asks as the closing credits play. I mumble in assent, tiredness overwhelming me. We both sit up, then he stands and pulls me to my feet. His firm hand on my back guides me to his bedroom, which is now our bedroom. As we step through the door, the familiar smell of the vanilla candle hits my nostrils. Every night I stay, he lights it a few hours before we retire to prepare our space.

"You're not going to sleep yet, Violet," he says darkly. We're standing in the middle of the room, and I glance at him. "I have a five-star rating to achieve first."

He walks over to the tall windows that look out onto the city below, turning and holding out his hand. I follow him, and he pulls me in front of him, wrapping his arms around my swollen stomach, then resting his chin on my shoulder. "Out there," he whispers softly. "The outside world. It's something we need to endure. For years, doing that has been tough. But now, Violet, having you here with me will make it so much easier. My home has always been my sanctuary, but with you in it, it's my heaven."

Warm lips touch my neck, starting below my earlobe and working downward. As they reach my collarbone, he pauses—the air passing his lips flutters across my skin. With each breath, my arousal heightens, his fingers drumming against my body. "You are so fucking sexy," he whispers, and flexes his hardened cock against my ass.

"I'm like a beached whale," I argue.

"Yeah, but you're my beached whale, and carrying our baby. That makes you completely irresistible."

The following morning, I wake up to him wrapped around me, his hand splayed across my seven month's pregnant stomach. He's snoring softly at my shoulder. When I look at the clock on the bedside table, it reads eight-thirty in the morning. My eyes pop open as Harry's phone starts to vibrate frantically somewhere in the room.

"Harry," I hiss, "you've slept in. What time were you meant to be at work?"

"Who cares?" He mumbles. "Let's stay in bed. It's almost Christmas. Maybe I'll call in sick." I chuckle, my whole body pulsating softly.

"When was the last time you called in sick?"

"I've never had to do it before," he says, "but I think today it's required."

"But you're not sick."

"I am. I have obsessive-compulsive Violet disorder, and I need to stay here with you." He wriggles his arms from around me, kisses my shoulder, then gets out of bed.

"Where are you going?" I ask him, turning onto my other side.

"I'll only be a minute." He's standing by the bed naked, scrolling through his phone.

"Now, that's a sight I could get used to in the morning," I say. He smirks then returns to reading whatever he was a moment ago. I shimmy over to him so I'm lying on his side of the bed, gazing up at him. With one hand, I reach out and cup his balls, and his cock hardens. He looks down at me, and I bite my lip. "That's an even better view now."

"Do you want something?" He raises an eyebrow. "Was last night still a four-star performance, or did I attain the magic five?"

"You attained and surpassed it," I tell him, my free hand moving between my legs, touching myself where I'm now tender from his fingers and mouth. "If you're going to call off work, will we have a rerun now? Practice makes perfect." I wrap my fingers around his length, and he growls, a primal sound from deep within him. It's something I've come to expect, and it speaks directly to my libido.

He lowers himself down to sit beside me, his cock standing tall against his stomach. With one hand, he traces my collarbone then runs it down over my breasts, twisting each nipple as he goes. I gasp at the delicious mixture of pleasure and pain.

"How is down here feeling today?" he asks, touching my pussy. "Tender? She had a lot of attention last night to obtain that magic star." I laugh, and unexpectedly he slides a finger inside me. "Wet already for me," he whispers. "Have you been a horny little vixen all night? Fucking me while you sleep?" Our eyes meet, and his burn. "I'm going to make you come again, Violet, then you're going to take my dick in your mouth, and I'll feed you."

***

On Christmas morning, we sit at the breakfast bar and dig into a plate of bacon and eggs. Communication seems to have quietened this week—it's as if everyone has taken a step back and is allowing us time together. Today, all we have planned is a food frenzy and time lounging around in our Christmas onesies. With no Mrs. D. at home, we were forced to purchase mountains of ready-to-cook fast food. Even though the calories to be consumed are ridiculous, I will savor every last greasy bite.

"Can I give you your presents now?" he says. I woke up ravenous and insisted we eat first. He mumbled something in challenge but gave in within moments.

"Okay, but you better not have spoiled me. I only got you a little something this year." He shrugs then jumps off his stool and wanders away along the corridor toward the bedrooms. He appears back holding a huge box wrapped in bright-red paper. "Harry, what have you bought? It's too much."

"Shut up, Violet," he says, taking me by surprise. "Just come here and open the fucking gift. You could have bought me a packet of condoms and it would be enough. Having you here is the greatest Christmas gift I could wish for." He places the box on the coffee table.

I walk over and start to strip away the paper. Underneath is a simple brown cardboard box. When I open it, it is filled with boxes of my perfume. I laugh out loud.

"Is one hundred bottles enough to keep you smelling like the place I want to bury myself night after night?" he says and grins. "You said you didn't know what it was. I found it. This isn't really a gift for you. It's for me."

"Greedy bastard," I tease.

"Your gift is down here." He takes my hand and leads me down the corridor toward our bedroom, but he keeps going. The room beside ours has the door lying open. When we step in, it's empty of everything except a single white crib in the center. "This will be our baby's room," he says, and my heart swells. I love how he uses the word "our" when describing the bundle in my belly.

"Thank you," I whisper, overcome with emotion. A sob of happiness catches in my throat.

"In the new year, I've arranged for a designer to meet with you and plan options for decoration. I assumed the little one would need to be in our room to begin with." He looks to me for reassurance, and I nod. "So that gives you plenty of time to design the exact nursery you want depending on the sex."

"You are fucking perfect," I say, turning to him and wrapping my arms around his neck. "What the hell did I do to deserve you?" We kiss, gently at first then with more intensity. He is showing me I'm his, and I'm submitting to his domination.

"The real question is, what did a boy like me do to land you in his bed? Don't sell yourself short. You, my darling, are the most amazing catch, and I still can't believe you're mine." Our kisses become more urgent, and I'm about to suggest moving to our bedroom when the buzzer sounds on the intercom system.

"Who the fuck could that be?" Harry mutters, annoyed.

"Ignore it," I tell him. "Let's get back to where we were." The buzzer sounds again. He lets me go and strides out into the hallway. I follow behind him, pissed at being interrupted by a bell.

"What is it?" Harry snaps down the receiver. "A present for Violet?" he repeats back to the caller, clearly confused. "From whom?" His brows draw together. "And it's safe? You've scanned it." Another pause. "Okay, bring it up." He replaces the handset on the wall. "There is a present from your mother at reception. It's been through security and is marked as safe."

"My mother? How would she be able to get something to me without my father knowing?"

He shrugs. "Your mother is a much more capable woman than you think."

There is a knock at the door. Harry walks across, opens it, and takes the small blue box from the security guard.

"Thank you," he says, passing him a note of some denomination I can't see. "Merry Christmas." He brings the parcel to the kitchen counter, setting it down on the cool marble. I wander over and run my hand over the paper, then pluck the gift card from the box, turning it over. My eyes pop from my head as my stomach falls.

"That's not my mother's writing," I stammer. "That's Aiden's."

"Asshole," Harry mutters, furious. He takes the tag from my fingers and turns it over to read the message.

Merry Christmas, Princess

Harry pulls the paper from the box. Inside is a mug with the image of our 4D scan printed on the side. But it's the words that make me run to the toilet to wretch up my breakfast.

Daddy can't wait to meet you, Baby Marley.

CHAPTER THIRTY

The Level Boardroom

Harrison

Violet holds on to me as if her life depends on it. She's sitting on my lap in the boardroom as everyone arrives, her head buried in my neck, tears still streaming down her face. She wouldn't stay in the apartment by herself, and there was no one here to help with Mrs. D. being away. So, she came with me. I don't like to conduct business in my home if I can avoid it. It's important that I have somewhere safe, away from the dark. A place the lights are always on.

"Merry fucking Christmas," Russell barks as he strides in, but stops dead when he sees us. "Violet, what happened?" He all but runs around the table and crouches down beside his sister. His eyes dart over her frantically, trying to detect the issue. It's the most vulnerable I've ever seen him. "Violet, is the baby okay?" he says, again, "speak to me please."

"Both Violet and her baby are fine," I reassure him.

His focus moves to me. "Has that bastard got something to do with this?" he snarls, and I nod. With one knowing look, the strain between us vanishes. We come together in silent solidarity to seek vengeance for the devastated woman in my arms. A woman we both love and have cared about for decades. Violet may be the catalyst we need to heal our broken friendship. She may not only bring me love but also return me my best friend.

Connor appears with Marshall and Hunter. He scans the room, and his eyebrows draw together when they land on the scene surrounding me. "No Damon?" he asks.

"Christmas day and he has a daughter," I answer. "He's going to call in."

The three men sit down, but Russell remains on his knees at his sister's side, reassuring her that whatever is wrong, between us all, we will fix it. She isn't going to get hurt. We will all work together, as a team.

Violet's crying calms, her body relaxing against mine. She doesn't look at anyone. Russell pulls a seat up next to her and sits down. Everyone's focus lands on me, waiting for an explanation as to why I called an emergency meeting here on Christmas day. As Violet had run from the room, dropping and smashing the mug on the floor, I'd pulled out my phone and hit SOS.

"Violet received a package this morning," I say. "Delivered here."

"How the fuck did it get to her?" Connor snaps, his expression switching from curious to furious in an instant. "Someone will be getting fired."

"It was a safe package," I reply. "The security team scanned it."

"You brought us here to tell us that? That Violet got a present." He rolls his eyes then glances at the men either side of him. "Come on boys, we'll get back to our beers."

"Have you and Russell swapped personalities today or something? Don't be so bloody stupid. If you would listen instead of interrupting, I'd tell you." The phone rings, I accept the call, and Damon appears on the screen attached to the wall.

"Merry Christmas," he says, a smile clear on his face. The delighted squeals of a woman and young child are audible in the background. "To what do I owe the pleasure?"

"A package was delivered here today for Violet, supposedly from her mother. It wasn't, it was from Marley." They all fall silent. "He's laying claim to our baby as the biological father."

"What was the gift?" Marshall asks. The men look between each other.

"A mug."

"A mug?" Connor repeats. "You dragged us in here for a mug? Come on, I know you two are in the first throes of love, but for fuck's sake could this not have waited until tomorrow."

Fuck, he has a bad attitude today. I wonder what's aggravated him.

"It had our 4D scan picture printed on it. That picture hasn't been shared anywhere electronically. The only copies we have are the hard copies we were given at the hospital," I tell him. I widen my eyes to emphasize my next point. "So, he's either managed to hack Violet's medical information, or been close enough to get a copy of the actual document."

"Shit," Russell mumbles. He reaches over and strokes Violet's back gently. "We've got you, Sis," he says, and her eyes flick to him. She holds his gaze warily. He's not exactly been the dependable big brother since she returned. He makes her nervous, he always has. She wriggles in my lap and sits up before standing and moving to her older brother. Her arms surround Russell's neck, and surprise flits across his face with her display of affection.

"Thank you," she says softly, and he smiles. "I love you, my brother." After releasing him, she turns back to me. "I'll go home. You will all have a lot to talk about. Probably things I won't want to hear."

"Probably not," I reply, trying to give her an encouraging smile which is difficult with the fury running through me now. If Aiden Marley was in this room, he wouldn't be walking out of it. "I'll walk you back."

"No need," she says, waving me away. "It's only across the hall."

"I'll go with you," Russell interjects. "You stay here, Waite. I want to see my little sister to her new home safely." I nod, accepting he wants to do this. That the gesture is him trying to start making amends. He rises and places a hand on her back, then guides her out of the room.

"Home?" Connor says as the door closes behind them.

"Yes, home," I reply simply. "Violet moved in permanently a few days ago."

A smile plays on his lips. "Good," is all he says.

"Has your evil twin disappeared now?" I ask him. "Fuck, you were an ass when you arrived."

He laughs then shrugs. "You interrupted my Christmas morning. I haven't even opened my presents yet."

Deciding that I don't want to know what is under Connor's Christmas tree, I change the subject. "I want to dispose of Marley," I state, "permanently." My words are clear and direct. "He is a complication Violet doesn't need around her. After everything he's done, it would be better if he didn't walk on this earth."

"That can be arranged," Hunter says, his face splitting into a grin. "What a start to the new year, offing a bastard like that. I may want to do it personally. It would be such good fun. I would make it slow and painful." He taps his lips. "I've always wanted to skin someone alive. He could be the ideal candidate."

"I don't think we can afford to finish him yet," Marshall interrupts. "He's high up the chain in the drug business, if not right at the top. I hate to say it, but I think he could be our link.

If we follow him, we'll find the man in charge, whoever he is. And the fact he reached out to Violet makes him vulnerable. He's more likely to give us an opportunity than someone who is hidden in the shadows."

"There was some new information that came in this morning," Hunter says. "There's going to be a drop tomorrow at a warehouse on the river at Dartford. This shipment is going to a gang in Glasgow. Joel Parker was told about it, and he called me, wanted to give us the heads up."

"How would he know?" Damon asks, his eyebrows drawing together. "I didn't think Parker dealt drugs?"

"He doesn't. But the man has more informants than the fucking MI5. If it is a gang, a mob, or a women's knitting circle, someone will be feeding intelligence back to him. He's fond of double agents." Hunter chuckles. "That sounded very James Bond, didn't it?" He lifts his hands and creates a fake gun before pretending to shoot Marshall, then blows the imaginary smoke on top of it. "But Parker is always good for information. He knows I've been wanting to shut this down; he was happy to pass it along. Plus, he owed me."

"Are you going expand on that? He owed you what?" Connor questions. "Chocolate coins? A new knife? A fucking brain?"

"The most valuable thing known to man," Hunter says with a smirk. "Information." He claps his hands together in obvious excitement. "And I put a couple of traitors who were stealing from him to everlasting sleep too." He lifts a finger and draws it across his throat. "It was a beautiful thing—they bled out and passed away peacefully surrounded by the boxes of liquor they had been light-fingered with."

"Why do I not believe that it was peaceful?" I mutter, and he grins wickedly. Clearly pleased with the memory my words provoke.

"There were a few minutes of high-pitched screaming when I poured some of the said liquor into the slices I made." He shrugs. "But it was beautiful. Art."

"You're a sick fuck," I tell him.

"But you love me," he replies, standing then jumping across the glass boardroom table and landing beside me. He leans down and kisses my cheek. "Don't reject me now you've got your own pussy, Harry." His hands move to his heart, and he flutters his eyelashes dramatically. "Even if you don't realize it, you will always be my one."

"Fuck off, you absolute psycho." He throws his head back and cackles, then returns to his seat the way he came, the glass vibrating beneath his heavy boots. The door opens, and Russell walks back in. "How is she?" I ask him.

"Settled. She's on the couch, wrapped in a blanket, watching some terrible dating show."

"Yeah, she likes that sort of thing," I say. "Anything with terribly tanned bodies, fake dating, and more ass on show than necessary. It's on my television every bloody night."

"My sister has managed to pussy whip you already," he jibes. "If she can do that at seven months pregnant, imagine what you'll doing for her when she's back to full working order. You'll be feeding her fucking grapes while fanning her with a palm leaf."

"Russ, I'd crawl across hot coals naked while the devil himself whipped me for her." The brothers glance at each other. "This is not a short-term thing. I love the bones of her and the child she's carrying. We are creating a family. A home. A life. Violet is my future. My eternity."

"Looks like I'm not getting rid of you, Waite," he replies with an eyeroll. "She chose you."

"She did."

"Well, consider this your warning. Fuck over my sister, and they'll find you floating in the river." He narrows his eyes. "Blood is always thicker than water."

"Oh, pipe the fuck down," Connor mutters. "Sometimes I think you've grown up, then you go all caveman. Waite has had Violet's back over the years more than we have. I'm happy about it. She could do a lot worse."

"Thanks...I think." I give him a skeptical look.

"You know what I mean—her last attempt at a lasting relationship was with a married man she didn't even know was married."

"You're right," Russell agrees. "Her benchmark is set pretty low." They both laugh out loud. Bastards.

Marshall, Hunter, and Damon do not get involved in the conversation. In all honesty, I forgot they were even here, lis-

319

tening. Damon clearing his throat moves my eyes to the screen. When he realizes he has my attention, he speaks.

"As heartwarming as it is to see you all agreeing and getting along for once, some of us do have family Christmases to get back to. Could we decide on a plan?"

"We need to be at this deal going down tomorrow. If Marley appears, we know he's the connection that will lead us to the main man, possibly Edward Chase. The informant was adamant Marley will be onsite tomorrow. It's his drop, and it's at the client's request," Marshall tells us, straightening in his chair.

"Imagine the chaos we could cause," Hunter says, twisting his hands together. "It's tempting to try to get our hands on the goods."

"Are we saying we'll try to intercept the shipment?" I ask.

"Yes," Damon says. "If he loses the shipment, it will help force those higher up out to do the next one. Once a man loses a few million pounds worth of stock, they suddenly lose their dependability. They may even do us a favor and take him out for us."

"What about his message to Violet?" Marshall adds. "Because that's what it is, a warning, that he knows the baby is his and he'll be coming for them."

"If he's the child's biological father, does he not have rights?" Damon says.

"He gave up his fucking rights the minute he pinned Violet to the wall by her throat," I snarl, and they all murmur in agreement. "We need to end him."

"Not yet," Connor says. "We don't know enough about him and how he's connected. Him being the father could be to our benefit; it gives him a reason to hang around. He might slip up."

"We are not using Violet and my baby as fucking bait," I roar, losing control. They all gape at me as I slam both hands on the table. Connor who was standing by the window walks over to me. He leans in close so we are nose to nose, his shrewd eyes assessing me.

"Your baby?" he says, raising an eyebrow.

"Of course it is. I'm the man who's here. I'm the man wrapping my arms around her and feeling tiny legs kicking through her flesh. Marley is nothing but a fucking sperm donor. Violet and the child she carries are mine."

"That gives me an idea," he says, withdrawing and walking back over to the window.

"Care to share it with the rest of us?" Russell snaps.

"You marry her."

"What?" Russell shouts. "No fucking way. They've only just gotten together. The last thing my sister needs..." He trails off when he sees Connor's expression.

"You don't know what our sister needs," he replies firmly with emphasis on the word *our*. "If you could wind that short memory of yours back a few months, you may remember wanting to throw her out on the street when she appeared here."

"We had been lied to," he argues. "Father told us she knew he was married. That her running to Chicago had been planned. The pain she caused Mother...I couldn't forgive her for it."

"A discussion with Father may be a good idea," Connor says, going off topic. "If I call him, talk to him about Violet and the baby. Tell him about Aiden getting in touch, he may allude to how involved he is with him. What their plans are now."

"Can we rewind please?" Damon says. "Marriage?"

"Yes," Connor replies, pulling out his phone and typing something. "Here it is. According to UK government website, a man can be registered on the child's birth certificate if he is married to the mother either at the time of conception or birth." He glances my way. "I propose you marry my sister before my nephew or niece enters this world. You list yourself as the father and Aiden will need to fight in court to claim any rights."

"It does make sense," Hunter says, twirling his knife between his fingers as he always does.

"Do you think she'll go for it?" Russell asks, and I shrug.

"There's only one way to find out."

CHAPTER THIRTY-ONE

Harrison and Violet's
Apartment, The Level

Harrison

"Harrison, never give yourself to anyone completely. Don't sign your life away. People can never be trusted fully. Once you give them your soul, they are free to use you as they please." My mother's words circle in my head. I may only have been eight when she said them, but I remember them word for word. *"Love, but don't submit. Always be the one prepared to walk away."*

We had been sitting in the kitchen one morning. It was only a few days before her death. I'd been eating the crumbs from the bottom of the cereal packet while she sipped an Oxo cube dissolved in hot water. Things in the house were getting more volatile by the day. I noticed the ladies had more bruises, normally around their eyes or on their arms. When we tried to sleep in the living room, us kids all huddled together, it was more difficult as the screams were getting louder. It was a terrifying place to grow up. I do wonder what happened to the others. I can't even remember their names now.

Last year, for the first time, I researched my past. My mother. Who she was, where she came from, and how we ended up living in a whore house. My birth certificate has no father listed, not that it was a surprise; she probably didn't even know herself. I remember asking who he was and if I would ever meet him. She would talk my queries away without ever answering the actual question.

"He isn't important."

"We only need each other."

"You don't have a father; you were a miracle. A beautiful result out of intense pain."

Then I found the marriage certificate. She had been married to a man called Waite. Jeffery Waite. The man who owned the whore house. The man who bundled me into his car wrapped in a blanket and threw me into a ditch. The man who teased me with chocolate and would watch me go hungry. He had stood in front of her, promising to love her, honor her, until death took one of them away. He did none of it.

***

I returned to my apartment an hour ago. Violet was curled on the sofa under a duvet, fast asleep. She looked so peaceful; I didn't want to disturb her. So, I've retreated to my office to contemplate what happens next. It was agreed that marrying her was the sensible decision. It would put another layer of protection between that maniac and us. It would give me parental rights over our baby. It would give me standing as their father. We would be a unit, not only in emotion but legally, tied together until one of us undid the knot.

I pull the copy of my mother's marriage certificate from my drawer. The phone number of the prison her husband is held in is written along the top. I've never called it. Even though visiting him has crossed my mind, there was never a true reason to.

Now, I feel there is. I need to understand how you can be married to someone then put them to work for you. Allow other men to have their pleasure with them. The thought makes my skin crawl like it always does.

After I pull my phone from my pocket, my finger rolls the contacts until I find the number of the prison governor. I know him well. Many of my clients have been held in custody here over the years. I've visited dozens of times in the past twelve months, always ignoring the fact that he was there too. But with the rapidly changing situation I'm in, he's the only person I know alive who can tell me more about my mother and her tragic life. These are questions I need answered before I can commit to Violet fully and propose we join together forever by signing on the dotted line.

The phone rings, and he answers on the first ring.

"You do know it's Christmas day?" he says in a jovial tone. "I know we get on, Waite, but this is a bit overfamiliar, don't you think?" He belly-laughs, then coughs into the handset. I automatically move it from my ear.

"I need to see a prisoner in your custody today," I tell him, not bothering with pleasantries.

"Today? Surely, it can wait. It's their Christmas lunch today. There is a lot of excitement, I can tell you. You're allowed to take a day off."

"This is a personal matter," I say firmly. "And due to the circumstances, I need to speak with him urgently."

He sighs, knowing I won't back down. "What is the prisoner's name?"

"Jeffery Waite. He was married to my mother. And I need answers."

***

HMP Belmarsh holds some of the most dangerous criminals detained in the United Kingdom. It houses murderers, rapists, drug dealers and thieves. The entrance to the building is relatively inconspicuous, being built in clean red brick, but inside the atmosphere is one of unrest. After checking in and going through the necessary procedures, I am escorted to a visiting room. It's a simple white space with high windows, a stainless-steel table, and four red plastic chairs surrounding it.

The man I'm visiting is already waiting for me. He's older now—the past twenty years haven't been kind to him. Most of his hair is gone, and he's withered to a man half the size I remember. But then again, I was a small boy the last time I saw him. His eyes, though, are the same. The same evil glint flashes from them as I look at him. The same nasty smile plays on his lips, the way it did as he ate that bar of chocolate while I licked the remnants of food from his plate.

He sits on his chair, leaning back with his legs spread wide. His wrists are secured with handcuffs in front of him. The steel gray sweatpants and sweatshirt he wears are standard. Every man I've visited wears them. Here, you are a number. A blended sea of the most deplorable individuals in our society.

"Well, boy," he says. "I never expected to see you again." He sits up straighter in his chair. "Come and sit down. Your old man wants to hear everything you've been up to."

Without speaking, I walk over and pull out the chair opposite him, then lower myself into the seat. The welcome he's given me has confirmed my worst fear. This man is my father. I suspected as much. The marriage certificate was dated nine months before my birth. I'd been conceived when they were newly married.

"You were married to my mother," I state.

His mouth splits into a wide grin. "That I was."

"Why did you marry her?"

"She was a good fuck." He shrugs. "If you're not married already, I suggest you choose a wife with a tight cunt." I ignore him.

"According to your records, you're detained here at Belmarsh on various offenses including slavery charges. You've been incarcerated for ten years now with no hope of ever seeing the outside again."

"So they say, but my lawyer is shit. I need a better defense lawyer. Know of any?" he says with a wink. "You've made quite a name for yourself in here, but I hear you cost a pretty penny. Fancy doing your dad a favor and taking a look at my file, see if there's a technicality you can get me off on?"

"You will never be my father," I growl.

"Oh, but I am, Harrison. It was my spunk that shot up inside your mother and created you. When you look in the mirror, you will see me staring back at you. You are a reflection of me, moving in a dark world, dressed up in an expensive suit. I've followed your career. Impressive. It was a good move to get involved with Edward Chase. He has every connection you'll ever need."

"I was eight," I hiss, furious. "It wasn't a planned encounter. His sons found me lying where you left me. Where I've ended up is the result of unconnected events spiraling out of control and throwing me down a dark path. You being the fucking instigator of it."

He chuckles then leans forward, holding my stare. "Ask whatever you came here to ask, then fuck off," he says. "To come and visit me on Christmas day, it must be important. Go on, tell Daddy what's bothering you."

"You are not my father," I repeat.

"Stop using my name then, Harrison Waite."

"That was my mother's name," I spit back. "I want to know why. Why you married her? How she ended up as a working girl under your instruction, and if that was always the plan? Why I never had a fucking family or childhood because of you, you bastard."

His eyes run over my face, considering what to say and how to react.

"No, it wasn't the plan," he says simply. "Your mother and I were in love. She fell pregnant on our wedding night, the first time we had sex. It was a shock. We were young and didn't have the means to start a family. We needed extra cash."

"So, you fucking pimped her out?"

"I got talking to a guy in a bar," he says casually. "Yet again, our rent wasn't paid and we were spending every fucking penny on baby milk." He chuckles. "You were an expensive little shit." He readjusts himself in his seat then touches his crotch. "This guy told me his wife had started fucking men for money on the side. Between the mounting debt and lack of options, it seemed like a good idea."

"Could you not have found a job like a normal person?"

"I wasn't in the best place. Things were difficult...I owed people, dangerous people, some money and couldn't be seen in public." He lifts his joined hands and waves them to signal he's moving on. "Your mother wasn't overjoyed at the suggestion, but as the days passed and you screamed with hunger, she relented and gave in. It was a positive business decision, although it destroyed our marriage."

"A positive business decision?" When I arrived here, I had the intention of sucking this man for information. I'd thought that he could give me some sort of answer for the fuck-up that was my childhood. Now, I realize he means nothing to me. His opinions count for nothing. I couldn't be further from him in reality. His DNA may flow in my veins, but I'm nothing like him.

"Absolutely," he says, his eyebrows drawing together. "I made a fortune in pimping out pussy. Your mother started that. It was a worthwhile sacrifice." I stand abruptly. "Leaving so soon?"

"You are the scum of the earth. You not only sacrificed your wife but also your son. I see now, you are no part of me. I'm a million times the man you ever were. All I feel now for you is pity. Sadness that you have lived such an abominable life, and sympathy for my mother who never found the love she deserved." He smirks nastily. "Laugh if you want, but I'm the one walking out of the door. I'll not be dying alone in a prison cell. That's you."

CHAPTER
THIRTY-TWO

Harrison and Violet's
Apartment, The Level

Violet

"Where did you say he was?" I ask Russell. When I woke, I was surprised to find my brother sitting on the other sofa, his eyes glued to a soccer match playing on the huge television that dominates the living room.

"Out," he says, glancing at me then turning back to the screen.

"Where?"

"He'll tell you when he gets back. Now, go back to sleep and let me watch this." He lifts the beer in his hand to his lips and drinks greedily. "Yes!" he cheers, jumping from the seat. "Get in boys! Goal! Merry fuckin' Christmas!"

"Men," I mumble, pushing myself up to sit. My baby kicks furiously at the interruption to their relaxation. "Ouch, stop that. It hurts. Mummy is not happy with you." When I look up, my brother is watching me, a peculiar look on his face. "What is it?"

"It's good to have you back, Sis," he says, and my heart strains. "I'm glad you and Waite have managed to sort things out. I know I don't always act like I care, but I do."

"We're getting there. We have a lot to learn about each other. It's been a long time since we were teenagers." I run my hands through my hair in an attempt to calm the strands. "I hope the two of you will be able to be as close as you used to be. You and Harry were inseparable. What happened?"

He swallows visibly, then turns to face me. Seconds pass before he speaks—he's considering what to say. Or, perhaps, whether to tell me the truth. My mind strays, and I wonder if a woman was involved. Did one of them get the girl? Harry hasn't mentioned anyone of importance, but there have been women, I know that. Did my brother lose his best friend over one of them? It seems a plausible reason.

"I'm jealous of him," he admits, surprising me. "I've never been able to understand..." He looks away, dropping his eyes from mine. Color coats his cheeks, and he takes a deep steadying breath. The strong man, who rules his friends with an iron fist, disappears, and all I can see is my big brother, broken and confused.

"Understand what?" I prompt, standing then walking over to sit beside him. I take his giant hand between my two small ones. "You can talk to me, Russ. I'm your sister. I will listen."

"I never understood how he ended up a better man than me. It doesn't matter what he fucking touches, it works." He doesn't look at me, keeping his focus firmly on the floor. His skin flushes, glowing red at his throat and the top of his chest where his shirt sits open, embarrassment and discomfort visible at speaking about his insecurities.

"Not strictly true," I say, raising my eyebrows, and he glances up. "He failed to save me from that plane. Then he managed to get himself bound on the ground outside." He laughs, and so do I, the mood lightening. I return to being silent, leaving room for him to continue to talk if he wants to. My brother doesn't open up easily; this is a special moment that he chose me to speak to.

"When we all went to study law, I was a few years ahead. Being the oldest and in front is something I was used to." He inhales deeply, his large chest rising and falling. "Then we set up the firm. Harrison came into his own, winning cases that many more experienced lawyers had turned down. He made a name for himself. Clients flocked to us."

I look at my older brother, and my heart shatters. He was so used to being the man in charge. The winner. The best. My father applied unimaginable pressure growing up about his expectations of him, the grades he expected him to attain while complying fully with our father's demands. If there had been any bad behavior in our home, Russell took the brunt of the punishment whether he was guilty or not, always protecting both Connor and me.

Harrison had become a regular visitor to our home when he was sixteen. He was clever and charming. My mother smiled when he spoke, and my father praised his work ethic at the private school he attended, courtesy of our family. Even though they were close, I had seen annoyance flit across my older brother's face when my father bestowed his approval on Harry. It was something Russell rarely received. When he spoke to him, there was always the insinuation he could have done more, been more successful. Just more.

"I got angry," Russell says. "We fell out over a case that was his but I wanted." He rubs at his forehead, wiping away invisible sweat. "He relented and gave it to me. I lost. Our client went to jail, and it was my fault. I missed something."

"What happened then?" I cajole. This needs to be out in the open. Whatever is eating at him needs to be said out loud so he can let go of the resentment and hurt.

"Harry took over, found the technicality, and won on appeal."

"That would have been a kick in the teeth," I say, hoping to convey understanding and empathy. "I appreciate how difficult that would have been for you, Russ. I do, but I think your issue is with our father and his unfair expectations. His relentless control and demands. Harry was always gifted—he would never have come this far if he wasn't." He squeezes my fingers, acknowledging my statement. "But that doesn't make you any less of a man. His success isn't defamation of you; it should give you pride."

"What makes you say that?" he questions, and I smile at him.

"Without you, Harry might never have been found. He wouldn't have become the incredible man he is today. He would probably have never attended law school or had the life he does." He rewards me with a soft smile in understanding. "And I would never have found him. So, for that alone, brother, I thank you." I reach forward and wrap my arms around him. "Please sort this. He loves you like a brother. Don't let insecurities and our father ruin what is true friendship."

The apartment door opens, and Harry walks into the room. When I glance up, I see he's smiling. His eyes search for me, then focus, pinning me to my seat. My mouth dries. I can tell by looking at him he has plans for us. Something to celebrate. There is a quiet determination behind the smile; normally I see that when he has my legs spread with his head between them as he entices my body to let go and orgasm. My nipples hardened beneath the soft tank top I am wearing. He gives me a knowing look, then his attention moves to Russell who is walking toward him.

"Thank you for coming and sitting with Violet," he says, holding out his hand. Russell takes it firmly, shaking it, before pulling him into a bear hug. Harry's expression changes to momentarily stunned as the other man embraces him.

"I will do anything for my sister," Russell tells him. "I'm sorry for being an asshole these past few years. Your achievements are not grounds for me to be a dickhead."

Harry's mouth drops open slightly. His gaze runs over my brother's face—he's waiting for the catch. Russell releases him, standing straight and squaring his shoulders. "You have always been my brother. I love you like one. Did you find what you were looking for?" Harry nods. "You can fill me in later, once you've updated your girl."

My heart swells with my brother's acceptance of us. He glances at me and smiles, his eyes filled with genuine joy.

"Thank you," Harry replies simply.

"I'll be going. Merry Christmas, both of you." Russell moves back in my direction as I sit on the sofa, leaning down and embracing me. "Thank you, little Sis. You helped me see sense," he whispers in my ear. "I love you." Without another word, he leaves.

"Is there something you want to tell me?" I ask the beautiful man standing on the other side of the room.

"There are so many things I have to tell you and discuss with you, but right now, all I want to do is take you to bed." He strides over then offers me his hands. I take them and stand to meet him. "Would it be all right if we put this conversation on pause? Can I enjoy you first, then I'll tell you everything and what I want to suggest to limit Marley's ability to hurt you both?" He places both hands on my stomach then rests his forehead against mine. "Before things change, Violet, I want one more time like this."

"Before things change," I say, confused. The statement makes me nervous. "Do you have bad news for me? Tell me where you were, now, then we can go to bed. I won't relax until I know you won't leave me." His eyes are closed as he leans against me. I keep mine open, gazing up at him.

"I will never leave you through choice, Violet. For me to walk away, someone would have to drag me." He places a kiss on my forehead. "I went to Belmarsh Prison to visit my father," he confesses.

"Your father? He's alive?" The shock in my voice is evident.

"I suspected as much, but it was only confirmed today. He was the pimp who owned the whorehouse I grew up in. He worked his own wife."

"His wife?" I stammer.

"It's a long story. We can discuss it later."

"Answer me one thing—are you all right?"

"Yes," he says, opening his eyes and fixing them on me. "I discovered I was nothing like him. The fact his DNA flows in my veins doesn't define me. Family is what you make it." He leans down and kisses me gently on the tip of my nose. "I realized that where I came from isn't important. It's the man I am now that is." His hand rises, cupping my chin, and he runs his thumb over my bottom lip. "And from this day forward, you and this little bundle here will be my absolute focus. My life will be spent pleasing you. I adore you both more than I could ever show you."

My hands rise and wrap around his neck. He takes my mouth with his, kissing me hard enough to bruise my lips. When he withdraws, they sting a little. "You're mine, Violet," he growls. "You always fucking have been. Back when I took you for the first time in your bedroom, I knew it. That's what terrified me. Sliding inside you, our connection was undeniable."

"You said what we did was wrong," I mumble.

"Not wrong, but it wasn't how it should have been. I shouldn't have taken your virginity like that. It should have been special. We deserved the opportunity to try. It never came, and we captured the only opportunity we could."

"It was special," I tell him, "because it happened with you. And now we're starting a life together, we'll be navigating a lot of new challenges side by side."

"I thought we were going to bed first before the deep conversation started," he says with a smirk.

"Sorry," I mumble.

He slides a finger inside the neckline of my low-cut top, pushing downward so the material falls below my breasts, exposing me. He pinches my nipple between his fingers and twists gently. His eyes never leave mine, watching for every reaction to his touch. Warm, damp lips move to my neck as he continues his assault on my nipples with his fingers. His kisses are gentle, starting below my ear lobe and moving south. A moan escapes my lips.

"You like that?" he says, and I groan in response as he kisses my collarbone. His hands move to my sides, and he trails his fingers softly over the material of my top, up and down. My skin tingles under his touch, a familiar sensation appearing between my legs. "You're so sensitive," he whispers. "Your body reacts to mine on every level. I love feeling you tremble beneath my fingers."

"Make me shudder with those magic fingers," I say, and he chuckles. "Take me to the edge then push me over."

"Bedroom or couch?" His eyes fire as he asks.

My breathing hitches. "Couch." He nods in approval, then crouches and pulls my pajama shorts down my legs. I never even bothered getting dressed today. "Where do you want me?"

"Is on your hands and knees comfortable for you?"

"I'm sure I could manage that."

"Kneel on the sofa and place your hands on the armrest." He watches me get into position then moves beside me, tracing a single finger from the base of my neck down my spine to my ass. "Spread your knees wider," he orders. "Head down and close your eyes." I hear him move away.

"Where are you going?"

"You'll find out in a minute. Stay like that—it will be worth your while, I promise." There is the sound of doors opening and closing, then something being placed on the coffee table. The snap of leather being pulled from denim surprises me. I hear the belt hit the floor. When I take a peek, he's standing beside me wearing only his jeans, the button undone. "No looking," he scolds, slapping my ass hard. I snap my eyes closed but not before I see the bowl of ice cubes sitting on the table. Fuck, he has a plan. "Are you ready?"

"Yes," I whisper, breathless. My mind is whirling with the possible uses for an ice cube. He places three on my spine. One at my shoulder blades, one halfway down my back, then a final one just above my ass crack.

"You're going to hold that position, Violet, 'til they melt," he says. "I want you to focus on them dissolving slowly, running over your body. This one." His finger skims the skin at the lowest one. "Will seep down here." He runs the finger between my butt cheeks. "To here." His finger arrives at my pussy, and he touches my already wet lips. "If they fall before they've melted, I'll punish you. I want you to use the time to think how I'll make you feel tonight and how I'll make it happen." He moves to stand in front of me. "Eyes open, head up."

When I move my focus upward, I'm eye level with his crotch. He slides the jeans down his legs. He's not wearing any underwear. His cock hangs heavily in front of me. Bringing both his hands to my hair, he wraps the strands around his fingers then moves his hips toward me. "Open," he says. I comply, and he slides his cock into my mouth. "Remember, don't let those cubes fall." His thrusts are gentle to start with. I'm focused on the ice-cool trickles moving over my body while he pumps between my lips. With each thrust, my arousal heightens, then I feel the cube at my shoulders slide—it smashes on the floor.

"Oops," he says, withdrawing and walking to my side. He takes my hair once again in his hand, pulling my head backward. His other cracks off my backside unexpectedly. I wince, and the remaining ice cubes follow the first. "Bad girl," he growls, then slaps me again. "But fuck, you look good like this." One more blow hits my skin. "Did that hurt?"

"Yes, it stung," I stammer. He massages my backside with nimble fingers where he laid the blows.

"I owe you an apology then," he says, lying down on the sofa, lining his face up with my pussy. "Sit. Get those legs on either side of my face and sit the fuck down." I push myself up, nervous that he's underneath me at my current size. "Sit down," he growls, wrapping his arms around my thighs and pulling me onto his tongue. He licks at my clit; on instinct I move, enjoying the buzz building, needing the friction. He tightens his grip, encouraging me lower, then slips his tongue inside, running it around my entrance.

"Fuck me, Violet. Let those perfect juices flow into my mouth. I want to drink you down. I'm a thirsty man." I flex my hips harder, and his mouth eats urgently, wanting to savor every last mouthful. His tongue returns to my clit, and he pushes hard. I let go and give him what he wants. Me. My orgasm surges, my whole body trembling with pressure then the delicious release.

After, we lie in each other arms, wrapped in a blanket on the sofa. He's behind me, one hand protectively on my stomach. He props himself up on his other elbow and looks down at me.

"There's something we need to talk about," he says, and I glance at him. "Marley has made it clear he intends to make contact when our baby is born." My heart sinks. After a wonderful few hours, the issues still need to be discussed. "We need to block any claim he has as best we can. How do you feel about getting married?"

CHAPTER
THIRTY-THREE

Harrison and Violet's
Apartment, The Level

Harrison

"Married?" she stammers, and her mouth drops open. "You want to get married?"

"No," I answer on impulse.

She frowns.

"Well yes, I do, but a shotgun wedding wouldn't be my choice." I pinch my nose between my fingers. "Fuck, this is coming out all wrong."

"You think? Suggesting marriage then telling me you don't want to. Get your shit in order. I've got fucking whiplash." She turns away from me and stares at the opposite side of the room. I place my hand on her shoulder, unsure what to do. Her mood has flipped from blissfully satisfied and content to openly furious.

"Violet, I do want to marry you." She sniffs loudly. "But what I'm about to suggest isn't the way I would want to do it. This is about protecting our child from Marley." She doesn't respond, but I know she's listening. "Under UK law, a man can be listed on a birth certificate if they are married to the mother at the time of conception or birth." I pause to let her process what I've said. "If we get married before you give birth, I can be put on the document. It will give me parental rights, and Marley would have to challenge us in court."

"Harry, I'm due in a matter of weeks. How is this even possible?"

"We have to give twenty-eight days' notice before we can obtain our marriage license. Do you think you would be able to hold on until then?"

"I'll schedule the birth with the baby, shall I?" she snaps, then bursts into tears. "It doesn't work like that."

"It needs to if we want to put this roadblock in Marley's way. We can plan toward this. If you go into labor before we do the paperwork, then once we're married, I can apply for parental rights. But that gives him time to challenge us. It would be better this way." My attempt to console her backfires dramatically. She wriggles from my grasp and pushes herself up to stand, rocking back slightly on her heels as she loses her balance. "Violet, we need to talk about this."

She whirls to face me. Still naked from the waist down, she pulls her top up over her plump breasts. "Fucking sort the paperwork, the documents, and your rights," she hisses, pushing her hair out her face. "I'll sign whatever you need me to." Without picking up her shorts, she walks off in the direction of our bedroom. I watch her bare ass disappear in disbelief, at a loss with what the issue could be. The door slams closed, and the pictures vibrate on the walls of the apartment. I go to shout at her to be careful, then promptly close my mouth, not wanting to provoke another reaction.

When I glance at my watch, it tells me the time is ten o'clock. Needing advice, I call the only person that I can have an honest conversation with—my only friend who has had a real relationship and a wife. Damon answers on the second ring. "Please don't tell me you have another bloody emergency. We are sitting down to a glass of wine after getting the little one to bed," he says. "My Christmas is only just beginning." His nanny giggles in the background.

"I've fucked up, but I'm not sure how." He sighs. I hear his chair scrape across the floor. "I told Violet about the idea of getting married."

"Okay, and what did she say?"

"She asked me if I wanted to. I said no, this wasn't my ideal way to commit to someone forever."

"Please tell me you didn't use the word someone." He groans, obviously thinking I'm an idiot.

"No, I didn't. I told her that we need to give twenty-eight days' notice, so she can't have the baby until the end of January at the earliest, which is close to her due date. We need to get the paperwork in order."

He laughs, then coughs as if his drink has gone down the wrong way. "No wonder she's pissed at you," he says, still chuckling. "I thought you were a smart bastard who was good with women. Can you not see where you went wrong?" I don't answer him, pissed off that he thinks I messed up and have no idea what to suggest as my error. I was being honest. "Waite, you proposed marriage then talked about the bloody paperwork. Never mind the fact you advised she should hold the baby in. Let's not even mention the comment about not wanting to marry her."

"Shit..." Reality dawns on me hard. "I was trying to be proactive."

"Proactive isn't a key requirement in a proposal. Whether this is a shotgun wedding or not, Violet will still want to feel like you're marrying her because you love her. It would be different if it was purely transactional, but it's not. You've been playing the daddy card for weeks. It's time to step up and show her you mean it." He pauses, then sniggers. "Put a ring on it, as it were. You better go do some groveling."

"Suppose I'll have to," I mutter. "Thanks, mate, have a good night."

"Oh, I will," he replies and disconnects the call.

I wander down to our bedroom. Violet is already in bed with the duvet wrapped around her. When I approach, she's sleeping soundly. Tear marks stain her eyes. Guilt bubbles in my stomach. I did this to her with my own stupidity. Not wanting to wake her, I return to the kitchen and take another beer, then settle myself on a bar stool with my laptop to come up with a plan of how I can make amends.

***

Violet

I'm woken by music playing along the hallway. It's soft and melodic, nothing like the techno crap Harry usually plays. Blinking my eyes open, daylight seeps through the crack in the window blinds. The clock tells me it's eleven in the morning. Hell, I must have needed sleep. I don't remember Harry coming to bed. I'm not even sure if he did after our argument. It wasn't much of a quarrel; it was more of a temper tantrum on my part. Thinking back now, I was being a little irrational, but I'd never admit that to him.

We are going to get married but not because we've chosen to. It's a necessary procedure we need to go through to try to ensure the safety of our child, of the baby growing in my belly. The detail stings. Harry is marrying me now because he thinks it's the right thing to do. The accelerator on our life plans is firmly on the floor, and we're moving fast, potentially before either of us is ready to.

The music increases in volume. I extricate myself from the bed and wrap Harry's huge white bathrobe around me before going off in search of him. When I reach the living room, the blinds are down, and soft light from candles flickers around the room. There are vases of flowers scattered around the space. Roses. Red roses. Dozens of them if not hundreds.

I can't see him. Where is he?

"Marry me." His strong voice says from behind me. I turn around, and he's down on one knee with a ring box open, displaying the most stunning solitaire diamond ring. "Violet Chase, make me the happiest man on this planet and agree to be my wife."

I gasp in shock; this is completely unexpected. I was ready for round two of our debate. "Not because of anything other than my love for you. Because you and I were meant to be together from day one." Those eyes that melt my panties fix fast and take hold. My heart pounds in my chest. "The past fourteen years should never have happened the way they did. The universe has brought us together now because we were always meant to be us. We need to take this chance."

I gape at him, then my eyes drop to my toes as I register my ragged appearance. This is not the outfit or situation I ever imagined getting engaged in. When I woke this morning, I never thought I'd see Harrison Waite down on his knee with a ring ever.

"How did you organize all this? The day after Christmas," I say, glancing around the room, still in shock at the setting. It's an effing holiday, and he's somehow managed to procure a room full of flowers, a million scented candles, and a kickass diamond ring. The situation is impossible to comprehend.

"I know people. It doesn't matter. Marry me."

CHAPTER
THIRTY-FOUR

An Abandoned
Warehouse, Dartford

Harrison

"She said yes," I tell Damon as he sits beside me in the car. It's the middle of the night, and we are sitting opposite an industrial unit where the supposed exchange will be taking place. There is no sign of life, not even a light in the parking lot.

"I'd be disappointed if she didn't," he replies. "After your piss poor attempt, that was certainly a statement you made." He chuckles. "How much did the ring cost you?"

"Don't ask," I grumble. "Let's just say there was a high out-of-hours fee on both the ring and the flowers. Neither of the business owners were happy about being interrupted at midnight on Christmas night. I had to pay them handsomely for the privilege."

"It'll be worth it when you get the paperwork in order," he says with a wink. "I still can't believe you proposed using legalities as a reason. Connie would have killed me if I'd done that. She'd probably never have married me." He pauses, his thoughts clearly moving to his late wife. He's happier now, but there are times I know he still misses her. He always will, no matter how much life moves on. She was always taken from him. It was never a choice.

"Not my best idea," I agree, "but I seem to have salvaged the situation, luckily."

"So, what's the plan? When will the big day be?"

"We can give notice on the fourth of January, I can't get an appointment before then with it being the holidays. We need to wait twenty-eight days before the ceremony. I'll book the registrar for the 1st of February and pray she doesn't pop this baby out before then." I roll my eyes. "Knowing my luck, she'll have them the day before."

"Well, at least you only have to deal with a bridezilla for a few weeks. The months that led up to my wedding were torture—every detail was checked, double-checked then cross-checked on a spreadsheet." He runs his hand through his hair, smiling to himself. "Twice."

"Hopefully Violet will be too busy finishing cooking our baby to bother too much," I say.

"Don't be so sure. Weddings and women are intense subjects, especially when it's theirs being organized. I bet you one hundred quid that she will have your coffee table filled with wedding magazines within the week." He grins, raises an eyebrow, and holds out his hand. "Fancy a small wager?"

"Let's make it interesting," I reply, taking his hand. "Make it a grand."

"Careful, you have a wedding to pay for."

My cell rings, breaking the conversation. Marshall's voice fills the car. "I'm not liking this, boys," he says. "Something is off. Perhaps they've been spooked."

"Stop being such a negative bastard," Hunter chides. "They'll be here. Our information is good." At that moment, a small red car pulls into the parking lot of the unit we're watching. My phone rings again—it's Russell. I add him to my current call.

"We're all on the line," I tell them.

"Is this some sort of joke?" Russell snaps. "A big drug deal going down using a *Fiesta*. What sort of bloody gang is this?"

Damon snorts beside me and shakes his head. "Not every drug lord drives a Rolls Royce," he says, "I've been on plenty of stakeouts to know that the most inconspicuous cars work best."

"That's not a car," he says, annoyed by Damon's challenge. "It's a fucking go-kart."

"It looks like only one person is inside," I say, trying to get our *focus* back on the unfolding events. A man steps out of the tiny vehicle and closes the door. He's dressed all in black with his hood up; it's impossible to see who he is. He hides the key on top of the rear tire then walks away behind the building. There's an underpass on the other side of the industrial estate.

"We'll place a tracker on the car then follow him," Connor says. There is the sound of opening and closing car doors. "Keep us updated. I'll stay on the line." We watch as Connor appears from an alleyway to the right of the unit. I only know it's him as the reflective band we all agreed to wear, in case of a gunfight, wraps around his dark sleeve. He pauses in the shadows then runs across to the small red car and bends down, placing a tracker under the back bumper. He disappears in the direction he came from.

"Tracker in place," he says. "Russell, do you still have eyes on the driver?"

"Sure do," he replies. "He's heading for the river. I'll meet you at the rickety old bridge unless he diverts off course." Connor grunts acknowledgment then the only sound on the line is their breathing as they both run.

We continue to observe the deserted industrial unit for ten minutes—no movement, nothing.

Finally, two large black vans with their lights off drive past the parked car. They slow slightly but don't stop. They circle the streets for ten minutes, passing the little vehicle countless times. On what must be their tenth drive-by, the van at the back stops and a tall lean man climbs out. He walks across to the small car and retrieves the key as his partners drive off without waiting.

"Are you up for partaking in some car theft? With only one man, we can intercept," Damon says. He raises his eyebrows. "I know you fancy yourself as a secret agent. I'll even let you drive."

"We're going in," I tell the men listening on, excitement coursing through my veins. I've always wanted to pretend I'm in the *Fast and The Furious* movies, though I'd have preferred better wheels. "If we get the car, we can drive it to Damon's garage, strip it down there, and see what we find."

"Okay," they respond in unison.

Damon and I climb out of the car. There is an eerie silence; nothing is moving or calling into the night. My eyes scan the area, constantly looking for additional threats. We creep toward the man who is leaning into the driver's side of the vehicle. He doesn't see us approach until Damon has his gun trained on the back of his head. Damon's captive automatically throws his hands into the air.

"Name," Damon barks. When the man doesn't respond, he pokes at his head with the gun. "Name."

"Logan," he replies, surprisingly relaxed at having a gun trained on him.

"Who do you work for?"

"No one," he sneers. He is half in and half out of the car, one foot still on the concrete outside. He hasn't sat down on the driver's seat.

"Okay, Logan. If you want to play that game, can you tell me why you are collecting this particular car this evening?"

"I like to joyride. This one seemed like an easy catch," he says, his face contorting into a dark smile. I stand behind Damon watching Logan's reactions through the back window with my fingers resting on the gun at my belt. "It's not as if there is any value to it. No one would miss this piece of crap." He turns, looks over his shoulder and raises his eyebrows then waggles them. Damon responds by dropping the nose of the gun to his lips.

"Open," he orders. "It will be less messy when I blow your head off."

"A bit dramatic, don't you think?" Logan waves his hands, shrugs his shoulders, and moves to step out of the vehicle. "Here. If you want this little rust bucket so bad, have it."

"Don't fucking move." Logan stops immediately and glares at his opponent through narrowed eyes. "Who were the men in the black vans?"

"My..." he pauses, "partners in a joyriding club." I roll my eyes in frustration. This guy is a jerk. "We cruise around, find abandoned cars, race the streets then dump them."

Damon looks from Logan to me. "What do you think, Waite?"

"This seems too easy," I say, my confidence wavering. "It can't be this simple. One man to stop us stealing a load of heroin."

"Sometimes it is," Damon replies. "With fewer men involved, it's easier to move goods quietly." I accept his justification, but it doesn't make me feel any better. "It could be a decoy, but that's unlikely with the source of the information," he adds. "And with no contradictory location mentioned, I wouldn't think so."

Logan sighs audibly, bored. Damon lifts the gun and cracks him hard over the head with the butt. His victim falls to the ground unconscious. I grab his feet and pull him out of the way so he's lying ten feet from the car—close enough to catch if he runs but far enough away to not attack us from below.

We both stare at the vehicle—it's old. Rust coats the wheel arches and extends up the trunk. The front windshield is cracked across the center. The material of every seat is stained with age and ripped open, exposing the yellowed stuffing.

"Classy," I mutter. "My first heist and I get a shit-mobile." Damon chuckles and moves to the side to let me pass. I sit down in the driver's seat and turn the key in the ignition. "Why would he steal it if they didn't know what was in it?"

"He knew," Damon replies. "They always use their most disposable gang member for these things. Someone who won't be missed."

"Shall we wait to get it back to the garage to search it?"

Damon nods.

When I close the door, it squeals with pain as the parking area explodes with light, all the seemingly inert streetlamps coming on at once. Damon raises his gun as the front door of the unit opens and Aiden steps out. His lips are twisted into a smug smile.

"That was easier than I thought," he says. I reopen the door, but he holds his hand up. "I wouldn't do that if I was you. You're sitting on a pressure pad. Take the weight off it and..." He creates fireworks with his fingers. "Boom. No more Harrison Waite." He shoves his hands in his pockets and shrugs. Now, I best be going. I have some drugs to deliver." We watch him walk off, our jaws on the floor. We've been set up and, like fucking idiots, walked straight into the trap.

"Waite, do not move," Hunter barks down the line. "Drive to the disused warehouse on the river."

"Will the fucker not just blow up?" I snarl, panicked.

"Unlikely," Hunter says, but his tone doesn't emanate confidence. "Do you remember? Where we extracted some information from that pretty boy. Oh, that was a brilliant night."

"Yes," I reply, unable to say much more and ignoring his idiotic comment. The scenario plays out in my mind—me getting blown to smithereens. Pieces of me splattered all over the parking lot mixed with twisted metal. My first thought is Violet and our baby. Without me, she'll be more exposed, more vulnerable to him. "Russ," I say, sheer terror I haven't experienced since a child consumes my body. "If the worst happens, make sure that bastard never gets near them. Keep them safe."

"We've got you, brother," he replies firmly. *Brother*. At least if these are my last minutes on earth, I'll leave knowing we've fixed our relationship. "Meet us at the warehouse. We'll get you out of there, and you can look after them yourself."

Every mile takes an eternity. The heap of junk I'm driving moves at a painfully slow speed. "Don't overdo it," Hunter says—he's coaching me as we drive. If I get out of this alive, I will never attend a sting again. I'll be staying firmly behind my desk and becoming a pen pusher. "Keep the pressure on the pedal constant. When you get to your destination, do not switch the car off. Put it in neutral and park on a flat piece of land so you don't need to apply the handbrake. Limit all movement. We don't know how sensitive that pad is." My eyes are trained on the road in front of me. My heart beats so hard it could break my ribs. "Answer me," he barks.

"Yes, I understand," I snap. Damon is following behind in his *Focus*. He stays fifty or so meters away, keeping a safe distance from the effing bomb I'm driving. You couldn't make this shit up.

"It's polite to reply," Hunter says with a chuckle.

"Manners are not exactly top of my priority list," I bark back.

"For a privately educated man, Waite, your attitude leaves a lot to be desired." Hunter snorts with laughter. I scowl at him though he doesn't know it. Nothing about this situation is fucking funny.

"If I get out of this..."

"When you do," he interjects.

"I'm going to kick your ass."

"That I can't wait to see," he replies. "I look forward to it."

The warehouse comes into view. I drive toward it; the gates are already pinned open for me. My friend's cars are parked to one side along with a few other dark vehicles I don't recognize. The group of men stands in the center of the vast space, and Connor lifts his hand, signaling for me to drive to him. I come to a stop beside them, and the car cuts out. Everyone takes a collective breath.

"I told you not to fucking switch it off!" Hunter blares, storming up to the car and dragging open the door. He grabs my throat. "Do what I fucking say!"

"I didn't," I argue. "It cut out. Stop being a bloody neanderthal and help me out of this mess." I dig my nails into his skin, and he snaps his hand away. Another man I don't know approaches the car. He's tall and slim with glasses perched on the end of his nose. A computer nerd by the looks of him. Without a word, he crouches down at my side, then moves to his knees and peers under the seat.

"There's a timer," he says. "We have five minutes." He looks up at me, and I blink back at him.

"Who are you?" I ask, my voice harsh.

"Dan," he replies. "And as much as I'd love to introduce myself further, I'm sure it can wait until we're on safer ground."

"Fuck," I mutter, running a hand through my hair.

"Mr. Waite, please don't move. I haven't got time to do a full inspection of the device but considering it didn't explode when you sat down, I can assume removing pressure from the pad will cause it to detonate."

"So, it won't explode when the timer counts down unless I get up?" I ask, hopeful.

"Oh no, it will most definitely explode then."

"I'm fucking mincemeat no matter what," I growl, infuriated to be caught like this. To have been one-upped by a man I hate.

Dan ignores my outburst. "Mr. Waite, I am going to attempt to rebalance the pressure as we move you off the device. Hopefully this will stop the detonation. But as soon as you are out of the car, you need to run."

"Can you not deactivate it? You know, cut a wire or something?"

"Unfortunately not, it's too risky. I've seen too many people blown to bits by an incorrect wire being severed." He stands and walks around to the passenger side of the car, opening the door and kneeling on the seat. "I want you to move slightly to your right. I am going to apply weights to the pad as you move in an attempt to trick it."

"Have you completed this task successfully before?" As soon as the question leaves my lips, I regret it.

"Once," he says, not looking at me, too busy laying out small weights in the storage compartment between us. "The other times, well, let's just say most of them survived. I'm still here anyway." He looks me straight in the eyes. "We have around three minutes. We will get you out of here if you do everything I tell you."

I nod, take a breath, then turn to Hunter who is standing at the driver's door. Russell and Connor behind him. "Now fuck off," I tell them. "Get clear of this heap of shit." Without a word, they all turn and walk away.

"What's that?" Dan asks, distracting me by signaling to an envelope on the dashboard I didn't notice. He reaches for it and passes it to me. My name is written across the front. "Read it once you're out of here. Now, start moving very slowly." Another man has appeared at my side, crouched down watching what must be the timer.

"Two minutes," he advises. "But it's speeding up." Dan is placing a weight onto the seat each time I move.

"Now, I need you to step your right leg out of the vehicle and put half your weight on it." I do as I'm told. "Timer," he asks. The man beside me squints around my leg at the bomb below my seat.

"One minute."

I glance over. He's holding the final weight.

"When I place this down, you run. We all run." I grunt in response. The man watching the countdown stands. With the mystery envelope firmly in my grasp, I rise and run when the small piece of metal is placed on the seat.

Those of us still in the vicinity of the car scatter like marbles. Within seconds, the explosion erupts, throwing us all forward. I land on the hard ground on my hands and knees. Gravel punctures my skin. Everything stings. When I turn around, I see the sad little shit-mobile already burning bright, ashes flying up into the sky with the flames. My men and friends stand around the outer edges, watching on. They all move toward me, surrounding me like I'm a sacrifice. The envelope is still clutched in my fist, somehow.

"A love letter, Waite?" Marshall says, gesturing to the paper in my hand.

"It was in the car," I tell him. "My name is on it."

"This is all fucking freaky."

"Well open it," Russell says. When I glance up, he's standing above me staring down. I push myself up to sit, and the men gather in closer as I pull a photo from the now grubby white casing.

A picture comes into view. A woman. A naked woman lying on a bed with her legs spread wide. It takes me a moment to process who it is. Violet smiles sexily into the camera, her eyes aroused, ready to be taken. Across the bottom is a message.

Remember, I've been there too.

I rip the image up and throw it away. "What was in the envelope?" Connor asks firmly. He's standing at the back, watching silently. He's too far from me to have a look at the image.

"Something you wouldn't want to see," I say, my heart beating hard in my chest as my anger explodes.

"This bastard is going down," Russell growls. "I saw that photo, and no one does that to my sister."

CHAPTER THIRTY-FIVE

Harrison and Violet's
Apartment, The Level

Violet

I've lain awake all night, waiting. He's not home yet, and I'm getting worried. The clock shows six in the morning. Mrs. D. pops her head in my bedroom door again—she returned this afternoon from her stay with family and hasn't left me alone. "He's on his way," she says with a smile. "And he's in one piece."

A relieved breath pushes between my teeth, my whole body immediately relaxing. My emotion takes over and sobs promptly burst from me. Big watery tears run down my cheeks. I sit up as she walks over to the bed and sits down, wrapping me in her arms.

"Let it out," she whispers.

"I'm being ridiculous," I mumble against her shoulder.

"No darling," she says, pushing me back and looking into my eyes. "You're a heavily pregnant woman who has been through hell. It is perfectly normal to feel like this. Cry as often as you want, but ensure you laugh as much too." She smiles kindly, then kisses my forehead before cuddling me once more.

Ten minutes later, our bedroom door opens. Harry walks in, stopping when he sees us. I glance up at him—his face is almost black, covered with an unknown substance. The knees have been removed from his jeans. Blood stains his hands and up his arms. "It's all right Vi," he says, softly, "I'm home." He moves over to my side; Mrs. D.'s arms release me as he takes hold, and I start to cry again. I bury my face into his chest, he rests his chin on top of my head like he has done before. "I'm home," he whispers again ferociously, then tightens his arms around me.

"I'll leave you both to it," Mrs. D. says. Harry mumbles his thanks, and she leaves, closing the door quietly behind her.

I take a deep breath, trying to contain the emotion spilling from me. After screwing my eyes tightly shut, I open them then straighten my shoulders so I can look up at him. He smiles, and my nerves calm. He's here, and he's alive. "What happened?" I ask. His gaze runs over my face, considering what to say. "Tell me the truth."

"It was set-up. There was a bomb," he says, and I gasp, completely stunned. I knew this world was dark, but never did I think an evil device like a bomb would enter my life.

"A bomb!" I squawk.

"I'm all right." His voice is firm. "I'm sitting here next to you. But I won't pretend it wasn't fucking frightening." I take his hands, turning them over. They're covered in dried blood; the scratches extend up his arms beneath his shirt sleeves. I undo the button at his wrist and push the material upward. He winces as it moves across the damaged skin.

"You need to get these clean. I'll run you a bath," I tell him, swinging my legs out of bed. He touches the base of my back when I rise.

"I like you wearing my clothes," he says, his voice raspy. I pull down the cotton t-shirt that was in the laundry basket. It smelled of him and gave me some comfort while lying in our bed alone. The fabric strains over my swollen midsection, my belly button and nipples visible. "But I like you even better out of them." My stomach flips.

"Now is not the time," I scold, and he laughs.

"Any time is the right time," he challenges, then runs his fingers between my legs.

"No, I'm going to run you a bath." I smack his hand away and he rolls his eyes.

"Spoilsport," he mouths, and I lean down to kiss him. Our lips press gently together, and he touches my hip with his fingers. "I thought I was going to lose you both before we even got started," he says sadly. "It was the most soul-destroying reality I could ever imagine, not having this life with you." I don't need to say anything—he's said it all. Life without this would be pointless.

***

The steaming hot water sits a few inches below the top of the tub. I've added some bath salts with aloe vera to help ease the sting of his wounds. "Bath's ready," I call, and he appears in our en suite, walking up behind me and wrapping me in his arms. His lips come to my neck; he dusts it with gentle kisses.

"Are you going to join me?" he whispers in my ear. "There's plenty of room for two." I lift the t-shirt over my head in answer then turn and unbutton his shirt. It drops to the floor in a pool of dirty white cotton. I drop to my knees and unfasten his fly, pulling his destroyed jeans down over his taut behind then repeating the process with his boxers and socks.

I kneel in front of him, hands on my knees. His cock hardens. Pushing myself upward, I run my tongue from his balls along his length, and he moans, a deep guttural sound from the depths of him. "Bath, before we get carried away," he says bluntly. I stand, pushing my simple black thong to the ground.

He takes my hand, leading me to the side of the bath. I step in, and he supports my weight, ensuring I don't lose my balance. "On your knees," he orders. I comply. He lowers himself into the tub, facing me. The water sloshes over the sides, splashing off the white-tiled floor. I take a sponge from the small glass shelf that holds the shampoo, then pick up one of his hands, turning it palm up. Slowly, I dab the sponge over his skin, cleaning away the remnants of a terrifying night. He closes his eyes, his face contorting when it stings. I repeat the process over every inch of his skin, cleaning away the grime.

Once the obvious dirt is gone from his body, I pick up the blue bottle poised on the shelf and squirt a blob of creamy liquid into my hand. He's sitting with his back against the end of the bath. I move forward to straddle him. His hard length touches my lips as I sit, and he groans. Taking the shampoo, I rub it into his scalp. With his eyes still closed, my nipple grazes his lips. His tongue darts out and licks the bud, then he takes it in his mouth, sucking gently as I wash his hair.

"I need to rinse your hair," I mumble, breathless. The plastic beaker sits on the side. He murmurs in agreement but keeps sucking, his pressure increasing with every second. I rub my pussy against him. This is the closest we've been to full intercourse since our night back in June when I first appeared. We've done everything but.

After pouring cups of water over him, the suds slide slowly over his skin. I use my thumb to clear the excess from his eyes. He opens them, smiling like I'm a meal he wants to devour. Pushing my hand below the surface, I take hold of him, lining him up at my entrance.

"Violet," he warns, "you wanted to wait." He lifts his eyebrows, and his hands move under my ass, holding me up.

"I don't want to anymore," I hiss, my chest rising and falling, arousal bursting from me. My pussy screams to be filled with him. This is something I want to do for him, for us. I almost lost him. I want to show him exactly how much he means to me. "Let go of my ass so I can fuck you, Harry. This is happening now."

He releases me slowly, and I sit down, sucking him in. At this moment, I feel him in every part of me—in my pussy, throughout my body, but most of all encompassing my heart. We are connected in the most intimate way we can be. The two of us, together, finally.

I go slowly, my hips rocking to a silent beat. My bump is pressed up against his abs, even though he lies at an angle. He groans softly as I move. His hands sit on my hips, supporting but not interfering with my rhythm. My orgasm builds with each touch of him within me, pushing my body closer to release. I stroke his cheeks with my fingertips, holding his beautiful face within my grasp—his eyes have never left mine. Each of us watching the other's every reaction as I took control of his body and used him for both our pleasure.

"You're mine," I say fiercely. "And I am yours."

"Are you asking or telling me, Vi?" He flashes me a cheeky smile, and I stop riding him. He squeezes my skin, flexing his fingers to encourage me to resume my movements.

"What do you think?" I say with a smirk.

"I think you're being a tease again and it will result in that perfectly pink ass of yours being spanked. Move." I shake my head. One strong hand lifts; his fingers pinch one of my nipples and twist. My body convulses from the unexpected sensation.

"Move," he growls. My pussy spasms at the order, and I rock again, short sharp movements as the tip of his cock hits my g-spot. "That's my girl. Ride what you own. I'm here for you to do as you please. Show me who I belong to."

His words are too much. The orgasm that's been building since I took him within me shatters my body. Sheer ecstasy ripples across my skin as I come undone and he takes control of my hips, guiding them to finish what I started.

"I'm not done," he whispers. "And neither are you. Keep fucking me." His grip becomes stronger, more demanding. Our roles reverse, and he now has control, using my body to his benefit. Then I feel it, that sensation when a man comes, his cock jerking and giving me what I needed. Him.

As we step out of the bath, we wrap ourselves in the soft white robes hanging on the back of the door. On entering our bedroom, Harry's phone vibrates madly on the bedside table. "What the fuck now?" he grumbles, walking over and peering at the screen. "Connor," he says almost to himself then accepts the call. I don't hear what's said, only Harry telling him to come over. Five minutes later there's a knock at the front door.

My brother walks in, stressed. He paces around the room. It's so unlike him. "Violet," he snaps, "what social media do you have?" I blink, confused by the question.

"Only a Facebook page I think, but I don't use it. I've not been on since I came back from Chicago."

His focus lands on me, his eyes boring into mine. "Is it private?"

"I don't know. Why? I never used it. There's nothing on there."

"What is this about?" Harry interjects bluntly. He moves to the kitchen counter and opens his laptop, then types in the familiar blue website address. His page appears, but it's not under his name. "I don't have a personal page," he says as a way of explanation. He types my name into the search bar and my photo pops up. He clicks on it, and my profile opens.

I scream. Harry slams the computer closed. "Fuck's sake Connor. Could you not have fucking warned us?" he yells.

"They've been shared across various porn sites," he replies as I drop to the floor.

"Those were private photos," I wail. Aiden has posted and shared intimate pictures of us. Pictures we took to be used when we were apart. His identity is hidden, but mine is in full view for everyone to see.

"What is your password?" Harry says, bringing my attention back to him. He is standing looking down on me from above. "If he's not changed it, I'll deactivate your account now. We'll need to get the cyber team on this to see what they can do about the rest." His voice is calm, but when I look into his eyes, all I see is pain. I can't imagine how it must feel for him to see me with someone else like that. If it had been the other way around, I'd be devastated.

I tell him my password and it works. "He knows your personal information, Violet. You need to change all your codes and passwords for any accounts you have." He pushes the computer toward me while holding his hand out to help me rise, immediately releasing it when I stand. "I'll go and make some calls about getting the pictures tracked and taken down," he says as he walks off down the hallway with his phone at his ear.

Connor comes to stand beside me. "I've spoken to Father," he says quietly. "He's in full support of Aiden having contact with your child. They're close, Violet. Closer than we could ever have imagined. He's given Russ and I an ultimatum. It's either Harrison or him. We chose Harry." I glance at my brother, and he places his hand on my back.

"Thank you," I say honestly. "By choosing Harry, you're choosing me."

Harry reappears as I log into all the accounts I can remember, changing each one's details. He stands on my other side, looking over my shoulder and the screen. "I'm sorry," he whispers. "It's not your fault." His lips touch my hair. "It was a shock seeing you like that. I love you."

I close my eyes, a tear escaping down my cheek. My heart aches for both of us, my embarrassment and his pain. Aiden becomes more and more evil as the days pass. I hardly recognize him.

"Call Damon. Have him arrest Marley on the grounds of image-based sexual abuse," Harry says.

"We'll struggle to prove it's him," Connor replies.

"He will have been the only person other than Violet with access to the images. These were shared with the intention to cause distress and without consent. I want him fucking arrested for it," he snarls. Connor holds his hands up.

"Okay, okay, I'm making the call."

"What are you going to do?" I ask him quietly. My eyes are trained on the ground, my cheeks still burning with humiliation.

"I'm going to fucking bury him." He places one finger under my chin, encouraging me to look at him. "Violet, you have done nothing wrong. This is one of the lowest ways a person can abuse another. He will pay for this, either through the judicial system or by my hand. You are not to allow him to hurt you. Do you understand me?" I blink at him, shame engulfing me for the first time in months. "Couples conduct these types of relationships all the time. He had no right to share these images. Taking them was consensual for both of you, but he has broken the law. I will ensure he pays."

***

1ˢᵗ February 2023

"You ready?" Samantha says, smoothing down her fitted pink dress. She makes an incredible bridesmaid, all slim and neat, with rosy cheeks and smooth skin. On the other hand, I feel like a beached whale at almost full term and wearing a cream satin dress that cascades over my now huge bump. My breasts are swollen, straining against the fabric. Every part of me feels ready to burst.

"I'm just glad we got here," I tell her, and she laughs.

"Yes, the false alarm two days ago certainly caused panic. Fucking indigestion." She smiles warmly, then applies another layer of rouge to my cheeks. "You look beautiful, Violet. Twenty minutes to go." We are in a dressing room provided at the registry office. There is only our little group attending. We gave notice to be married as soon as we could, and life has been quiet since.

Aiden was arrested for sharing the images and has since been released on bail. Hunter's team is monitoring the drug ring, but they are wary of being passed bad information again. The whole thing had been a set-up aimed to ruin us and break Hunter's ties to Joel Parker of Glasgow. They hoped to turn us all on each other so we would destruct from the inside out.

The clock strikes quarter past two. "Fifteen minutes," Samantha says, jumping up and down clapping her hands. There is a knock at the door. "Go away," she shouts. "You can't see her till she's walking down the aisle."

"Waddling," I mumble, and she scowls at me.

"It's the registrar," a voice calls back. Samantha skips over and opens the door. A terrified woman dressed in a black suit is pushed into the room. My father stands at her back, his gun lodged at the base of her spine. Aiden follows in behind him and closes the door. He grabs Samantha by the wrist and presses his weapon at her chest.

"Pretty," Aiden says with a sneer. "You certainly outshine the bride. How is my baby momma?" He focuses on me. "Pregnancy does nothing for you. I'll be happier when that thing is out of you, but we'll need to get you a personal trainer."

"What are you doing here?" I ask, my eyes trained on my father.

"I'm here to walk my daughter down the aisle," he says. "What else?"

CHAPTER THIRTY-SIX

Tower Hamlets Register
Office, London

Violet

The five of us stand in the dressing room glancing between each other. The registrar whimpers at the end of my father's gun with her eyes screwed shut. She shakes visibly. "Fucking pathetic," my father mutters.

"How did you get in here?" I snarl at the two men I hate most in the world.

Their appearance is a shock. Harry has been anal about our security detail since Christmas. He had multiple meetings with his team to discuss how I would be protected today. I'd drawn a line at having a security guard in my dressing room, but our enemy must have navigated around at least ten men to get in here, including my man on the door.

Aiden holds up a small knife soaked in blood. "With force," he says with a smile. "There will be a few corpses to clean up."

"Marley, tell your men to hold their position and secure any of the bastards still breathing," my father barks. "I'm sure the groom isn't aware of our arrival yet; the operation has run smoothly so far. I want our entrance to be a great surprise." His focus moves to me. "How many men between us and the ceremony room?"

"I don't know," I reply with a shrug, feigning confidence I don't have.

"Daughter," he snarls, "be careful how you respond. I will make your worst fears come true." He gestures to my stomach.

"Two."

"Take three men, and take them down quietly," he says to Aiden. As he turns to carry out the instruction, Samantha speaks.

"Is this him?" she snaps. "The married prick who fucked you over?" Aiden nudges her with the muzzle of his revolver. "Spineless idiot," she continues. "You should be ashamed of yourself. First, you live with her under false pretenses, and now you're gate-crashing her wedding."

"Don't push it blondie," he growls. "I'd be happy enough to fuck you, then put a bullet in you. Keep talking, and I'll stuff that pretty little mouth with my balls so you can't speak." He leans in and runs his tongue up her neck.

"Ew, gross," she squeals. "Violet, I am severely concerned about your taste in men."

My mouth drops open at her bravado. She looks at Aiden and glowers. "Do you seriously think this is the first time an asshole has pointed a gun at me? I've given men head for money; you don't scare me." She lifts her foot and slams her stiletto down hard on his highly polished shoe. He yells as she elbows him in the ribs and wriggles from his grasp. He clicks off the safety, pointing the weapon at Samantha's head. She groans and rolls her eyes.

"Don't fucking think about it, Marley," my father warns. "Tie her hands together and put her in the corner. We can deal with her later. Right now, I want to focus on my beloved daughter."

Aiden pulls his belt from his dress pants and proceeds to secure Samantha's arms to her sides, before removing his tie and wrapping it around her neck like a leash. "Good girl. I can't wait to receive a cock suck from you," he says, squeezing her breast with his free hand, then yanking the restraint hard. She stumbles, the heel of her shoe snapping in the process.

"Dickhead," she hisses, and he tugs it again.

"Sit," he orders. "Little bitch, do as you're told, and I may even rub your belly." He ties the belt to a heavy chest of drawers then leaves, returning a few minutes later. "The team is clearing the way," he says and grins wickedly.

377

"I'm meant to be getting married in ten minutes." I look at my father and his eyes come to mine. "If I don't appear, they'll come looking for me." A dark smile flickers on his lips.

"I'm counting on it. You will be getting married, just not to the person you intended," he replies. He tightens his grip on the registrar's arm, and she squeals. "The name of the groom will be changing; you'll need to update your records."

"I can't do that, sir," she stammers. "All marriages in England are subject to twenty-eight days' notice." He lifts the gun and hits her on the side of her neck with the butt of it.

"It wasn't a request; it was a fucking order." She falls to the floor, cowering and shaking like a wounded animal waiting to be eaten. "By whatever means necessary, this will happen."

"Why do you care who I marry?" I say, interrupting him and regaining his attention. "You've disowned us all according to Connor. Bloody leave us alone."

He walks toward me and pushes at my stomach with his finger. "This is mine," my father says viciously. "I'm here to collect my property."

"Take your filthy hands off my baby." We lock gazes and I glare at him openly. Suddenly, I'm not afraid. He's nothing but a spoiled bully used to getting his own way. "You will never see your grandchild. As far as I'm concerned, you never existed. They won't even know your name."

"I won't see them," he says, openly furious at my disrespect. "I'll fucking own them." He leans in, his nose inches from mine. "Now daughter, listen to me—this is what is going to happen."

I take a step back from him, and he grabs my wrist. "Don't you dare walk away from me." I pull it from his grasp, and he slaps me hard across the face. "Today, you will marry Aiden as I instructed you to. But not before I kill that traitorous boyfriend of yours, and perhaps your brothers."

***

Harrison

"Where is she?" I hiss to Russell. He's standing beside me as my best man. His hand grabs my shoulder in support.

"It's normal for the bride to be late," he says, jovially. Today he's been annoyingly bright, in complete contrast to his usual broody self. "I'm more concerned we're missing the registrar." He runs a hand through his dark hair as he senses my nerves. Two days ago, Violet thought she was in labor. We rushed to the hospital, gaining a speeding ticket in the process. It turned out to be a bad case of indigestion, *which resulted in the most expensive box of indigestion medicine ever purchased and a clipped alloy wheel.*

"If she's gone into labor and fucked off to hospital, I'll bloody throttle her," I grumble, and straighten my tie for the thousandth time.

"Calm down, Waite," he cajoles. "I'll go and see what's going on." He saunters off down the aisle I'm waiting for my bride-to-be to walk up. Connor smirks at me.

"Cold feet?" he suggests, raising an eyebrow. "Maybe she's a runner. Though she couldn't run very fast. I'm sure we could catch her."

Russell disappears through the double doors which lead to the small ceremony space we stand in. It's plain and simple, with white walls and terrible pine woodwork. The chairs set in exact rows are red velvet and badly worn. I'm standing in front of an old wooden table with a few neat piles of paperwork. It looks more like a meeting room than somewhere you would get married.

Violet never bothered with any of the fancy trimmings you normally get at a wedding. Not one wedding magazine had appeared in the apartment. No flowers, chair covers, or tiaras were purchased. She ordered herself and Samantha a dress each, told me to wear my best suit, and that was it. Damon balked handing over the one-thousand-pound wager he lost, but I leaned on him hard enough to get it anyway. We spent it on my bachelor party—most of it disappeared into the slot machines of a casino in the city while we drank champagne.

A few minutes later, Russell appears back. His eyes find me, and the look on his face tells me we have an issue. I hear Edward Chase before I see him. "I understand congratulations are in order," he calls across the room. "I am disappointed, Harrison, that you didn't have the courtesy to ask my permission for my daughter's hand in marriage. With the education I provided for you, you should know better."

It takes me a moment to survey the scene. Violet walks in front of her father and next to a woman I assume is meant to be marrying us. Samantha is being dragged along with something tied around her neck by Aiden. They all stop at the top of the aisle. Violet stares at me, her face blank. Her hands are placed protectively over our child.

"There has been a slight change in the proceedings," Edward says with a sly smile. "You'll all be pleased to know there will still be a wedding today, but not the one you were expecting. I'm delighted to invite you all to attend the marriage of my daughter, Violet, to Aiden Marley." Marley claps his hands together then walks over to stand next to my girl, pulling Samantha along with him. He's carrying a gun in his hand. Damon, Marshall, and Hunter move to stand, but I signal for them to stay seated.

Marley wraps his free arm around Violet's waist, then leans in and kisses her cheek. He nips the skin between his teeth and bites. Her hand shoots out and pushes him hard in the chest, and he stumbles backward. "Bitch," he snarls lifting his hand to hit her. Russell grabs his wrist, crushing it between his fingers. Aiden turns the gun on him, aiming it at his forehead.

"Russell, Aiden, this is no way to behave at my daughter's wedding," Edward growls. Aiden glares at his opponent, then drops his weapon to his side.

My eyes dart around the room in search of the security detail we employed. They should never have gotten near the place, never mind being able to abduct the bride. My despair and fury war with each other. It's clear for every man we have, Edward

Chase has two or more. I can only assume they've been taken down one by one.

"Shall I walk you down the aisle, my daughter?" Violet's father says, moving beside her and linking her arm through his. They walk slowly toward us, followed by the rest of the party. "Any funny business and I'll shoot the mouthy one," he says. "Tell the few men you have left to stand down, Harrison. You wouldn't want to be responsible for the death of Violet's best friend, would you?"

Four more men I don't know appear at the back of the room, each one holding a firearm. I glance at Connor; he nods in the direction of the men in acknowledgment. This is going to end badly. My only concern is to get Violet and our baby out alive.

Hunter sits silently, his eyes trained on the floor. Damon crosses his arms across his chest and pushes back on his chair, surveying the scene as it unfolds. Someone is going to have to make a move. The question is who will it be?

"What do you want, Edward? Where are our men?" I ask, deciding to try to take control of the situation. It's the first time I've used his Christian name to address him.

"Dead, maimed, or trussed up I expect," he says with a smile. "They put up a good fight, but you're all amateurs, that much is clear." He laughs boldly, confident that he has won. "Step down, then you and your friends can walk away unscathed. Violet will marry Aiden here as she was meant to. You can return to your city-boy life with your fast cars and cheap women," he says. "Say goodbye to one another, as you won't be seeing each other again after today." He pushes Violet firmly in her back. She staggers, and I catch her in my arms.

"She's fucking pregnant," I snap, and he laughs.

"That is something I'm aware of. The father of the child, my grandchild, is also mindful of the situation. Hence why we are here today to ensure the correct man marries my daughter. After the birth, Violet will return to Chicago with Aiden, and the baby will stay with me."

All eyes fall on the old man speaking. "That was our agreement." He looks to Marley, who nods. "As of today, I have disowned each of my children. None of you will inherit anything from me. This child will become my sole heir, and as such will be raised by myself and my wife."

"Over my dead body," Violet screams, pulling herself from my arms and throwing herself at her father. A gun fires, then the whole hell is let loose. All the men jump to their feet, running into the chaos. We are outnumbered. The room is filled with feminine screams.

I search frantically for Violet then I spot a bundle of white fabric lying between the chairs. Samantha is crouched beside her, desperately trying to wriggle from her restraints.

As I weave between the warring bodies, Edward's arm hits me square across the chest. I look up into the eyes of the man I used to consider a father figure. A man who spent hours helping me learn to read. A man who gave me opportunities beyond my wildest dreams but also applied pressure to my life that took it out of my control.

"We need to talk," he says sharply, lifting his gun to my chest. "Turn around and walk to the back wall." I follow his instructions, my eyes searching the room to try to figure out who's winning. Bodies are scattered across the floor; men kneel over men throwing punches wildly. "Put your hands against the plaster and spread your legs wide." I feel the gun muzzle touch the base of my neck.

"You, Harrison, surpassed any expectations I ever had of you. You became everything my sons failed to be." He tuts softly under his breath. His lips come to my ear as he stands behind me. "Until a few months ago, I was proud of you, but then you set your sights where they weren't allowed, defying me in the process. In this family, we do not tolerate betrayal." He takes a step back, and I feel the gun rise against the back of my head. "Today, I am rebalancing the scales." He presses the cool metal harder against my flesh. "Goodbye, my son." And the gun goes off.

***

Violet

I stand over my father holding the smoking gun. The blood drains from his face as my waters break. Harry spins to face me, his eyes running from the top of my head to my toes. I crumble to the floor, and he drops down beside me, wrapping me in his arms. "What's happening?" I whisper, terrified to look at the scene behind me. "Who's winning?"

"We are," he tells me. "The boys are securing them all now. The police will be on their way. It's over." I glance at my father; he's looking up at the ceiling with vacant eyes. "You were incredible. You saved me," Harry says, fiercely, and kisses my cheek.

"I think you need to call me an ambulance." Panic flits across his face with my words.

"Are you hurt? Did they hit you?" he splutters, his hands running over my body, looking for a wound.

"No, I'm in labor."

CHAPTER THIRTY-SEVEN

The Bex Corrigan-Jones Respite Centre

6 months later...June
2023

Violet

The good-looking doctor with dark hair and bright blue eyes stands on the small stage erected in the center of what used to be a farmhouse courtyard. There must be two hundred people here to celebrate the opening of the *Bex Corrigan-Jones Respite Centre*. Dr. Ben Jones is thanking everyone for coming and explaining how it came about that he and the beautiful red-haired woman next to him, Antonia, have gone about renovating what was a dilapidated farm, then turning it into a haven for families with terminally ill members. Dr. Jones lost his wife to cancer five years ago. The center is being opened in her memory.

"Look," I whisper to Samantha, nudging her ribs with my elbow. "He's not wearing a wedding ring anymore."

"He's a bit old for me," she replies with a smile.

"Experienced, not old." She bites her lip and scrunches up her nose. "He's got four kids so he must have a good idea of what to do."

"Do you both have to discuss this while I'm sitting next to you?" Harrison hisses. "Actually, does it need to be talked about at all?" He's sitting beside me with our almost six-month-old daughter, Evie, in his arms. She's sucking greedily at the bottle he's feeding her. Once she's finished, he arranges the cloth over his shoulder and burps her gently.

"Samantha is a single woman," I tell him. "We are looking at what options are available to her. A lady has needs."

"I think Samantha has plenty of options that satisfy said needs," he says, glancing at her. "Isn't that right, Samantha?" She flushes a delicate shade of pink and giggles. "From what I've been told, the providers of the satisfaction of your needs are fighting over you."

"May the best man win," she answers, and raises the champagne flute she's drinking from toward him then takes a sip.

Harrison laughs and shakes his head. "Bloody tease. Russell and Connor are at each other's throats, and you're enjoying every damn minute."

"That I am," she says. "I hope they can learn to get along; it's impossible to choose between them. I wish they could understand that."

"Trust you to get yourself involved in a throuple with my brothers," I whisper, feigning annoyance. Secretly, I'm in awe. She handles both of them expertly. Never did I think Russell would be under a woman's thumb, but he is. "You'd be better off losing both of them and getting some fresh meat," I joke. My eyes return to the doctor on the stage. "No wedding ring and experienced. That could be a lot of fun."

"Violet Waite, please stop eyeing up other men. Remember, you are a married woman with a ring on her finger," Harry interjects. "Whose husband will detach the limbs from any man who tries to get in your panties." I turn to face him. His eyes are dark, and he flashes me a cheeky smile. "I'll be the one removing those panties later, so you know who is boss. That's a promise."

The crowd bursts into a round of applause. Dr. Jones lifts a hand thanking everyone and walks down the stairs from the platform. His female companion follows him. They embrace once off stage, then she turns and walks over to a group of women who call her name. He approaches us sitting in the front row.

Harrison rises and takes his hand; they shake firmly. "Congratulations," Harry says. "What an incredible facility you've built here. A true honor for your late wife."

"It wouldn't have been possible without generous donors such as yourself and your good lady here," he replies. "How is this little one?" He tickles Evie's chin with a gentle finger.

"Noisy," I say, and he laughs.

"Yes, mine are all teenagers or older now. They don't get any quieter, I hate to tell you." His focus returns to my husband. "Thank you again. Your donation made the difference between opening on schedule or having to delay. I can't thank you enough."

"No thanks needed. You were there when Violet needed you and we were strangers." Harrison wraps his fingers around my waist, our daughter safely tucked into his other arm. "Now we are friends, and I will be there when you need me. Go and enjoy your success. I need to be getting my girls home." We say our goodbyes, then Harry ushers everyone to the car. Samantha climbs into the back seat. "Where do you want to be dropped off?" he asks her.

"The Level," she replies with a smile.

"Dare I ask who you are visiting?"

"The good brother," she says with a wink.

We all arrive back at the gigantic apartment block I now call home. The private lift at the rear carries us to the boardroom. Samantha kisses my cheek then skips off in the direction of Connor's apartment. "It's going to end in tears," Harrison says, and I shrug.

"I don't know. She seems to care about them both equally. Maybe they could learn to share." His eyes pop wide open.

"Share. You expect a man to share a woman with another man for the rest of his life." His voice drops to a rumble. "I don't share, so don't get any fucking ideas." Evie is sleeping soundly in her car seat, which he carries effortlessly in one hand.

"All relationships look different," I say. "Don't knock it until you've tried it."

"We will not be trying it," he snaps, then stalks off in the direction of our apartment. "That ass of yours is going to sting tonight for even suggesting that. Be prepared not to be able to sit down tomorrow," he calls over his shoulder, and my pussy clenches. Pissed-off sex with my husband is fucking hot.

Upon entering our home, I find my mother sitting on the sofa with her legs curled beneath her, reading a book. "Did you have a nice time?" she asks as Harrison walks over and places a kiss on her cheek.

"Hello Mum," he says. "Yes, it all went incredibly well. The team has done such a good job. The facility will be a lifeline for some who need it."

"That's wonderful. Let me see my granddaughter," she coos. "There's my girl. You're coming to Nana's for a sleepover tonight. What a big girl you're becoming." She unfastens Evie from her car seat that Harry placed on our coffee table and bundles her into her arms. "We are going to have an amazing girl's night," she tells her.

My daughter has given her a focus these past months as her life destructed. After my father recovered from the gunshot wound to his back I inflicted on him, he was arrested on drug-dealing charges and is currently being held in Belmarsh Prison awaiting trial. It turned out that our suspicions had been correct—the drug ring was headed up by him with Aiden playing a secondary role.

Harrison purchased a downstairs apartment in our building for my mother to move into after being left destitute. All our family assets have been frozen awaiting the outcome of the case against my father. The charges mount day by day as more men jump ship and add to the allegations. He will be incarcerated for a very long time and most likely will never see the outside world again. The knowledge is bittersweet. My heart breaks that my father is such a terrible man but swells that my husband has been part of the team that took him down.

Aiden Marley disappeared on the day of our failed wedding. He slipped out the back door amongst the chaos and hasn't been seen since. His face is currently plastered across the internet and television screens as one of the most wanted men in the United Kingdom. Whether he will be found remains to be seen. If the information Damon received is correct, he had been siphoning cash from each drug deal for years. I would imagine he is sitting on a Caribbean Island somewhere surrounded by women and flashing his cash. I hope he chokes on a piece of coconut.

The Level Boys still have their Wednesday night get-togethers in my home. I provide them with cases of beer and unlimited pizza if Mrs. D. has the night off. They watch soccer and talk about work. It's wonderful hearing them together as friends.

The six of them make an incredible team, but since Evie was born, they've not undertaken any vigilante justice as far as I'm aware. However, I'm not convinced I would be told if they did. Harry knows my feelings about him trying to emulate an MI5 agent—he's been instructed to remain behind a desk for now.

We married in March when Evie was six weeks old. It had been a fresh spring day, the sun peeking through the clouds with the birds beginning to sing with the improving conditions. We never told anyone, simply booking the registry office and pulling two random witnesses from the street. The elderly couple had been delighted to assist us in our ceremony. We wore casual clothing of battered jeans and black t-shirts. With my trusty Converse on my feet, I walked down the aisle to the man I've loved all my life while he held our daughter to his chest. Our vows were simple but perfect. Love, trust, and live together until one of us no longer walks on this earth.

Evie lies contently in her grandmother's arms. It's wonderful having her close by again. My mother has been missing from my life since I was nineteen. She's a new woman without the restrictions my father placed on her. Her freedom is being enjoyed with new female friends and her family. My brothers and Harrison ensure she wants for nothing. In return, alongside Mrs. D., she keeps our homes functioning and provides on-tap childcare. The two women are firm friends; every Friday they attend a bingo club in the city. I am certain it's because the caller reminds her of Bruce Willis.

"We will be going," my mother says, passing me my daughter. I cuddle her fiercely and drop a kiss on her forehead.

"I'll see you tomorrow," I whisper. "Mummy loves you so much." Harrison comes to my side, and we both stare down at the little girl who completes our home. He is an incredible father, supporting and loving both of us completely. He places a matching kiss where mine was. My mother retrieves her from my arms before walking out of the door with her.

"So," he says, turning to me as it closes. "We have an empty apartment and hours to fill. What does my wife want to be doing?"

"You," I answer bluntly, and he responds with a sexy smile.

"There is the small matter of our conversation from earlier. Your thoughts on sharing as a positive aspect within a relationship. It's not something I would be prepared to consider." He takes my hand and leads me to our bedroom, pushing open the door. We step through. "I promised you an ass you can't sit on," he says. "I always keep my promises." He guides me to the center of our room. "Stand here. Don't move." My mouth dries in anticipation of what is to come.

He removes his suit jacket and hangs it meticulously in the wardrobe. Then he unbuttons two further buttons on his shirt before slipping off his socks. The crotch of his black suit trousers fills with his growing erection. The sight makes my nipples harden. He is going to fuck me hard. The fire in his eyes tells me as much.

"You have been a naughty girl today," he says quietly, as he approaches me from behind. His hands slide around my middle and across my almost flat stomach. Evie has left her mark, but my husband doesn't care. He adores the signs that I created his daughter. That I am a mother. "You're lucky I didn't bend you across the table earlier and show you why sharing is not an option." I giggle, and he responds by nipping my neck firmly with his teeth. His fingers move to my shoulders, slipping the thin straps of my summer dress down over my arms. The blue cotton falls to the floor. He unhooks my bra, and it goes the same way. I'm left with only my white lace panties, which are removed seconds later.

He strolls around my naked body in a circle, one finger remaining on my skin at all times. It glides over my breasts, touching each nipple briefly, then across my back. His eyes never leave mine; I turn my head to follow him as he moves. His free hand goes to his pocket. He pulls the black satin mask I'm so familiar with out into the open, then secures it across my eyes. As he moves in front of me, he takes both my wrists in one hand and ties them together with something soft I can't see. My body buzzes with excitement. I love when he takes control like this, when I can only feel him and hear him. With my sight gone, every other sense is heightened.

"Walk forward," he orders firmly. Our new bed has four tall posts, one on each corner. "Hold on here." I take firm hold of the hard wood. "Lower," he growls. I bend at the waist, moving my grip down. His fingers run from the base of my neck and down my spine, stopping at my butt cheeks. The room fills with soft music, classical and romantic. "Lower," he orders again then knocks my legs wider with his bare foot.

I sense him standing behind me. He presses himself against my ass, his cock rubbing against my skin through the fabric. His palm moves between my legs, laying across my pussy. He leans over me and drops a kiss onto my back before withdrawing his hand and slapping me hard. I groan. "One," he counts. "Bad girls get punished, then they get fucked." His touch disappears again before reappearing with a sting. He slides one finger inside me. "Two, and hell you're wet already, you dirty girl." The final blow comes, and I open my legs wider, knowing he will replace the pain with pleasure. "Three," he says gruffly, his arousal evident.

He lowers himself between my open legs facing my clit, his hands resting on my thighs. I feel his mouth on me, gently exploring my lips. I bend my knees slightly, wanting more. "You are the sweetest delicacy I've ever tasted," he whispers. "I could eat you all fucking day." His laps become more urgent, his hands twisting around my legs and pulling me down onto his mouth. I let go of the pole and wobble.

"Hold on," he barks. "I want you to come like this. Bent over, tied up, and sitting on my face." His teeth nip my clit as my legs buckle momentarily. Unfazed, he keeps on sucking brutally. The sensations coursing through my body intensify—I curl my toes. "Let go, Vi. Let those juices explode onto my tongue." My stomach clenches, and I erupt, flowing onto his lips. He drinks down greedily, his nails digging into my flesh. He wriggles out from underneath me, rises, and takes my bound arms, turning me to face him before removing the blindfold.

I blink at him as the dark gives way to the daylight. He's still dressed in his shirt and dress pants. He gently unties what I now see is a robe belt from my wrists. His hands cup my face, and he kisses me, a kiss that is both soft and domineering. I drop my fingers to his cock, holding him firmly through the material. As I undo his zipper and slip his pants down over his ass, I say, "Shall we make a start on creating that football team?"

***

Thank you!

If you enjoyed Harrison, I would appreciate it if you would take the time to leave a rating and review on Amazon, Goodreads, or Bookbub. Reviews are so important to authors. It really does help. Thank you for reading.

Review on Amazon here: https://mybook.to/Harrison

***

Bonus Scene

If you're not quite ready to let go of Harrison and Violet yet, sign up for my newsletter and receive a bonus scene.

Sign up here: https://dl.bookfunnel.com/mveawtt6vj

Damon

The Level Series: Book
Two

October 2020

Connie

"This time," he growls, "this time you will be." I'm pressed against the mattress as he slams himself inside me. He groans and we lose ourselves in one another, but my pleasure does nothing to dampen my fear. Tears roll freely down my cheeks. "This time, Connie. This time we'll make it happen."

I'm ovulating. Every month we relive the same scenario. The days arrive that give us a chance of adding a new member to the family, and we chase the dream with gusto. Sex every twelve hours, vitamins, minerals, and no alcohol. I lie in bed once he's completed his end of the bargain, terrified to move in case his swimmers are diverted from their path. In the past sixty months of trying, we've never achieved one positive pregnancy test. Not one.

My husband is a big man, and his strong arms hold his body above me, dwarfing mine. The physique I love to touch grazes my skin as we move together. Inside, he fills me—every time we make love it takes time to adjust to his size.

His thrusts become more urgent. My body sucks him in and holds on for dear life. The familiar roar erupts from him as he reaches his peak, his hips pushing hard before he releases, emptying himself fully. His lips lower to my forehead, and I close my eyes beneath his touch.

"I love you, Bubbles," he whispers. "We will make this happen somehow."

"I love you too," I tell him. He rolls off me, then immediately exits our marital bed, wiping himself down quickly with a towel before starting to get dressed in dark jeans and a matching plain hooded top. I lie with my hips propped up on a pillow and watch him. You would think after eighteen years together this would get boring, but it never has.

Damon McKinney was my teenage dream. We found love in our youth and have enjoyed each other ever since. He was the boy next door, two years older than me. We used to play together as young children. Then he grew up and moved on, being allowed out with his friends on his bike to the local park while I had to stay home. I'd play in my front yard so I could shout to him as he came and went. He always lifted a hand in greeting and smiled, but we rarely spoke until I turned sixteen.

It was summer, and I was growing up fast, doing all the things I shouldn't have been doing. We met at a friend's party, high on alcohol and life. He kissed me and that was it. I've been his ever since.

"Will you be late tonight?" I ask him, glancing to the window. The autumn winds are picking up as winter threatens to appear. The brown leaves of the trees outside sway in the strong breeze, every so often tapping the glass.

"I don't know, Bubbles. This case I'm working on is turning into a bit of a headache. The team is struggling. We have a debrief on the latest operation at four o'clock." He glances at his watch. "Which I am going to be late for."

"Thank you for coming home," I say softly, and he glances at me. "I know this has all become tedious." He walks back to the bed and sits on the edge beside me, cupping my chin in his palm and running his thumb across my lower lip.

"Making love with you is never tedious. Don't ever think that." His eyes bore into mine as he speaks. They're deep green, the color of ferns. His dark hair is cropped close to his head. "We will do whatever it takes to create this baby, I promise you that. But Bubbles, we need to start considering other options if this month is not successful."

I tense, not wanting to have this conversation, not wanting to accept the reality of not being able to carry my own child. I know as well as he does that I won't be pregnant. Five years of negative tests have proven that it isn't possible. The demoralizing fertility appointments only compound the fear.

"I know," I whisper, as I sit up and twist my hands in my lap. "Maybe we should consider surrogacy." He visibly relaxes before my eyes. That huge frame which has held me as I sobbed so many times when blood stained my panties eases as the tension ebbs away. Both his hands come to my shoulders, and I peek up at him. "I'm sorry for being stubborn."

"Allowing another woman to carry our baby is a huge decision. Your uncertainty is understandable, but we need to live our lives. The monthly stress and timekeeping isn't good for either of us." He brushes his fingers against my cheek, wiping away a stray tear. "And as much as I love coming home for a mid-afternoon rendezvous, I want to be doing that for us to enjoy each other, without the end goal in mind. It's time to let go, Connie. Someone else can play a part in this."

"The doctor did say my chances of maintaining a pregnancy are low," I say, and he nods. "We're not getting any younger." He takes my hand and squeezes it between strong steady fingers.

"Mid-thirties is not old," he teases. "We only have a few gray hairs between us. We can make this happen, but we need to use the resources available to us. We've tried, and it hasn't happened. I'd rather have our baby by other means than none at all."

"Okay." I push the single word past my trembling lips. My emotions are bursting to the surface with the acceptance that unless a miracle has occurred today, I most likely will not be carrying our child and bringing them into this world. The realization both frees my heart from the terror and breaks it simultaneously. If I'm ever to be a mother, it will not be in a natural way.

***

January 2021

My husband and I shrug out of our winter jackets before taking a seat in the sleek, modern office of our agent, awaiting our initial meeting with the potential surrogate. British winter has hit hard this year, and every road is covered with ice. A cup of tea has become an essential at every time of the day to warm up.

The process of finding a surrogate has been made relatively painless by hiring a specialist to provide suitable female candidates. Officially, in the United Kingdom, a surrogate cannot be paid for their service; however, you are able to cover her expenses. This specific agency is headed up by a highly sought after fertility doctor who will provide surrogacy services beyond the tight constraints of the law, allowing for more leeway on both sides of the agreement. Only those with deep pockets and golden connections have access to his expertise, and luckily, we have both.

Damon being at a senior level in the police force meant we needed to complete the process with as much discretion as possible. He didn't want our personal life known to any more people than necessary, or government organizations and charities trawling through our business. Therefore, through a friend, we were introduced to this highly private matching service for childless couples and young healthy women needing a financial boost. It seemed an ideal solution to my empty womb and heart.

Emma Becker is a law student struggling with ever-increasing living costs and student debt. At the age of twenty-two, she is thirteen years my junior and in the first throes of adult life. In the sole picture I've seen of her, she was fresh faced with long blonde hair and stunning blue eyes. The flowers decorating her head implied she was free and enjoying life. Today, we will get to ask her why surrogacy is a route she wants to pursue and the reason she chose us.

The frosted glass door swings open. Our agent, Grace, walks into the room followed by Emma. Emma is tall, and her hair flows down her back to her ass. She has a fuller figure than I imagined with wide hips, large breasts, and a nipped-in waist. My stomach drops at the thought of this woman living in our home with us. Damon and I have been on our own for over fifteen years, since we moved in together in my late teens.

She smiles kindly, strolling over as we both stand. She takes my hand first, shaking my sweaty fingers firmly, then turns to Damon and repeats the process. I look to my husband trying to assess his reaction. His face is blank except for a polite smile.

"Shall we all sit," Grace says, gesturing to two leather sofas placed in an L-shape to the side of the room. "Over here is more comfortable."

We all move into the space. Damon and I take one sofa, while Emma and Grace sit on the other. My husband's arm wraps around my shoulders; he emits strength I don't have. I feel him willing me to be all right with this.

"So as you're both aware, this is Emma, who has been matched with you as a surrogate. Emma has assessed your file and is happy to proceed with the process."

"Thank you, Emma," Damon says, and all eyes in the room fall on him. "We both appreciate the potential opportunity you have given us."

"You're welcome," she replies, her ice-blue eyes moving between us.

"This is my understanding so far," Grace says, lifting the paperwork from the coffee table between us. The contract.

Surrogacy contracts in the United Kingdom are not enforceable by law, but it is best to have one, even under these circumstances. Luckily, we have a few lawyer friends who have been able to assist with its construction.

"Emma will become pregnant by means to be agreed upon. She will carry your baby until birth, then sign all parental rights to yourselves after the birth as per UK law. In return, you will provide her with a safe place to stay and expenses for living costs during this time period. It has been noted she will provide you with breast milk, if possible, for up to six months after the birth, but will move into alternative accommodations at this point, off the premises of your primary property."

"In a nutshell, that's correct," Damon agrees. "Emma will stay with us so we can support her during the pregnancy, and so

Connie will have an active role. After the birth, we will provide an apartment for six months."

"Excellent. Do you have anything you want to ask Emma?" Grace says, her gaze moving to me. I take a breath; this is a question I need to get off my chest.

"Only one," I reply. "Why?"

"Why what?" Emma questions, her voice is sharper than I expected. She straightens her shoulders, giving me the impression of a terrified girl trying to be strong. My resolve to go through with this falters. She's so young—is it right for us to ask this of her? But if we don't, someone else will. And I want my baby.

"Why surrogacy, why this agency, and why us?"

She cocks her head to one side, surveying my face. Damon fidgets, uneasy with her mannerisms, I think. He's protective, very protective. No one is allowed to say a word against me, especially when it comes to our inability to have a family. The last time we were at a family gathering and the subject of children came up, he marched me out of the room before the tears could fall.

"In all honesty," she says, "I'm floundering. I have no money and most likely will lose my home. My studies are going well, but I need a secure place to stay while I complete my degree. This is something I can do that won't invade my time too much. It will reduce my living costs and let me chase my career." She pauses for a moment. "Everyone in this room knows we're out with the realms of the law here. Normally, it's a requirement for surrogates to have maintained a healthy pregnancy. This agency places more importance on reproductive health and keeping your mouth shut, so it was a good opportunity to improve my circumstances. Also, knowing how much the introduction fee you're paying is, I figure you must really want this baby and will provide them with a good life." I gawk at her and she laughs. "I don't want children of my own. My family are gone, and I have no support. My reasons are selfish, but I hope that doesn't disappoint you."

"Not at all," I respond. "I appreciate your honesty."

The meeting continues and we discuss the sensitive topics of how the arrangement will work. It is agreed she will move in with us for a two-week trial before we decide to move forward with the surrogacy. However, as the introduction is part of the fee due to the agency, Damon hands over the five-thou-sand-pound cash payment safely counted in a padded brown envelope. The balance of twenty thousand pounds will be due on the initial round of treatment.

We all stand, ready to say goodbye. Grace and Emma shake our hands, then we walk out the door further forward in the process of getting our child.

***

It's a bright winter's morning at the end of January. The sun streams in our window as Damon and I sit up in bed drinking cups of tea. It's his routine on the days he's home: he goes downstairs first, makes two drinks, then brings them back to our bedroom. We chat, relax, and make love until we feel like getting on with our day.

Today is not so peaceful. Emma has come to the end of her two-week stay with us, and we need to decide whether to move forward with the process. She has asserted she is happy to.

"Bubbles," he says, "if you want to go ahead with this surrogacy now is the time to say. If not, we can end it here and look at building our lives without a child."

My heart strains. One part of me is warring with the other, questioning whether I can watch another woman birth my child. Closing my eyes, I take a deep breath. If we don't try, I'll always wonder what if.

"Yes," I answer him. "I want to try." He wraps me in his arms as the tears come, the loss and hope contradicting each other with their rawness. His lips drop to my ear and he kisses me softly.

"I love you, always. This time next year we will be sitting here holding our baby. You are such a strong woman, never forget it. I am so proud of you."

***

It was decided that we would try a round of embryo implantation first via the same agency, although the process offered high costs and a low chance of positive results. When the test showed negative, Emma apologized.

"Don't ever say sorry," I told her. "This isn't a guaranteed thing. We'll have to speak to the clinic about another cycle." Having her in my home hasn't been as awkward as I thought it might be. She's at the library a lot of the time and spends the rest of her day studying in her room. She is completely career focused.

"Implantation isn't the only option," she says. "It's my egg we are using. There's always the natural route."

That had been another blow. My eggs were now considered infertile or beyond use; they recommended using a donor. Emma had stepped up again.

"You want to sleep with my husband," I snap, and she bursts out laughing.

"No, we can use a syringe. An artificial insemination kit." My eyebrows shoot up and I blink at her in confusion. "Damon can do his thing and we put it in a syringe, then transfer the sperm into me." Her voice is level, calm, and completely at ease with the suggestion. My heart rate skyrockets at the thought. "It means we can try multiple times a month at the optimal time, and more importantly." She pauses, focusing on me. "If one month it doesn't happen, we can try the next easily."

"It does make sense," I stutter, unsure. "But I'll need to speak to Damon."

"Of course," she replies with a smile. "I'll send you some instructional videos I found online." She takes both my hands in hers. "I want to make this happen for you, Connie. My studies have improved amazingly since I moved in. You have helped me without even realizing it. If I can do this for you, I will."

***

Emma's optimal time to become pregnant rolls around. Damon holds his plastic beaker and wanders off to the toilet to do his duty. He returns ten minutes later with the contents, passing them to us. We're standing at the kitchen counter, syringe poised.

"I'm out," he says, walking off, and we both giggle. I pour my husband's semen into the syringe, then we both head to her room. Sliding a syringe filled with my husband's sperm up another woman's vagina isn't something I ever thought I would do, but so be it.

The previous weekend, I had suggested to Damon that perhaps natural conception would be best. He'd balked then lost his temper. "I am not sleeping with another woman," he barked. "How can you even ask that of me?" His face had turned bright red as he stormed around the room.

"It was only a suggestion," I muttered, annoyed.

"You need to stop watching those weird videos online," he shot back. "We are using the syringe method. No arguments."

"But sperm..."

"Bubbles, I don't care if it increases our chances to ninety-nine percent. I am not putting my dick in another woman's pussy. Is that clear?" He turned to me, furious eyes holding me to the spot. "Don't ever ask that of me. It's always been you, and I will not have you be able to think of me with another woman, whether the relationship was business or pleasure."

In hindsight, he was right. The thought of him having sex with someone else would have killed me. But in that moment of madness, it had seemed like a sensible suggestion. Creating a baby can become all-consuming, especially when you can't do it yourself.

***

Two weeks later, Emma comes bursting into the living room. It's a Tuesday morning, so she doesn't have classes either at the school or online. I've been surprised how many classes she has delivered remotely rather than in the classroom. Damon is tying his shoes, getting ready to leave for work.

"I'm late!" she shrieks. I'm sitting on the sofa in my huge snuggly robe drinking a massive mug of tea. Her voice causes me to jump, and a little liquid splashes over the side onto my pristine velvet sofa.

"For where?" I ask her, confused, as I dab at the stain with my robe.

"My period," she says, looking at me as if I'm a fucking idiot. She waves a box in her hand. "I'm off to pee on this stick. Wait here." She skips off out the door in the direction of the bathroom then appears back five minutes later placing the white pregnancy test on the table between us all. "We need to wait ten minutes then look. We want two blue lines."

I roll my eyes at her. She hasn't a bloody clue how many of these things I've looked at over the years. Hundreds, if not thousands. They always had one effing line.

She stares at her watch. "Time," she announces. "You check, Connie."

I lean forward to look at the little stick, and two blue lines blink back at me. "We're pregnant," I whisper, shocked. Emma starts to dance around in celebration. Damon leans over, embracing me and kissing my temple.

"We're going to have a baby," he says.

My body floods with emotions—happiness, joy, pain, fear, sadness, relief—a heady cocktail which is hard to understand. My gaze moves to the young woman who has made this possible, and all I feel is deep appreciation for her. Gratitude that we found each other when we both needed it.

"We better get baby shopping," Damon says, diverting my attention to him. He flashes me a breathtaking smile. "It's happening, Bubbles. You're going to be a mummy."

***

June 2021

Emma's pregnancy, our pregnancy, has finally been announced to the world with the simple explanation that she is the surrogate mother. Our baby is due in December, and I can't wait to meet them. Life is feeling hopeful, as if we're almost near completion of our goals. So far there have been no complications apart from a bit of morning sickness, but Emma charges on doing what she needs to do. In a strange way, she's become the little sister I never had, helping around the house and talking about girly things. We've enjoyed the summer sunshine together, lying out on our loungers while talking nonsense.

Damon was recently promoted at work, which is demanding more of his time. He's moving through the ranks quickly, and has been headhunted into the National Organized Crime Unit in recent weeks. It's a role that will put pressure on him in the workplace and push him to move in darker, more dangerous, circles. A lot of his job we can't discuss, but I know things are changing for him and for us. When we're out of the house, he is that bit more cautious, his eyes scanning the situation as we go about our day. It makes me uneasy.

I've made a quick stop to get some groceries for dinner. The supermarket is quiet on a warm Thursday afternoon. I park in a spot in the far corner of the parking lot. Damon treated me to a shiny SUV in preparation for our new addition; it's bright red with four slick black alloys. I don't want it being dented by an asshole that can't drive.

As I walk across the pavement toward the wide entry doors, a man dressed in black with a baseball cap steps out of a small white van. He steps into my path, stopping me in my tracks. "Connie McKinney?" he asks curtly.

"Yes, who's asking?" I snap back.

"It won't matter. You don't need to know," he replies, then flashes me a nasty smile. "You won't be here." His arm rises, and he presses cool metal to my chest. I glance down at the gun then back to him. "Goodbye," he says, and shoots.

***

Damon is available to order here:
https://mybook.to/damonbook

Acknowledgements

This is my first acknowledgment page. I do apologize for not writing one sooner, but to every person who has shown me support this past year – thank you.

Book number eight, which for me is incomprehensible. It's hard to believe that in less than two years, what started as '*I will try to write a book*'...became this. I have so many people to thank who have helped and supported me along this crazy journey.

First of all, my friend Joann, the person I gave six chapters of a random story that popped into my head, and asked her to read it. Her enthusiasm and feedback are what propelled me to write more.

Shirley who cheered me on for the beginning reading chapters as I went.

Without these two ladies, I most likely would never have gotten beyond a few lines on a Word document.

Jessica, a new friend from across the pond, read my completed manuscript and gave me constructive feedback. Her positivity and reassurance that Loving Dr. Jones was good enough to pursue pushed me to look at publishing my book seriously. Now, she is a key part of my team and still helping me with developmental editing, copy editing, and proofreading.

Tasha and Tiffany, both took the chance to read my first book as ARC readers. Now, they help me with the BETA process, reading as I write. I feel so lucky to have found amazing cheerleaders and friends.

Lilibet and Lakshmi who were willing to give up their time to be the final eyes on this manuscript. In an attempt to catch those pesky typos. I am still convinced there is a 'typo fairy'.

Mercyann Summers and Carolina Jax, our daily chats and brainstorming are one of my favorite things about this journey. We laugh, celebrate, and moan together.

TL Swan, the woman who inspired me to attempt writing between her amazing books and selfless videos which explained the process of becoming an author.

My fellow Cygnets, a brilliant group of writers in which I have found both friends and mentors.

Extasy Books took the risk on a brand new author and published four of my novels within a year. Thank you for the amazing opportunity and education.

The girls of The Spicy Book Nook, a multi-author Facebook reader group that was set up in 2022, when everything needed to become an author seemed so much to take on. We did it together.

My incredible street and ARC teams, who take time out of their lives to read, share, make content, and talk about my books.

Every person out there who has bought one of my stories, thank you so much. Whether you are a friend, family member, or stranger, I feel so grateful you chose to spend some precious time on my book.

Finally, my long-suffering husband and daughter, Gavin and Talia, who have been living with fictional characters since I woke up one morning and decided to write a book. Their support has been constant and without it, the journey would have been near impossible.

About the Author

VR Tennent writes contemporary fiction for women filled with love, heartbreak, and spice. She never promises a happy ending, but guarantees a rollercoaster of emotion. Her flawed characters will navigate their journeys through life, often making controversial decisions in the process. Be prepared to laugh, cry, and scream in frustration as you read.

In January 2022, she decided to put pen to paper and write a book after joining the writer's group of her favourite author. Five months later she was offered a publishing contract on that very book.

Sign up for my newsletter at www.vrtennent.com

Find me on social media

Facebook: https://m.facebook.com/vrtennentauthor/

Instagram: https://www.instagram.com/vrtennentauthor/

TikTok: https://www.tiktok.com/@vrtennentromanceaut hor

Goodreads: https://www.goodreads.com/author/show/22716361.V_R_Tennent

Bookbub: https://www.bookbub.com/authors/vr-tennent

Also By VR Tennent

Moral Dilemmas Series
https://mybook.to/Moraldilemmas
Loving Dr Jones   **https://mybook.to/lovingdrjones**
Surviving Heartbreak **https://mybook.to/survivingheartb reak**
Rebuilding My Future **https://mybook.to/rebuildingmyfu ture**

Guilty Secrets Series
Locked **https://mybook.to/locked**

Under The Sun Series
Discovering Me **https://mybook.to/discoveringme**
Embracing Us **https://mybook.to/embracingus**

The Level Series

HARRISON

Harrison **https://mybook.to/Harrison**
Damon **https://mybook.to/damonbook**
Chase **https://mybook.to/chasebook**

<u>Wild Blooms Series</u>
Heather and Heartache **https://mybook.to/heatherandhea rtache**

Made in the USA
Las Vegas, NV
20 July 2024

92647748R00249